Chris Hockley was born i
honours degree in sociol
from Manchester Univer
Technology. He became
papers in Sussex, Bristol,
Street. He is currently a
newspaper and lives in L with his wife and two
sons.

By the same author

Steel Ghost

CHRIS HOCKLEY

Seven Little Girls

Grafton Books

A Division of HarperCollinsPublishers

GraftonBooks
A Division of HarperCollins*Publishers*
77–85 Fulham Palace Road,
Hammersmith, London W6 8JB

A GraftonBooks Paperback Original 1991
9 8 7 6 5 4 3 2 1

Copyright © Chris Hockley 1991

The Author asserts the moral right to
be identified as the author of this work

A CIP catalogue record for this book
is available from the British Library

ISBN 0-586-21124-1

Printed in Great Britain by
HarperCollinsManufacturing Glasgow

Set in Times

To Jake and Jody, for all the lost games . . .

Acknowledgements

My thanks are due to Dr Gib Parrish of the Center for Disease Control in Atlanta, Georgia, whose research into the phenomenon of Sudden Unexplained Death Syndrome planted the seed of an idea for this novel inside me, and who was willing to help once the seed started to grow.

Thanks also to Maeve Ennis for letting me sleep in her dream laboratory at University College, London, even though she learned nothing from me.

To Jean Clarke, David Knox and my brother Roger for sharing their experience of faraway places with strange-sounding names. And to Joy Chamberlain for her breath-takingly perceptive advice.

Sometimes life is real
Sometimes life is a dream

And sometimes, life is one long nightmare

1

Pearl's dream was ecstatic – and she could not know how badly it would end. Her new man, the most caring and wonderful human being in the world, was making love to her in a woodland garden. The Garden of Eden. She was Eve and he was Adam.

She found herself calling him Adam, though something in the dark recesses of her soul reminded her that his real name was Elliot.

'No matter,' she whispered in his ear. 'You can call me Eve if you want.'

'Eve,' he sighed, running a finger along the undulations of her spine. 'Eve, Eve, Eve. I love you, Eve.'

She felt a burning sensation, a burst of fire scorching the inside of her ribcage. She wanted to give herself to him. She wanted him to take her, no questions asked or expected. He sensed it and was tense with anticipation.

He was floating in mid-air above her. She looked up at his magnificent nakedness, his skin soft and creamy against a backcloth of unblemished blue sky, his dewy perspiration making his body hair sparkle in the sun. Something was lifting her, making her comfortable. She glanced to one side. A giant hand with the texture of lamb's wool held her in its palm, while its fingers pushed seven silk cushions in the colours of the rainbow beneath her. How she adored the sensation of silk on flesh. The giant hand stroked her as if she were a sleeping cat. She stretched and purred.

Adam floated down towards her, drifting from side to

side like a feather dropped from a cloud. He grew larger and larger until she could look inside his rich brown eyes. She saw sprays of purple, red and pink on his retinae, like fireworks in a clear night sky. He was mesmerizing her, tantalizing her. His skin touched hers and she was powerless.

He was inside her without the slightest push, without the slightest pain. She groaned with the sweetest pleasure as she felt him and sucked his shoulder until she tasted his blood. He was the most vital she had ever known. Strong. Uncompromising. Yet as succulent as a ripe peach.

'Crunchy-peachy, that's what you are,' she told him.

'You're beautiful, Eve,' he responded. 'I love your smile. I love your hair. I love your arms, your legs, your breasts, your tiny hips. I love the fleshy dome of your womb. I love all of you. I want all of you.'

He pushed and pushed until she thought she would die. She arched her back so he could penetrate deeper. He sent electric shocks through her nipples with his lips. She pushed her nose under his and forced his mouth open, sliding her tongue inside to drink him.

The giant lamb's-wool hand picked them up as they lay entwined – and gently, so very gently, turned them over.

Now he was behind, exploring new frontiers inside her. She folded her arms around the edge of the cushions – and enjoyed. She could feel the pressure building in her body. She began to whimper. It was almost a sad cry, like the tears of joy and sorrow that come with meeting a long-lost friend who must soon be on his way again.

It was a cry that said: 'I've never been so happy, though I know it cannot last.'

All the joy, all the sorrow and every other emotion she possessed flooded out of her as she climaxed. She heard

10

Adam shout her name. 'Eve! Pearl! Eve!' And she knew Elliot was happy and sad, too.

She lay there for a moment, with Adam heavy on her back, before the giant lamb's-wool hand tucked itself under her belly and raised her into the air.

The cushions vanished and below her was the carpet of the woodland garden, green and fertile with the vigour of late spring. Birds sang, daffodils pushed proud and erect through fresh blades of grass. It was all so magical, so perfect.

Too perfect. Too good to be true.

Pearl was unsettled and, for the briefest of moments, her eyelids flickered open and she was in the bedroom of her apartment in New York.

She saw the cuckoo clock she had brought back from Switzerland to put on her wall. Two luminous green hands fixed on a tiny wooden chalet, with a gaily-dressed milk maiden dangling beneath on a swing. She saw a pile of skirts and sweaters overflowing from her wardrobe. And she saw her new photo of smiling, crunchy-peachy Elliot, its corners curling as it rested against a bedside lamp that was still alight.

'Stay here,' she murmured aloud. 'Don't go back. It was good but now it's bad. Don't go back.'

Her mind would not listen to reason. She slept again and returned to the woodland garden. For the first time, she realized she had been there before – and that something had happened on that day. Something that could not be more divorced from making love with Adam. Something terrible.

'Not the Garden of Eden,' she told herself. 'Just woods. Woods outside Geneva. The school picnic.'

Her nostrils caught the scent first, but it was not long before she saw them. Bluebells. Knots of them scattered

11

here and there, bent by the breeze and *laughing*. Laughing at her.

'No. Please, no. Not now. If there is a God up there, make them stop.'

A red squirrel appeared and darted through the blooms, the tufts on its ears making the bells jangle as the creature brushed against them.

'Go away! I told you I never wanted to see you again.'

The squirrel looked at her and smiled. Mischievously, it shook its head from side to side to make the bells ring louder, before scurrying behind the trunk of a fallen pine tree.

Pearl heard voices. Shrill young voices that betrayed fear. The voices of her dearest friends when they were six years old, gawping at the awful spectacle that was unfolding before their eyes in the clearing beyond. Pearl knew she was with them. One of seven little girls united by an unbreakable bond and a growing sense of dread. They stood rooted to the spot, staring open-mouthed at a man and a woman facing each other in the clearing beside the rusty wreck of an old car long since abandoned by its final owner.

It was Stefanie who transmitted a need for action. 'The tree trunk. Hide, Pearl! Hide, Louise!'

'What's he doing?'

'Hide, Kipini! Hide, Sari!'

It *was* Stefanie. Pearl could hear her as clear as day.

'Hide, Mai-Lin! Hide, Dany!'

'What's he doing?'

'He's hurting her. Listen, she's crying.'

Pearl caught a snatch of their teacher's frantic cry, blown this way and that by the breeze as she searched the woods for her lost charges.

'*Girls, girls. Where are you, girls?*'

'Over here, Mam'selle,' Sari called.

'Ssssh!' Stefanie hissed. 'They might hear us.'

'Who?' Louise asked.

'The man and the woman.'

'Ugh! There's a squidgy mushroom on this tree trunk.' Sari grimaced at her discovery.

'Ssssh!'

'I won't shush.'

'You must. They'll hear us.'

Pearl could hear and see as if she was watching a movie on television. She wanted to stop it. Switch off the picture, turn off the sound. But she could not reach out. She became aware of a growing sense of smell and tried not to inhale as the air became thick with the scent of fresh pine. Silver birches and sycamores swayed as the breeze picked up. The squirrel, alarmed, ran away through the bluebells.

'*Girls, girls!*'

'Mam'selle wants us.'

'We can't go now.'

'Even if we wanted to.'

'I want to.'

'You can't go, Sari.'

'What's he doing now?'

'She can't get up.'

'Why not?'

'He won't let her.'

Two more voices, one deep, the other pitched higher. It was them. The man and the woman.

'*All I want to know is why?*'

'*If you do not know, you should know.*'

'*I don't understand.*'

'*It is time to tell the world – and be done with it.*'

'*No! It is a secret and shall remain a secret.*'

13

'*You cannot expect me to agree to that. Not now. Not after what I told you.*'

'*You must! You have to . . .*'

'*I do not HAVE to do anything. You do not own me.*'

Stefanie butted in. 'She's angry.'

'She speaks funny,' said Dany.

'She's not American.'

'Or English.'

'Neither am I,' said Mai-Lin.

'You speak funny, too.'

'Look!' Kipini cried.

'What's he doing?'

'Oh, dear sweet Jesus. Don't let him do that.'

A glint of sunshine reflecting from metal or polished stone. Four fingers on his left hand. That's right, only four. I counted them. Perhaps he cut one off.

'*Girls! Les enfants! You must come back to me.*'

'I want to go back to Mam'selle.'

'Be quiet, Sari.'

'Ssssh!'

'He's hitting her.'

'He's angry with her.'

'He shouldn't do that.'

'He's hitting her.'

'Oh no . . . please don't, M'sieur. Please . . .'

Pearl was helpless. She looked over her shoulder. Adam was Elliot again. She reached out to him, pleaded with him to help her. But he was dissolving like sugar in boiling water. Soon, nothing remained of him – and she was left with her six little friends.

She clung on to Dany behind the tree trunk. She closed her eyes, but still she could see. She pushed her fingers in her ears, but still she could hear. There was no escape.

'She's not moving.'

14

'Do you think she's . . .'

'Yes.'

'What's he doing now?'

'Oh, no.'

'No! No! Leave her alone.'

But the man didn't leave her alone. The seven girls watched in shocked silence, numb with confusion and fear.

The breeze turned into a wind. Dark clouds spread quickly from the horizon, blotting out the sun. As the first drops of rain clattered on to a row of docks beside the tree trunk, the man turned round.

'He's seen us.'

'He's heard us.'

'He's covered in red.'

'He looks strange.'

'I don't like him.'

'He's seen us.'

'He's coming for us.'

'What shall we do?'

'Run!'

'I can't. My legs . . .'

'His face – there's something wrong with it.'

'Look, he's coming.'

'Help! Mam'selle! Mummy!'

'Leave us alone!'

Pearl watched the man stride towards them through the brambles and across the moss. Behind him, a scarecrow appeared from nowhere, its limp form dressed in black rags and dangling from a tree on a rope. As the wind picked up, it swung to and fro, making the rope groan like a wounded soldier. Yet the man did not let it distract him. His eyes, glowing crimson amid the instant gunmetal gloom of the woods, made it clear he had only one thing on his mind.

'He's still coming,' Dany called.

'NO!' Pearl screamed as he reached them. 'GO AWAY, NASTY MAN!'

Pearl was overwhelmed by the horror of the vision. She could not control it – and it came to control her. It clawed at her mind, pulled great chunks from her flesh, pummelled her bones to dust. At the very horizon of her consciousness, she was somehow aware that she was convulsing. Froth spewed from her mouth.

A door opened. A man rushed into the bedroom. There was a scream of alarm.

'Christ, Pearl, what is it?'

If only anyone knew . . .

2

The key rattled resonantly in the lock and the side of a fist thudded against the thick metal door.

'Get up! Slop out! Make your bed! Up, up, up!'

Knapp was already awake. He stirred every morning at 6.30 and waited fifteen minutes – or 900 seconds, counted one by one – for the inevitable rattle, the inevitable thud and the inevitable cry from the corridor outside. Always the same pitch, always the same volume, always the same emphasis on the final 'Up!' The disembodied harbinger of another day in Mogden secure hospital, a day in which the empty routine would follow the precise pattern of the day before, and the day before that, and the day before that.

It was February. Knapp knew it would still be dark outside, though it mattered little in this room, which had no view, no contact with the rest of Mother Earth. Its only window was set in the door and barred, its only light was artificial. Soon, when the charge nurse reached the switch cupboard, the pale-blue security nightlamp that glowed with a dull sheen high above his bed would be replaced by the unshielded glare from the single white bulb that hung desolately from the cracked ceiling.

And yet, and yet . . .

Knapp sighed with a heaviness that reflected the contradictions and ironies of his situation. The room was a symbol of privilege, granted to him in return for his work in the library and the administration office. And the lightbulb was a symbol of trust, granted because his consultant was convinced that, unlike many others in this place, he would make no attempt to twist it from its socket, smash it and use the sharp edges to carve bloody fissures in his wrists. Without such concessions, Knapp would still have been in one bed among forty-five others in the ward around the corner, and he couldn't have that.

He had spent the best part of six years in that ward before he realized what had happened to him, why it had happened and what he could do to rectify it. From that moment to this had been another twenty-four years, taking him past his sixtieth birthday.

Thirty years – *THIRTY YEARS* – inside this dank, draughty, God-forsaken relic of Victorian monstrosity. Locked away thousands of miles from his homeland. It did not bear thinking about.

Yet not a moment went by without such thoughts. It dominated Knapp's soul, scratched at the inside of his skull with great claws of bitterness. The waste, the unfairness, the frustration, the conspiracy against him. It was all there, mixed together in a sludge of silent, but simmering protest.

And it was all *their* fault. The seven girls. The seven little snoopers. Without them, he could forget the past. And without them, he could yet build a future.

The future . . . ah yes. It would be at Kennedy's side, just as his past would have been had he not been cruelly robbed of the opportunity. Oh, he knew all about Friday, 22 November 1963. Dallas. The Texas School Book Depository. The mystery man on the grassy knoll. The screams of Jackie as she was spattered with blood. He knew every detail, down to Exhibit 134 presented before the Warren Commission: a photograph of Lee Harvey Oswald holding the same rifle that was found in the depository.

18

He also knew there had been *NO* assassination. He had read countless newspaper articles and books telling him there had been, watched hours-long television documentaries trying to pin the blame on the Mafia, the CIA, Russia, Cuba, the FBI, Uncle Tom Cobbleigh and all.

But it had been a sham. Kennedy had been too smart, too great a man to have got himself shot. In Knapp's estimation, he had simply *tired* of being President, for his own reasons, and had decided to get out – to take a rest – by fooling the world in the cleverest way imaginable. Faking his own death in front of television cameras that made the world a witness.

Just as surely, Kennedy would one day return to take up his rightful position at the head of mankind. It was his destiny and he knew it, whatever the personal considerations that had forced him into hiding and Jackie into the arms of the fat Greek shipping magnate.

By now, like a good wine, Kennedy would have matured into something extraordinary, something to be savoured. He was waiting for the right moment, that was all. The moment when his valued associate Donald J. Knapp was ready to stand at his side again. The moment when the perfect partnership would be restored in all its former glory.

Knapp was prepared to accept whatever duties Kennedy called upon him to perform. He would seek out the great man and take up his position the instant he removed the only obstacle in his path. The seven little girls. They had destroyed him once and could destroy him again.

Unless he destroyed them first.

Knapp knew he would soon be free to settle the issue. Hagerty had told him so in his last letter. It had arrived from Washington a week ago, addressed to Michael

Crosby, the name by which Knapp had been known since his arrival at Mogden. Like all Hagerty's letters, it had been left unopened and unscrutinized by the hospital censors, and had been delivered to him in person by Ashe, the Medical Controller. It was more breezy in tone than Hagerty's habitually bland scrawlings, and ended with the news of his imminent release and a PS which read: 'By the way, I've chosen another new name for you to celebrate the occasion. Evan P. Dallenbach. How do you like it?'

Knapp did not like it, any more than he had liked Michael Crosby. But just as before, he saw the necessity for it and adopted it at once. He kept it a secret from everyone, even Ashe. One more secret to go with all the others. It was a timely boost to the covert world of private thoughts and intentions which he had nurtured and honed inside his ten-by-ten domain. Thoughts and intentions which kept him apart . . . and kept him superior.

The lightbulb flashed on. Knapp felt his pupils shrink and steeled himself for his daily ordeal of mixing with the stinking collection of the insane, the demented and the deluded that fate had decreed to be his fellow travellers in time. Some were murderers, rapists, arsonists and the like. Some were inside Mogden because of the severity of their illnesses rather than their offences. Some disturbed souls were there simply because there was nowhere else for them to go.

Whatever their circumstances, Knapp found them all disgusting. Over the years, helped by the possession of his own room, he had distanced himself more and more from them, until contact was the minimum required to avoid violence. It was not that he was afraid of physical confrontation. He was tall, six feet and the rest, and strong enough. But in Mogden, whether you were assailant or victim, your name went down on an Incident Report. And that was one more barrier to freedom.

A polite 'Good morning' here, a courteous 'How are you today?' there. It was all that was needed.

At times, he could feel their burning resentment, the charring laser beams of their eyes as they glared at him, the venom in their sneers and their insults. But what did they expect a man of his stature to do? Join them for a game of football on the Airing Court? Now that really would be grotesque.

Most of them had learned and left him alone. Many, it seemed, had even become wary of him. Some had become frightened. Which was appropriate. Knapp remembered a frowning Kennedy turning to him a year before he won the Democratic Presidential nomination and asking, 'Donald, do you think it's true what they say? That good leaders are the loneliest men on earth?'

Knapp did not doubt it then and did not doubt it now. It was a price that had to be paid.

He climbed from his bed and put on his dressing gown and slippers. His door was pushed open by an unseen hand and the deafening cacophony of the ward swept in. Knapp gripped his chamberpot and walked into a corridor suddenly swarming with rejected humanity. He was bumped by another patient, making some of his urine spill over the edge of the pot and on to his ankles.

'God!' he cried out, wincing at the wetness. The other man looked up at him, ready to snarl a challenge. But then he saw who it was, and scurried back into the crowd before Knapp had a chance for retribution.

The toilet was abominable. Bodies pushing other bodies. Elbows jabbing into ribs. Grey-skinned men squatting in cubicles with no doors, their pyjamas

21

crumpled at their feet. The stench of excreta. Nurses watching everybody and everything they did. Every damn thing.

'No bog paper,' someone called.

'Use your fucking fingernails,' a nurse responded.

'Screw you, screw.'

Knapp knew he should have been immune by now. But he wasn't, and suspected the same was true of everyone pressed against him.

He washed and shaved hurriedly, his sole motivation being a compulsion to get out of the toilet as soon as possible. The instant he slipped his toothbrush back into his washbag, he barged his way through the throng of vested armpits and returned to the ward for his next dose of degradation, morning roll call.

'Line up! Line up!' The same emphasis on the final 'Up!' from the same charge nurse.

Knapp stood off the end of his rank. Only a yard or so, but sufficient to keep him apart from the rabble. He ignored an order to close in and the charge nurse did not press the point, contenting himself with a resigned scowl in Knapp's direction.

It was a relief when the interminable head-counting was over, and he was allowed to return to the refuge of his room.

He cast an eye around its absurdly high walls as if rehearsing for the day of his release. He had done his best to make something of it. Put up abstract paintings by a particularly artistic inmate who used vivid colours as a reaction against his dour surroundings. Filled shelves with books, cheered up his iron-frame bed with a striped blanket donated by some charity or other. His privileged existence had endowed him with a radio, a record player, a desk and a television on which he could follow his Open

22

University courses. But in a crass gesture by the authorities to prove who remained in control, he had not been allowed to decorate. His walls, like all others throughout the building, were unplastered brick covered with a drab shade of dusty ochre paint, effectively killing any hopes Knapp ever entertained of treating the room as anything but a cell.

He dressed in one of the two suits Hagerty had sent him along with the letter. But he had no mirror and did not know how he looked.

'Very stylish, Mr Crosby. Very stylish indeed.'

Jute, a weasel-like nurse who combed strands of loose sandy hair laterally across his skull in a vain attempt to disguise the onset of baldness, arrived carrying Knapp's breakfast tray. Knapp turned. Not for the first time, Jute was stopped in his tracks by the man's towering size and the aura of inner strength and importance that went with it.

'Don't patronize me, Jute,' Knapp said severely.

'No . . . er . . .' Jute's voice was edged with uncertainty. 'I didn't mean it to sound like . . .'

'No matter.' Knapp waved a dismissive hand and motioned to Jute to leave the tray on the desk. The smell of frying lard swept into his nostrils and made him retch. He did not trouble to examine the food. It never changed. A plate of egg and bacon swimming in fat; a piece of dry, cold toast and a cup of tea filled so carelessly that most would be in the saucer.

Jute, a born opportunist, was quick to react.

'I'll have it if you don't want it,' he said eagerly.

'So you can sell it to someone else for a couple of cigarettes? C'mon, Jute, I know you better than your thieving mother. Besides . . .'

23

'You're hungry enough to swallow anything – and it's better than eating in the canteen with the loonies.'

Jute expected a chuckle or at least a flicker of the eyes to acknowledge such a darkly astute observation. But Knapp remained as impassive as ever – and Jute stayed as confused as ever.

Rumours abounded about why Crosby, an American, had been locked away in a British secure hospital for the criminally insane. About why he received letters and parcels from a mysterious benefactor in Washington DC. About why he had immersed himself in complex academic studies. And particularly, about why he never gave away *anything* of himself to others. But to Jute's annoyance, no hard facts had emerged.

'The Controller wants to see you,' the nurse said. 'I'm to go with you after you have finished your breakfast.'

'He follows me here, he follows me there, he follows me everywhere,' Knapp responded.

'Not my choice,' Jute said defensively.

'So I don't get lost,' Knapp continued. 'After all, the corridors here only lead to other corridors. And they all look just the same. Could be confusing for a madman, don't you think?'

The mocking sarcasm was lost on Jute. He fiddled uneasily with the master key dangling from his waist on a leather strap, and asked bluntly: 'Why does the Controller want to see you?'

'You don't know?' Knapp said with surprise.

'No, but I bet you do. You always do, don't you?'

Knapp was gratified by the implied deference.

'I am to be released. Set free. Out of the pen. Over the wall.'

'It's not a jail.'

24

'No? Look around, Jute. Do you see patients or pris-
oners? Nurses or warders? Treatment or punishment?
Doctors or judges? Only consultant psychiatrists can sign
a release form.'

'So yours has been signed. It means they've made you
better.'

'*They* made me better?' Knapp was outraged. His lips
thinned and he spat his next words. 'I made *myself* better
decades ago. And since then, what? They made me wait
. . . and wait . . . and wait. I have been here thirty years,
Jute. Nothing much in the scheme of things, eh?'

Jute searched for a way to escape the tirade.

Knapp saw his unease and yelled, 'Should I stop
shouting, making a scene? To protest about my treatment
is to *prove* I am psychotic, right, Jute?' He stopped short
of losing his temper completely, mainly through sheer
exhaustion at having played the game for so long. He
looked benignly at the nurse and said quietly, 'I ask you,
Jute. I ask you to tell me why I was not released *years*
ago?'

Jute had no answers. Though Crosby's medical file had
for some reason remained locked in a safe, he could make
an educated guess at its contents. A classification graduating from 'Improved' to 'Suitable for Transfer to Conditions of Lower Security' to 'Suitable for Release'. Yet,
if such recommendations had indeed been made, Ashe
had never acted upon them. And for all Jute knew, the
Home Office, the final arbiters, had never heard of
Michael Crosby.

Jute felt stickily uneasy and in the end could think of
nothing but spinning around and rushing out. Knapp
heard the click of his heels echoing in the corridor and
counted the paces. Five . . . six . . . seven. The noise
fading now, to be replaced any second by the clanking of

25

keys, the turning of a lock, the sliding of a bolt and the groaning of a door. And then Jute would click on into the bowels of North Riding Wing.

Someone had to pay. They would all pay. Knapp sat at his desk and thrust his head between his hands, concentrating his thoughts on the mission that was to come, a mission for which he had been preparing since the day he was given his own room and his own privacy.

He was ready in both body and mind.

To keep his body supple, he had put himself through a vigorous workout each and every day. Sometimes in the gymnasium, more often simply in the space beside his bed. Sit-ups, push-ups, squat thrusts, trunk curls. Even without a mirror, he knew he was in superb shape for a man of sixty.

To keep his mind alert and, above all, disciplined, he had plunged himself into the study of quantum theory in all its infinite aspects. He had taken to it after pulling a book from the library shelf entitled *Quantum Physics: Illusion or Reality?* which he felt reflected his own situation admirably. And Hagerty had kept him supplied with each new book and research paper on the topic, of which there were hundreds.

The subject was vast, complex and dynamic, which suited a man with nothing but time on his hands. Moreover, it combined scientific fact with philosophy and mysticism – throwing up wonderfully gruelling contortions for the brain to unravel. In the 1970s, he had sailed through two Open University degree courses in physics and chemistry to add to the Harvard law diploma he had obtained as a student. And six years ago, he had become an Oxford University Master of Science by correspondence after writing a thesis on quantum mechanical tunnelling in biological systems. He knew he had reason to

26

be proud – and there was no doubt his achievements had impressed Mogden's medical boards. But then again, what the hell did they know?

NOTHING!

For all their probing and all their tests, they had never uncovered the clues. Clues that had been filed away in his mind for three decades. Clues that would lead him to the girls. Clues that were with him again now, dancing in front of his eyes.

He saw the woods in Geneva . . . he saw Yelena . . . and Hagerty . . . and Napier and Lipton. He saw the school crest on the girls' blazers. Two white swans with intertwined necks on a curly silver line representing water. He remembered two names, Pearl and Dany. He remembered an Oriental girl – and a black girl the others called something like Bikini. He raised his left hand in front of his eyes and remembered how he lost his ring finger, remembered how it was severed below the knuckle. He remembered how through the blood and through the flailing arms, he heard Napier's plummy voice cry, 'Dear Lord, it could have been my daughter watching you butcher . . .'

Knapp had felt a surge of power within himself ever since he received Hagerty's letter. It was like a massive cobweb-coated generator being started up again after aeons of decay and neglect. Now that power was about to be released. All that time wasted, but *nothing* could stop him now.

3

'Finish your apple, Dany. The others are waiting.'

'I won't be long, Mam'selle.'

'Do not speak with your mouth full, child.'

'But – '

'No buts. It is rude.'

Dany chewed hard. The other girls stared at her, some willing her on, others pouting with impatience.

'Oh come on, Dany,' Stefanie groaned. She was eager to begin the adventure.

Dany swallowed the remnants of the apple, core and all.

'Well done, Dany,' Mam'selle said. 'Now gather round, girls.'

The girls gathered round. Mam'selle was young, in her first year as an infants' teacher. She had long ash-blonde hair and a pale skin that made her rosy cheeks look as if they had been painted on, like those of a circus clown. She was wearing one of her favourite pink gingham dresses, which Sari thought looked like a tablecloth. The girls liked Mam'selle's softness and friendliness, partly because she reminded them of their mothers – and partly because they knew that should they be mischievous, they could normally get away with it.

'It's a lovely warm spring day, so let's make the most of it. We'll collect some wild flowers of as many different types as possible. Then we'll take them back to school and I'll show you how to press them.'

'Press them?' Pearl had never heard of flower-pressing

– and as usual had formed a question by repeating the last two words of the previous speaker's sentence.

'You put the flowers in the middle of a book,' Stefanie volunteered. 'Then you leave them for a bit and they come out all dry and flat. Mommy does it sometimes with the roses in the garden.'

'The garden?'

'The one in Geneva, silly. Oh, I guess you don't have a garden, do you? I forgot you lived in an apartment.'

'We had a garden in Washington,' Pearl said defensively.

Mam'selle swept a delicately-boned hand in a circle around her, indicating the perimeter of the clearing which they had chosen for their picnic.

'Do not go any further than the very edge of the trees,' she said. 'Do not leave my sight. Is that understood?'

'Yes, Mam'selle,' the girls chorused.

'Now we have twenty girls here. Let us see if we can find twenty different flowers. Who will be the first to find the white petals of the wild strawberry? There are some here, I saw them earlier. Off you go now.'

The girls did as they were told, short stubby legs stamping awkwardly over clumps of grass and tangled knots of fern, eyes glued a yard in front of their feet as they searched for primroses and pansies. Mam'selle settled on a rug with a copy of Balzac's *Le Père Goriot*, grateful for the lull after the frenetic squabbling of the picnic. Girls will be girls, she told herself, but *must* they be so noisy? Before she caught up with Balzac's story, she watched the children fan out towards the edge of the clearing and wondered when the seven would break away, as they always did.

A second after the thought crossed her mind, Stefanie, all ribbons, bows and silky auburn curls, veered left. And as if she were the Pied Piper, she was followed in turn by Pearl, Dany, Kipini, Mai-Lin, Louise and Sari.

'Like glue,' Mam'selle muttered under her breath, grinning at the speed with which her prediction had come true. Her eyes flicked down to her book. '*Page quatre-vingts-dix*,' she said aloud, pleased to be thinking once more in her native French. '*Arrivé rue Neuve-Saint-Geneviève, il monta rapidement chez lui . . .*'

The girls formed a circle. They pulled the creases from their white cotton dresses, flicked dust and fallen hairs from their crimson blazers and straightened their straw bonnets. They wanted to be smart for the ritual that sealed their membership in the secret society. They called themselves the Seven Swans, a name taken from their number, the name of their school – L'École Internationale des Cygnes – and a line from the carol they had learned the Christmas before last. Seven swans a-swimming, six geese a-laying, five go-wold rings.

'Who are we?' Stefanie yelled.

The others sang out in unison. 'We are the Seven Swans. And we'll hiss and we'll spit before we will split.'

Kipini could not stifle a giggle. It happened every time she said 'spit'. The others glowered at her, anxious to get on with the ceremony. Stefanie held out her arm so her hand was at the centre of the circle. Her neighbour, Dany, followed suit, wrapping her wrist around Stefanie's like the necks of the swans on their blazers. Pearl was next and then the others, until they all had hold of each other.

They struck up the final line of the chorus. 'Swans don't cry, swans don't lie. Swans stay together until they die.'

Stefanie, a rebel from the day she could crawl, glanced towards Mam'selle as they broke apart. 'C'mon,' she said.

'Come on where?' Louise asked nervously.

Stefanie nodded to the edge of the woods and said, 'The adventure. Remember?'

When Mam'selle next looked up from her book, they were gone.

Memories swirled around the souls of the six remaining Swans as they watched Pearl's coffin being lowered into the ground. They clung to each other for support, excluding husbands, boyfriends and surviving parents, in order to share one private, united moment of grief.

'I can't believe it.' Dany shook her head sorrowfully, feeling a stream of warm tears flowing across her cheeks. She was on the point of collapse and held tightly to the fabric of Stefanie's dress. 'I just can't believe it.'

'No one can,' Kipini offered.

'Do you remember the school reunions?' Louise said. 'How we huddled together in a corner, dressed in our very best ball gowns, talking about our skiing holidays and the time we met Senator Kennedy in the Palais des Nations? Pearl was so thrilled.'

'We all were,' said Mai-Lin.

'And now she has been taken from us,' Sari said in a spiritual way, which made them all cry harder.

Curran – Pearl's brother and Dany's husband – stood to one side with his father. He listened to the priest saying a prayer, but did not hear the words. It was the first funeral he had been to since his mother died years ago, and he was unsure of his emotions. Between deep crevasses of hopeless grief, he found himself thinking that it all had to end for everyone some time, that he could be next, and – ridiculously – that the family burial plot, amid gently swaying palms on a man-made hillock overlooking the Atlantic rollers between Miami and Fort Lauderdale, was a fine location for a last resting place. It was where

Pearl would sleep for ever. And it was where he, too, wanted to spend his eternal days, even though he had long since lived in Britain.

He looked at the six women draped in black beside him and marvelled at the strength of their bond. They had come from all corners of the globe to be together, just as they had gathered many times before for happier occasions. Sari from Australia, Mai-Lin from Bangkok, Kipini from some plantation or other deep in the Kenyan bush. Louise had travelled with him and Dany from England. And Stefanie had flown in that morning from California.

How sad, how very sad, that Pearl could no longer be with them.

'Ashes to ashes, dust to dust . . .'

They threw flowers on to the coffin as the priest recited his final dirge. When the gravediggers began to fill in their hole, it became too much to watch. The six women wheeled away bereft of anything but a naked hollowness inside.

Curran went to comfort Dany, but was intercepted by Stefanie. She had been away and had not learned of Pearl's death until fourteen hours before the funeral. Now, she needed to know what had happened.

Curran wondered what he should say. Was he to tell Stefanie here and now, at his sister's graveside, how Pearl had died as he watched? How she had tossed and turned on her bed, drenched in her own sweat as if gripped by some dreaded tropical fever. How she had screamed for help that he could not give. How foam gushed from her mouth like a waterfall the instant before her body went limp . . .

'You were there.' Stefanie had taken too many tranquillizers, and was barely coherent. 'You must tell me.'

For some reason, Curran tried to make it sound matter-of-fact, as expected of a journalist writing daily of disaster and tragedy. But he discovered as he spoke that personal involvement was another matter – and his hesitant voice betrayed his anguish. 'I was staying at her apartment in New York. A sort of holiday, you know. You've heard about Dany and me . . .'

'I know your marriage is in trouble,' Stefanie said sympathetically. 'As if you both didn't have enough with all of this.'

Curran grunted wearily, but continued his story. 'Pearl wasn't there all the time. Some magazine had commissioned her to write a feature on the early days of the United Nations, and she popped over to Geneva to research the European end. Anyway, when she came back, she wasn't well. She found it hard to sleep, she ran a temperature and kept having these God-awful nightmares.'

Stefanie checked behind to make sure Dany had not been left alone. When she saw Pearl's father at Dany's side, she slipped her arm through Curran's and walked with him up a grassy slope to the waiting cortège of limousines.

'Go on . . .' she urged gently, knowing that like her, Curran was bleeding inside.

'She said that if she wasn't going to sleep, she may as well make the best of it. She went to an all-night party. Somewhere in the Village, I think. I didn't go – she was with Elliot. After she came back, she made it through to about five the next evening, then said that if she didn't crash out, she would pass. I said OK and switched on the TV as she went to bed. A couple of hours later, I heard this terrible crashing and bumping from her room. I went to see what was going on – and there she was. All

33

over the place, screaming and having a kind of fit. I tried to bring her round, but there was noth. . .' His voice tailed off as he was stabbed by guilt that was as real as it was irrational.

Stefanie squeezed his elbow into her waist. 'Was there an autopsy?' she asked.

Curran gathered his thoughts, gulping mouthfuls of fresh coastal air for sustenance. 'They found a slight abnormality in the conduction system of her heart. They said it wasn't much and may not have been the cause of death, but in the absence of anything else . . .'

'A congenital defect? Your mother died from a heart attack.'

'I don't know.'

'Perhaps you should have a check-up.'

'I don't know. I don't know.'

'She wasn't on drugs or anything?'

'No. She drank quite a bit, but don't we all . . .'

'No heroin, no coke?'

'No, Stefanie.' He used her name deliberately, knowing of her chequered history of creative highs and drug-racked lows. 'I told you. I told you what the autopsy found.'

'I'm sorry.'

'God, Stefanie, I'm sorry, too.' Curran's despair overcame him. He stopped walking, pushed his face into cupped hands and felt his palms being dampened by his tears. Stefanie put an arm around his bent shoulders.

'It should be me comforting you,' Curran muttered hopelessly.

'I've got the Swans,' Stefanie said. 'They'll help me. We'll help each other.' She tried to be brave, but felt a renewed thrust of pain as she listened to Curran's muffled, aching words.

'I just wish she had come round. Just for a minute. Just so I could've said goodbye.'

'Left here, driver. Follow the white van ahead.' Hagerty closed the Jaguar's glass partition with a rigid finger. Chauffeurs were such notorious eavesdroppers.

The car's suspension made light of the rutted tarmac track. But even so, Hagerty knew he would be in for a rough ride as soon as they picked up Knapp. He wiped condensation from the window and stared out.

Dawn was trying its hardest to push through the bulbous charcoal clouds above, but was fighting a losing battle. Even if it won, Hagerty thought, there was precious little for it to illuminate. If there was a bleaker landscape anywhere on the planet, he had yet to see it. A stark moorland valley between two stark moorland ranges. Only the odd limestone rock broke the relentless rolls of barren turf. And the sole sign of life came from twitching twigs of heather, freeze-dried by the north-east wind that ripped through the Pennines in winter. Even in the warmth of the Jaguar, Hagerty flicked up the collar of his coat.

He turned to aim a reassuring smile at Martha, Knapp's daughter. She tried to respond. But she was too nervous and her face stayed taut and watchful.

Hagerty worried about Martha. He had always worried about Martha, though not for the reasons she thought. He knew she regarded him as a sort of kind uncle, more than just a friend of her father's. A patron who had known her since she was a babe in arms, and who had stayed in touch with her to help her over her father's incarceration and her mother's death.

The truth, if only the poor kid knew it, was that she was what Hagerty called a 'pipe-joint'. Under pressure, pipe-joints leaked. And the result could be a catastrophic flood. Martha didn't know much. But she knew enough to cause havoc if ever she blabbed. And that was why Hagerty had taken her under his wing. To make sure she didn't.

When she was sixteen, soon after her mother died, Hagerty took her to one side, sat her on a sofa, told her that her father was still alive, where he was and why he had been sent there.

'You know he was a very fine diplomat when you were born,' he said. 'Probably the best at the United Nations in Geneva. And that he was destined for great things, maybe in the White House.'

The teenager nodded.

'And your mom told you he had to do some kinda secret work, and that he was killed doing it.'

The teenager nodded again.

Hagerty remembered clearing his throat to inject his voice with sincerity. 'Well, Martha dear, only half of that was true. He did get involved in secret stuff. He had to go to a building in England. A building below ground, under Downing Street. Have you heard of Downing Street?'

'It's where the British Prime Minister lives,' the girl said.

'That's right. Only he was under a great deal of pressure. National security, that type of thing. A lot depended on him and I'm afraid it all became a little too much. It does sometimes, you know, even for the strongest of us.'

'So what happened?' Martha had said directly.

'He went a little crazy and set fire to the building. An awful lot of really secret British documents went up in smoke – you know, there weren't many computers around then, everything was on paper. And three people in the building were killed.'

'So they put Daddy away?' Martha had understood instantly, which was a relief.

'Yes, they did, honey. In England, because that's where he did what he did.'

'So is he OK now?'

'He's better, honey, much better.'

Hagerty could see Martha's eyes lighting up as if it were yesterday. From that moment on, she knew her father was *ALIVE*!

And that is why she was a pipe-joint.

Of course, they had talked it over many times since and Martha had asked him to shade in the grey areas. But his story of the revered diplomat turned agent, who in a moment of madness had flashed over into berserk arsonist, had remained essentially intact.

From time to time, Hagerty felt stabs of guilt at such deception. But then again, he was in the business of lying, a high-up at State who liaised with the CIA over disinformation that could be pumped into the system to be picked up by the Reds. All cock and bullshit, all part of the game. And his lies about Knapp – for the truth did not remotely concern espionage or arson – were utterly essential.

To protect Knapp, to protect himself and to protect Napier and Lipton.

A careless sparrow flew across the path of the white van in front and was hit. It spiralled lifelessly through the air and thudded against the Jaguar's windscreen. Martha jumped as if the dead bird had been a grenade, and the shock fuelled the tension that had gripped her body.

'Oh Jesus . . . oh God,' she uttered. She looked at Hagerty, her eyes begging for help.

He placed his hand on hers. 'It's natural to be frightened,' he said warmly. 'You were tiny when he was taken away. You only met him when you were eighteen, across a desk in a funny kind of hospital. You don't truly know him. Sure, it's natural to be frightened.'

'I feel sick,' Martha complained. 'It's worse than just the jitters.'

Hagerty patted her wrist. 'Don't worry. It'll be fine. It's just good to know your father is well enough to come out and join the rest of civilization, isn't it?'

'I suppose – but I can't help it. Oh Jesus . . .'

Martha pulled away from Hagerty so she could wring her hands. Hagerty saw her knuckles turn white and her fingertips glow crimson with trapped blood. He felt like telling Martha to get a grip, to put a block on her damn neuroses before they careered out of control. But he clung on to his patience, mainly because a part of him, at least, understood her.

At times, he wondered if she would flip, just as her father had done. After all, alcoholic fathers often sired alcoholic children. That sort of link was a proven medical fact, so maybe it applied to conditions of the brain. Hagerty hoped and prayed it did not, for then Martha would be a pipe-joint that could blow apart, let alone leak.

No, he had convinced himself that Knapp's daughter was merely *damaged*, like a bent key that doesn't quite fit in the lock. The evidence of her years as a woman backed up such an assumption. She had left a trail of broken romances like the debris from a crashed jet.

One after another, poor misguided men had fallen head over heels in love with her. She was pretty, she had an air of vulnerability that made their hearts balloon. And there

38

was no doubt that on occasions, she had returned their love.

But she was so damn *contrary*. One minute she would want her hand to be held. The next she would pull it away. One moment she would be desperate for a strong man to move in with her. The next she would complain resentfully of his intrusion upon her privacy. The guys were on a hiding to nothing. And most, Hagerty was sure, had given up through sheer exhaustion.

Yet who could blame her? A girl who had never known her father. A girl whose mother had died as she battled the hell of puberty. A girl whose perception of life had been turned upside down by the news of what had really happened to her daddy.

Maybe she had never truly grown up. Maybe, even now, even at the age of thirty-odd, she *needed* a father. Hagerty knew she had lifted Knapp on to a pedestal higher than the Empire State, even though she had only her imagination to go on. Hagerty knew because he had encouraged her. It was one more layer of sealant over the pipe-joint.

'What's his new name?' Martha said suddenly. 'Tell me again. I keep forgetting.'

'Dallenbach,' Hagerty replied. 'Evan P. Dallenbach. He won't like it, but it's – '

'Necessary. I know. Like it's necessary that Donald Knapp must stay a dead man if he is to have any kind of life.'

'Good girl.'

'Please don't call me that.'

'What?'

'Girl. I stopped being a girl a long time ago.'

'I'm sorry.'

Martha looked shame-faced at Hagerty. 'I didn't mean to snap,' she said. 'I'm sorry, too.'

'That's OK,' he said calmly. 'It's natural to be frightened today.'

Hagerty channelled her on to small-talk to keep her occupied. He asked her how her job was going, whether she was satisfied by Pan Am's latest pay award to its stewardesses, whether she preferred London to New York, whether she would like to fly another route.

But his scant concentration evaporated totally when the Jaguar turned a corner and the turreted silhouette of Mogden hospital came into view.

'Good Christ . . .' Hagerty glared disbelievingly at the cluster of people standing thirty yards from the main gate in a haze of silver thrown up by powerful lights. He knew who they were long before the Jaguar rolled to a halt behind the white van on the gravel circle outside the gate. Press. At least sixty of the bastards.

Hagerty peered out at them, grateful for the car's smoked windows that prevented them peering in at him.

Photographers and camera crews jostled for position behind a makeshift cordon of striped tape set up by the posse of policemen keeping watch nearby. Sheepskin-coated reporters stood to one side smoking cigarettes and rubbing their hands to keep warm. Technicians checked their equipment amid a fog of condensed breath. Television front-men combed their hair.

'Why are they here?' Martha asked.

'Tip-off,' Hagerty replied with concrete certainty.

'About us?'

'No.'

'About Daddy?'

'Impossible. It's to do with the man he's coming out with. Shit! I should've realized some mercenary little

40

asshole could do this. I should've . . .' Hagerty, more fretful than Martha had ever seen him, grabbed the carphone. He punched Mogden's number and asked for Ashe. 'I'll stop your father coming out now,' he told Martha breathlessly.

At the same moment, the small side door beside the main gate was unlocked and heaved open.

Knapp had been warned about the press by Ashe, but was unconcerned. He had faced them without fear many times before and would do so again now. He stood with Jute at the rear of the queue, staring at the bell tower above the gate and thinking how – mercifully, unbelievably – he would never see it again. He felt as cold as the wind which buffeted his ears but was glad he had not worn a coat over his suit, as appearances were essential when facing the representatives of the voting public.

Up ahead, the door had opened and the famed murderer Harold Whittaker was about to step through, surrounded by a bizarre grouping of uniformed policemen, white-coated medics and the imposing, silver-haired figure of Ashe. Knapp chuckled at the attention poor Whittaker had apparently attracted. He may have wiped out his family as they sat down to Sunday lunch. He may have chopped his domineering father into little pieces and popped bits and bobs of him into the oven to roast. But inside Mogden, he was hardly the inhuman, savage beast portrayed by the newspapers. More like a frightened rabbit of a man. He had been eighteen when he rid himself of his family. Now he was fifty-five. He looked seventy-five.

Whittaker shuffled out to meet his fate, lost in a heavy duffle coat and gripping the same leather-cornered suitcase he had carried into Mogden all those years ago. As the queue moved forward, so Knapp followed.

41

Amid the early-morning gloom, Mogden was lit up by arc lights and a battery of flashing cameras. Through the door, Knapp saw Whittaker dip his forehead to hide his face and heard the reporters firing a volley of questions.

'How does it feel to be free, Mr Whittaker?'

'What was it like in there?'

'What are your plans now, sir?'

Knapp fleetingly wondered what the TV boys would ask him, but as he reached the door and finally crossed the threshold between captivity and freedom, he was suddenly overcome with a terrifying feeling of dread, the like of which he had experienced only once before.

He looked out at the vast, open landscape stretching before his eyes and heard an uncompromising voice bellow at him from the horizon. 'Here I am. The big wide world. Step right this way . . . if you dare.'

He had not been a part of it for so long. And now it was confrontational. Hostile. It didn't want him to be there.

In an instant, Knapp was gripped by a fearful panic and felt a powerful urge to turn on his heels and sprint back into the protective, enclosed womb of Mogden hospital. But he was sharp enough to realize what was happening, and fought with all his might. He stared back at the morose moors, returned the cold gaze of the limestone rocks, cocked a snook at the taunting sprigs of heather. He took the world on at its own game. And slowly, gradually, he began to overcome it.

The camera flashes were still popping, even though Whittaker had been surrounded by his guardians and could barely be seen.

Knapp straightened himself, lifted his chin to give himself an air of nobility and raised his left hand into the air, holding it steady to give the photographers a picture of profound solidity, an image that would doubtless be appreciated by Kennedy. He waited for requests to change his pose. And he waited for quick-fire questions from the reporters. But to his surprise, none came.

The scavengers, it was clear, were more interested in picking up a tawdry story about the 'beast' Whittaker than discussing how Knapp felt about the latest appointments at the White House. They had broken through the cordon to swarm around Whittaker's posse – clicking their buttons, thrusting their microphones and straining their vocal cords. Yet Whittaker, almost crouching now, reached the sanctuary offered by a white van without breathing a word.

Jute, following orders, pushed Knapp's elbow to direct him towards the Jaguar. They slipped through the mayhem without fuss as the reporters, frustrated by Whittaker's invisible rat-run, turned to besiege an unprotected Ashe.

Jute said an almost regretful 'Goodbye, Mr Crosby' and left Knapp standing with his ankles enshrouded by the Jaguar's spiralling silver exhaust fumes. Knapp looked back to see if anyone would yet notice him. But no one did – not even Ashe – and he felt a stab of hurt.

The rear door of the Jaguar opened with a discreet click. Knapp heard Hagerty's monotone voice issue its greeting from the dark interior. 'Mr Dallenbach, I presume.'

Knapp stood still for a moment, as if he needed further guidance from Jute . . . or anyone. But finally he turned, worked his way around the flank of the Jaguar, dipped his shoulders and climbed inside.

'Daddy!' Martha shrieked with delight and hugged him like a favourite teddy bear, pushing her head against his chest.

Hagerty, smiling, reached across her and offered his hand. 'Mr Dallenbach,' he repeated.

'If you say so,' Knapp replied vaguely.

'I say so – and you are,' Hagerty confirmed. He lost no time in thrusting a sheaf of documents at Knapp. 'Passport, birth certificate, health insurance and so on and so on. They underwrite your third identity. Take good care of them.'

'I will. Thank you.' Knapp was careful to be both formal and courteous, as his position demanded in such a situation.

Martha told him excitedly how thrilled she was to see him *properly*, instead of smiling at him from the other side of a barren wooden table. 'After Mommy died, I felt so alone. It was awful, terrible. But now I've got you again, Daddy – and you've got me. We're going to have some great times together. I'm going to show you the world. It's changing *so* fast, you won't believe it.'

Knapp, irritated by her babbling, ignored her. He was more intent on investigating the wonders of the Jaguar. He ran a finger along its polished walnut panels, pressed his behind into its soft cushioned seats, flared his nostrils to take in its smell of unblemished newness.

As Hagerty tapped the glass partition and the chauffeur drove away, he turned to look out of the car's back window. The white van was trying to inch through a solid wall of photographers, all desperate for a final crack at scooping a picture of its passenger. One was on the bonnet, pointing his lens through the windscreen, his leg being tugged by a young constable caught off guard by the bestiality of it all. Knapp glanced beyond the scrum to take his leave of grim, charmless Mogden hospital.

As it shrank into the distance, he found himself lost in

a mist of disbelief. 'Thirty years,' he muttered under his breath.

'What?' Martha asked.

'I won't be going back.'

'Of course not, Daddy.'

'Only forward. From now on, only forward.'

'That's the way to go.'

The mist cleared. Knapp felt a wave of relief sweep over him, followed an instant later by a renewed surge of power.

Awesome power. Fantastic power. Power beyond the dreams of man. The generator was running at full tilt. And this time no one – not even *them* – would switch it off.

4

Curran was glad to be back at work. Newspapers demanded speed and concentration. Deadlines left precious little time for self-pity. A triumph of adrenalin over valium. It was what he needed.

'Take "Whitrel", will you?'

Curran was jerked from his thoughts by the strident demand of Hockenhull, his chief sub-editor.

'How's it spelled?' Curran asked.

'Whit as in Whittaker, plus rel as in release.'

'Oh, Harold Whittaker getting out of Mogden.'

'That's it, here's a picture to go with it. Have a look before it goes to process.'

Hockenhull threw the picture across the desk. Curran studied it. It showed Whittaker caught in no-man's-land between the hospital gates and the police van, with his entourage behind.

'It's a Reuter pic,' said Curran, surprised.

'Yeah. The Reuter bloke was the only one to get a decent mug of Whittaker apparently. Our idiot got an extremely interesting picture of the inside of a bloody van. All right if you want to know how big the inside of a van is so you can move a wardrobe. Fuck-all use to a newspaper.'

'Typical,' Curran sneered. Like his thirty or so comrades on the sub-editors' table, Curran nurtured a traditional contempt for the paper's reporters and photographers. Fact-finders and shutter-snappers, yes. Stylists, no. The field workers, in turn, dismissed the subs

46

as office-bound rewrite hacks with no idea of the *real* world.

'Where's it going?' Curran asked Hockenhull.

'Page-one picture story in the shoulder of the splash. It hasn't got much of a run. Just a few lines of poetry to go with the pic. The instructions are on the copy. Headline's done. Says SUNDAY LUNCH MANIAC FREE AFTER 37 YEARS.'

'Bit of a mouthful.' Brookes, Curran's neighbour on the subs' table, chuckled at his own joke.

'Shut yours and get on with your own story,' Hockenhull said.

'No laughing on ze table!' someone imitating a Nazi called out. 'Ve haf vays of making you suffer.'

Curran tapped his keyboard to call Whitrel on to his terminal screen. The reporter's story, phoned in to London from Leeds, was more than ten times longer than the space finally allocated for it by the editor. Curran read it carefully to glean the main facts. The reporter's version was bland – to be generous – and Curran quickly decided to write his own. Four paragraphs would have to say it all.

He split his screen so he could read the reporter's story on one side while he created his own on the other. Before he began, he took one more look at the photo in the hope that it would inject him with at least a degree of inspiration.

A sub called McKeachie – a new recruit suspected by the editor of having too much of a bleeding heart to survive in feet-first tabloid journalism – looked over his shoulder. 'Ironic, isn't it?' he said.

'What is?' said Curran, trying to concentrate.

'I mean, the guy is freed from a nuthouse because he's finally OK in the head. So we use a picture of him looking like a loony. Wild, scared eyes, the lot. And we call him a maniac in the headline. He doesn't stand a chance, does he?'

'A better chance than me if I don't write this before the first-edition deadline.'

'Yeah, piss off, McKeachie, and let the man do his work,' Hockenhull barked without looking up. 'What do you want the fucking headline to say? Ordinary man goes for a walk outside hospital?'

'What did he do, anyway?' McKeachie persisted.

'Brought the final curtain down on four people,' Brookes said.

McKeachie, raised in a more violent era in which four dead was peanuts, said: 'So why put him in a place like Mogden?'

Brookes, an authority on notorious crime, groaned at McKeachie's ignorance. 'The four were his father, his mother, his sister and his eighty-two-year-old grandmother. He used an axe on 'em. Did terrible things with their remains.'

'Christ,' McKeachie said.

'He had been jilted by a girl and thought they were laughing at him,' Brookes continued. 'They didn't laugh for bloody long.'

'It was one of the most horrific cases of its time,' Hockenhull said as he bit into a sandwich. 'Like the Moors Murders, the Yorkshire Ripper, that sort of thing. No one has forgotten the name of Harold Whittaker. Neither will you now, McKeachie. So piss off back to your seat.'

The editor, a bullish man named Christie, appeared on the far side of the newsroom, stomping brusquely across the floor. He was still twenty strides away when he caught sight of Curran.

48

'Ah, Curran. First day back?' Christie spoke no louder than normal, but his throaty voice carried across the newsroom as if he had shouted the words from the top of a mountain.

'Yes,' Curran replied dutifully.

'Everything all right?'

Curran felt sick. Why did Christie *always* have to talk about private affairs in public – and in such an attention-seeking tone?

'Fine,' he lied. It was not worth saying anything else.

'Good.' Christie wheeled away to face the night editor. 'Right, Eddie, the game's up. What are we going to do with this bleedin' paper?'

'Fine . . .' The word echoed around Curran's head as he drove home – and he let out an ironic laugh to ward off a growing sense of hopelessness. His sister, to whom he had always been close, was dead. And his marriage to Dany was crumbling in his hands like a piece of stale cake.

If only he could turn the clock back to the time when the lives of the two perfect friends had first crossed his own. Dany had flown the Atlantic to spend the summer with Pearl. And Curran, footloose and fancy-free after graduating from university, tagged along with them.

It had been idyllic. Long, hot, silly Floridan days. A whirlwind visit to New York that captivated Pearl enough to make her want to live and work there. A growing fondness for Dany that grew into love, signed and sealed in a rowing boat on the Everglades. If only it had lasted for ever . . .

Hockenhull, bless the bugger, had gone easy on him and had given him no pressure-cooker work other than the Whittaker release story. With a half-hour cut from his shift thrown in, he was home by 1 A.M.

49

Dany was still up, lolling in an armchair with an empty bottle of red wine on the floor beside her. Curran sighed. Dany was not in the habit of drinking, and became aggressive when she did.

She did not greet him and he said nothing to her. She shrugged her shoulders as if to say, 'Who cares, anyway?', climbed clumsily to her feet and brushed past him. She returned a minute later with another bottle of wine, the corkscrew stuck in its neck. 'I can't do it,' she said, thrusting the bottle at Curran. 'Don't have the strength.'

He nodded towards the empty. 'You managed before.'

'That was hours ago.' Dany's speech was slurred and her natural, olive-skinned beauty was equally distorted. Sad, red-rimmed eyes, crinkled clothes and drooping shoulders. Let out on the street tonight, she would be picked up for vagrancy.

'You're drinking too much,' Curran scolded.

'Hah!' Dany let out a sarcastic laugh. 'That's rich, coming from you.'

'Pearl was tanked up before she died, that's all.'

'Was it drink that killed her?'

'No, but – '

'So . . .' Dany snatched back the bottle and tugged on the corkscrew herself. It gave on the fourth pull, taking Dany by surprise so that a thick globule of wine leaped from the neck of the bottle and fell on the carpet.

'I'll get a cloth,' Curran said. 'And a glass. I'll have one with you.'

'Please yourself.' Dany slumped into the armchair, leaning forward with effort to fill a glass lurching precariously between the surface of a coffee table and the edge of a magazine.

Her languid indifference made Curran's blood boil. He

left the room, but did not fetch the cloth. He needed to calm down and made a detour to look in on Yvette.

He kissed the child as she slept and pulled her duvet over her exposed shoulders. She stirred slightly, but did not wake. Curran caught a pungent whiff of something sweet and guessed that Yvette, whose podgy little hands went everywhere they shouldn't, had again helped herself to a dab of her mother's perfume or somesuch.

He backed away, took a deep breath and turned in a circle, smiling at walls covered with Yvette's drawings of her favourite cartoon characters. They were good, especially Goofy. And Curran, like every other parent, wondered if Yvette possessed real artistic talent. Whatever, the sketches gave the bedroom an atmosphere of happiness. And for Curran it had become a refuge worlds away from the joyless dungeons where he and Dany bitched and clawed at each other.

He glanced back at the sleeping girl, a picture of innocence and peacefulness. It had not always been so. Curran remembered how she would cry floods as yet another argument flared up in front of her. Six weeks ago, she had become so upset she could not breathe, and collapsed to the floor weeping and gasping at the same time. It came as a frightening jolt to Curran and Dany, forcing them to recognize their cruelty. Since then, they had made a pact to throw up a façade of contentment whenever Yvette was around. And to a large extent, they had succeeded.

In truth, Curran thought, it had not been too difficult. He had a deep reservoir of love for Dany, and she for him. Someone had pulled the plug, that's all, and it was dribbling away little by little. No one's fault. No one to blame. Their arguments were born out of frustration that they could do nothing to stem the flow.

Curran spoke aloud to Yvette, as he often did while she was asleep. Perhaps she couldn't hear. But she couldn't argue, either.

'Now we know the truth, we'll make it quick and clean. You won't see your mummy and daddy fighting. Maybe Mummy will find someone else pretty soon. Maybe I will, too. You're only six, sweetheart. When you're grown up, you won't remember a thing.'

By the time Curran returned to the lounge, cloth in hand, Dany was clearing up the spilled wine.

'Someone had to,' she said as he walked in.

Curran watched her swaying on all fours. She looked so ridiculous. He bent to help her to her feet.

'Danielle . . .'

'Don't call me that!' she snapped, flicking his hand from her shoulder. 'You know I hate it. It was what my mother called me when I was a naughty child, damn her.'

'Easy . . .'

'Snobby bitch! She got her hooks into Daddy as soon as he set foot in Geneva. An English knight in shining armour, whisking her on to the back of his proud white stallion. What a catch for a Swiss peasant woman! The diplomatic service. The United Nations, for God's sake. Parties, galas, dinners, the full bit. Christ knows what Daddy ever saw in her. She must have been a good fuck, that's – '

'Stop it!' Curran hauled her from the carpet and sat her in a chair. She burst into tears. He looked down on her and felt pity. An unhappy childhood, a marriage turned sour and now the death of her best friend. The wine had mixed it all together.

He grabbed the bottle and took it to the kitchen, giving Dany time to compose herself.

After he returned, they chatted for an hour, about Pearl and about Yvette, while Dany sobered up.

'Yvette smells of something,' Curran said.

'It's talc.'

'What?'

'Talcum powder.'

'You don't use it.'

'Mother left it here. Yvette managed to get it all over the bathroom and all over herself. She looked like a ghost.'

'Did you scold her?'

Dany did not speak, but her eyes replied. They said, 'No, of course not. How could I when she is going through so much already?' Curran understood.

Fatigue overcame them just before three. Dany rose to her feet gingerly and stretched.

'Anyway, how did you get on tonight?' she asked through a yawn. 'What did you do?'

Curran was surprised. The last time Dany showed an interest in his work was months ago.

'Get to bed, I'll show you tomorrow,' he said.

'No,' she insisted. 'I want to see.' She smiled for the first time since his arrival. 'Really . . . I mean it.'

Curran shrugged his shoulders. In truth, he was glad she had asked. He found the paper and passed it to her. 'A few small stories inside,' he said. 'But mainly the poetry with the picture on page one.'

Dany held the paper in front of her and tried hard to steady it. It took time for her eyes to focus, but when they did she felt a shard of coldness inside her as if she had been pierced by a sword made of ice. A shiver escaped down her back and she began to tremble. She tried to look away, to prise her eyes free from what they were seeing. But she could not. The newspaper demanded her attention, entranced her as surely as if she was on a hypnotist's couch.

Curran saw what was happening. 'What is it?' he asked, his voice sharp with alarm. 'Dany, what is it?'

She found it hard to talk. Her lips froze as the coldness penetrated her entire body. 'Picture . . .' She managed to utter. 'Him.'

Curran watched as Dany's trembling grew until she was shaking from head to foot. Only one thing could cause such a reaction. Fear. Stark, uncompromising fear.

He moved quickly to quell it. 'Whittaker? He's harmless now. As harmless as a baby. It says so in the story.'

It didn't work. Dany's eyes, shining like diamonds, bore into the page. Her shoulders shuddered as the page sent its message back to her brain. The muscles around her lips twitched as if she had been wired up to a battery. Curran was sure that if he left it a moment longer, her hair would turn white.

He ripped the paper from her hands and flung it to the ground. Dany looked at him in horror, as if he had committed some awful crime. She ran into the kitchen, tugged ferociously at the cork of the wine bottle and poured herself another drink.

Curran followed her. 'Dany . . .'

She spun round and fell backwards against the sink. 'Don't touch me!' she screamed. 'Leave me alone!'

5

Dany returned to her childhood in her dreams. She kicked
her heels as she waited to play hopscotch with the others,
though for some reason she could not fathom, they had
gathered for the game in the depths of a gravel pit. The
base of the pit was vast, its surface muddy and strewn
with puddles.

'We can't chalk hopscotch squares here,' she announced
to anyone who was listening.

Kipini ignored her. Singing a Kenyan tribal song from
her homeland, she dug a piece of chalk from the mud and
used it to map out a perfect hopscotch grid, its shiny white
lines glistening in the sunshine.

Dany, proved wrong, pouted and looked away. It was
a funny place, she thought. The pit's walls, which surely
should have been slopes of loose gravel, appeared to have
been hewn from solid rock – angular and sharp-edged like
that found towards the peak of a Himalayan mountain.

'I'll go first!' Stefanie announced.

'You're always first,' Sari groaned.

'Any objections?' The challenge was delivered with a
show of confidence and strength beyond Stefanie's years.
Sari, her natural timidity returning instantly, caved in and
shook her head.

Stefanie threw a large flintstone into the first of the nine
squares clearly numbered by Kipini's piece of chalk. She
lifted one leg, hopped on to the square, picked up the
flintstone without wavering, turned round and hopped
back.

'Easy,' she said with a smirk. She slid the flintstone on to square two.

Dany, certain it would be hours before anyone else had a chance to play, sat down with Pearl.

The bright afternoon sun warmed their faces. Yet why couldn't it dry the puddles? And why, even though they were sitting in mud, did their little white dresses not become soiled?

'Search me,' Pearl said like a grown-up.

'It's because the water in the puddles isn't wet enough,' Mai-Lin ventured.

'That's stupid.' Dany mocked Mai-Lin by pulling the sides of her eyes until they became slits. 'Chinese velly silly.'

'I'm *not* Chinese!' Mai-Lin protested.

'Thailand's near China, isn't it?'

'So?'

'Stop arguing.' It was Louise. She didn't like arguments. They made her feel sick inside, like when she ate too much treacle tart.

Stefanie tripped over herself as she hopped back from square five. 'Shit!' she cried out, and the others all giggled. Stefanie threw the flintstone to Kipini. Then, her attention diverted, she pointed far away to the sides of the pit and said: 'Look! What's going on?'

Before their eyes, the walls began to crack as if they were being baked by the sun. Soon, great fissures appeared, accompanied by snapping sounds so loud that the girls covered their ears. From each of the perpendicular chasms, smaller faults spread out horizontally until the whole vast bank was criss-crossed by gashes and tears. The process carried on until the wall – once so solid and so uncompromising – became a crazy paving of individual rocks. The girls spun on their heels. It was happening all around them. As they watched, rock turned to stone, stone turned to pebble, pebble turned to gravel and gravel turned to powder. In less than a minute, towering black walls of basalt had been transformed into towering white walls of talcum.

'Biscuits,' Louise said out of the blue.

'What?' the others chorused.

'It's just like Mummy's biscuits. They always crumble in your hand and then you can't eat them.'

'Well, are we going to play or aren't we?' Stefanie had had her fill of the surrounding spectacle and was impatient to resume the game. 'Who was next?'

Kipini realized the flintstone was still in her hand and squeaked: 'Me.'

The others turned to watch her progress across the hopscotch grid. Behind them and around them, the walls of talcum began to slip and slide, great plumes of white spewing from top to bottom like avalanches of snow. Behind the faces of the avalanches, fantastic forces were at work, lifting the powder which had just fallen back to the peak, so it could fall again. The result was a wall that moved forward inch by inch without losing height.

Kipini reached the third square before losing balance and stepping out of the grid.

'My go!' Dany shrieked. She was good at hopscotch and even at the age of six had developed a competitive edge that usually found itself matched against Stefanie's.

'Go on, Dany,' Pearl urged from the sidelines. It gave Dany heart. She knew Pearl was a special friend.

The towering banks of talcum closed in relentlessly, soaking up the puddles on the pit floor and roaring as if they were galleries full of bullfight spectators baying for blood.

Pearl groaned. Dany had been too casual and had

thrown the flintstone beyond the second square. Stefanie, though she too was fond of Dany, could not suppress a wry smile.

Mai-Lin took the flintstone and with an athletic spring in her heels, bounded across the squares with growing confidence.

The others cheered and clapped. The oncoming walls had blotted out the sun, yet their dresses still shone, their faces still glowed. By the time Pearl took the flintstone, they were totally absorbed by the game. Nothing could disturb them.

Pearl fell at the first hurdle. The flintstone hit a twig poking from the clay in square one and bounced outside its borders.

'I told you to be careful,' Stefanie said.

'No you didn't!' Pearl objected.

'When?' Dany chimed in.

'When I first saw the twig.'

'You're making it up, clever clogs.'

The white walls loomed high above them, turning them into tiny silhouettes. Their faces were splashed with droplets of talcum, but they didn't mind. Even when the leading edge of the powder crept up to their feet, they were unconcerned.

'Right,' Louise declared. 'Stefanie and Mai-Lin are on five, Kipini's on three, Dany's on two and Pearl is still on one. You go next, Sari, and I'll go last.'

The white dust rose above Sari's ankles, but it did not impede her progress. She made it to square three before getting in a tangle as she twisted around.

The others laughed. Sari was the plumpest and most ungainly of the group, as well as being the most timid. She had to put up with a constant stream of mockery. But she had been blessed with a forgiving temperament and her Aunt Sally status did not trouble her.

'I'm ahead of you,' she quickly pointed out to a giggling Pearl.

Louise took the flintstone. By the time she leaped for square one, the drifting powder had reached her midriff. Yet it was not solid. She bounced through it as if it was morning mist, great clouds of talcum billowing from her clothes as she spiralled through the air. And she whooped with delight as she returned safely from square five to take the first-round lead.

It was only when Stefanie returned for her second attempt that the girls realized what was happening.

'It's going up my nose, making me want to sneeze,' she said.

'We're sort of sinking, aren't we?' Pearl said.

'More like being rained on by white stuff,' Mai-Lin observed.

'I'm scared . . .' Kipini was the first to admit it, though she was not the only one to feel a sudden rush of fear.

Dany looked up. It was as if she was standing at the foot of a great white drainpipe, with just a tiny circle of sky at the top. The drainpipe, a screaming vortex of dust like the eye of a hurricane, was becoming narrower by the second. Dany felt the powder spilling over her shoulders and touching the base of her neck. The force of its great bulk pressed in on her sides and would not allow her lungs to expand. 'H . . . help,' she cried hesitantly. Then more urgently: 'Pearl! Stefanie! Help me!'

There was no reply. The other girls – all of them – had been overtaken and consumed by the powder. A great white curtain had come down in front of them – and they were gone for ever.

Dany would be next. She knew it. The pressure was too

great. She heard a snap and felt an agonizing pain in her side. A rib, perhaps, or a collar bone. Rolled balls of talcum pushed into her mouth. She tried to blow them out, but it was far too late.

Tentacles of powder crept into her nostrils. She could no longer breathe. The converging walls of the drainpipe rose ever upwards, covering her eyes. She could no longer see.

She was drowning in a solid sea, being crushed by a liquid wall.

The last pocket of hot air in her chest expanded as if someone inside her was blowing her up like a balloon. It scorched her flesh, cracked her bones. She felt the drainpipe close above her head . . . and prepared for the ultimate terror of death.

Dany woke with a start – breathless, bathed in sweat and with a heart racing as it had never raced before. She coughed and spat, and brushed herself from head to toe with manic fingers. When she was sure her hair, her skin and her clothes were free of the powder, she staggered to the toilet and vomited to cleanse her insides.

Panting, she returned to the bedroom, taking tiny steps as she did when she was a child. She glanced at Curran. He was sleeping on his back with his head turned away, oblivious of Dany's ordeal by suffocation.

Half of her desperately wanted to wake him. She needed help. She needed someone to see her tears, to listen to her story and to tell her everything was all right.

But she was back in the real world now. A world of despair and of a husband and wife with a chasm between them. A world in which keeping a distance meant clinging on to the remnants of confidence and self-esteem.

She ran downstairs and grabbed the bottle of wine. She was trembling so much she could barely prise the cork free – and this time it was not because she had been drinking.

She could not remember being so frightened. 'Walls closing in,' she muttered aloud. 'That's the stuff of mad women.'

She was not sure if she was mad. But as she stood in the kitchen, shaking in her nightdress, she was certain that her dream had been more – much more – than just another nightmare. 'Omen?' she mumbled, asking herself the question. 'Foreboding of evil?'

She told herself not to be stupid, but gulped wine from the bottle as if it were the elixir of life itself.

Knapp had lost the habit of flying and could not relax in the plane. The ascent from Heathrow Airport, so much steeper and faster than the early jets had managed thirty years before, had unnerved him. And every two minutes, he jerked his head sideways to look out of the window, worried that at any second he would be sucked down into the ocean far, far below. The plane was too big. It was carrying too many people, too much luggage. How could it possibly stay airborne?

He was furious that such an elementary fear had encroached upon the single-mindedness he knew was essential for the task that lay ahead, and moved to allay it before it became a total diversion.

He pressed the call button on the panel above him. Martha, a natural jeans girl who looked somehow uncomfortable in her pressed cotton uniform, was at his side a moment later.

'Get me a large bourbon on the rocks,' he said.

She looked at him dubiously. 'Are you sure?'

61

'Are you sure *what*?' Knapp barked.

Martha realized what he was getting at and said: 'Are you sure, *sir*?'

Knapp would not let her off the hook. 'Would I ask for a bourbon if I wasn't sure I wanted a bourbon?'

Knapp's neighbours glanced at him from behind their newspapers. Hagerty watched the confrontation from eight rows back.

Martha blushed and replied: 'Of course not, sir.'

'Well then.'

'It's just that . . .'

'Stop arguing, girl, and fetch the drink!'

Martha glanced at her father over her shoulder as she walked to the galley. He was a bag of nerves. Jittery, unsettled and a face lined with angst. Maybe one drink – just one – would not hurt.

By the time she returned, Knapp had lost himself in the foreign pages of the *New York Times*. He did not even look at her, just waggled a finger to show her where to leave his bourbon. She felt an urge to make a fool of him by curtseying, but resisted temptation at the last minute.

It was not until the jet was halfway to New York that she got the chance she wanted. She joined Knapp as he waited for the toilet, though he refused to acknowledge her presence. She looked around to make sure no one was watching or listening. 'What was that all about, Daddy?' she said in a virtual whisper.

At first he would not answer. But when Martha persisted, he hissed: 'What was *what* all about?'

'The slave treatment.'

'You mean the drink?'

'What else?'

'You heard what Hagerty said.'

'That we should ignore each other and that no connection should be made between us.'

'Exactly. For the sake of my anonymity and your career. So why don't you follow instructions?'

'I did.'

'No!' Knapp became agitated. 'You failed to accord me the respect that my rank merits.'

'What? I don't understand.'

'Exactly. You don't understand. That is why I had to be firm. It is only to be expected.'

Martha was still perplexed and studied Knapp's face for clues. There was none. He was as stoic as he was determined. His lips were rigid and he betrayed neither gratification nor remorse. He reminded her of a Buckingham Palace sentry under siege from photo-snapping tourists. No smiles, no scowls, just implacable dignity. Her father was a mystery, as he had been to her since the day she was told he was still alive.

'Just don't overdo it,' she pleaded.

'Hold your tongue!' he said firmly. 'Remember your place and your duty, child.'

'I am not a – ' Martha stopped herself as the passenger in the toilet unbolted the door and came out.

Knapp strode into the lavatory without a backward glance. Why could the girl not understand? Why could she not realize that all he wanted to do was step inside the toilet and CLOSE its door so that no one – no one – could see him.

Martha felt lost and wished she could recapture the exultation she had experienced just a few hours before, when she saw her father emerge from behind a screen of photographers and reporters at Mogden hospital.

She leaned her head on the toilet door and said quietly: 'I'm sorry, Daddy. I know it's hard for you. You must be absolutely exhausted by it all. Try to get some sleep when you come out of there, OK?'

There was no reply.

Curran's heart was heavy as he left the solicitor's office. It had been a soul-destroying experience in many ways. He loathed lawyers as a breed. Greedy money-grabbers feeding off misfortune, tragedy and other money-grabbers. In a fit of aggression, he had charged the solicitor with being such a man, to which the solicitor had replied: 'Rather like tabloid-newspaper journalists, wouldn't you say?' Curran would have hit back, but the lawyer took the wind from his sails by insisting on progressing with the business in hand.

'Are you *positive* divorce is the only answer?' he asked.

Curran had thought long and hard before he arrived. And though he was racked with guilt and sorrow and every other emotion associated with failure and regret, he had no hesitation in replying: 'Yes.'

'And does Mrs Curran feel the same way?'

'Yes.'

'On what grounds do you expect your divorce to become absolute?'

'To be decided.' Who the hell cared, as long as it went through without the ugly strife that had scarred most divorcees he knew?

'On my advice?'

'And on the advice of my wife's solicitor.'

'Of course . . .'

'I don't want you to carve us up between you. Understand?'

'Mr Curran!'

'I'm not apologizing.'

So it went on. Curran couldn't wait to leave and get on

64

with the other business of the day. He took a tube to Covent Garden and walked past the stalls and sandwich bars of the market arcade to the British Library's science reading room, an inglorious yellow-brick building in a dusty side street around the corner from the Aldwych Theatre.

His object was to purge his desolation by throwing himself into a closer investigation of Pearl's death. He could not explain it, but something had been gnawing away at him ever since he told Stefanie what happened at the funeral.

Like him, Stefanie had found it difficult to comprehend how a still-young woman, apparently fit and with everything to live for, had been killed – taken out – by a sudden, massive heart attack. And like him, Stefanie had searched in vain for a logical explanation.

He remembered the mortuary surgeon's uncertain diagnosis. Slight abnormality in the conduction system . . . nothing much . . . but in the absence of anything else . . .

'Just one of those things,' the guy had drawled with neither care nor concern.

But maybe, just maybe, there *was* something else. And if there was, Curran was determined to find it.

An Asian library assistant in a sari brought six medical textbooks to his chosen study desk, and he leafed through them energetically. He dallied briefly on sections about conduction systems, making a mental note that millions of people with minor abnormalities lived perfectly long and healthy lives. But for the most part, he ignored anatomical detail and concentrated on chapters dealing with the clinical characteristics of cardiac arrest.

The terminology used by the authors was daunting, and Curran had to summon the last reserves of his concentration to absorb it. Words like acute myocardial infarction, arrhythmias and ventricular fibrillation seemed somehow to blur into surrounding phrases. But gradually, as he read deeper into the subject, a pattern emerged and light was thrown on darkness.

He learned that Pearl's pump had stopped pumping; that this had led to an inadequate cerebral blood flow; that she would have suffered irreversible brain damage within four to six minutes of the arrest; and that this would have been followed soon afterwards by what was unemotionally described as biological death.

He learned that his efforts to revive her by thumping her sternum and giving her mouth-to-mouth had been the correct action to take. And with some relief, he learned that the chances of saving her life, given that her heart had gone haywire, had been slim.

Contributing professors told how patients' skin turned either ghostly pale or cyanotic blue, depending on what happened to haemoglobin pigments in the blood.

Photographs showed heart victims with jugular veins standing out on their necks like mole runs; with jaundiced yellow eyes that looked as if they would glow in the dark; with clubbed toes and fingers; with blotches caused by mini-haemorrhages on the inside of their eyelids; and with tongues like raw beef.

But nowhere – *nowhere* – did Curran find a reference to the strange nebulous lather that shot from Pearl's mouth at the moment of death.

He left the library more puzzled than he had been before he went in – and more convinced that Pearl's death had *not* been just one of those things.

6

Visions burst and splintered across Knapp's mind. He was an eagle, a great soaring bird. So mighty and with such a wingspan that no other bird could climb into the highest realms of the heavens to join him. He floated alone above the clouds, peering through gaps in the silver mist to study the landscape far, far below.

He saw the verdant green canopy of a forest, sliced into curved-edge sections by glistening ribbons of river and delta.

There were no buildings to impinge on the lushness of spring. No tarmac. No concrete. No glass. Just open countryside for as far as his eagle eyes could see. It made him feel free and it made him feel proud.

He became aware of a thermal pushing up against his belly. Relishing a warm wave of pleasure, he tilted his body and spread his feathers so the current of hot air took him ever upwards with no effort on his part. Spiralling. Gliding. Controlled by the elements, yet in control of them. It was an exhilarating sensation – and he let out a raucous call to express his euphoria. Given the choice, he would fly for ever and never return to his eyrie on the bluff.

The thermal petered out. He allowed himself to drop for a second. Then, with two beats of his vast wings, he was on his way again. Over a lake and across a ridge of hills. Valleys radiated from peaks and pushed deep shadowy scars in the tree canopy. He tucked his head between his shoulders to feel the breeze on his crown and to gaze beyond his talons for signs of life on the ground.

It was then that he saw it. A black dot on a clearing, like an inkspot splashed on a sheet of green paper. It was stationary at first, but soon began growing, expanding outwards, until he realized it had left the ground and was rising through the air towards him. A sleek, swift bird of a type he had never encountered. A bird with a sharply pointed black beak and a tail of flame. A bird set on challenging his rule of the skies.

He tried to avoid it, tried to whirl away from its path, but it was hopeless. The flamebird was too fast, too direct, too awesome. It sliced through the feathers of his starboard wing, burning the flesh that held them in place.

He gave a scream of pain and prayed the flamebird would not return. It did not, but the damage was done. Without his feathers, he was a cripple. For a few precious seconds, he stuttered on as best he could. But he was a shadow of the monarch he had been an instant before. He had been conquered, crippled, by a superior force. Though he urged himself to keep going, his muscles tired and his strength sapped. In the end, everything gave out at once. The eagle became a stone and plummeted towards earth at ever-increasing velocity.

Falling . . . falling . . . falling.

Knapp wailed as he hit the ground. He half opened his eyes – and saw Martha looking down at him. Her face was alarmed, but her voice was calm and reassuring. 'It's all right, sir. Just a bit of bumpiness. We'll be landing in New York within an hour and a half. Why don't you go back to sleep until we begin to descend . . .'

Knapp tried to become an eagle again. But the great bird was dead and could not be regenerated.

Instead, he travelled on foot. Across fields and through

forest until he came to the edge of a city. As he tramped the streets, looking for a sign that would tell him where he was, a great roar from a crowd swept over the rooftops towards him.

It stirred his curiosity, and he determined to find out what had caused such a cacophony. He waited for another roar to set his direction, and walked cautiously towards its source.

Before long, he was in a stadium. An ancient, weathered amphitheatre like the Colosseum, only far more immense. It was packed with hundreds of thousands of people. Perhaps even a million, who could be sure? On a stage in one corner, the old Russian leader Khrushchev, his face red with anger, was addressing the multitude. He did not have a microphone, yet his every word was as clear as a bell. He was in the middle of an onslaught against the United States. An American U2 spy plane, he snarled, had flown over Soviet territory and had been shot down by a Russian rocket. As he spoke, the crowd cheered and waved little Soviet flags pinned to lollipop sticks. A shimmering haze of steam rose from the sea of red. It spurred Khrushchev on to a savage attack.

'The day chosen for such an aggressive act by the United States was the First of May – the most festive day for our people and the workers of the world. The Soviet government will lodge a strong protest with the United States and will warn it that if similar aggressive acts against our country continue, we reserve the right to respond to the hotheads of the West with measures which we shall find necessary to ensure the safety of our country.'

The crowd were stirred to fever pitch. To a man, they shouted: 'Down with the aggressors! Down with the bandits!'

'The incident is a danger signal to the whole world,'

Khrushchev went on. 'Who was responsible? The President or the Pentagon? I warn both that the Soviet Union has rockets that are ready to be fired around the clock.'

'Down with the aggressors!' the crowd chorused. 'America must pay for its banditry!'

As Knapp watched, Khrushchev's face became Eisenhower's face. The crowd ripped the little red flags from their sticks and replaced them with the Stars and Stripes.

Eisenhower's tone was more conciliatory. 'We will hold an inquiry. We will find out who was responsible. We will ask the Soviet authorities for more information. Questions of war and peace are clearly involved in incidents of this kind.'

Eisenhower's face became Kennedy's face – and Kennedy's became Knapp's.

Now it was he who was addressing the assembly. 'There is a crisis,' he told them. 'But it will be solved.'

He allowed himself a pregnant pause before bellowing: 'And *I* am the man to solve it!'

The crowd, inspired, rose to their feet and clapped until their hands were raw. Knapp acknowledged their idolatry by raising his left hand and holding it firmly until the clamour subsided. As his audience sat to listen again, one of their number, a woman in the front row, remained on her feet.

Knapp was transfixed by the sight of her. She was between twenty and twenty-five – and the most beautiful girl he had ever seen. Slim, petite and wearing her vivid red hair bold and long, she wore a check jacket, a black pencil skirt and a beguiling expression of apprehension. As he gazed in her direction, she smiled at him, her lips curling sweetly into the shadowy recesses of her high Slavic cheekbones.

Knapp felt an irresistible force growing inside him.

There were hundreds of thousands of eyes fixed upon him, but he could see only her. He had to hold her and he could not wait until later. He had to hold her now.

His aides, loyal and understanding, patted him on the back as he skipped down the steps of the rostrum. Once on the ground, he broke into a run. Past the brass band and past the choir, until he was with her.

She held out her arms – and he slid his around her and pulled her into him until he could feel her warmth. The crowd cheered as he stroked her hair. They swooned as his fingers touched her face and they cried 'Hurrah!' as his lips met hers for the first time in years.

'Yelena,' Knapp whispered. 'I've been so lonely without you. Never leave me again. I love you, Yelena. There has been no other. I love you.'

Knapp lost himself in her supple femininity. He felt a nervous excitement in his chest which he had forgotten could exist. How wonderful that such a reunion had happened here, like this, a complete surprise. No man could dare ask for more.

He rubbed his face in the nape of her neck. He wanted to seal his nose and mouth with her skin, to become intoxicated by her, just as he had been before.

Yet something was wrong, something amiss, something that would prevent him taking her away with him. Something that would snap off his love before it had a chance to blossom again.

It was not Yelena. She was moist and tender – and he could sense she was ready to give and to receive.

No, there was a presence, an evil force determined to destroy their partnership, as there had always been. A force of seven demons, seven daughters of the Devil. He glanced beyond Yelena's shoulders to confront them.

They were there as he knew they would be. Motionless.

71

Expressionless. Unmoved by the ecstasy of those who surrounded them. They stared at him with cold, penetrating eyes.

'We can see you,' one said in a deep, rolling voice that came from the fiery heart of the earth.

'We know what you are doing,' said another.

'And we know why,' said a third.

The three who had spoken pointed accusing fingers at him. The four other girls watched implacably as they waited for his reaction.

Knapp acted quickly. He told Yelena to wait for him and rushed back to the rostrum.

He raised his arms for quiet, then launched into a tirade that bordered on the hysterical. 'They are to blame for everything!' he told the people. 'And they are here!'

'Where?' the people cried.

Knapp showed the crowd where the seven demon daughters sat, in the row behind Yelena. 'In our midst!' he screamed. 'Directly in our midst.'

'And what will you do?' the crowd chorused.

Knapp placed his right hand on his heart in order to deliver a sworn pledge. He calmed himself and waited for more than half a minute until the masses were quiet. When he was ready and when there was no sound to disturb him, he said: 'I will eliminate them.'

Dany could not sleep – and took her frustration out on Curran the moment he walked through the door. 'It's 3 A.M. for Christ's sake,' she said. 'No wonder we're falling apart at the seams. Bloody ridiculous hours you work. You come home while Yvette and I are asleep, and you're asleep when we get up in the morning. I ask you, what a bloody life!'

Curran wished he could react with the resentment he

felt inside, but after a harrowing visit to the lawyer's, hours poring over medical textbooks and a busy shift at the newspaper, he was simply too tired. He brushed past Dany and sat at the dining table, unravelling the aluminium paraphernalia of an Indian takeaway he had bought on the way home. Dany followed him and threw herself into a chair opposite, her relentless glare challenging him to take her on. He knew he could not escape with silence alone.

'Be honest,' he said eventually. 'What difference does it make whether I am here or not?'

His apparent calmness only aggravated Dany further.

'Oh yes, oh yes. All very well for you to come and go as you please, Mr Very Important Journalist. And *who* makes sure Yvette is dressed in the morning? Who makes sure she is at school on time? Who picks her up in the afternoon? Who feeds her? Who –'

'You know I work into the early hours,' Curran interrupted. 'I have to sleep some time.'

'I work, too. I have a heavy schedule in front of me. I don't suppose that counts.'

'Of course it counts.'

'Then why are you making it more difficult for me? Why won't you share the responsibilities of bringing up a child?'

'I do!' Curran protested. 'And what's more, you know I do. Do you want me to sit here and detail my every moment with her? Saturday 4 P.M. to 5.30: played Escape from Atlantis with Yvette. Sunday 8 A.M. to 8.15: made Yvette three pieces of toast. One spread with Marmite, two with honey. Sunday 8.30 A.M. to 9.30: watched –'

'You're being facetious.'

'You're being dogmatic.'

'Christ!'

73

Dany tried to cling on to the remnants of her self-control. It wasn't easy. She had barely slept for forty-eight hours and had been further exhausted by worrying about the trauma of her dream.

Curran's next remark could have been the final straw. 'I saw a lawyer today . . .' He wiped his lips with a serviette as he said the words, hoping in some way that the fabric would absorb them and muffle their message.

Dany stared into his eyes for what to him seemed like an eternity. He caught a quiver in her lips, a tremble in the muscles of her chin. But she suppressed both, and did not cry.

'So . . .' she said quietly.

'So,' he replied. 'Are you going to throw my curry over me?' He hoped she would. It would help relieve his crushing sensation of guilt. She, too, wished she could pick up the meal and hurl it into his face, so dark, oozing, brown liquid like shit would drip from his eyebrows and from his nose. It would be a fitting comment on what she thought of him at this precise, this awful, this dreadful moment of their lives. She knew that some of her friends, placed in the same position, would do just that. But she was not the type.

Was it a strength or a weakness? Dany did not know. Right now, all she knew was that she hated Curran, she hated herself and she hated everyone.

'We both know it is inevitable,' Curran said in little more than a whisper. 'It's a crying shame, a criminal waste. But it's inevitable.'

'Yes.' Dany sighed at the inevitability of the word inevitable.

They tried not to row as they talked about Yvette's future. Curran said that at such a tender age, etcetera, for purely practical reasons, etcetera, he understood that

74

Yvette perhaps needed her mother more than her father. And though it would hurt him grievously, he thought he could come to terms with seeing her every so often.

'With your hours, she goes for days without seeing you now,' Dany said, this time without malice. 'She's at school before you wake up and you're at work before she comes home.'

'All girls love their fathers,' Curran responded. 'I shall have to look forward to the time when Yvette can think for herself and will come to stay with me of her own accord.'

'Wherever that might be . . .'

'Wherever that might be.'

Dany tried to sleep again, but at 5 A.M. she was back downstairs. She watched an old black-and-white movie on TV, shifting from side to side on the sofa, unable to find a comfortable position.

She told herself she had every reason to be restless, what with all that had gone on before they went to bed. But her subconscious knew better. Even while she was awake, she was dreaming. Even as she watched TV, she was seeing images other than those on the screen. And they had nothing to do with divorce, or what would become of her, or how Yvette would take it.

Each time she slipped into another world, she was a child. Scared to the point of being petrified. Helpless to the point of being a naked, newborn baby. She shared her fear and her helplessness with other children – her friends – and that was a comfort. But once, she saw herself clinging to the side of a wrecked yacht in the midst of a great storm at sea. The others, in turn, were clinging to her. And she knew that if she let go and drowned, they would all drown. In a way, it would be her fault. It was an awesome responsibility.

She opened another bottle of wine, searching her mind for clues about why she should suddenly feel so vulnerable.

Was it because she and Curran were finally on the verge of splitting up?

'Maybe, but I don't think so,' she muttered aloud. 'I knew it was coming.'

Was it because she feared for the future?

'Maybe, but why then am I going back to the past?'

Was there a hidden meaning? Freudian perhaps. Did it have to do with sex?

'Always a possibility, but I don't feel deprived.'

She glanced around the lounge, asking the walls if they knew anything that could help her. Her eyes alighted on the unruly pile of papers, magazines and directories beneath the table that served as a prop for the phone.

She climbed from the sofa, ignoring a heavy head brought on by the wine, and scooped up an armful. She flicked through them, paper by magazine by telephone directory, tossing each aside with a certainty that they could not tell her anything. Until she came to Curran's paper of the day before – and its picture of Harold Whittaker's release from Mogden secure hospital for the criminally insane.

The tips of her fingers went cold as she touched the newsprint, as if she had dipped them into a bowl of crushed ice. It relayed a shudder throughout her body and she knew that here, on this page of this newspaper, was something that had come into her life. Without invitation and without subtlety, like an unruly gatecrasher at a party.

What she did not know and could not know was *WHY*?

Acting swiftly to quell her anxiety, she crumpled the newspaper into a ball and threw it into the expansive open grate that dominated the room. A box of matches rested on the marble mantelpiece above, and Dany reached up for them. Her hands were shaking so much that pulling a match from the box became a major task, but she managed in the end. She struck the match and held it to a loose corner of the paper.

Dany watched as it flared up – hoping that the flames would burn away the hidden, secret blackness within her that had begun to fester like a cancer. She stayed there, on her hands and knees, until the last flake of scorched paper had ceased to glow.

It was then that she realized she was too late. The cancer, or whatever the hell it was, had her in its grip – and would not let her go.

Dany stood by the hearth again in the morning, surveying the small pile of ash left in the grate, her flesh damp and tingling with the residue of sleeplessness. The sight of Curran, standing awkwardly in the door with a suitcase, only compounded her wretchedness.

'It's for the best,' he said. 'Until things begin to get themselves sorted out. Zak has offered me a bed in his flat.'

'A friend in need is a friend indeed,' Dany muttered without thinking.

'Do you mind if I keep a key and come and go?' Curran asked.

'It's still your house.' Dany avoided saying 'home'.

'Only I haven't had a chance to talk to Yvette yet. I thought if I popped in and out, now and then, I can seize the right opportunity. And it will show her that Mummy and Daddy do not intend to tear her world apart. Maybe

77

I'll even sleep here sometimes. In the spare room. What do you think?'

Dany's gaze shifted back to the fireplace – and she felt a stab of irony. She remembered when they had humped it home from the antique shop. It cost a small fortune, but they didn't mind. They told each other – out loud – that they had bought it to 'restore the Victorian magnificence' of their home. But they both knew the real reason. They wanted to make love in front of burning logs.

'It wasn't sex, was it?' Dany said, remembering Freud.

'What do you mean?'

'Sex. Screwing. Is that what's gone wrong between us? Do we revolt each other?'

Curran smiled and shook his head.

'Then why haven't we made love for months?' Dany challenged.

'Other things. Other wrongs. Sex tailed off when love tailed off, not the other way around. For God's sake, we've still been sleeping in the same bed.'

'*You've* been sleeping . . .'

Dany's head fell to one side like a heavy flower on a withered stem – and Curran understood.

'Did you dream again?' he said.

'All the time,' Dany muttered. 'It's terrible.'

'Same sort of thing?'

'The girls. Me and the six others.'

For a moment, neither knew what to do. Dany experienced all the old feelings of wanting to share her fears and of needing help from the only man she had really known. Curran, for his part, was reluctant to leave her like this.

Dany sensed it. She took a breath of courage and whispered: 'You'd better go.'

He smiled gratefully, turned and shuffled through the

front door, his suitcase heavier than it had been a moment ago.

Dany did not watch him leave. The pain would have been too great. As soon as the door clicked shut, she concerned herself with how she was going to get through the day.

Her first priority was to phone the TV studios. She worked part-time as a production assistant, her hours varying according to Yvette's schooling demands. She specialized in wildlife programmes – her love of animals enduring long after it had been passed on to her by Kipini – and she had been eagerly anticipating today's shooting of a studio discussion about ivory poachers.

Dorothy, a secretary near retirement age, took the call.

'Tell them I can't make it,' said Dany. 'I've been floored by flu.'

'Such a pity, dear,' Dorothy sympathized. 'And you had been so looking forward to it.'

'I know. It is a shame.'

'Never mind, dear. Make yourself a hot-water bottle, go to bed and sleep.'

Dany hung up without another word.

Sleep? If only she could.

7

Knapp was installed in a Midtown Manhattan apartment by Hagerty and Martha. It was a modest affair considering its Fifth Avenue address. Just one large open-plan reception room with offshoots to a single bedroom, shower room and kitchen. But it was expensively furnished. Teak tables and desks, brass fittings and soft leather armchairs. Its wooden floor had been recently sanded and varnished. A variety of deep-hued Persian rugs were scattered arbitrarily as if the person who laid them was certain they would be shifted. There was a television, a video, a hi-fi system, a phone. And the kitchen boasted every labour-saving device known to man and womankind.

Hagerty blew a film of dust from piles of instruction booklets arranged neatly beside the cooker.

'These'll tell you how everything works,' he said with a smile. 'Let me know if you have any trouble with the terminology.'

'I'll manage,' Knapp said coldly. 'I haven't forgotten how to wire a plug.'

'No . . . no . . . of course not.' Hagerty sauntered to Knapp's side, waving an arm at the vivid mosaic of snow-capped mountains that dominated the facing wall. 'I had it done specially,' Hagerty said. 'You always liked going up in the Alps.'

Knapp nodded and said, 'I did.' But his face displayed no hint of a cherished memory, and he did not look at the mosaic for long.

Hagerty turned and pulled back the drapes shielding a

balcony window. 'New York, New York,' he enthused as he absorbed a panorama stretching across Central Park's reservoir. 'So good they named it twice.'

This time Knapp did not look at all. All he wanted to do was to walk slowly around the apartment, to relish its openness and its cleanness, to touch this and to poke that, to try to unravel the mysteries of the battery of buttons that confronted him. But he knew such behaviour would betray both weakness and ignorance, and that was out of the question.

He threw his newspaper on the sofa, slumped down beside it and gasped, 'Whew!' as if he was a jaded civil servant just back from another tiresome day at the office. Perhaps they would go and leave him the hell alone. He needed time and, above all, space to himself. It was the only way he could get on with what he had to do.

He could not wait a day longer. Girls had to be traced and found. Girls had to be eliminated. Girls had enjoyed charmed lives for far too long.

Hagerty, though he had so much more to show, was left high and dry. And Martha, who knew how much effort Hagerty had put into preparing the apartment, was embarrassed.

She busied herself by making coffee and turning on radiators, but grew increasingly perturbed by the awkward silence that was descending on them all like a heavy morning mist. As she brought the men their cups on a tray, she decided to grasp the nettle. 'You don't have to stay here if you don't like it,' she said breezily. 'We can always find somewhere else.'

'Absolutely,' Hagerty confirmed. 'Though we thought you'd relish being here. Martha's place is just a few blocks away.'

'I can pop in, help you out, see if anything needs doing,' Martha said.

'I'm not a cripple,' Knapp said, eyeing them both sternly as if to warn them not to underestimate him. He looked around the room in a gesture of compliance. 'The apartment's fine. I'm very grateful.'

Hagerty recognized insincerity when he saw it, but decided to laugh it off. He shrugged his shoulders and muttered, 'Oh, well . . .'

'It'll be better once you sprinkle a little bit of your own personality around,' Martha offered.

'It's fine as it is,' Knapp insisted.

Martha looked at him and wondered why he was treating her like a stranger. It made her nervous and hesitant. 'I . . . I just want . . . *need* to know that you're comfortable. It's important to me, Daddy.'

'Why?'

Knapp did not elaborate. He just left the question hanging in the air. Cold. Harsh. As if it had been blown in to the apartment by a north wind. It swept Martha off balance and she did not know how to cope. Half of her wanted to understand him, to be patient, to allow him time to come to terms with his new life. The other half wanted to challenge him, to demand from him how he *dared* to talk to his daughter like that.

Hagerty sensed her dilemma. He asked for more coffee, then followed her into the kitchen as she went to fetch it. 'Look,' he said quietly, taking her by the hand to reinforce his message. 'I know it's difficult for you. Perhaps this is the most difficult day of your life. But it's difficult for him, too. It's been a while . . .'

Martha felt a tear escape her eye and dabbed at it before it tumbled down her cheek. 'I know,' she said, her voice faltering. 'It's just . . .'

She did not know what she wanted to say. Hagerty's arm slipped around her shoulder. The kind uncle spoke to her gently but firmly, giving her the benefit of his worldly wisdom. 'It may be best if you go.'

'Go?' She was surprised. 'I just got here. We all just got here.'

'Let him be. For a while. A short while. Maybe you can even come back tonight. But just give him some time on his own. He's not used to being with other people – ordinary people. That's all, I'm certain of it. Listen to me, Martha. Hear what I say.'

Martha listened and thought. And in the end, she decided to take the kind uncle's advice.

She hugged Knapp and kissed him on the cheek as she left – and tried not to feel hurt when he did not return the embrace.

'I'm flying tomorrow afternoon, but I'll come by in the morning,' she said.

'As you wish,' Knapp replied.

'OK . . . 'bye then.'

'Goodbye.'

She gave a little wave as she walked through the door – and cried all the way to her apartment.

As soon as Martha left, Hagerty became more business-like – and Knapp responded in similar fashion. They faced each other across the table, arms crossed and heads held erect. The situation reminded Knapp of the visiting room at Mogden, and he could not suppress a glance over his shoulder in case they were being watched by a nurse. But the only other figure in the room was a ceramic skier plunging down the mountain mosaic, and he turned to concentrate on Hagerty's outpourings.

'The address of a Wall Street bank,' Hagerty said,

flicking a business card across the table. 'A substantial lump sum was invested for you some time ago, on which there will by now be a good deal of interest. In addition, you will be able to draw a weekly pension. The account is in the name of Evan P. Dallenbach. Details of how to get at the money are on the back of the card. The passport I gave you can be your initial ID at the bank. You won't starve . . .'

'Thank you, Hagerty,' Knapp said.

'Uncle Sam never forgets a servant.'

Knapp was about to point out that Uncle Sam had forgotten him for thirty years, but Hagerty jumped in with a volley of questions. Knapp gave his answers without delay.

'How much do you recall?'

'Everything.'

'Do you remember when your name was Knapp?'

'Yes.'

'Do you remember Yelena?'

'Yes.'

'Do you know why it was necessary for us to do what we did?'

'Of course.'

'Do you know why you became Crosby?'

'It is obvious.'

'Do you know why you are now Dallenbach?'

'It's as good a name as any other.'

Hagerty was pleased. Mercifully, the man's brain was as sharp – and as formidable – as it had ever been. Hagerty did some memory-jerking of his own, recalling the time when they stood with Napier and Lipton in a bar at the Palais des Nations, pondering their meteoric rise to diplomatic prominence with some bemusement and toasting the future, which they felt sure would be the most exciting era since time began. Hearts raced as they considered how they could play leading roles in the making of history. Confidence and youthful vigour oozed from their very flesh. Hagerty remembered listening to Knapp's habitually incisive analysis of the day's nego- tiations between the Western powers and the Russians – crucial negotiations that would determine the starting line for the Paris summit between Eisenhower, Khrushchev and Macmillan.

'The Comet . . .' he muttered.

'I beg your pardon?' Knapp said languidly.

'What we used to call you, because you were bigger than a shooting star.'

Knapp looked away and thought of other things. No use delving into the past when the future was waiting.

'How strange is fate,' Hagerty whispered to himself.

'Speak up, man!' Knapp protested. 'I simply can't hear what you're saying.'

'I said how strange it is to think where you were only this morning.'

'The hospital?'

'Was it as bleak inside as it looked from outside?'

Knapp glared across the table with a ferocity that took Hagerty by surprise, and gave his answer a bitter edge that matched his sudden anger. 'You could have found out for yourself if you had taken the trouble to visit.'

Hagerty threw up his arms in an exaggerated display of innocence. 'God! C'mon . . . you know that was absol- utely *impossible*. You know the reasons. You just told me how you remembered everything. I couldn't visit. It would've . . .'

'Destroyed you just as it destroyed me!'

'No . . . yes, dammit.' Hagerty felt he needed to defend himself. 'We were all sucked into it. Me, Napier, Lipton.

We were all in those fucking woods. We all did what we had to do. To save you, for Christ's sake.'

'To *save* me? You had me locked away for thirty years!'

'It was *necessary*. You just admitted it yourself. You needed help.'

'I didn't know what I needed,' Knapp countered. 'I was so pumped full of chemicals I didn't even know what day it was. I had lithium for blood, Hagerty. Can you imagine that?'

Hagerty shook his head compliantly in an attempt to parry the onslaught. It was a small gesture, but to Knapp it was a beacon. A giant red stop sign that made him realize how close he had come to losing control, and thus losing any chance to rebuild his life. For the moment, he reminded himself, he had to carry on playing the game with Hagerty, just as he had played it with the medical examiners in Mogden hospital. Only Hagerty was smarter. Knapp decided to become more circumspect, but to retain the undertow of resentment that Hagerty would doubtless expect.

'I went through three phases inside Mogden,' he said calmly. 'Phase one: years of sedation during which I was in no position to hold any opinions about anything. Phase two: as my medication was wound down and the crap clogging my head dispersed, the shreds of my life as a diplomat made me realize why it had been necessary to place me in such an establishment. Phase three: an absolute certainty that I was well enough to resume a life outside the perimeter wall.'

'And so you are,' Hagerty offered. 'In the last twelve months, your health has been described as – and I quote – "excellent" in three medical board reports.'

'The last twelve months?' Knapp could not stifle a sigh laden with despair. 'It has been excellent for many – so many – years. Yet you chose to keep me inside. It was you, wasn't it? In the background, pulling strings. Leaning on Ashe. Were you appointed as my keeper by Napier and Lipton, or did you appoint yourself?'

'There was no conspiracy.'

'No? So why did the hospital censors allow your letters and parcels through without scrutiny?'

'I kept in touch because I wanted to.'

'You're a powerful man.'

'Not that powerful.'

'Powerful – and afraid.'

'Afraid? Afraid of what?'

'That it will all come out. Even after all this time.'

'No!' Hagerty was adamant. 'I took steps to make sure.'

'Which included keeping me locked away. Out of sight, out of mind.'

'Never out of mind. Believe me . . .'

'It could still wreck your career.'

'It's already been wrecked. I could've climbed higher. Director of the CIA, perhaps. Or maybe it could've been me in Henry Kissinger's shoes. I was the one who had to explain your disappearance to people – influential people.'

'And what did you tell them?'

'That you'd run off into the sunset with Yelena.'

'And they weren't impressed . . .'

'I was your closest friend. They thought I could have stopped you.'

'So you're resentful, too.'

Hagerty had to smile. It had happened again, just as it had always happened before. He had been turned inside out by a superior mind, a match for which he never expected to encounter. All he could do was marvel at how, within hours, Knapp had reasserted his authority.

He dipped his head in a mock show of deference. 'It's both humbling and comforting,' he said. 'It's never pleasant to have one's limitations exposed, but it's just *great* to have you back on song.'

Knapp dismissed the praise with a wave of the hand. 'Whatever you say, you still have a lot to lose,' he said. 'But don't worry. I'm not one of your damn pipe-joints. That's what you used to call them, isn't it?'

Hagerty nodded – and marvelled again.

'Napier,' Knapp said abruptly. 'Now there's a man with a great deal to lose.'

'You've followed his progress?'

'In words and pictures. It's been interesting to see how the newspapers have built him up over the years. The dashing young Member of Parliament. The ambitious junior minister. The progressive Home Secretary . . . and the implacable Prime Minister.'

'Yes,' Hagerty mused. 'A lot to lose.'

'And Lipton? What of him?'

'Knighted Whitehall mandarin. The voice of the Foreign Office, though totally unknown to the public.'

'So . . .' Knapp sighed. 'You all did well.'

Hagerty noticed the sorrowful lilt in Knapp's voice. It had been neither grudging nor envious, but it carried an unmistakable tinge of regret.

'You would have beaten us all to it,' Hagerty said. 'The destiny of the world would have rested in the hands of Khrushchev, you and Kennedy.' His face became suddenly pained as another memory was revived. 'Poor Jack,' he muttered.

Knapp smiled inwardly. Poor Jack? Oh no. More like Genius Jack. Hagerty had just been taken in like all the others. Knapp was tempted to tell him the truth about

Kennedy's great illusion. He knew it would make Hagerty's day, for Hagerty, too, had been close to JFK. He *would* tell him soon, but it was too early right now. There were other things to be done first.

No need to reassure me, Hagerty. I'll be back up there shooting with the rest of you soon enough. As soon as we're *all* safe. As soon as the seven girls descend into the hell they so richly deserve.

'Yes, poor Jack,' he said.

Louise had never spoken in public before and felt sick at the prospect. She had tried to think of a way to worm out of it. But there was none, save for throwing in the towel and allowing them to forge the road through the grounds of her stables without a murmur of protest.

Even the thought filled her with indignation. She was not an aggressive person, but cherished the whiff of independence that the stableyard gave her. She had built it up quietly and patiently over the years – and now she had ten ponies, two full-size horses, 104 pupils for her riding lessons and scores more on the waiting list. In the summer, she was hoping to build a barn to house an indoor jumping ring.

It was a business that allowed her to escape the raucous hurly-burly of her husband's 600-acre farm and the incessant crudity of the farmhands. It was a business that did not rely on stabbing others in the back in order to make a profit. And it was a business which was hers.

Now it was threatened by people who wanted to lay a cold strip of navy tarmac through her rich Suffolk meadows, in order to service villages invaded by the Londoners from whom she thought she had escaped years ago. Arrogant Londoners who said they hankered after the country life, yet demanded roads to take them to their office jobs in the capital. Ignorant, fashion-chasing Londoners who had as much sympathy for fresh air and grass as she had for the grime-laden, exhaust-choked alley-streets that were their natural habitat.

She could have waved the white flag. Looked for other fields for her horses and her barn. But it had been *such* an effort to build up the school. She was certain she could not go through it all again.

So here she was, on the rickety stage of a church hall, sitting on a hard wooden chair behind a trestle table and in front of the piercing eyes of the hundred or so ruddy-cheeked folk who were likewise affected by the plans for the road. Beside her, the village schoolmistress who had agreed to chair the meeting was going through her preamble, welcoming the audience, thanking the church for the loan of the hall and so on.

Any minute now, Louise thought, she will say my name and announce my speech.

Oh God.

She felt her heart thumping in her chest and was sure the people sitting in the front rows could hear it. She was cold and she was exhausted. She had not slept the night before for worry. She glanced at her shaking hands and noticed they were as white as snow. It made her think of the time when Lake Geneva iced over and she went with the other girls to feed the swans and the ducks.

The swans had been fierce enough, but when a flock of geese arrived to demand their share of bread and biscuits, all hell let loose. They hooted and they honked. They lurched forward in a wave of wing-flapping aggression. They were insatiable – and finally put poor Louise to flight.

She remembered Stefanie calling after her as she ran.

'Look at Louise, everyone. Can't even say boo to a goose!'

Oh, for just an ounce of Stefanie's courage now.

'. . . And now I would like to call on Mrs Louise Daniel to put you all in the picture. Louise.'

The schoolmistress's strident voice brought Louise back to the present. She could delay no longer. This was it.

An awful silence settled over the hall, broken only by the squeaking of Louise's chair, scraping on the stage as she climbed slowly to her feet. In the front row, a reporter from the local paper, his pencil ready to take shorthand notes, added to her sense of dread. She checked her own notes, scribbled on a piece of scrap paper, and wished she had taken more care to write them clearly. The audience, static and expectant, waited for her to speak.

'Er . . .' She hesitated, remembering a well-meaning friend's advice never to start sentences with 'Er . . .'

'Thank you all for coming here . . . er . . . tonight. It is perhaps the most important . . . er . . . issue . . . or controversy if you like, that this community has faced for . . . er, well, years.'

She could not bring herself to look up from her notes, but could sense their eyes boring into her. She felt like a medieval pickpocket about to be hanged in public.

Poor cow, they must be thinking. Poor, pathetic cow.

She had rehearsed her speech time and again in front of the dressing-table mirror.

Thank you all for coming here on such a (cold/wet/damp/mild) night. She had intended to use the outside conditions to make her audience feel at home. Promise to warm them up if the night was cold, or promise not to delay them should the night be heaven-sent for walking to the pub. But she had already forgotten to include the reference to the weather.

Oh God.

How many more mistakes before the end?

When she sat down after twenty minutes, there was a ripple of polite applause. She could not have dared to hope for anything else, but she felt more and more foolish as following speakers prompted cheers, raucous shouts of 'Hear hear!' and stamping of feet.

As everyone filed out into the night, there could be no doubt it had been a tumultuous meeting that signalled a bloody fight to the end with the road builders.

Yet Louise was immune to the back-slapping, the hand-shaking and all other actions of mutual encouragement. She stayed in her chair behind the trestle table, staring vacantly at the clock above the hall's double-doored entrance, still tense though her personal ordeal was long over.

'Louise?' It was the schoolmistress, collecting her hand-bag after saying her farewells. 'Are you staying here, dear? Camping out? I should think it'll be a trifle draughty.'

'No, Mam'selle. I'm going home.'

The schoolmistress was in a hurry and did not hear clearly. 'Well, come along then,' she said as if she was talking to a reluctant pupil. 'It was a wonderful meeting, don't you think?'

'Yes . . .' In truth, Louise had absorbed very little of it since saying her own piece. It could have happened on another planet.

'That'll give the town hall something to think about. I should say so. Oh, do come on, Louise. The caretaker wants to shut up shop.'

Louise got to her feet and slid her arms into a heavy sheepskin coat. As she pulled on a pair of mittens, the schoolmistress noticed the deathly pallor of her skin.

'You all right?' she asked.

'Yes . . . no . . . I don't know,' Louise stuttered.

'Only you're as white as a ghost.'

'I feel as if I've seen one.'

'I hope you haven't got flu coming. There's a lot of it about.'

'I had a sleepless night last night, that's all.'

'Worrying about your speech?'

'I suppose so.'

'You needn't have. It was wonderful.'

Louise nearly choked at the schoolmistress's gushing insincerity. The speech had been mediocre at best, awful at worst. It had certainly *not* been wonderful.

'Anyway,' the schoolmistress went on. 'Whether it's flu or the legacy of a bad night, you'll be better after a good rest. Can I give you a lift?'

'Thanks, but I've got the Land Rover.'

'See you at school tomorrow then.'

'Probably not. Timmy's ill. I think I'll keep him at home.'

'What's wrong with him?'

'Flu.'

'Ah, well there you are, then.'

Louise found it difficult to concentrate as she drove home. Every oncoming car seemed to have at least six headlights, a problem made more acute by black ice that reflected harsh rays off the lanes that wound from the village to outlying homesteads. She skidded on one bend and was fortunate to keep the Land Rover out of a ditch. It was with relief that she saw the saffron light that hung outside the farm.

She paid £5 to the eighteen-year-old farmhand who had been babysitting Timmy and watched the lad cycle away. Her forehead was throbbing, twisting and pumping, and felt like two lead bars swivelling on scales. She placed her palms on either side of her skull and pressed, hoping to squeeze out the migraine like toothpaste from a tube.

She vomited, but it didn't help. She sat in front of the fire, nursing her pain and feeling alone and frightened. It was a lonely place, three miles from anywhere. And not for the first time, Louise was certain that a ruthless gang of villains and ne'er-do-wells was on its way to get her. She would be screaming for help as they held her down, but no one would hear.

She jumped when the door swung open at midnight, but it was only her husband, Robin, returning from a Farmers' Club outing.

He was shocked when he saw the state she was in and tried his best to comfort her. He poured her a brandy, but she refused to drink it. He held her in his arms, but she wriggled free.

'Louise, darling, what on earth is the matter?' he asked finally.

She was frantic. She didn't know, so how could she answer?

8

Knapp pushed the furniture around his apartment, partitioning the main lounge area until he could see definable sections like separate rooms.

'What good is a mansion without nooks and crannies?' he mumbled as he toiled. Some of the furniture, particularly the sofa, was heavy – and Knapp was forced to admit he was not as young as he was. Yet he carried on with dogged determination, striking up a conversation with himself to keep his mind active while he was engaged in purely physical work.

'I think the dining table should rest just here, don't you?'

'You have fine taste, sir.'

'That's what the Republicans said when they found out about me and Marilyn.'

'Marilyn?'

'Monroe.'

'Marilyn Monroe?'

'C'mon, Donald, don't give me that. The whole world and his dog knows about me and Marilyn. And you, you sly fox . . . you were probably one of the first to find out.'

Knapp chuckled as if to admit he had indeed known all along. He picked up a dining chair.

'So, Donald, what do you think? Should we have two chairs on either side of the table, or one, assuming we have one at each end for host and hostess?'

'That depends on how many people you are planning to entertain, sir.'

'You know how Jackie loves to throw a party.'

'But, if you'll forgive me, sir, although this is indeed a beautiful house, it will never be able to accommodate the massed ranks of Washington society.'

'So, one chair on either side, then?'

'I would recommend it.'

'Then I'll do it, Donald. You know I always value your advice.'

'Thank you, sir.'

Knapp pushed one chair under either side of the table and one at each end. There were two spare. He took one into the bedroom so that important visitors would have somewhere to sit if ever they needed to see him when he was ill. He slid the other under the desk which he had pushed into a corner near the door. He had already put the telephone, writing paper, a pair of fountain pens, ink and a blotter on the desk. And as soon as he could cover its plain pine top with a sheet of thin claret leather, he would have a fine and distinguished study.

'So, on to the reception room. I do wish there was a fireplace, don't you, Donald?'

'Central heating is efficient, but soulless. A fireplace gives a room character.'

'And somewhere for the Soviets to throw their vodka glasses!'

'Indeed so. Have you seen anyone? Zorin? Kuznetsov? Gromyko?'

'Not since the Cuba thing. We really showed them there, didn't we, Donald?'

'Bloodied their noses.'

'Kicked their asses.'

'Only you could have done it, sir.'

'Nonsense. You make it sound as if I was the only American involved in the whole damn escapade. What

96

you forget is that I had a back-up team of immense talent, drive, loyalty and determination. People like Adlai Stevenson and Bob McNamara. And people like you, Donald.'

Knapp decided to move the sofa once again. It was facing a wall which Hagerty had covered with shelves and books. That was OK. Most of the books were new and their classical binding and gold lettering held out the promise of quality as well as quantity. A stimulating sight, all in all. But the sofa was too *close* to the wall. Newspaper photographers and TV camera crews were certain to demand frequent pictures of him 'relaxing at home' and would doubtless ask him to lounge on the sofa with a cigar, a bourbon and a magazine. But where would they stand to shoot their pictures or roll their film? No, the sofa would have to come back another yard or so to give them elbow room. Knapp sunk to his haunches and curled his fingers under the base of the sofa, ready to pull.

'While you're here, Donald . . .'

'Sir?'

'I . . . I know I should have mentioned this earlier, but – '

'Go right ahead, sir.'

'I . . . I'm so sorry about your wife.'

'Ruthie?'

'Yes, Ruth. Of course. Ruthie. I'm sorry . . .'

'Thank you for your concern.'

'It must have broken your heart. She was a wonderful woman.'

'Wonderful, yes. But sadly not immortal.'

'Like the rest of us. Er, tell me, Donald. What exactly happened?'

'Cancer. Lung cancer. Too many cigarettes for too many years, I guess.'

'Shame, shame, shame. Life is not fair. And neither is death. She was a wonderful woman – and you were so devoted to her. A perfect couple. Shame, shame, shame.'

'I had planned my entire future with Ruthie. Sometimes things go awfully wrong.'

'I know they do, Donald. There was Yelena . . .'

'You know about Yelena, sir?'

'And the seven little girls.'

'So, sir, you know what must be done if I am to rejoin you in the White House.'

'Of course.'

'I know how to do it.'

'I don't doubt you will be thorough and professional, Donald.'

'I already have clues. They went to the school where Napier sent his daughter. I remember its name now. L'École Internationale des Cygnes. They had swans on their blazers.'

'So you'll be paying the school a visit?'

'You know what schools like that are like. Exclusive. Ostentatious. Downright stuck-up. They'll have records, reunions. They'll keep track of their little Arabellas and Lucindas so they can boast of their success when they become fully-fledged *femmes fatales*.'

'Quite so. That's impressive forward thinking, Donald. I wish you luck. And when you're done, you'll know where to find me.'

'I will – and it will be the dawning of a new era.'

Knapp let go of the sofa with a gasp. He felt his face glowing like a hot coal and could sense that the veins in his neck were standing out with the strain of uncommon effort. It was time to rest.

He walked slowly to the shelves and plucked a book that had been left by Hagerty in the centre of the display, turned at right angles so its glossy purple front cover was fully visible. Knapp allowed himself a smile as he read its title. *Quantum Mechanics of Molecular Conformations* – the long-awaited new edition of what had been rightly hailed as a master work.

Knapp fixed himself a bourbon on the rocks and settled down to read its foreword.

Yet suddenly, as his eyes flicked across the very first paragraph, it dawned on him that he no longer had any call for either its message or its challenge. The need for survival, pure and simple, had passed. Now, he was a free man, with things to do and places to go.

He threw the book in a bin and grabbed his coat.

Curran did not want to go to the party. His mind was preoccupied with a creeping realization that Dany's fevered sleeplessness was an uncanny carbon-copy of what had happened to Pearl before her death. But Zak, a man with Polish roots whose full name was Zakowski, insisted.

'Don't be a dodo,' he scolded. 'Besides, what else are you going to do? Mope around and feel sorry for yourself all night? That's not going to help anyone.'

Curran glared at his friend. Zak, a movie freak who worked in the head office of a cinema chain, was infamous for being self-opinionated to the point of arrogance. He could rarely see other points of view and took pleasure in slapping down innocent remarks made in small-talk as if they were serious propositions. Women, in particular, counted themselves among his targets and did not like him for it.

The result was that Zak could sustain little more than one-night stands. Yet it seemed to work out. Zak was happy without commitments and his fly-by-night lovers were fleetingly impressed by his brashness, his generosity, his startling vigour for life – and the way he always made things happen rather than wait for someone else's lead. Curran admired the same qualities. No one was perfect – but Zak was better than most. Apart from anything else, he had been the first to offer a bed once he learned how things were with Dany.

'It's at a hotel near the airport. Sweaty bodies wall to wall – and hundreds of beds to heave them into.'

Curran thought Zak sounded like a sixteen-year-old and told him so.

'Better than sounding like a ninety-six-year-old,' Zak replied instantly. 'Now get changed and let's go.' He pushed Curran's suitcase towards him with a foot. 'Trish won't wait for me all night, you know.'

'Who?'

'Tantalizing Trish the temptress. She's an actress. A nugget of nubility with the pout of Bardot, the legs of Garbo and the lips of Vivien Leigh. Hang on in there, babe, Clark Gable's on his way.'

At first, the party was hard graft. Curran didn't know anyone apart from Zak, and Zak was busy wooing Trish with lavish cocktails and stories of Hollywood in the 1930s.

Curran bumped from awkward encounter to clumsy introduction and met the usual bunch of people who couldn't understand how on *earth* he could work for a popular tabloid.

'Lying scandal rag full of crap,' one dinner-jacketed guest said bluntly.

Curran, who had long ago given up trying to explain his craft or even pointing out that his newspaper was read and enjoyed by twelve million or so people each and every day, called him a pompous prat and moved on.

When he met attractive girls, he felt bashful, almost shy. He was out of practice at flirtatious conversation, out of practice at watching for tell-tale signals transmitted by interested females, out of practice at simply being available. In a brief moment of panic, he wished Dany was there with him. But then again, she would have been too tired – and he was tired of her.

It was only a hefty punch in the shoulder from an exasperated Zak that spurred him into action. He decided to look for a girl in the same situation as himself.

Alone and unsure.

He found her within ten minutes. She was sitting on a stool with her back to the bar, supported against its chromium-tube surround by her elbow. She was tall and lean – and showed off her legs by wearing black tights and a leather mini-skirt. She had long blonde hair, outgrowing a perm and naturally bleached into streaks as if she had just been on holiday. Her round-featured face could have been mellow were it not for the dark way in which she was looking at the dancers swaying to a Dire Straits number away to her right.

She is wondering why they are having fun, and she is not, Curran thought to himself. Truth is, she is holding herself back. Why?

He watched her for a while, saw her picking at her fingernails, scratching the nape of her neck, flicking imaginary specks of dust from her skirt. When there was nothing else to be done, she took a pack of cigarettes from her handbag and slipped one into her mouth so it dangled from her top lip. Her lighter would not spark, and Curran saw her shaking and cursing it before hurling it back into her handbag with startling force. She fared little better with a box of matches, her undue haste in trying to strike one foiling attempt after attempt. Finally, in a flurry of elbows and blurred wrists, she succeeded, inhaling deeply as if to reward herself for all that effort. Yet her subsequent puffs were markedly stunted. She blew out her little clouds of smoke the instant after drawing them in to her throat. And she stubbed out the cigarette before it was half finished.

Curran briefly wondered if she was on a date. But no perspiring man staggered back from the dance floor to take her hand and none of the other drinkers clustered around the bar took any notice of her. She was nobody's girl tonight.

Curran cleared his throat and made his entrance. He asked if anyone was using the stool next to hers and she shook her head blankly.

At first, she was reluctant to answer his questions and he felt more foolish than ever. But then she accepted a drink and managed a hesitant smile as he passed it to her.

'What's your name?' he asked at last.

'Martha,' she replied. 'Martha Knapp.'

Louise turned in her bed for the thousandth time and mumbled, 'No! I'm not coming.'

Stefanie wouldn't have it. 'Oh come on, scaredy cat,' she sniped. 'You're the only one who doesn't want to come.'

'I'm not so. Sari wants to stay here, too, don't you, Sari?'

The others turned to Sari. She looked at her feet and did not say a word.

'Thanks a bunch,' Louise moaned.

'Look, we can't stand here arguing,' Stefanie said. 'Mam'selle will call us back soon. We've got to go.'

'I'm not coming, so there.'

'We'll go without you then.'

'Into the woods,' said Dany.

'To play Swallows and Amazons, or tag, or hide and seek or something,' said Pearl.

'Bags I hide first,' said Dany.

'You're always first,' said Mai-Lin. 'It's not fair.'

'I'm going,' Stefanie announced. She glanced back to the middle of the clearing. Mam'selle was still reading her book and was not looking. Stefanie crept into the undergrowth, taking care not to tread on any twigs that might snap and alert Mam'selle to their adventure.

'We're supposed to be looking for flowers,' Louise protested. 'Mam'selle will be angry if we don't.'

Pearl spotted a wild strawberry at her feet. She bent to clip its delicate white bloom and waved it in front of Louise's nose before slipping it gently into a pocket with a degree of care that seemed incongruous with her outward show of aggression. 'There'll be more in the woods,' she said with certainty.

'We'll get lost.'

It was Louise's last stand, but it was as futile as Custer's. Stefanie, crouching in a thicket of fern, waved for the others to follow. One by one, they disappeared from the sunlight of the clearing into the shade of the woods.

Louise shivered as she slipped under the canopy of branch and leaf. She was sick with worry, not only at the prospect of detention when Mam'selle found out, but because she was sure there was danger ahead. A tiger, perhaps. Or a three-headed monster that would bite off her head and her arms all at the same time.

'Do they have tigers in Switzerland?' she asked Sari.

'I don't think so – but there are some lions,' Sari replied.

'Don't be silly,' Kipini, the expert, said with authority.

'Snakes?' Louise asked.

103

Kipini pointed to a red squirrel scurrying towards its tree across a mossy hillock covered with bluebells. 'There's nothing more beastly than that here,' she said.

Louise was not convinced. She tried her best to join in the hide and seek game, but could not concentrate. The other girls threw fallen pine cones at her and laughed at her timidity.

'Gotcha!' Stefanie yelled as her cone whacked Louise on the arm. She spun on her heels, instantly bored by such baiting, eager to move on to the next excitement. 'Who's gone? Who's hidden?'

'Dany and Pearl,' Kipini said.

'Where are they? Let's find them.'

Sari pointed to an ancient oak tree away to the right and said: 'Dany's there. I saw her running.'

'Oh, blooming heck, Sari,' Dany moaned as she emerged. 'Did you have to tell everyone?'

Sari looked sheepish and muttered, 'Sorry . . .'

'Start again!' Stefanie ordered stridently.

'Sssh!' Pearl came out from behind an azalea and held a finger to her lips.

'What's up?' Stefanie demanded.

'Sssh!' Pearl repeated. She pointed along a dirt footpath leading further away from the clearing. The others stood as still as statues and kept silent.

Voices!

Two voices, one bass, the other high-pitched. Mai-Lin thought they sounded strange, like her mother and father sparring before one of their fights.

'Let's go and see,' Stefanie whispered.

The girls crept towards their quarry stealthily, their ears pricked for further guidance on where to find it. They left the footpath to follow the trail across bramble and a criss-cross tangle of pines blown down by a recent gale.

They saw the two people as they emerged from a tunnel carved through a laurel bush by previous adventurers. Thirty yards ahead, through a glade of young silver birch and more venerable sycamore trees. A man and a woman, he holding her elbow and she wrenching her arm, trying to break free from his grip. They were both angry – and every one of the girls, even Stefanie, instantly felt they should not be where they were.

'The tree trunk. Hide, Pearl! Hide, Louise!'

'What's he doing?'

'Hide, Kipini! Hide, Sari!'

'What's he doing?'

'Hide, Mai-Lin! Hide, Dany!'

'Hide yourself. Get down.'

'He's hurting her. Listen, she's crying.'

'*Girls, girls. Where ARE you, girls?*'

'Over here, Mam'selle,' Louise called out as she twisted on to her back, but no one heard. Why hadn't her husband come to bed? She needed him at her side so desperately.

'Why can't *they* hear Mam'selle?'

'They're too far away.'

'It's the wind.'

'They're too busy arguing.'

'Ugh! There's a squidgy mushroom on this tree.'

'Ssssh!'

'I won't shush.'

'You must. They'll hear us.'

'Look!'

'What's he doing?'

'Oh, dear baby Jesus. Don't let him do that.'

The breeze stiffened, making the laurel leaves behind them rustle. Louise was dazzled by a glint of sunshine reflecting off something the man was holding.

'*Girls, girls!*'

'Over here, Mam'selle.'

WAKE UP, LOUISE. YOU *MUST* WAKE UP. *NOW*. WAKE UP NOW.

Filthy grey clouds appeared above the trees, scudding across the sky and blotting out the last of the brightness. With no apologies, they bombarded the girls with huge droplets of rain which made their bonnets bounce on their heads.

'*Girls! Les enfants! You must come back to me.*'

'Over here, Mam'selle.'

SOMEBODY COME AND GET ME. PLEASE . . .

'He's hitting her.'

'He's doing nasty things to her.'

'Oh no . . . please don't, M'sieur.'

'No! No! Leave her alone!' Louise shouted at the top of her voice, yet all her cry achieved was to alert the man to her presence.

He turned where he stood and looked through the sycamore glade to where she was hiding with the others. He spun on his heels and walked towards them. One stride, two strides, three strides. Louise counted them all. Nothing could stop him. His ankles glided through knotted clumps of grass. His clothes were caught by outstretched arms of bramble, yet the fabric did not rip. Time after time, his head crashed against low tree branches, yet he did not blink an eyelid.

'He's coming to get us.'

'He's covered in red.'

'What shall we do?'

'Run.'

'I can't. My legs . . .'

'Stop! Go away, nasty man.'

But he didn't stop. He kept coming, coming – his thick, hairy arms ready to grab them and tear them apart; his

106

twisted face and wet mouth ready to devour them. He was a monster. The Bogey Man. Everything they were frightened of when they closed their eyes at bedtime.

As Louise watched his approach, his neck sprouted into three branches. A head grew at the end of each. Gnarled, warted and yellow, like a diseased pumpkin. Each pair of lips parted to reveal rows of razor-sharp wolverine teeth.

Louise remembered the fairy tale. *All the better to eat you with* . . .

Mai-Lin cried out. 'He's nearly here.'

The three-headed monster leaned forward to snap up its first child.

'Help! Mam'selle! Mummy!'

'Too late.'

'*No!*'

'Louise, darling, what's the matter?'

She could not reply. Her mouth was full of spittle and she had to rid herself of that first. She felt a man's hands on her shoulders, shaking her until she was sure her skull would fall off.

Her breathing was ragged and shallow and sometimes stopped altogether. She slipped in and out of consciousness, sensing only snatches of the flurry of panicked activity that broke out around her.

'Louise! Darling, please.'

A cold hand slipped underneath her left breast and pushed down hard on her heart. It relaxed for a moment, then pushed again. Relax. Push. Relax. Push. Relax. Push.

Two fingers slid in between her teeth and forced her jaw open. The man's lips met hers and formed a seal. Hot, sticky breath entered her and inflated her lungs.

'Come on!' A sound of encouragement, coming from

107

far, far away. 'Come on, you can make it. That's my strong girl.'

The smell of the woods drifted away. In its place, the wind brought a whiff of antiseptic. Like household cleaner, but stronger. She opened her eyes for a split second. She saw a white ceiling with peeling paint. She was aware that she was moving. She was on her back on a hospital trolley, that was it. Flashes from strips of neon burst into her head. She counted them. One, two, three, four – and got up to nine before closing her eyes again.

'Do something!'

'I'm trying my best, sir.'

Louise knew the doctor's best would not be good enough. The terror had gone now, but it had devastated her body. However hard she tried, it simply would not work.

'Please, I beg you.'

'Stay calm, sir. I won't let her go.'

Thank you, doctor, Louise thought. They can do such wonderful things these days.

Tubes in her mouth, in her arms and in her bladder. A plastic mask across her nose. Needles in her veins. An awful hissing sound from some machine or other.

'Stay with us. Stay with us!'

Thanks once again for your best efforts, doctor.

She did not hear his final words.

'I'm sorry . . .'

9

Curran met Martha again the next time she was in town. He took her to a small, unpretentious Italian restaurant in Richmond, a few miles from Heathrow Airport, and ordered clam tagliatelle and a bottle of Frascati.

It was awkward at first. They had exchanged simple introductions at the party, and now it was time for a meatier understanding. Martha, mindful of past disasters, was wary of this new interloper in her life and was reluctant to open up. Curran, for his part, had forgotten what it was like to get to know a woman, one to one for an entire evening, and found the experience as daunting as it was stimulating.

The date could have foundered in the mire of fresh acquaintance, but both needed a diversion from more pressing matters and were determined to make it work. Curran, curious about why such a looker had not been snapped up long ago, was not one to leave curiosity unsatisfied. 'So then,' he said. 'No husband, no Steady Eddie . . .'

Martha responded with a puff of the cheeks. 'Oh, I'm just a good pair of pins in a uniform to most guys – a suitable partner for the Mile High Club. You wouldn't believe the amount of nudge-nudge wink-wink bullshit I have to put up with each and every flight.'

'I can imagine,' Curran offered.

'I don't imagine you can,' Martha insisted. 'Men face different kinds of hassle.'

'You're on the prime route for crap. New York–London.

High-powered transatlantic businessmen looking for an extra-marital kick.'

'Did you do that?'

'When I was with Dany?'

'Sure.'

'No.'

'And since you hit the buffers?'

'I haven't looked for it, to tell you the truth. And when it happens, you know, an attraction for another girl, I still feel guilty. It holds me back. Like we say in the papers, I make my excuses and leave.'

'Jesus, your fly must be bursting.'

Martha was immediately embarrassed by her own boldness. She muttered, 'Oh God . . .' and looked away, pretending to be suddenly absorbed by the mock lines of washing the restaurant owner had hung across the ceiling to remind him of Naples.

Curran, relieved that the ice had been broken, laughed out loud.

But Martha took it the wrong way. 'Please don't mock me,' she said with a sudden harshness.

'I . . .' Curran did not understand.

'Only I don't like to be mocked.' She fixed him with sharp eyes that warned him to take care.

It was a message Curran was quick to absorb. 'I'm sorry,' he said sincerely. 'I wasn't – '

Martha's face instantly flushed with guilt and regret. 'God . . .' she said, holding up her hands as if she could not believe her own actions. 'No, no, you don't have to be sorry. It's me that must apologize.'

'No . . .'

'I'm a little edgy, that's all. I've had an exhausting week. Excuse me.'

They both felt the ice begin to freeze over again at the

edges, a sensation accentuated by their silence as a waiter served the tagliatelle.

Martha took it upon herself to hold the cold at bay. 'Where's your home?' she asked. It was not penetrating, but it was better than nothing.

'Fort Lauderdale, Florida,' Curran replied.

'Nice. So how'd you end up in England's green and pleasant land?'

'I met Dany. Came here to live with her. I'm sort of mid-Atlantic now, like those awful disc jockeys.'

Martha encouraged him to talk about Dany. He was reluctant at first, and asked Martha every two minutes if he was boring her. She shook her head and listened, but even so he gave her a truncated version of how he and Dany had fallen in – and out of – love.

'So what about you?' he countered as soon as he could. 'Where's your place?'

'New York,' Martha said blithely.

'A real live native New Yorker?'

'Oh, come on. How many of those are there? Actually, my family comes from Illinois and I was born in Switzerland.'

'Does that make you Swiss?'

'No, sir.' She saluted like a soldier. 'I'm momma's apple-pie American. My father was a diplomat. I was born while he was working at the UN in Geneva.'

'That's amazing!'

'What is?' Martha was perplexed by Curran's incredulity.

'My father was in the service, too. And Dany's. And both worked in Geneva. That's how I came to meet Dany in a roundabout sort of way. Through my sister Pearl. She was Dany's closest friend at school there. They were tiny

111

then – six or seven – but they always kept in touch afterwards.'

Martha was alarmed, though she tried not to let it show. She felt her toes curling inside her shoes.

'When was your father in Geneva?' she asked nervously.

'Late fifties, early sixties. Yours?'

Martha hesitated, then said, 'About the same time, I guess.'

'Wow!' Curran slapped the edge of the table with his fingers. Practically the whole restaurant glanced in his direction, but he raised his voice even higher. 'Maybe our folks *knew* each other.'

Martha stiffened in her seat and took a forkful of tagliatelle to give herself time to consider her reply. When she was ready, she said, 'I wouldn't know. I was just a baby.'

'What did your father do in Geneva?' Curran persisted.

'I don't know.' Martha's voice was harsh again. 'He was pretty high up, that's all I can say.'

'Oh . . .' Curran took the hint and allowed the subject to drift. 'My pop was just a newcomer, a junior, so they probably didn't meet after all.'

'Probably.'

'So, is your father still alive?'

'No,' Martha replied without hesitation. 'He died a long time ago.'

Now Curran understood. A girl without a father. A sadness rekindled whenever she talked about him. It explained a lot about the solitary air that had surrounded her at the party – and was in danger of engulfing her again now.

As he watched her sipping her wine, her eyes refusing to meet his, he knew he did not want that to happen.

'After the meal, I'll take you for a walk by the Thames,' he said soothingly. 'It's beautiful round here, and the air's fresh by London standards. No aircraft gasoline fumes at any rate.'

Martha's common sense told her to call a taxi, to leave the restaurant without Curran, to climb on her 747 the next morning and to put 3,000 miles of ocean between herself and him.

But then he stretched an arm across the table and placed his hand softly on hers. Now, she was forced to look at him. And she saw nothing but sincerity, warmth and a billowing fondness.

She was lonely. He was lonely. And since when did common sense rule the heart?

She could not prevent the words slipping from her mouth. 'We can go for a walk,' she said. 'Or we can go to my hotel room.'

Knapp chose to walk. At first, his step was brisk, aided by a stout gold-topped cane thoughtfully left by Hagerty beside the door of his apartment. But the further he trudged, the more Manhattan bore down on him.

It was so vast – and yet so cramped. Its rulered avenues of outstretched buildings, heaving themselves up towards snow-laden clouds one after another after another, formed grim concrete corridors that had no beginning and no end. It was Mogden hospital by another name in another place.

Walk! Don't Walk! Walk! Don't Walk! Even the street signs bellowed orders with the relentless ferocity of the vilest charge nurse. Was this freedom to which he had come . . . or had he walked through the gates of hell?

During his years of isolation, he had tried his damnedest to keep pace with the world. He had read newspaper after newspaper. He had studied their photographs to reflect on changing shapes and sizes. He had watched television documentaries to absorb moving images of life.

But nothing could have prepared him for this *savage* onslaught. Everything was different. People were different, the clothes the people wore were different. The stores the people shopped in were different, the stuff sold to the people by the stores was different. The cars driven by the people were different, and the streets through which the cars rumbled and blared were different.

The very air was different. Different smells. Different texture. Different colour.

He leaped from the path of a fuzzy-haired kid swerving along the sidewalk on a skateboard. He was knocked aside by a strutting young blade wired up to a Walkman. And his fascination in watching a man withdrawing money from a cashpoint was rewarded with a torrent of abuse and a violent push which sent him tumbling to the ground.

As he pulled himself to his feet, he looked up as if pleading with the Gods to pluck him out of this new dungeon. But it only compounded his claustrophobia, for there was precious little sky – precious little hope – to be found beyond the terrible towers.

His only way out was to remember it as it was.

Streamers and confetti pouring from office windows as Jack's motorcade eased its way through the masses blocking Broadway. The Democratic Presidential candidate, shy but earnest, returning their waves with a smile as wide as Nantucket Sound, his crinkled brow keeping out the harsh sun and accentuating his boyish good looks. Jackie in a wide-brimmed hat, radiant in the knowledge that she was pregnant again.

And after the campaigning, a break at the Kennedy compound at Hyannis Port. The white-railed verandahs

114

where they all posed for pictures. Touch football on the lawn with Bobby and Ethel, Teddy and Joan. Jack smoking a slim Cuban cigar especially imported from London, laughing at a right hand painfully swollen because he had shaken those of so many well-wishers. Taking his leave of the old man, Joe, with his habitual kiss on the forehead.

'You'll win it on TV,' someone called. 'You're four years younger than Nixon – you look four goddamn decades younger.'

The Kennedy Mystique. The New Frontier. That was what was in the air then.

Jesus, how it had been polluted since.

'Smoke, smoke, smoke. Crack and tabs. Smoke, smoke, smoke.'

Knapp was shaken from his rage by the monotone chant of a half-breed pusher who had fallen in behind him, and looked around to find himself amid the pools of snow-white light beamed out by 42nd Street's porn palaces. He knew neither how he had got there nor how long it had been since he was shoved to the ground by the man at the cashpoint. But he also knew it was where he wanted to be.

'Smoke, smoke, smoke. Hey mister, c'mon. Do some biz, man.'

A hundred leather-jacketed, sullen-faced turkeys lined the sidewalk, with apparently little else to do but stand and stare. Knapp felt threatened and tapped his cane sharply on the flagstones as if sending out a warning to keep predators at bay.

'Smoke, smoke, smoke.' The half-breed kept up the chant as he trailed Knapp's footsteps. In the end, Knapp turned to confront him. He was in his early twenties, a curious mixture of Hispanic and Indo-Chinese, wearing a woollen bobble hat and red lumberjack shirt.

'Get off my ass!' Knapp snarled.

The pusher did not argue. He wheeled around, found another ass and followed it. The hookers saw what happened and moved in. If the guy didn't want dope, he wanted sex.

Knapp fleetingly wished Hagerty had slotted him into Washington, where this sort of thing was so much more organized and discreet. He knew why Hagerty had chosen New York, but what was it to him if Martha lived around the corner? When he left her and Ruthie – when he was *forced* to leave them – she had been in diapers. No use trying to suck back water from under the bridge. Rivers only flow one way.

If he counted Martha, there had been three women in his life. Now he needed a fourth. Just for one night, before he took the plane. Maybe even an hour or two would do, as long as he found one. No one could be surprised at the burning, bestial feelings that were emanating from deep within him. Not after they had been suppressed for such a long, long time.

A scrawny redhead aged about seventeen was the first to offer herself. She waited patiently while Knapp went through the ritual of looking around to see if he was being watched. He had Kennedy's name to protect, as well as his own.

'Yes,' he said at last. 'Where is your office?'

'Office?' The redhead thought for a while, then chuckled. 'Oh that. Yeah, I got an office that needs new springs. Only a block away.'

'That's no good.'

'What?'

116

'I'll meet you across the city. Somewhere in Brooklyn, maybe.'

'What?'

Knapp grew impatient with the girl's ignorance of the basic facts of life.

'Don't you understand?'

'What?'

'Look at my clothes, the shine on my shoes, the gold top on this cane.'

'So?'

'So it is dangerous for me to be seen here, child. I have a reputation and a station in life to safeguard.'

Now it was the girl's turn for impatience. 'Look, bud, you wanna stick your dick in my fanny, right?'

Knapp, disgusted by the hooker's crudity, admitted it reluctantly.

'So why the conditions?' the girl cried. 'Is it part of the buzz, or what? You're a guy, I'm a whore. Let's go and do it.'

'Not here . . .'

'What are you? A cop?'

'Do I look like a cop?'

'None of the best cops do.'

'I'm not a cop.'

'So what are you doing here, Mr Smart Clothes? If you're the kind of guy you say you are, this is the last place you'd come sniffing. You'd be all cellular telephones, hotel suites and Amex gold cards.'

'I don't know anywhere else. I haven't been in New York for a while. For Christ's sake . . .'

The girl grew tired of wasting precious earning time and stuck a finger under Knapp's nose. 'Go fuck yourself,' she sneered. 'Ain't no one round here gonna do it for you, that's for sure.' She spun on her stilettos and marched back to her lookout post, five yards from the entrance to a peep show.

Knapp, fuming with indignation, walked on.

The same thing happened with the next five girls. Willing to do business, unwilling to leave their home territory.

'It's a dangerous job,' one tried to explain. 'All kinds of weirdos. At least we can rely on some sort of protection around here.' She glanced at a bunch of heavies twenty yards further up the sidewalk. Knapp got the message and moved on.

It wasn't until he reached the end of the street that he struck lucky. A Polynesian girl, not a beauty but less haggard than most of her kind, who said she understood his need for discretion. 'But you'll have to pay me for a whole night,' she insisted.

'Do you imagine money is a problem?' Knapp said loftily.

She shook her head and apologized.

Knapp accepted it with a mellow smile. 'What's your name, sugar?'

'You can call me Miss Twilight.'

Knapp laughed.

The girl's face reddened with the anger of a teenager who has suffered enough mockery from her elders. 'I'm part-time,' she hissed. 'I'm supposed to be at violin class tonight. Shall I give you my name and telephone number so you can tell my mother what her daughter is really stroking with her bow?'

Knapp told her of a hotel he had known since way-back-when in a hidden Brooklyn square behind Hicks Street, and said she should meet him in the cocktail bar next door in two hours. He gave her a down-payment of fifty dollars and promised her 300 more if she showed.

After they separated, he shopped at Macy's for a jute sack, a car tow-rope and a briefcase in which to put them. He considered hailing a cab, but rejected the idea on the grounds that an alert cabbie would surely recognize him. On the subway, he would be just another face in the crowd.

The little bitch kept him waiting – and for a moment he wondered if she had taken the fifty and run. But she showed after twenty minutes and was thoughtful enough to apologize. He wanted to go to the hotel room immediately. She dug her heels in and hit him for a large pina colada, sipping it provocatively through a straw while twirling the cocktail's little paper umbrella between the thumb and forefinger of her right hand.

Knapp enjoyed the tease and reached across to stroke her jet-black hair. She did not pull away – and he realized he had found a gem among rhinestones.

'How old?' he asked.

'Off limits,' she replied.

'What is?'

'Asking my age.'

No more than sixteen, Knapp thought when he saw her naked in the hotel room. Her breasts were light and pointed, with smooth nipples of a pinkish colour at odds with her Pacific heritage. Her creamed-coffee body carried not an ounce of surplus fat and her short but supple legs extended from round and athletic buttocks, suggesting she could outrun a gazelle. Knapp was especially entranced by her pubic hair, glistening in the pale light of a tablelamp, and yearned to feel its warm, damp welcome.

And yet, as she took off his clothes and ran her fingers across his chest and down his thighs, he remained as still as a statue and did not become aroused. She pushed

119

herself against him where he stood and for the first time in thirty years, he felt the unrestrained glory of a woman's skin against his. But this, too, failed to make him erect.

Perplexed, the girl asked him what he wanted from her. His gaze switched to his cane and briefcase, resting against the side of the bed. The girl became alarmed.

'Are you going to hit me with the stick?' she cried. When he shook his head, she said hopefully, 'Do you want *me* to hit *you*?' But his expressionless reaction told her he did not want to be beaten, either.

He said nothing and retreated into his shell, his penis languid and unwilling. The girl felt a stab of fear in her chest. She had come across a silent type like this before – and the encounter had ended in weals and bruises which she hid from her mother for a fortnight.

He sensed her trepidation and moved to calm her. 'It's all right,' he said quietly. 'You'll come to no harm.'

'What then?' she asked nervously.

He took three strides to reach his briefcase and clicked it open. He pulled out the sack and the rope and held them up before her eyes. She could not restrain a gasp and wondered if she ought to make a dash for the door.

He threw the sack to her. She caught it in her hands. It was clean and smelled fresh, but what the hell did he want to do with it?

'Put it on,' he said.

'What do you mean, "Put it on"?'

'Just slide it over your head, as if you were putting on a dress.'

She opened the neck of the sack and looked inside it. 'Do you mean climb into it?'

'No. I said to slide it over your head.'

'But . . . there's no hole in the bottom . . . for my head to go through.'

120

'No. There's no hole.'

The girl realized what he was driving at, but could not believe it. 'You want me to cover my face? So you can't see me?'

'It's loosely woven. You'll be able to breathe.'

'Jesus . . .'

Knapp could see her fear growing and felt that he owed her an explanation. His manner was abrupt, but sincere. 'I'm sorry,' he said. 'It's the only way I feel able to do it. I have to put the sack over the top half of your body.' He glanced at the rope. 'And tie you up.'

'Jesus . . .'

'I won't hurt you. I promise. It's the only way.'

She said she didn't know, she wasn't sure. If he were her, she said, how would he feel?

'I won't hurt you,' he repeated. 'How much did I offer you before?'

'Three hundred.'

'Five hundred for the night.' He nodded towards the sack, still hanging from her hands. 'And that.'

She was swayed by the money and by the way in which he let her rummage through his clothes for a gun or a knife. After receiving further assurances that he would not slap her or punch her, or use his stick on her, she agreed. It was a chance. She knew it. But it was a chance she was prepared to take. She slid the sack over her head and waited.

Knapp told her to lie on the floor while he tied her. He folded back the trailing edge of the sack so the girl was exposed from the waist down, then made a lassoo with the rope and slipped the loop around her torso, tightening it until she told him to stop. He made sure the sack was held in place, then rolled her over on to her stomach. He wound the rest of the rope around and under her

121

shoulders, pulling them back so her wrists crossed at the base of her spine, and finished by tying the loose end of the rope to the loop with a reef knot.

He told the girl to kneel with her legs apart so that her head rested on the edge of the bed, and helped her into position. She braced herself for his entry. When she let out a whimper of anguish, he promised once again he would not harm her.

He was as good as his word. He eased himself in little by little until her natural resistance subsided. Only when he was sure she was ready, when he knew he would not rub against dry flesh, did he allow himself a rhythm.

At first, he clung on to the underside of her shoulders, a leverage afforded by design due to the way in which he had tied the rope. But as his sensation grew, he freed his hands to stroke the fine down that filled the valleys of her back and kissed the stubby protuberances of her lower vertebrae.

Now he could enjoy her flesh, her smoothness, her radiating heat, her mounds and curves that led to her secret places.

When he climaxed, he gave out a long howl of pleasure and dug his fingers into her buttocks. After a while, when his last pulse was over, he leaned forward to whisper in the cocooned girl's ear. 'Why? You knew what would happen. Why, Yelena, why?'

10

Curran turned the key of his door, feeling callous and shameful. His mind was in turmoil as he asked himself question after question.

Why, when he had just experienced one of the most wonderful nights of his life, could he not feel lasting satisfaction?

Why, when his marriage was over and done with, did he still feel guilt?

Why did he have a barely controllable urge to tell Dany about Martha? Why did he feel he was cheating her?

There were no answers, only more questions as he found Yvette in the hall, clinging to a half-naked doll as heavy tears tumbled down her cheeks. It was late morning, yet she was still in her nightdress. It was a school day, yet she was at home. Her hair was still tousled from the night before and a garish orange stain surrounded her mouth where she had tried to help herself to a jug of fruit juice. She fell into Curran's arms, held him tight and cried and cried.

He patted her lightly on the back and said, 'There, there.' She was cold – and he noticed her feet were bare.

'Where's Mummy?' he said as her sobbing subsided.

Yvette pointed upstairs and said: 'In bed.'

'Is she ill?'

'I don't know.'

'Have you had breakfast?'

Yvette shook her head and looked sorry for herself.

'Have you washed?'

'No.'

'Well, I'll tell you what.' Curran tried to sound cheerful, though it was an effort. 'You go and scrub your face. Get all that yukky orange off it, and clean your teeth. And as soon as I've seen what's wrong with Mummy, I'll make you lots and lots of toast. You can have Marmite, honey, peanut butter, anything you like. What do you say?'

Yvette looked up at him curiously, as if she knew he had left home and was checking to see if he still loved her. But then she smiled, pearl-drop lips pushing dimples into fleshy cheeks, and he knew she was all right.

He bounded up the stairs two at a time and swept into Dany's bedroom – for that was now what it was – ready to shout and scream at her.

The sight that confronted him – and the smell of stale wine that had seeped into every corner of the room – made him shudder.

Dany was asleep, but awake. Tossing maniacally amid tangled sheets smothered with burgundy stains, her eyes closed but her mouth open and jabbering incomprehensibly. Her duvet had fallen to the floor, sending a collection of empty bottles sprawling. A wine glass lay amid them, its stem broken as if Dany had dropped it, or thrown it, from the bed.

She jerked over again as he watched, turning her back to him. Through strands of her hair, he noticed that the bottom sheet had been ripped. By being tugged from side to side as she tossed, perhaps. Or had she torn it deliberately with frantic fingernails?

Dany cried out as if she was being attacked.

Curran ran around the bed and took her by the shoulders. He shook her violently and shouted: 'Wake up! Snap out of it!'

Her eyes opened immediately. Wild, accusing eyes,

boring into Curran as if he had committed some heinous outrage on her. Her jaw dropped open and she panted and dribbled like a rabid dog. Curran instinctively let go of her and took a step back.

Her expression changed as if someone were turning a knob behind her back. From the venom of a cobra, through relief, to the docility of a lamb. She wiped her mouth with the back of her hand and frowned at him as she tried to focus. 'It's you!' she said. 'Stephen, it's you! Oh thank God, thank God, thank God.'

She burst into tears, climbed on to her knees and hurled herself from the bed into his arms, forcing him backwards into the seat of a chair. He held her in the same way he had held Yvette. Her hands gripped his hair and clung on for dear life. It hurt him, but he stayed silent.

She was beside herself and could not stop crying. Time after time, she repeated: 'It's not him. It's you.'

Curran felt a dampness spreading across his thighs and realized Dany had wet herself. He held her tighter and told himself he would never let go.

Yvette appeared from behind the bedroom door, her crinkled face asking a thousand questions. 'Has Mummy been sick?' she said. 'Are you looking after her?'

Curran glanced down at the head of matted hair in his arms, then looked vacantly at Yvette and said: 'Yes, I'm looking after her.'

Dany pushed her lips into the nape of his neck. He felt them move as she spoke, but could barely hear her fractured words. 'Robin rang. Louise is dead. In her sleep, just like Pearl. Oh Stephen . . .'

Knapp bristled with impatience and resentment as he stood in the queue at the bank. He was not accustomed to having to wait for service and promised himself that he would soon see to it that he would never again be forced to stand in line.

The wait stoked an angry mood caused by the girl whore. Had he not treated her well? Had he not fed her with steak and poured her champagne during lulls in their activity? Had he not kept his word that he would not hurt her?

Then *why* had she reacted so wildly when he warned her once again to be discreet? Why could she not see that their meeting should remain a secret, that she should never talk of it, even to her friends? Why did she curse and insult him when he told her he had a reputation to protect?

He had been forced to slap her face, even though it meant breaking his promise. And he had been forced to threaten her with reprisals if ever news of their rendez-vous leaked to the press or to associates. 'You will pay dearly, Miss Twilight. I shall find you, and you will pay dearly.' Those had been his exact words – and he meant them.

'Next!' Knapp had reached the head of the queue. He gave the clerk the number of the account that Hagerty had opened for him, showed his passport as identification and asked for his balance. The clerk twirled around on his seat to check on the computer behind him. After he passed on the required information, Knapp drew out $5,000 in cash and travellers' cheques, warm in the knowledge there was more where that came from – and that this simple fact had transformed the clerk's attitude to one of deference.

Thank you very much, sir. We hope to see you again, sir. Three bags full, sir. That was the way it should be.

Knapp took a cab to JFK Airport. When TWA told him their next flight to Geneva was full, he tried Swissair.

126

They had a plane leaving for Zurich within two hours, with a connecting flight to Geneva. Knapp booked a seat.

'How would you like to travel, sir?' he was asked.

'I'm on government business,' he replied. 'The correct impression must be made. I'll go first-class.'

He travelled 3,500 miles in distance, but thirty years in time. As he leaned back in his press-button seat to sleep, his mind drifted to a bar in Évian les Bains, a small town on the French side of Lac Léman, reached from Geneva by a short boat ride. He was with his closest colleagues. Hagerty, his lieutenant in the American negotiating team, and Napier and Lipton from the British side.

They had gone to the bar for a break from work, but the upcoming Paris summit inevitably dominated the conversation. How could it not, when there was so much at stake? The end of the Cold War or the beginning of a new Ice Age, someone had called it. None of the four men – fresh, young, optimistic and thrusting though they were – felt such a statement was an exaggeration.

'Complacency,' Napier said, stroking a thick moustache which covered an unsightly childhood scar.

'Who?' Hagerty asked.

'Everyone on our side,' Napier replied. 'Eisenhower, Macmillan, the State Department, the Germans, the French. They all think a disarmament agreement is in the bag. The whole of Washington assumes everything is sitting pretty for the conference. Isn't that so, Knapp? You have your ear to the ground.'

'I'm afraid you're right,' Knapp admitted reluctantly.

'And yet nothing could be further from the truth,' Napier continued. 'Things are going tolerably well with the Soviets here, thanks to the Famous Four . . .'

'Who?' Hagerty said again.

127

'Us, you clot.' Napier allowed himself a brief chuckle before his natural intensity returned. 'But it's a different story in Washington and Moscow. The ground has already been fouled. Ike has put Khrushchev's nose out of joint by saying he is not prepared to spend longer than a week at the summit. Khrushchev has put Ike's nose out of joint by replying that the leaders should stay in Paris for as long as necessary – and insulting Nixon.'

'What did he say?' Hagerty, who had been away for a few days, was anxious to catch up on the news.

'He said that if Nixon took over the negotiations at the end of Ike's week, it would be like sending a goat to mind the cabbage patch.'

'Nixon a goat? So where's the insult?'

They grinned at each other. Nixon-baiting was always an entertaining amusement.

Knapp took a deep breath before launching into his customary summary of the situation. The others were happy to listen. Knapp had a God-given ability to put his finger on the nub of the debate and to express it concisely and precisely. He was seldom less than impressive and was universally admired by his peers. But emotions ran deeper than that. Knapp managed to combine ability with humility, a rare achievement and one which often turned mere colleagues into personal friends.

'If one listens carefully to Khrushchev, and if one is aware of the Russian mentality, one will immediately recognize that everything in the garden is far from rosy. We stand today less than a month from the Paris summit. A time when olive branches should be held out and taken. Yet what is the reality? In speeches to the Supreme Soviet, Khrushchev says he has little hope that the Western powers are *really* prepared to seek a solution to the problems of co-existence. He describes State Department speeches by Herter and Dillon as "provocative" and their approval by Ike as "unfortunate". He argues over the future of West Berlin. He calls West Germany "revenge-seekers" who want atomic weapons to eliminate the state of East Germany. He says France is "playing a very dangerous game" by supporting the Germans. He accuses Western hawks of trying to use the summit to show off the power of the Allies and adds that anyone who thinks this is possible "has as much chance of seeing his own ears". Is this the language of trust and of peace?'

The others shook their heads in unison and blew out their cheeks in exasperation. For eighteen months, they had worked hard in Geneva on behind-the-scenes talks with the Russians – and the result was a draft agreement containing countless clauses of mutual co-operation. All that was needed was a final nod and the signatures of the Big Three. So near and yet so far. The frustration was immeasurable. They looked to Knapp to give them hope, but he was not yet prepared to do so.

'These problems are daunting,' he said. 'But they are as nothing compared to the crux of the matter.'

'Which is . . .' Hagerty prompted.

'Which is that even though Khrushchev toured the United States last year, and even though relations seemed to be on the up, there has been a hardening of internal pressure on Mr K. The truth is that international tensions provoke national unity. And as these tensions diminish, so the Russian people tend to pay less attention to the party line. It is the eternal dilemma for every Soviet leader – and carries with it a devastating force. A force which could blow up the Paris summit with the power of a nuclear bomb. And yet here we are, gentlemen, talking glibly about disarmament.'

Knapp complemented his superbly ironic climax by

turning his back on the others and striding to the bar to order more drinks. As the barman poured the Scotch, he looked back at his three friends and played a game with himself, wondering what they would all be doing in ten years' time.

They were all high-fliers. All successful and in positions of gruelling responsibility for men in their early thirties. But, Knapp reckoned, only Napier measured up for greatness. Tall, suave and with an eye for the main chance, his manner of speaking was elegant and persuasive. He could say everything and nothing at the same time. He was not above playing tricks on opponents and often told outright lies if he felt they would serve his purpose.

Opinionated and righteous, and with the blue-blooded backing of a family estate and Harrow-and-Cambridge education, he would move into politics when the time was right, which would be soon.

Knapp chuckled to himself, for with Kennedy's blessing and encouragement, he had already begun covert preparations for election to the Senate. He would tell Napier soon, and despite their minor ideological differences, they would go forward to glory together. A successful Paris summit would be the perfect springboard for them both.

Hagerty? Not so stylish as Napier, but dependable, confident and quick to make decisions. A fierce and uncompromising patriot, he would follow a career which would see him in the forefront of maintaining America's prime position in global affairs. Too sensitive and argumentative to make a party politician, he would probably rise through the echelons of the State Department to high office.

Lipton had barely said a word since their arrival in Évian, which was not uncommon. A heavily-veined plump man without charisma, he was nevertheless capable of the most devastating aggression – that of issuing threats with a smile. His future lay in the British civil service as a buffer. He would be a valued go-between happy to advise and protect whichever master or mistress was delivered to him by the electorate. But above all, he would do all in his power to ensure the perpetuity and influence of Whitehall itself.

By the time Knapp returned with the drinks, the conversation had veered away from shop, which was a relief, and had assumed a more personal note.

'How's Ruthie?' Napier asked.

'Fine, just fine,' Knapp responded.

'And the toddler?'

'Martha? Oh, you know, staggering around on wobbly legs, bumping into everything and smashing all our china.'

Napier guffawed and said: 'Sounds jolly chaotic.'

'She's a menace all right, but a beautiful menace. You'll have to come round for lunch on Sunday, then you can see for yourself.'

'Love to.'

'Bring Fiona and Jasmine. By the way, how is Jasmine finding her new school?'

'Better. So much better. They're pushing her harder. Making her think.'

'Where is it?'

'On the outskirts of town. You must have seen the sign on the Lausanne road. Two swans with intertwined necks. And its name in silver Gothic lettering – '

'L'École Internationale des Cygnes. Yes, I've seen it.'

An expression of amazement crossed Napier's face. Knapp's eye for detail was extraordinary.

'You know,' Napier said. 'It's no surprise you've nailed your flag to Kennedy's mast. You're two of a kind. You've

131

both got it all. Good looks, rich talent, a happy family. The lot. Even the Russians say it about you.'

Napier spoke with neither envy nor sarcasm. Knapp wished he had done, because then he could have felt embarrassed. Instead, he felt a sensation which had been new to him only months ago, but was now becoming relentlessly familiar.

Fear. Stark, unembroidered fear.

It came to him only occasionally. Out of the blue, once every two or three days. But when it did, he felt as though he had been run through by a sword. He had tried to understand it, though it was not easy. After all, had he not been leaning against the bar just minutes ago, basking in the inevitability of his journey to the White House? And now this. He even had to fight to stop himself trembling.

The last time it happened, he thought he had found at least part of the explanation. As his career had blossomed so vividly, so the expectations of others had risen to unforeseen heights.

But were they being fair? Were they creating pressure? Was he suffering from stress, the silent and invisible killer? If so, how many years had it been gnawing away at him? And how much more of him would be claimed by the strain of the summit?

Was his self-confidence genuine, or was it a woeful and destructive sham? Above all, did he still possess the strength to keep his secret from them?

Yelena.

If they – if anyone – found out about her, he would be destroyed.

He needed to divert his mind. Quickly, before they noticed the terror in his eyes.

Thanking Napier for the compliments, he raised a glass

and proposed a toast. 'To the Paris summit,' he said grandly. 'Let there be *nothing* to stand in the way of its success.'

It did not work. The fear still mounted, the sword twisted in his gut, until he was convinced he would have to scream.

As the others supped their Scotches, he excused himself and made for the toilet, trying desperately not to break into a run. Once there, he locked himself inside a cubicle and thrust his head into the bowl the instant before he vomited. He sweltered and shivered at the same time. Beads of perspiration burst from his forehead and dampened the inside of his shirt. Paralysing colics swept across his stomach and abdomen. It had never been this bad.

He stayed there, motionless, for what seemed like an eternity, not daring to show himself until his recovery was complete.

Lipton came into the toilet to urinate. 'You all right, old chap?' he called with a chuckle.

Knapp crouched lower in the cubicle, suppressing a renewed urge to be sick.

No, I am not all right. When the summit is over, I must see a doctor. Secretly, but it must be done. Yelena will help me.

'Just like Khrushchev,' he said cryptically. 'Shitting bricks.'

11

Curran felt lost in a fog and pressed two fingers to his temple in a vain attempt to ward off a searing headache brought on by the impossible possibility of what was happening.

The seeds of suspicion had been sown as he spoke to poor Robin on the telephone – and realized Louise's death had been identical to Pearl's, down to the froth that tumbled from their mouths as they suffered their final convulsions.

'It was like protoplasm,' the farmer had said. 'Like the colourless liquid which oozes from a crushed plant. I caught some between my fingers as I tried to clear Louise's throat, and felt its texture. Thicker than water, yet thinner than spittle. A substance I have never before encountered in man or beast.'

'What did the doctor say?' Curran asked.

'He paid no heed to it. He said Louise died from a massive heart attack caused by the onset of severe stress, to which she was demonstrably unaccustomed.'

'Robin, had Louise been having nightmares?'

'She had been sleeping badly, yes. It made her awfully irritable, which as you know is . . . was . . . unusual for Lou – '

The change of tense from present to past was too much for Robin to bear. His voice wavered and he broke down as grief overcame bravado. 'I . . . I'm sorry, Stephen,' he stammered. 'Tell Dany that Louise will miss her so much. She'll miss all the Swans. They meant so, so much to her.'

Curran was unsure he could swallow the implication that Louise had departed to another place, but if it helped Robin . . . 'Yes, of course,' he said. 'And they'll miss her.'

He promised to call again later and said he would try to get to the farm on his next day off. But as he hung up, his thoughts turned instantly to Dany. He remembered how she had dribbled like a dog when he woke her. And like her two dear friends, she was being tortured by a succession of vivid, terrifying nightmares.

A connection was obvious – yet there could be none. Closer than sisters the three of them may have been, but they lived separate lives in separate places. How could they *possibly* be affected by the same terrible ailment? It simply was not feasible.

The unwritten rules of his trade began to bounce around in front of his eyes. Expect the Unexpected. Never Assume Anything. Nothing is Impossible.

Surely to God, *something* was happening. But what?

It was then that his head started to pound.

He walked slowly to the kitchen to find some painkillers. Dany, sitting flaccidly on a stool at the breakfast bar, looked at him through the steam of a large mug of black coffee, and pulled the corners of her dressing gown over her knees in a token attempt to look tidy. It was difficult for her to say what she felt. But no matter how pathetic, she knew this was her opportunity to come out with it. She tried to make it as brief as possible.

'Stephen, I know and accept that our marriage is at an end. But I know also that I need help . . . and I have no one else to turn to.' She sighed and added, 'There, I've said it.'

She looked away to give him the chance to say 'No.' Through the window, under the leafless apple tree that stood dormant in the garden, she saw a cluster of yellow and purple crocuses. Curran had given her the bulbs on Valentine's Day eight years ago.

'They'll come up at this time every year . . .' he had said, '. . . as an annual reminder of my love for you.'

She planted the bulbs and, just as he had promised, they pushed up through iced earth every February. Only now they were meaningless. Just another bunch of flowers. Dany told herself that if Curran would not help her, she would dig them out and throw them away.

Curran abandoned his search for tablets and turned to face her. He found himself walking over to her, cupping her cheeks in his hands, kissing her tenderly on the forehead.

Dany pulled back, torn apart by the contradictions and wounded pride clawing at her self-respect. Curran reached out. His hand caught the edge of her shoulder and fell limply down the length of her arm. When he spoke, his voice was barely more than a whisper. 'I'll help you,' he said. 'Of course I will. I'll do everything in my power.'

They talked about Dany's nightmares – or her visions, as she called them, because they were so much more powerful than ordinary dreams. She told how she could remember little detail, but even so, she was aware they always centred on the Seven Swans – and were always frightening. She motioned to an overflowing waste bin and its attendant collection of empty wine bottles, standing around it like sentries on guard duty.

'It's the only way I can stop the visions,' she explained. 'The drink washes them out of my head and drowns them.'

'But they come back,' Curran said.

'Each more photographic than the last. Weird visions. Inexplicable visions.'

'There's always an explanation.'

'You think so?' Dany's shrill voice reflected her disbelief.

'Tell me more. Tell me what you saw and how you felt.'

Curran listened intently as Dany told him what she could. And the more he heard, the more he became convinced that the visions meant something – and that unless they were checked, they could inflict vast and permanent damage.

'Do you think I should see a psychiatrist?' Dany suggested.

'Vultures,' Curran scoffed. 'Picking the bones of the inadequate and the stupid. You are neither.'

'A doctor?'

'Drug-prescribers. Referrers. Too basic.'

'Well, *what* then?' Dany said sharply.

'Trust yourself – and trust me. Contact the other Swans. Ask them if they're dreaming, too. Go back to the Geneva school. Find your Mam'selle. See if anything comes up.'

'I'm working at the studios for the next week.'

'Then quit,' Curran said without hesitation. 'This is more important. Two of your friends have died, Dany, and you're in trouble. Resist it. Don't let it drag you down.'

'And you? What'll you do?'

'Me? I'll be the keeper of your dreams. And I'll find out what they mean.'

Knapp waved farewell to Hagerty, Napier and Lipton and took off. It was good to be an eagle again and the vista of the Alps below him was a breathtaking example of glacial magnificence. White, open and virgin-pure, it was the perfect place to escape his pressing worries about the Paris summit.

He saw a dot far below, moving across the snow towards a mountain peak. He swooped down to get a closer look.

It was a woman, naked apart from a medieval leather mask topped with a small scarlet feather. Although the mask covered her face, Knapp knew it was Yelena, and cried a greeting. For a time, she ignored him. She carried on tramping through the snow, leaving delicate footprints that showed she had walked straight, whatever the obstacles in her path, for more than a mile. She was smooth and milky, and neither her flesh nor her nipples betrayed the wickedly cold temperature of the air around her.

Knapp cried out again, a raucous call sent from a male bird to a female as a sign of attraction. This time she turned – and he saw something that froze his blood. On a strap tied around her left wrist, out of his sight until now, she was carrying another bird of prey. Hooded, like her, it had eyes like diamonds and a plume of long scarlet feathers stretching from its rear quarters until they brushed the ground, melting every grain of snow they touched.

The flamebird!

'No!' Knapp screamed. 'This is treachery, Yelena. Betrayal. You cannot do this to me.'

But he knew she would and urged his giant wings to take him up to the heavens and away from this menace of the skies.

Yelena watched him climb until he was a speck. Then she let the flamebird go with an order to destroy.

Knapp saw it coming and knew escape was impossible. It was so fast, so ruthless. It tore into him and scorched his belly with its infernal heat, and he began his death dive.

He plummeted into the snow at Yelena's feet, gouging a hole in the snow. As the flamebird settled back on her wrist, as docile as a house sparrow, she stroked its crown and said: 'What must be must be.'

Knapp could still see her as he retrieved his luggage at Zurich Airport.

Curran found five books on dreams on the shelves at Foyle's, and bought them all. He began to read at work, flicking through pages during brief hiatuses in a routine shift of court stories and picture captions, on which he could barely concentrate.

'I know why you're reading that crap,' Hockenhull chided at one point. 'You're in a bloody dreamworld yourself today.'

Curran picked up his case from Zak's on the way home. He had told Dany it would be better if he moved back in, in case she should need help in the middle of the night, and her gratitude convinced him it was the right decision.

He used the spare room, poring through the books for hour upon hour, hoping that in one chapter, on one page, he would unlock the door to Dany's despair.

He concentrated on sections dealing with regression to childhood, but unearthed more confusion than hope.

Sigmund Freud wrote of adult dreams being prompted by infantile wishes and conflicts, and suppressed sexuality. Thus, dreams of a loved one's death could be interpreted as a hidden childhood wish to eliminate a rival; dreams of burglars and ghosts were juvenile memories of parents who came to the bedside of a sleeping child, the burglars being the sleeper's father, the ghosts the mother in a

white nightgown; dreams of trees and steeples represented the penis; dreams of containers like pockets and
boxes the female genitals; dreams of daggers and spears,
or fountains and taps, symbolized penetration and
orgasm; dreams of pleasurable movement like flying or
rocking on a seesaw represented the eroticism of mastur-
bation or sexual intercourse. And so on and so on.

Curran supposed it could be so. But while an infantile
conflict might be applicable to Dany's case, there was no
way of knowing what it could have been, or how it was
now being manifested. And the sexual element could be
safely ruled out. Dany took no pleasure from her dreams.

After further reading, Curran took the view of other
academics, including such notables as Jung, who accused
Freud of over-simplification. Some of these critics spoke
of a return to childhood as an escape from adulthood, of
maturity being too hard to bear. Women who dream such
dreams, they said, may have powerful maternal desires
that remain unfulfilled.

Again, there was a sniff of truth. Dany *could* be
searching for an escape route from the heartache of a
crumbling marriage. And before the rot set in, she had
often spoken of having a second child.

Hints here. Clues there. But nothing concrete. And
nothing that coincided with the circumstances of Pearl,
who had worn her sexuality on her sleeve and had never
wanted children; or Louise, whose family life was secure
and happy.

As dawn filtered through the curtains and birds sang,
Curran was forced to accept the reality: that despite
decades of research by some of the most formidable
brains in history, the workings of the human subconscious
were as much a mystery now as they had always been.

Thousands of theories, yes, but few facts. For a newspaperman such as Curran, who dealt only in facts, neatly presented one after the other, it was hard to stomach.

As he drifted towards the refuge of sleep, all he could do was to pray the answer was simpler. Was he failing to see the wood for the trees? What about the notion that dreams were simply garbage disposers, unclogging the mind of recent experiences which would not be retained as memories?

Taken alone, it could not explain Dany's recall of her early schooldays, for they were not recent. Yet there could be a connection.

Curran took stock of Dany's recent experiences. Pearl's death. The encounter with the other Swans at the funeral. The heavy drinking. The moment when she saw the picture in his newspaper of Harold Whittaker shuffling away from Mogden hospital . . .

That was what had put the fear of God in her. Perhaps that was what had triggered her visions.

Exhaustion overcame him as he tried to figure out *why*.

A pale-yellow moon illuminated the Gothic lettering and its attendant emblem of intertwined swans outside the tall school gates. Knapp drove past and parked the hire car half a mile on, then walked back until he reached the perimeter fence. It was five feet high and made of wrought iron painted crimson. Silver fleur-de-lys spikes topped its main support posts, but their purpose was decorative rather than constituting any serious attempt to keep out intruders. 'After all,' Knapp murmured to himself, 'it's hardly Fort Knox.'

Knapp made light work of climbing over. He heaved himself up until he gained a foothold, then sprung athletically into the air, using his wrist as a pivot to clear the barrier with inches to spare. He automatically glanced back to see if anyone had been watching. But at 2 A.M. on a frosty night in late February, the outskirts of Geneva were populated only by mice and owls. He congratulated himself on achieving the first results of his Mogden fitness regime, which, he felt sure, would serve him well in the crucial weeks to come.

The gravel drive leading to the school, a saffron ribbon in the moonlight, bent away to his left. He decided to stay as hidden as possible, and scurried into the copse of trees away to his right, where his black clothes would merge into the shadows of the night.

It was a logical progression of secrecy and stealth, for he had already rejected the alternative means of gaining access to the school records. It would have been simple to make an appointment with the principal, to pose as an Austro-American professor called something like Wendlinger, engaged on a United Nations project charting the lives of children from across the globe whose paths had crossed in infancy. But there were complications. What, for example, would the good principal make of newspaper photographs and TV film of him standing next to Kennedy upon their triumphant return to the White House? Recognition would be immediate. And then whither Professor Wendlinger?

'Stay low,' Hagerty had said back at the apartment. 'Don't make waves.' It may have been in another context, but it was sound advice from a man who knew all there was to know about secrecy and stealth.

Brambles tugged at Knapp's ankles as he picked his way through the copse. It was not large. He could not get lost in it. But its smells took him back to the more substantial woods further out of town, where he had walked arm in arm with Yelena. Earth freshly turned by moles, awaiting its crystalline encrustation by hoarfrost. Layers of rotting leaves, compressed by rain and snow, their smoky odour mixing incongruously with the fresh scent of pine from stoic evergreens. Soon, daffodils and bluebells would push up through the moss to add their perfume. Later in the year, ferns would curl open to line mile upon mile of tracks threading through the trees, and conical shafts of sunlight would roast secluded clearings. Clearings where he and Yelena would lay their blanket and make love until . . .

'Until it ended,' Knapp uttered. 'Until they ended it.'

The school emerged from behind the trees. Its three storeys of limestone shone fluorescently into the darkness around it, but no light beamed from its rooms. Knapp was relieved, but not surprised. Napier had once told him over dinner that the school served only diplomatic families based in Geneva and did not take boarders, and a discreet phone call from Zurich had ascertained that nothing had changed in the thirty years since. With no precious, valuable girls to guard, there was no need for the school to be anything but a hollow shell at night. Knapp was sure there would be a token presence. A concierge, perhaps. But it was long after his bedtime.

Knapp pulled on a pair of thin leather gloves, glancing resentfully at the flapping, unfilled pouch where his lost ring finger should have been, and scurried to the rear of the building. He chose a window at random and pinpointed the glass pane nearest its handle. He took a handkerchief from his coat pocket, fumbled in a flower bed for a large stone, and wrapped the stone in the handkerchief to give it a degree of sound insulation.

He tapped on the pane until it cracked, then pushed gently with a thumb until the broken glass worked loose. A small hole appeared as shards separated. Knapp squeezed a hand through it and bent his wrist to pull glass from putty one piece at a time, so it did not fall and shatter. He placed the pieces on the grass outside, then opened the window to climb in.

He found himself in a classroom, and flashed a torch to avoid bumping into desks or chair legs. He walked briskly through it, closing the door behind him so the cold draught from the broken window would spread no further.

The school was shaped in a square around a courtyard, and Knapp assumed the offices for which he was searching would be on the ground floor. As he paced its corridors, he shone his torch on every door he passed. Each bore a small brass plate indicating its role – Classe Quatre, Classe Cinq, Laboratoire de Biologie, Salle des Arts and so on – and Knapp smiled at how easy they were making it for him.

Amid a forest of pot plants, he found a more grandiose oak door bearing the nameplate: PRINCIPAL M. Didier Delestre, Licencié ès lettres. He tried the handle – and the door swung open without protest. Knapp's eyes, urgent now with the task in hand, followed the torch's beam as it swept around walls peppered with small oil paintings and a herring-bone carpet blistered by dropped cigarettes.

It was a large office, left uncluttered by Delestre's taste for elbow room. Its main features were an antique walnut desk bearing a computer terminal, a neatly stacked pile of documents and an intercom; a matching bookshelf; a plush leather sofa for visiting parents and a locked glass cabinet – brazenly wired up to an alarm system – containing recent sports trophies won by the school.

But there was nothing to interest Knapp, and he

turned his attention to a connecting door marked SECRÉTAIRE. It was slightly ajar and Knapp pushed it open with a foot.

The secretary's office was busier. More functional pine desks littered with word processors, files, envelopes, sheafs of headed notepaper and pens. Knapp noticed a safe built into the wall, but was distracted by yet another door. Its brass plate proclaimed its purpose, and Knapp felt a surge of elation as he read the word: ARCHIVES.

The door opened into a cavelike room of bare concrete floor and plaster walls, lined on one side with filing cabinets and on the other three sides by shelves piled high with magazines, newspapers, framed photographs and long rectangular boxes containing bunches of manila envelopes separated by index cards. Knapp began his search immediately . . . and the clues he had nurtured in Mogden reverberated in his head. A pot-pourri of faces he could never forget. Two names, Pearl and Dany. An Oriental girl – and a black girl the others called something like Bikini.

Two hours later, he had them in his grasp.

He saw them in class photographs, feigning innocence in their white cotton dresses. He saw them trying to hide prying eyes behind dark glasses on the ski slopes of St Moritz. He saw them gorging themselves at Christmas parties in the mountain lodge. He saw them sneering at their elders as they served salmon sandwiches to parents on the lawns.

In school magazines, he saw them grow through the years in which he had been locked away from the world. He saw them arrogantly clutching flutes of champagne as they posed for reunion pictures in their strapless ball gowns. He saw their destructive glee as they gripped a knife to cut a celebration cake. He saw them giggle, and laugh, and cackle, and crow.

The Seven Swans, they called themselves. Always together. Always side by side. Their bond made legend by eulogies from schoolmasters and mistresses who had no idea of the evil of which they were capable.

He read their reports, studied their personal files until he knew each as a father knows his daughter. He cross-referred between picture, magazine article and file until he had seven names, maiden and married, seven last known addresses and seven telephone numbers.

It was while he was noting them down that the light flashed on and a challenging voice rang out behind him. 'Alors, qu'est-ce que vous faites, hein?'

Knapp relied on instinct, surprised at the instant calm that settled on his shoulders despite being caught in the act. He could not turn, could not show his face. So he would let the concierge come to him.

At first, he could tell, the caretaker was reluctant and played for time. Knapp heard him stub out a cigarette with his shoe and sniffed its Gallic aroma.

'Dites-moi ce que vous foutez ici. Moi, j'ai appellé les flics.'

The voice was trembling. Even without seeing him, Knapp knew what he was like. Old, afraid. Blue overalls pushed out by rolls of fat. Fingers stained by the tar from untipped Mary Longs. A head as empty as his threat about the police. Faced with a motionless, silent quarry, he would not know what to do. And he would eventually come.

Knapp did not have to wait long. He heard the footsteps approach, felt the hand on his shoulder. And when hot breath kissed his neck, he made his move.

Gripping his hands together, he thrust them out in front

of him, then brought his elbow back into the concierge's stomach with a force he did not know he possessed.

The concierge squealed like a pig and fell to his knees with not a gasp of air left inside him. Knapp skipped to one side then took a step backwards, so now it was he who was behind. He kicked the concierge in the base of the spine, and as the caretaker's head whiplashed towards him, piled a fist directly into his neck.

The concierge slumped to the ground, cracking his head harshly on the concrete.

Knapp spoke to him, even though he could not hear. 'That's what happens,' he said gently, almost as if he was trying to soothe the old man's aches and pains. 'That's what happens when you take their side.'

Stefanie peeped around the curtain and grimaced at the sight that confronted her. An audience of between 140 and 160, gathered in rows beside the long catwalk that stretched across the hotel conference room. Rows of the chic and the elegant. Of men with sunglasses hooked on the breast pockets of their shirts, and women smoking coloured Russian cigarettes through jewelled ebony holders. Fashion writers, most of them, with attendant hangers-on. Stefanie pulled her head behind the curtain and stuck her tongue out at them. 'After my blood,' she muttered under her breath.

She *despised* them, and briefly wondered how the hell she had got into a business which forced her to be pleasant to such loathsome people.

It had seemed like a good idea in the early 1970s. Plenty of scope for fashion design then. Freer, more exhilarating times. Heaps of opportunity for innovation and experiment.

And she had been successful straight away, just as her

teachers and friends at school and college had prophesied. Hailed as a heroine at twenty-one and predicted by pundits to develop into one of America's pathfinding new-wave businesswomen, it had all seemed so easy.

So what went wrong? Nothing really, she thought to herself. I just didn't want it. Didn't want to mix in the world of deep-pile carpets, chauffeured limousines and people who kept saying 'super' when they meant 'awful'. Preferred to stay close to art-college girlfriends and guys I met on the Vietnam protest marches.

The result had been what Stefanie called 'interestingly catastrophic'. A succession of lovers, some good, some bad; two husbands, one dead and one who bolted over the horizon with most of her money; a brief addiction to heroin, bravely fought and conquered, though she still enjoyed dope and dabbled with controlled intakes of cocaine; and a steady fall-off in business that led to its extinction three years ago.

So now she was making a comeback, complete with new, sophisticated hairstyle and woman-about-town image. She was not sure why. She reckoned it had something to do with age and a renewed need for achievement. But mainly, she suspected, she wanted to put one over on the people who destroyed her.

The people on the other side of the curtain.

She would play their game. She would be a 'super' person designing 'super' clothes. She would pretend and fake. And then, when they had lifted her back on her pedestal, she would tell them what she thought of them and go off to do something else.

It would be sweet, but it would also be difficult. Just as she hated them, so they hated her. Few had forgiven her for ignoring them with such contempt. No one liked a smart-ass who didn't play it by the rules.

148

She could overcome their resistance only with determination and raw flair – and that was why tonight was so vital.

She took a deep breath and whispered: 'Sink or swim, Steffie. This is it.'

Briefly, she felt in need of a friend. Someone to hold her hand and to tell her everything would be all right. It reminded her of the morning, when she switched on her telephone answering machine and heard a message from Dany. 'Call me . . . urgently,' Dany had said. 'It's about Louise. Actually, it's about all of us.'

There was something wrong. It had been in Dany's voice. Stefanie would have phoned back there and then had not a panic-stricken seamstress called to say she was behind schedule for the show. Since then, she had not had a moment to spare, and there was no time even to *think* about it now.

She marched to the changing room, clapped her hands and yelled, 'Let's go, girls! Do it for me.'

The room was small and cluttered with racks of clothes. A group of twenty models elbowed each other and set hangers swinging as they slipped into their first exhibits. Stefanie helped those with the more clinging dresses.

Outside, a string band began playing 'When You Wish Upon a Star'. It was appropriate. The show was being staged in a hotel in Anaheim, around the corner from Disneyland, and Stefanie's collection was loosely based on Disney characters. Brilliant red, black and yellow combinations like Mickey Mouse; blue and white stripes with sailor hats like Donald Duck and so on.

'More West Coast casual and more fun than the classical shit put up by East Coast and European bitches,' she told her backers. Though they raised their eyebrows at her aggression, they were forced to agree. Stefanie, they told each other, was still a prodigious talent.

The show was frantic and nerve-racking. Stefanie stayed in the changing room throughout, making sure every one of her creations looked magnificent. Breathless models hurried in, stripped naked where they stood and grabbed the next dress from harassed assistants. Stefanie brushed them down, rubbed creases from hips and shoulders, pulled sleeves and winked her approval. The girls fixed shining smiles on their painted faces and hurried out again.

In less than forty minutes, it was time for the traditional climax: the wedding gown. Pure and sexy at the same time, it was a show-stopper. A figure-hugging white top slit to the base of the spine and criss-crossed by lace at the back, with a bomb-burst of smoky pink-grey feathers cascading from the hips to the knees.

It drew gasps from the critics – and Stefanie knew that at the very least, the show would not be a dismal failure.

As the band launched dramatically into music from *Fantasia*, she hurriedly pulled on her own outfit. It was a Mickey Mouse amalgam. A tight jet-black off-the-shoulder dress matching her newly dyed hair, yellow silk stockings that felt glorious against her legs and cherry-red shoes the exact colour of her lipstick.

After an appropriate wait to allow mounting antici-pation, she was pulled on to the catwalk and smothered with sticky kisses by her models. Then they scampered off to leave her alone to receive her applause. It was enthusi-astic and had to be genuine. Stefanie bowed and did a mock curtsey. Someone called out: 'You look great yourself, Steffie!'

'Thank you,' she responded. 'It's great to be back.'

* * *

It was 3 A.M., but no one wanted to leave the party. Stefanie, her every ounce of energy spent by the preparation, tension and trauma of the show, forced herself to keep circulating.

In terms of a show, it had been a success. Whether it had succeeded as a sales pitch was another matter. She would find out in a few days when the fashion writers delivered their verdicts. Until then, she had to keep smiling, keep talking and keep their glasses topped up with champagne.

It was not easy. As she had predicted, an undercurrent of resentment still lurked in the room's recesses. Most of the time, the critics were over-friendly, over-complimentary. Artificial, just as she had remembered. But they could not resist firing the odd barb.

'Marvellous collection, darling,' one bouffant-haired woman oozed. 'I do hope you can find someone to market it. After all, it may be awkward for you. After last time, I mean.'

Stefanie somehow managed to smile. 'I'll cross that bridge when I come to it,' she said diplomatically.

She moved on to receive the treatment from someone else. She fended off sarcasm, parried verbal assaults and ignored downright insults. But after another hour, she felt she was close to insanity.

If I stay in *this* room, with *these* shit-suckers, one moment longer, she warned herself, I am going to knee a rat in the balls or throw my drink in a bitch's face. And that will be that.

She excused herself by saying she needed to fix her make-up. She scurried to her hotel room and took a miniature ring box from a pocket of her suitcase. It contained low-grade cocaine, the only sort she could afford. She sprinkled a line on a coffee table and used a ten-dollar bill to snort half into each nostril. She gave herself five minutes before she returned to the fray.

It did the trick. She was still on her feet as dawn broke and the last of the critics weaved away from the hotel. No scenes. No arguments. No harm done. A fine collection and a 'super' public relations follow-up. It was all she could have hoped for, and for the first time, she began thinking of organizing a repeat show for potential clients.

She could not concentrate on it for long. Exhaustion overcame her as she said goodnight to her models, assistants and anyone else who was spending what was left of the night at the hotel. She took the elevator, staggered to her room and collapsed on her bed without undressing.

As they closed, her eyes caught a glimpse of the bedside telephone. Call Dany, she thought. Must call Dany. When I wake up, it'll be the first thing I do.

She had reached the limit of her endurance. Within seconds, she was in a deep sleep.

Feathers. Pink feathers, white feathers, blue feathers, black feathers. They pulled out of the wedding dress and floated away, transforming themselves into a jay as they spiralled through the air. The bird spread its wings and launched itself from the branch of a tree, clattering through the dappled shade of the woods and swooping low over the clearing before arcing upwards towards its new perch on top of the decaying wreck of the abandoned car.

Stefanie screamed. She did not care where she was, as long as it was not the woods in Geneva. She did not want to go there ever again.

She let out a second scream, even more piercing than the first.

'Ssssh!'

Stefanie spun around to see who was telling her to hush.

'Dany!' she said in surprise. 'I was going to call you . . .'

Dany did not reply. She was more intent on hiding behind the fallen tree trunk. Stefanie saw that all the others were there – and were doing the same. She squatted down beside them.

Kipini reached across to stroke her hair. 'Like the new style,' she said.

'I don't,' Stefanie countered. 'I only did it for them. Playing the game, that's what they call it.'

'Why do it?' Pearl said bluntly. 'Why put yourself through it?'

'Oh, stop going on at me, will you? I've had enough of that for one day.'

'Look!'

Stefanie, alarmed by Dany's cry, followed her gaze. In the distance, through a glade of silver birch and sycamore, a scarecrow hung from a tree, attached to a low branch by a length of rope. The breeze picked up and the rope creaked and groaned. A man watched the scarecrow swaying. Back and forward, back and forward, his head moving in unison with its to-ings and fro-ings.

The sky turned as black as night. In an instant, the woods were awash with thick sheets of rain as if a heavenly giant had upturned a shelf-ful of buckets above them.

'No! No!' Louise shouted.

The man heard and turned towards them.

'He's seen us!' Stefanie cried.

153

'He's heard us.'

'He's coming to get us.'

'He's covered in red.'

'He looks strange.'

'I don't like him.'

'Look! He's coming. He *is* coming.'

'He can't hurt us.'

'Yes, he can.'

'He's going to.'

'*Stefanie! Pearl! Dany! Where are you?*'

'Over here, Mam'selle.'

'*Kipini! Louise!*'

'She can't hear us.'

'*Mai-Lin!*'

'Mam'selle's going further away.'

'*Sari! Oh, Mon Dieu, where are you?*'

'What shall we do?'

'Run!'

'I can't. My legs . . .'

'His face – there's something wrong with it.'

'He's coming.'

'So are they.'

'Who?'

'Three more men. Over there. Look!'

Stefanie looked. It was true. Away to the right, three men in sodden black suits were dashing between the trees, punching their way through the rain with flailing arms, shouting and crying out. They were the length of a games field away. But even at such a distance, Stefanie could see their faces as if she was peering through binoculars.

The first had a bushy moustache like a squirrel's tail. The second was as round and purple as a beetroot. The third, the most frantic of the trio, had a big hooked nose, cheekbones sharp enough to cut meat and a meanness in his eyes that made Stefanie shudder.

'Stop!' the moustache yelled.

'Don't!' the beetroot pleaded.

'Jesus Christ!' the meanie screamed.

But the man covered in red took no notice of them, and Stefanie turned to watch his final approach. His feet pressed down on saturated leaves, making water ooze from beneath the soles of his shoes. He came to a halt a yard from the girls' refuge, towering above them with his hands on his hips. They looked up at him and whimpered.

'Help! Mam'selle! Mummy!'

'Louder, Sari. Shout louder.'

'Leave us alone!'

'Go away, nasty man.'

'He isn't.'

'He won't.'

'Run! We must run!'

'NO! STAY EXACTLY WHERE YOU ARE . . .'

It was *his* voice.

'It's too late. We're trapped. Goodbye, Dany. Goodbye, Pearl. Goodbye – '

The maid knocked lightly on Stefanie's door. When there was no reply, she carried on with her round. She had heard about the party – the whole hotel had. And she realized there would be more than a few who needed to sleep it off. She reported rooms that had not been cleaned to her supervisor. He grinned and made a note in his log so they could be tidied by the afternoon shift. He had been told Stefanie was the party hostess, had spent a great deal of money with the hotel and should not be hurried, and so left the next attempt to gain entry to her room until 4 P.M. When another maid told him there was still

155

no reply, he gave her permission to use the master key. The girl returned minutes later, white-faced and trembling. The supervisor asked her what was wrong.

'She was on the bed,' the maid gabbled. 'We tried to rouse her, but we couldn't. We think she's dead . . .'

12

The story was huge and developing all the time, making Curran's day the most gruelling for months. The IRA had detonated a bomb in the VIP car park before an England–Ireland rugby international at Twickenham, killing eight, including a distant relative of the Queen, and wounding twenty-six. Curran wrote the main running story, stretching across pages two and three, while Brookes took care of the forty-word caption for the photograph of devastation that took up the whole of the front page.

Eleven staff reporters and three news agencies were at the scene, all filing copy from carphones that was fed instantly into the newspaper's computer system. Hockenhull barked out catchlines of relevant new copy. Curran called each on to his screen to read, digest and pick out facts to be included in his piece. No sooner had he finished the story for one edition than Christie had planned the next and he was off and running again. New headlines, new layout, new photographs and new information.

A badly-mutilated woman did not survive the surgeon's knife, bringing the death toll to nine. More details came in about the murdered Duke – obscure yesterday, a name known to the world today. One of the wounded was his wife, the Duchess, yet to learn of her husband's grisly fate. There were new quotes from eye-witnesses found by diligent reporters, some of them differing from previous accounts of the outrage. One said the victims had been enjoying a champagne picnic around a hamper placed on a portable table. Another said they were simply walking past the planted car when the bomb was detonated. There was condemnation in the Commons and from statesmen and women around the globe. The IRA issued a proclamation crowing about a major strike at British imperialism.

By the time Curran had written four different versions of the story, each more vivid, authoritative and comprehensive than the last, it was close to midnight. He pushed his chair away from the terminal, rubbed sore eyes and reflected on nine hours' solid, manic work, sustained only by coffee, the odd sandwich and the powerful drug of a good story.

His shift was over, but he did not want to go home. Though logic told him he should be dog-tired, his heart was beating too fast for sleep.

'Coming to the boozer?' Hockenhull suggested. 'I'll buy you a nightcap or three.'

Curran shook his head.

Hockenhull misinterpreted his reluctance. 'Let it be, will you? Nothing much more'll happen now. The late-shift boys can handle it. Bollocks to the IRA.'

'You go. I'll catch you up.'

'Ach, for fuck's sake!'

Hockenhull, still wound up like a spring from the evening's rigours, needed a drink and could not wait for indecision. He stomped away towards the lift without offering further enticements.

Curran watched him go. The sight of Hockenhull accelerating as his nostrils caught the scent of Young's Ordinary Bitter was faintly amusing. But as Curran's mind was freed from thoughts of bombs, blood and severed limbs, so it was filled with the obsession that had been only temporarily diverted to the recesses of his consciousness.

Dany and her dreams of dread.

Curran glanced around the newsroom and was relieved to discover that the two men he had been hoping to talk to before the bombing story broke were still at their posts. Salmon, number three on the picture desk, and de Udy, chief crime reporter and one of the few field operators respected by Christie and the rest of the production staff.

He asked Salmon for a blow-up copy of the Whittaker release photo that had frightened Dany so much, before wandering across to de Udy.

'You look knackered,' de Udy observed as he watched the pale figure's approach.

'So do you,' Curran said.

'Good paper, eh? All over one to seven and you bastards got my by-line right for once.'

'Top stuff, wasn't it?'

'Yeah, some picnic.'

They laughed at the black joke before de Udy said: 'What can I do for you?'

Curran, sensing that de Udy, too, was anxious to reach a bar, came straight to the point.

'Remember Harold Whittaker?'

'The Sunday-lunch man – yes . . .'

'Have you been keeping tabs on him since his release from Mogden?'

'Sort of. I did a piece a few days ago, but it was spiked and didn't make the paper.'

'Saying what?'

'Oh, he's got a job as a surface worker in a Nottinghamshire coal mine. Union fixed it for him.'

'Sounds a decent yarn.'

'I thought so. I found the whole thing quite moving. You know, such a notorious bastard shoulder to shoulder with good working folk after all this time. But the newsdesk didn't want to know. Said that although we carried that page-one piece when he was freed, it didn't get much of a reaction, especially from younger readers. They said Whittaker was yesterday's man and they had enough modern-day nutters on their hands, thank you very much.'

'Did you speak to him?'

'On the phone.'

'What was he like?'

'Ah, you wouldn't believe it. Meek and mild, mellow and content. All that stuff.'

'And do you believe he is meek and mild?'

'I checked with his supervisors. They all think he's a wonderful little fella. Wouldn't hurt a fly, they said. Represents a threat to no one. A triumph for the government's new rehabilitation scheme. Gin and tonics all round in Whitehall. Speaking of which . . .'

De Udy checked his watch and said: 'Better not push our luck. I know the Crown's OK for lates, but it's after bloody midnight.'

'Hockenhull's buying,' Curran said absently.

'By the way,' de Udy said as he pulled on his coat. 'What's your interest in Whittaker?'

'Personal.' It was weak, but Curran could think of nothing else and hoped de Udy, whose curiosity matched any cat's, would be too tired to care. The crime reporter frowned suspiciously, but did not take it further. Curran thanked him, told him he would see him in the pub, and went back to his desk to wait for the blow-up.

The subs' table began to fill up as the late shift came back from their break to work on the final edition. Curran was asked to brief Brannigan, the sub taking over the IRA story.

'And when you've done that, take a look at this.'

It was McKeachie. He was on late copy-tasting, reading the wires coming in from Reuters, AP and UPI to see if there was anything interesting enough to be used by the paper.

'I'm going for a drink, then I'm going home,' Curran called out wearily.

'Please yourself, but you'll be sorry you missed it.' McKeachie cast his bait, knowing full well that Curran would be unable to resist taking it. His confidence was not misplaced. Curran, slinging his anorak on a vacant chair, came to look over his shoulder.

McKeachie lowered his voice to talk privately. 'See. After what you told me about Dany . . . and those books about dreams you brought in . . . I thought you'd be interested.'

The story on McKeachie's screen, like hundreds filed into London in the early hours, came from America, where it was evening and things were still happening. It told of a symposium at a medical institute in Atlanta. The subject was sleep and sleep-related illnesses, and the story quoted a London-based sleep researcher with the Irish name of Ciera O'Connell, telling the assembly of the case of a middle-aged man who complained he was on the brink of suicide because, for the past decade, he had not slept longer than three hours a night, and frequently did not sleep at all. He exhibited all the red-eyed symptoms of chronic insomnia: headaches, listlessness, desperation, foul temper, an inability to concentrate or communicate. But when she got him into her laboratory, the researcher discovered he in fact regularly slept a normal eight hours. Her conclusion, therefore, was that the man was *dreaming* that he was awake, a theory reflected in the working headline above the article, THE SLEEPING INSOMNIAC.

'It says she is based in London,' McKeachie said as Curran read. 'I thought she might be able to help. Sounds like she knows her stuff.'

Curran slapped McKeachie gratefully on the shoulder and pressed a button on his keyboard to obtain a print-out of the story.

'Brilliant!' he exclaimed. 'A sleep researcher. Why the hell didn't I think of that when I read the books?'

'You're too fucked to think of anything.'

'Sleep researchers? I didn't know such creatures existed,' said Brannigan, who had overheard.

'That's because they only come out at night.' McKeachie imitated an owl to give his joke extra shine.

'Thanks again, McKeachie,' Curran said. 'I owe you.'

He rushed over to the printer, which shared a purpose-built recess with a neglected yukka plant. As he watched the machine spray the Atlanta story from computer memory on to paper, Salmon handed him a rolled-up poster-sized photo of Harold Whittaker's release from Mogden.

Curran skipped the pub and went straight home. He pinned the blow-up to a wall opposite his bed and turned a spotlight on it so it was the only clearly visible feature of the room. He spent the night laying back on his headboard, scanning the photograph through a golden haze, staring into Whittaker's eyes for a clue about his macabre hold over Dany.

He remembered how she had shivered as she looked at the front page of his newspaper. 'Picture . . . him,' she had uttered that night. And after her most terrifying nightmare, she had hurled herself into his arms and whimpered, 'It's not him, it's you.'

Curran knew he would never forget the purity of her fear. Yet de Udy talked of a wonderful little fella who

162

wouldn't hurt a fly. As another dawn broke, Curran rammed a fist of frustration into his pillow. 'Nothing adds up,' he muttered aloud. 'One and one make three. Two and two make five.' He looked up as if praying for divine guidance. 'Oh Christ,' he said. 'Sometimes I wish you were really there.'

But in the final reckoning, he knew it was up to him.

He managed two hours' sleep, but his mind was still racing when he awoke. He toyed with the idea of showing Dany the blow-up, but swiftly rejected it on the grounds he would be dabbling with the unknown. One glimpse at the photo had turned her white before. And now, with its drama enhanced by its size, it could destroy her. Whatever the chances of a breakthrough, it was simply not worth the risk.

Dany had gone by the time Curran climbed out of bed, but left a note saying she was taking Yvette to school before going on to the TV studios to deliver her resignation.

The message ended: 'Booked on BA flight to Switz 10 P.M. tonight with Yvette. Will call you at work from airport. Wish me luck!!!!'

Curran showered quickly, plucked the picture from the wall and drove back to the newspaper office. He went straight to the reference library and commandeered its microfiche, ignoring a half-hearted protest from the head librarian.

He ran through years of past issues of *The Times*, reduced to a minute proportion of their original size and grafted on to film. He studied the case history of Harold Whittaker from beginning to end, looking for something – anything – that would suggest a crossover between his life and those of the Seven Swans.

It was only after four hours of mind-bending research that he finally conceded there was none. He could not feign surprise. After all, he told himself, what possible connection could there be between a murderer from a humble family in the north of England and seven privileged children whose fathers were diplomats and who spent their formative years in the sheltered, feather-bedded confines of a private school in Geneva?

'None,' he muttered aloud. 'I haven't found it – and I never will.'

He turned again to the photograph of Whittaker's release and studied it remorselessly. He was not sure what he was looking for. Only that it would be something else. Something new. Something bizarre, perhaps. Something he had not thought of before.

He persuaded himself to open his mind, forget past assumptions. After so many hours of useless investigation, it was clouded and took minutes to react. But he told himself determination would win through and ordered himself, as if he was both military general and private, to stick to his task.

After another hour, he spotted something that made his pulse race. It was not much, and he prayed he was not stirring false hope within himself. But it was *something*.

There was a man, another man, in the crowd behind Whittaker and the Mogden director, Ashe. He was not significant. Just another face among faces. Pushed into the background by the frenetic circle of guards and medics who were hustling Whittaker to freedom.

But in the midst of such a grim, humourless gathering, he was *smiling*. And he was actually *waving* at the camera!

Why? What on earth possessed him to do such a thing at such a time? Surely, bizarre was an apt description for his actions.

Curran looked closer, until his nose was almost touching the photograph, and immediately found another curiosity. The man's left hand, the one he was waving with such apparent bonhomie, had only four fingers.

Curran leaped from his chair and ran from the library. He took the lift up to the newsroom, banging its walls in a futile attempt to make it go faster. Once in the newsroom, he rushed across the floor, past an amazed Christie and his colleagues on the subs' table, to the reporters' enclave.

To his relief, de Udy was there, tapping out a statement issued by the widowed Duchess from her hospital bed. Curran grabbed hold of his chair, spinning it around so the crime reporter was forced to face him.

'One more favour,' he gabbled.

De Udy was too stunned to respond.

'A name inside Mogden hospital,' Curran pleaded. 'A contact. Someone who knows inmates and staff. The person who told you Whittaker was being released.'

De Udy was not sure. Like most self-respecting reporters, he did not easily part with the names of hard-won contacts, particularly those prepared to risk their jobs by leaking information to the press.

'Please!' Curran was desperate. 'It's very important to me. I'll tell you about it one day. Please . . .'

De Udy unlocked a drawer and took out his contacts book, leafing through it until he reached the section under M for Mogden.

'Jute,' he said without looking at Curran. 'He's a male nurse. Good, but expensive. You'll have to pay top whack.'

De Udy scribbled a phone number in his notebook and tore out the page, handing it to Curran.

'Take good care of it,' he said. As Curran thanked him,

he added: 'Take good care of yourself, too. It's not normal, you know.'

'I know,' Curran said.

Knapp put the phone down and smiled. He had expected that, with luck, one of the seven might have been eliminated by Mother Nature, and so it had proved. So awful, so tragic, Louise's husband had whined. Knapp wanted to tell him it was nothing more than the treacherous little bitch deserved, but instead he offered Professor Wendlinger's condolences and said he would call back at a more appropriate time.

Taking a red-inked fountain pen in his hand, he stroked a perfect thin line through Louise's name, then studied the remainder of his list. He had written notes beside each alphabetically-ordered name.

The girl Dany: no reply.

The girl Kipini: father answered. Not there. In bush, on plantation. Linitria Sanctuary, part of Kuypers Memorial Foundation. Access by light aircraft from Nairobi.

The girl Mai-Lin: Bangkok police force.

The girl Pearl: no reply.

The girl Sari: professional mother. Married to Sydney architect.

The girl Stefanie: no reply.

Knapp glanced at his watch. Time for one more call before he prepared himself for the evening ahead. He went back to the top of the list and dialled London. The phone rang for twenty seconds before it was answered. Dany, who had heard it as she thrust Yvette into a taxi outside, was breathless. 'Dany Curran,' she panted.

Knapp said nothing. There was no need.

'Hello, who is it?' Dany said. 'Stefanie? Is that you? Did you try to get back before?'

Knapp hung up and smiled again. Name confirmed. Location confirmed. Appointment with death confirmed.

He was soaking in the bath when he heard a tap on the door.

'Daddy?' a muffled voice called. 'It's me, Martha.'

'You have a key, don't you?' Knapp shouted.

'Yes.'

'Well then. Use it.'

Martha silently cursed him. Her arms were full of food bags, she had used her toe to rattle the door and now she had to drop the bags to search for the key in her purse. But she was determined to make a chirpy entrance and walked into the apartment humming a Paul McCartney song.

'Where are you?' she said as soon as she saw Knapp was not in the lounge.

'In the bath,' he said.

'Oh. That's why you couldn't open the door.'

'It could have something to do with it.'

Martha fetched the food bags and carried them to the kitchen. 'I've got forty-eight hours free,' she announced. 'I thought I'd start by cooking you a good meal. How does pepper steak and crisp-dry fries sound?'

'Fries give you heart disease.'

'Then I'll do sauté.'

Knapp washed his hair and hosed himself down with a hand-shower. He wanted to look his best and was prepared to take his time over it. It was not every day you got the opportunity to meet Khrushchev.

'What are you doing in there?' Martha cried as she put on an apron to beat the steak.

'What do people usually do in bathrooms?'

167

'Same as you. But sometimes they come out afterwards.'

There was no reply and Martha resigned herself to conducting a conversation through the bathroom door. 'What have you been doing?'

'Why do you want to know?'

'Girls are usually interested in what their fathers get up to.'

'I've been doing nothing that will interest you. Walking around. Travelling.'

'Travelling?' Martha was surprised. 'What do you mean, travelling?'

'I spent a few days in Europe, that's all.'

'Daddy!'

He sensed her shock and felt resentful.

'What do you expect me to do? Stay in all day and watch TV? Do you want me to be a prisoner here, too?'

'Of course not.'

'I have things to do, places to go, like any busy man.'

'Of course, Daddy, but – '

'So, then.'

Martha felt like a yacht knocked off course by rough seas. She reminded herself of Hagerty's advice. Be patient. Stay cool. Hang on in there. And wait for him to warm to you. All the old clichés, but sound nevertheless.

'Who did you fly with?' she asked innocuously.

'Swissair.' Knapp climbed from the bath and reached for a towel.

'You know, as a parent you're entitled to huge reductions in fares with my airline.'

'Unnecessary. My finances are adequate.'

'Sure, but why look a gift horse in the mouth?'

'Why depend on charity?'

'It's not – ' Oh, what was the use? Martha concentrated

168

on grilling the steak and preparing what she hoped would be an especially spicy pepper sauce to compensate for the tasteless trash she was sure her father – a noted gourmet, so she had been told – had endured these past years.

She would wait until she could see him. Until they could talk properly. And over the meal, she would tell him all about the new man in her life. A mid-Atlantic journalist. Now *that* was sure to interest him. All fathers liked to keep a weather eye on the romances of their daughters.

Knapp emerged from the bathroom in his underwear and socks. Martha went to kiss him, but he turned away, flicking a finger in the direction of the bedroom. 'There's a shirt on the bed,' he said. 'Iron it, will you?'

'*What?*' Martha could not believe her ears.

'Hurry, girl, I don't have much time.' Why, oh why could she not understand that a sense of urgency was required on such occasions? Khrushchev – the head of state of the Soviet Union, no less – could not afford to wait. He had a summit in Paris to attend.

Martha could not move. She leaned against the bathroom door staring at the ridiculous figure of a man standing with his back to her, refusing to look at her, refusing to acknowledge her as anything but some sort of skivvy.

'Why not slip on a T-shirt?' she said tentatively.

Knapp growled like a dog. 'Because I must look my best,' he said as if the answer was painfully obvious.

'I don't care what you wear.'

Knapp spun round. His icy stare rooted Martha to the spot even more firmly. 'What does it matter what *you* care?' he said. 'Now iron that shirt while I find my dinner jacket.'

'Dinner jacket?' The penny dropped at last. Martha felt

a flicker of exasperation cross her chest. 'Daddy, you're not going out, are you?' She glanced at the cooker. The pepper sauce was beginning to boil. She needed to turn down the heat before it was ruined, but even as she saw the danger, something told her that any attempt to head it off would be futile. Knapp's silence in response to her question confirmed her fears.

'Do you have an appointment?' she asked.

'Of course,' Knapp replied. 'And I am proud to keep it.' He raised his voice and blood flooded into his face until it was crimson. 'Now iron that shirt!'

Martha felt her patience ebbing away. She tried to control herself – and instead of yelling 'No', she simply shook her head.

'Do it, girl.' This time it was a military order, delivered with a menacing snarl.

Martha could contain herself no longer. 'You do it!' she cried.

She turned to make for the kitchen, intending to pull the bubbling sauce away from the ring. Knapp followed her, grabbed her by the shoulder and wrenched her around. He raised an arm in the air and brought it down again, slashing her across the face with the back of his hand. She screamed in disbelief and pain and tried to fight free, but he hit her again. The force of his blow sent her crashing against the cooker. The pan containing the sauce flew up and flipped over, sending splashes of scalding liquid across her ankles.

'Insolence!' he shouted. 'I won't have it!'

Martha caught a glimpse of her handbag through the tears welling in her eyes. She grabbed it, ducked under Knapp's shoulders and made for the door, snatching her coat from the sofa as she went.

He made no attempt to stop her. He knew it would only waste more time.

'Delighted to see you, Mr K,' he muttered as he surveyed the mess in the kitchen. 'You'll have to excuse my daughter. She had no idea . . .'

13

Dany drove along the autoroute linking the satellite town of Nyon to Geneva. It was a clear day with the first warmth of spring in the morning air. To her left, across glittering Lac Léman, Mont Blanc shone through lesser peaks like a freshly cut jewel. To her right, neatly clipped grass verges, manicured beds of early daffodils and luxuriant green fields told her she was indeed back in Switzerland. She wound down her window to enjoy the smell of pasture.

So far, it had been an encouraging visit. Her mother, residing like an ancient Central European monarch in an orchard-enveloped manor house on the outskirts of Nyon, had been more pleasant than usual, making a fuss of Yvette, offering the use of her car and even warming to her task of giving moral support to a daughter in distress.

Yet the tension that had scarred their relationship since Dany's teens was never more than a whisper away. When they talked about the Swans, Dany asked if Pearl had called in during her last – her very last – trip to Switzerland.

'I didn't expect her to,' the mother said almost huffily. 'You said yourself she was busy – researching some magazine article or other. She didn't have time for a wrinkled old baggage like me.'

'Nonsense.'

'Nonsense my backside. That's exactly how you think of me, too.'

Dany let out an ironic half-laugh as she turned off the

172

autoroute. It had always been like that. An ordinary conversation turned into yet another unnecessary tiff caused by her mother's constant, ridiculous challenges. Memories were made of this.

There were more at the school, returning one by one. Images that slowly but surely pierced the haze curtain thrown up by the passing of years. Images that turned reality into fantasy and fantasy into reality.

So little had changed. The winding gravel drive leading through the rhododendron bushes and the copse; the woodshed at the end of the garden where they used to hide from Mam'selle; the austere limestone building enclosing a cobbled courtyard with its oxidized copper fountain; the bell tower – target for decades of grimaces from children as it rang to tell them playtime was over – and the playing fields at the back, where strident physical-education mistresses attempted to pass on the rudiments of lacrosse to small girls with large sticks and puzzled expressions.

As she climbed from her car, Delestre rushed from the door to greet her. He squeezed her elbows and they exchanged a kiss on each cheek.

'Madame Dany,' he gushed. 'I was so pleased to hear you were coming.'

Dany was warmed by his enthusiasm. A dapper French Swiss, wearing a beige suit with a red rose pinned to its lapel, he had taken over as principal five years ago from a tweeds-and-breeches Englishwoman inappropriately named Miss Spice. Dany had met him only once before, at a charity gala the previous summer. Yet his handed-down knowledge of the Seven Swans had been all but complete, and he had spent the evening urging Dany and the others to fill in the gaps.

173

He ushered her to his office, but on the way they passed Dany's old classroom. Delestre stopped, turned and waited for the request he knew would be made in the next second or two.

Dany chuckled at his sly grin. 'I always like to go in, you know,' she said.

'Every time you return,' Delestre said, his lips widening into a smile.

'May I?'

'But of course, my dear. It belongs to you.'

Delestre nodded to the teacher as they entered to assure her everything was in order. Dany stood in the corner, fixed by the eyes of twenty-four curious little girls lined up across the room in six rows of four, all wearing white cotton dresses and crimson blazers embroidered with intertwined swans. The desks were made of different materials – pine and white melamine – but had remained in the same places as their chipped oak forerunners. The paraphernalia of drawing books, crayons and paint pots was scattered across the broad shelf under the panoramic window, just as it had always been. The class calendar, pinned to a cork board, had survived as a treasured tradition, the spaces alongside each day ready to be filled in as a diary of events by a chosen girl of the week. Even the teacher, hair pinned up in businesslike fashion, reminded Dany of Mam'selle. And the way she clapped her hands to restore her pupils' attention . . .

'Uncanny,' Dany murmured under her breath. She turned to Delestre and whispered: 'Do you know what happened to Mademoiselle Barthié?'

'Who?'

'She was my teacher. It's the reason I am here. To try to find her.'

'Ah yes, as you told me on the telephone.' Delestre

looked imploringly at Dany and shrugged his shoulders with a Gallic flourish. '*Je m'excuse*. Teachers come and go, you know, and I don't know about her like I know about the Seven Swans. But shall we try to find out?'

Delestre guided Dany to his office, singing as he walked and waving an imaginary baton in the air. Dany steeled herself to tell him about Pearl and Louise, already regretting the shadow she would cast over his natural sunniness. Briefly, she wondered if she need tell him at all. But she knew she had to. To leave him in ignorance would be unjust. In the end, she came out with it – just blurted it out – as Delestre offered her a seat.

The principal was mortified. '*Mais ce n'est pas vrai,*' he kept repeating, and slumped breathlessly into his chair as if he had been punched in the stomach. 'But how? When?'

Dany told him what she knew. Two deaths of chilling similarity – and her strange dreams of infancy.

Delestre absorbed it all without uttering a word. Half a minute after Dany fell silent, he was still shaking his head in disbelief. 'So,' he said finally. 'Is your search for Mademoiselle Barthié connected in some way to these terrible happenings?'

'She may know something that could explain the dreams.'

Delestre gazed vaguely around the office and tapped his fingernails on his desk. 'I wonder . . .' he muttered.

'Pardon?' Dany could barely hear him.

Delestre looked directly at her, his face a mixture of bewilderment and alarm. 'My dear,' he began. 'A few nights ago, this school was broken into by a man who was found in the records room by Monsieur Bousquet, our concierge. Monsieur Bousquet was savagely attacked. His spine and ribs were damaged, and his skull fractured in an assault of the most appalling violence. The doctors say he will survive, but he is still on a life-support machine.'

'Oh Lord . . .' Dany shivered in her seat, as if the water vapour in the air around her had suddenly been turned into minute spheres of ice.

'The strange thing is,' Delestre continued, 'that this man was not a burglar. We had a thorough check, and nothing was taken. Not even a paperclip. However, the attack on Monsieur Bousquet was severe enough to warrant police forensic tests. And you know what they revealed? That the man had pawed through several files, including the pupil registers for 1959 to 1964 – '

'That's when I was here,' Dany interrupted.

'Magazines and newspaper cuttings with stories and pictures about our annual reunions and other major events, and the master list of current addresses of past pupils. *Alors*, the only thing poor Monsieur Bousquet has been able to tell police was that the man was tall and had grey hair – he was no juvenile delinquent. So why was he here? Who was he? And what was he looking for?'

Dany took up the line of thought. 'You think he may have something to do with me . . . with us?'

Delestre puffed out his cheeks and looked uncertain. 'Who knows? But it's a coincidence, yes?'

When they crossed into the records room, Dany knew it was more than a coincidence. She could *feel* the man's presence as if he was standing next to her, as if his breath was mingling with hers, as if at any moment he would reach out and touch her.

She wanted to leave, to run from the room as fast as her legs could carry her. But Delestre was already poring through the staff files cabinet – and she knew the need to find Mam'selle was more desperate than ever.

She shook herself like a dog in a vain attempt to rid her flesh of the man's enveloping aura.

'Are you cold?' Delestre asked.

'No . . . yes,' Dany stammered. 'I . . . I think I may have a chill coming on.'

Delestre, sullen now and barely able to concentrate, took another ten minutes to flick back through the years to discover Mam'selle's fate. Dany, unsure of how much longer she could bear to be in this tainted place, willed him on.

Finally, he pulled a folder from its rack, opened it and thumbed through a sheaf of documents. 'She resigned at the end of the summer term 1960,' he announced. 'At the end of your second year here.'

Dany squinted over his shoulder and said: 'She didn't say anything to us. Didn't let on she was leaving.'

'My dear, it was such a long time ago, and you were just a little girl,' Delestre pointed out, waggling an upright finger. 'You would not have remembered.'

As memories swirled and expanded, Dany became certain that Mam'selle's secrecy had been complete. But she did not want to contradict Delestre, and asked simply: 'Does it say anything else?'

Delestre read aloud. 'Mademoiselle Claudine Barthié. DoB: 14 August 1939. Address: 269 Chemin de la Grosse Pierre, Plan-les-Ouates, Genève. Tel: 28 62 37. Joined staff: 18 September 1959. Post: General teaching duties. Nominated class: Class 2B. Resigned: 24 July 1960. Reason for resignation: Personal. Notes: Resigned without notice. Informed principal on 24.07.60 she would not be returning for new academic year. Believed to be moving away from area, to another canton. References: Not requested.'

The entry was completed by the restrained signature of Gloria L. Spice.

Delestre slipped the file back into its drawer. 'References not requested,' he repeated as he slammed the drawer shut. He flapped his fingers imitating the flight of a bird. 'A young lady in a hurry to get away, wouldn't you say?'

And to leave the past behind, Dany thought.

She knew now. There were no ifs, buts or maybes. As she stood there, gazing blankly at the closed drawer, she *knew* Mam'selle would have wanted to leave the school as soon as was practically possible. What's more, though it was out of reach, buried deep in the tangled fibres of her soul, she was sure she knew why.

The intruder's presence became intolerable. It was creeping through her pores, permeating her blood, soaking into her bones. She was awake, yet it was just like her dreams. He was coming for her. He was out to get her.

She bolted from the room and ran until she emerged panting into the sunlight.

Delestre, startled, hurried after her. 'Madame Dany,' he yelled. 'What is it?'

Dany looked over her shoulder. All she could see was a chasing man – and she knew she had to get away before it was too late. She leaped into her car and started the engine. She pressed the accelerator too hard, and let the clutch out too fast. Her rear wheels spun on the gravel and for a moment, one terrifying moment, she thought she was trapped and that he would get her. But then the wheels bit and she sped away.

'Safe – but for how long?' she gabbled aloud. 'Oh, Mam'selle, where are you?'

* * *

Mademoiselle Barthié was seventy miles away in Le Locle, an isolated little town high in the Jura mountains, where the winter snow had yet to melt. Wrapped in a quilted coat, she tramped past the hill where children and teenagers gathered to ski, sledge and flirt.

'*Bonjour, Mam'selle.*' A cry rang out from a small boy as he tumbled off a toboggan at the foot of the slope.

Mademoiselle Barthié returned his greeting, but her thoughts were elsewhere, with Pearl and the potted life story she had spouted excitedly when she turned up in Le Locle out of the mists of time. How she had become a journalist. How she worked on weekly papers in Florida before her father fixed her a job on the *New York Times*. How she had turned freelance and was now taking lucrative commissions from magazines. And how the latest involved a feature about the early years of the United Nations. An offbeat feature, one in which she could include her own experience as the child of an American diplomat based at the UN in Geneva.

'Intrepid journalist tracks down cherished ex-teacher,' she said in headlinese after Mademoiselle Barthié got over the shock of how the little girl had grown so.

If only Pearl had contented herself with sweet reminiscences over a glass of sherry. If only she had not been so headstrong. If only she had not insisted on dragging her dear Mam'selle back to Geneva, back to the harbour-front hotel where they had their afternoon teas in winter and back to the woods where they had their picnics in spring and summer.

'Remember the Seven Swans?' she said, laughing as they followed a track through the trees. 'Swans don't cry, swans don't lie. Swans stay together until they die.'

'And are you still together?' Mademoiselle Barthié asked with genuine curiosity.

'Always have been. Always will be, even if for the most part it comes down to letters across the ocean. Oh, Mam'selle, why didn't you come to the school reunions? They were so splendid.'

They had been walking in a glade of sycamore and silver birch when Pearl saw the rusty remains of the car, abandoned long since to its decaying and crumbling fate. The sight of the car had changed her at once from carefree woman to frightened rabbit of a child. She had run away through the trees in a flurry of elbows and heels, with no direction or purpose other than to get away from where she had just been.

When Mademoiselle Barthié finally caught her up, she was leaning over with her head between her knees, vomiting violently beside the road that ran by the woods.

Pearl could not explain it. Mademoiselle Barthié remembered more than she dared reveal. The first flush of panic when she realized the girls had gone – and the agonizing stomach cramps as she searched for them, shouting their names one after the other.

They drove in silence to Geneva railway station, where Pearl said she was sorry and asked Mademoiselle Barthié if she would mind taking the train back to Le Locle.

Mademoiselle Barthié shook her head sorrowfully as she dug her moonboots into the ice to begin the long climb towards her home. The parting at the station had been a month ago, and she had not heard from Pearl since. No phone calls, no goodbyes. How could someone reappear in her life like a flash of lightning, then vanish just as quickly?

The pavement was slippery, despite the grit that had been sprinkled on it earlier. Mademoiselle Barthié kept her shoulders hunched and her bespectacled eyes pinned to the ground to seek out ruts that would give her more grip. She did not see the black-coated figure waiting outside her apartment block. The first she knew of him was when he slipped a hand under her elbow to help her on to the steps.

She looked up and peered at him through misted lenses. As the condensation cleared and he came into focus, she let out a gasp and uttered, 'You . . .'

His skin was more leathery, his jowls looser and his hair greyer. But even under an extra layer or two of fat, the features were the same. The large, hooked nose, the bloodshot eyes and the dimpled chin. The angular, flesh-less cheekbones pointing down to thin, humourless lips. As Mademoiselle Barthié stared at him, he emitted an air of unconcerned authority that could only come with high office.

Hagerty returned her gaze. The beginnings of a smile creased his jaw, but it did not mellow him. She pulled her arm from his hand and scurried for her door.

Hagerty called after her. 'I'm sorry if I alarmed you. May I come in?'

'*Non!*' Mademoiselle Barthié turned to face him. 'No, you may *not* come in.'

His tone hardened immediately. 'Then I'll say what I have to say on these steps. And you will listen.'

'Oh no . . .'

Mademoiselle Barthié knew at once she was no match for a man such as this, and groaned at her own inad-equacy. She let him in, even made him coffee. When he took his coat off, she shuddered. He was wearing a black suit, just as he had been in the woods thirty years ago. Just as his friend had been wearing, too. Two men in black suits, shepherding the seven lost girls back to her side.

He sat her on a sofa and stood above her, keeping her

181

trapped with harsh, unbending eyes. Just as she expected, his mood was hostile.

'How much do you remember?' he asked.

Mademoiselle Barthié felt obliged to answer. 'I remember losing the girls. I remember the fear I felt as I searched for them. I remember the blessed relief when you and your friend brought them back to me. I remember the terrible state they were in . . .'

'And the stories they told you about what had happened?'

Mademoiselle Barthié hesitated before saying, 'What stories?'

Hagerty became impatient. 'Ah, come on now, Mam'selle – that's what they called you, isn't it? – they must have told you stories. Kids always do.'

'Yes . . . all right . . . yes.' Mademoiselle Barthié's admission was little more than a whimper. She wished the man would go away. Just go away and leave her alone.

'And they were different to the story I told you.'

'Yes.'

'And what did you make of them?'

Mademoiselle Barthié tried to summon at least a degree of courage. She took a deep breath and said, 'I felt they were closer to the truth than your explanation. I may be only an infants' teacher, monsieur, but I am not stupid. I knew at the time that what you were saying was false, that what happened involved more serious matters. Strange Americans and Englishmen deep in the woods of Geneva. Spies, perhaps. Agents. You were out of breath when you returned the girls, monsieur. And there was blood on your shirt . . .'

'But you didn't do anything about it, did you?'

'As you pointed out so forcefully, to do so would have cost me my job, possibly my whole career. It was me who

182

lost the girls in the first place. And there was something terribly wrong about the whole affair.'

'So you waited an appropriate length of time, until the end of term, and then you resigned. You even left Switzerland altogether, didn't you? Took up a post at the École Primaire du Sud Ouest in Biarritz, France. After that, you worked at seven other schools and playgroups in the Basque region. You only returned to Switzerland three years, two months and fourteen days ago. And you had the good sense to set yourself up in a small, unassuming little town like Le Locle, as far away from Geneva as practicable given the size of the French-speaking part of your country.'

Mademoiselle Barthié was stunned by the man's detailed knowledge of her movements. A chill ran down her flank, as if she had stepped from sun to shade. Inexplicably, she felt the need to defend herself. And as she did, a solitary tear ran down her cheek and dropped from her chin.

'I carried a heavy burden of guilt wherever I went. I was too concerned for myself. I should have made it my business to discover what happened. I should have spoken out. I should – '

'No!' Hagerty's insistence was total. 'You acted properly. Never forget it. *Never.*'

Mademoiselle Barthié took off her spectacles as more tears cascaded from her eyes. She did not understand. 'Why?' she cried desperately. 'Why were you there then? Why are you here now? Who are you? What do you want with me?'

'I want nothing more than to remind you.'

'Why?'

Because you are a pipe-joint, Hagerty thought. One that I would have resealed before Knapp's release had I not been summoned to Camp David by the President's people on the weekend I was due in Europe. But one that I am resealing now.

'Because the time is appropriate for such a reminder,' he said.

'Why?' Mademoiselle Barthié repeated, her voice cracking. 'For pity's sake, *why*?'

'That must remain my affair, Mam'selle.'

'And what of me?'

'You?' Hagerty's cold half-smile returned. 'You are happy in your work, aren't you? You are content to be helping the young children of Le Locle.'

Mademoiselle Barthié nodded and tried to palm away the dampness on her face. Hagerty reached out and took her chin in his fingers. Without undue force, he turned her head until she was looking directly into his eyes.

'Then let's keep it that way,' he said.

Curran met Jute in the public bar of a stinking, smoke-stained pub in the centre of Leeds. At first, Jute was nervous and hesitant – flicking his weasel eyes around the bar as if he was certain that his superiors at Mogden hospital would choose this pub of all pubs, and this night of all nights, to walk through the door. But three double Scotches and Curran's promise of a £200 fee loosened his tongue.

Curran showed him the blown-up photograph and asked him to identify the tall man waving to the camera in the background.

Jute chuckled at the familiar faces on the picture. 'A patient called Crosby,' he said instantly. 'Released at the same time as Whittaker.'

'A patient . . .' Curran repeated vacantly, already trying to slot this new piece of information into the puzzle.

He asked Jute to tell him everything he knew about Crosby.

Half an hour later, the potted profile was complete. An American in a British institution, yet retaining influential connections in the United States. A brilliant academic, yet kept within secure walls. A solitary figure who never spoke of his past and who was never mentioned by Mogden's controllers. A man who upon release had been picked up by an unseen acquaintance in an official-looking car with smoked windows, which had whisked him away to an unknown destination. A man of mystery whose crime was as secret as his true personality.

'He was unique in being completely in control of himself,' Jute concluded. 'Not like the others, who always give away a little of their madness here, a little there.'

'So you're saying he was sane.'

'He had no time for idiots.' Jute laughed at his joke, but Curran remained poker-faced, pushed the nurse's whisky glass to one side and said pointedly, 'Neither have I, Mr Jute. Was the man sane?'

Jute's grin vanished. He had had enough dealings with pressmen to realize they demanded value for money.

'That was his opinion,' he said. 'You couldn't get close to the bugger, but you could *sense* he was desperate to get on with his life outside. Christ, the frustration that must have built up inside him . . .'

'For how long?'

'How do you mean?'

'When was he admitted?'

'Long time ago – but I don't know the exact date.'

'What?' Curran cried disbelievingly.

'I told you, his records were kept secret from underlings like me. Word was they were held personally by Ashe.'

'Who?'

'The Medical Controller.'

'Can you get to them?'

Jute raised his eyebrows and said, 'Difficult . . .'

Curran took the hint. He tossed Jute an envelope containing ten £20 notes and promised, 'There'll be more.'

'I'll try,' Jute said, his mouth creasing into a satisfied smile. 'I'll surely try.'

The phone rang as Curran walked through his front door at 3 A.M. Dany was drunk and hysterical, and he could barely decipher her disjointed jabberings.

'I can't sleep. I can't find Mam'selle. No trace of her. There was a break-in at the school. A tall man with grey hair did it. He's after me, Stephen. He's after all of us. He killed Pearl and Louise. I don't know how, but he did. He did, Stephen. What am I going to do? Oh God, what am I going to do?'

Curran tried his utmost to calm her, but it was difficult on the phone. 'It's all right,' he said thoughtlessly, ignoring all she had said. 'Where are you?'

'At Mother's. But where do I go from here? Don't know where Mam'selle went. No trace of her.'

'Then come home. It was worth a try, but if it's a blind alley . . .'

'Has Stefanie called? Have any of the Swans called?'

'I've been out.'

'Then we haven't got anywhere, have we?'

Curran could have told her about Crosby, but the revelation would inevitably have led back to the newspaper picture. Besides, he had yet to find a connection between Crosby and the Seven Swans. Instead, he told Dany about the sleep researcher Ciera O'Connell. 'We'll ask her to help,' he said. 'She can look inside your dreams, find the answer.'

Given a ray of hope, Dany managed to compose herself, though her words were still slurred. 'It's there in my head,' she said. 'I can feel it.'

'We'll go to see her as soon as I get back from New York.'

'New York? When are you going there? Why?'

'To help Dad clear out Pearl's apartment. And to see if there's anything in her place that will help us. She died after going to Geneva. You're dreaming about Geneva. There might be something.'

It was only half the reason. For the past forty-eight hours, Curran had felt an irrepressible yearning to see Martha. Not only was she a new and exciting lover, she was also his grip on normality. He *needed* time with her like a fish needs water and a diver needs oxygen. As the thought crossed his mind, so did a streak of guilt.

He offered Dany an idea in a vain attempt to purge a nagging sense of wickedness. 'I'm flying out tomorrow,' he said. 'Zak has promised to keep an eye on you. But if you come home, we can spend tonight together – and talk.'

'Yes,' Dany said wistfully. 'I'd like that.'

Dany screamed as Curran forced her down. He held her wrists against the mattress and pushed roughly into her. She tried to bite him, to hurt him, to make him let go, but it was useless. His rage gave him the strength of two men.

'What are you doing, you bastard?' she shrieked. 'Get off me. Leave me alone. You're hurting. I don't want you, bastard. I don't want you.'

'You never did!' he shouted. 'Never really wanted to

please me, to love me. Now see how it feels to be taken, sweetheart.'

Dany jerked her shoulders off the bed, taking Curran by surprise. They cracked foreheads in the confusion. Dany cried out in pain and felt a streak of warm blood ripple across her taut skin. Curran was unperturbed. He pinned her down again and accelerated his thrusting, powering his way into her until his pelvis cracked against hers.

Dany screamed again. The leak in her forehead mixed with the tears from her eyes, sending winding streams of pastel pink tumbling over her cheeks and her nose.

'Never really loved me,' Curran yelled. 'Always slow in bed. Always oh-all-right-then. Never keen. Never willing. Never hungry. Never sexual. The flesh of a furnace with the heart of a fridge.'

'Lies!'

Dany asked herself what had happened to the considerate man who had tried to soothe her over the telephone. What had turned him into an animal? Her indignity was complete and she prayed he would stop. But he did not. He pushed and he pushed until she was sure she would be split in two. She watched his chest and his trunk redden and saw veins and arteries swelling in his neck. Globules of sweat from his head dropped on to her breasts. He looked down at her, eyes glowing with outrage, as if she was the lowest form of vermin.

'Help!' she yelled out of the blue. 'Somebody help me.'

She felt a tugging on her shoulders and wondered what was happening. An instant later two pairs of tiny hands slipped under her armpits and pulled.

'We'll help you,' said Pearl.

'We'll save you,' said Stefanie.

Kipini and Mai-Lin leaped on to Curran's back and clawed at him with their nails.

'Leave her alone, nasty man,' Mai-Lin cried.

'Don't hurt her,' said Kipini. 'You mustn't.'

Louise and Sari, too timid to join the fight, jumped up and down excitedly beside the bed chorusing words of encouragement to their friends.

'Go on, save her! Save poor Dany.'

Curran yelled in agony as his back was scratched. He tried to buck like a wild horse, to throw the swarming predators off him. The diversion was just what Pearl and Stefanie needed.

'Swans will hiss and spit before they split,' they declared. 'One, two, three . . . pull!'

With one massive, united effort, they tugged Dany free. In an instant, she twirled her body away from Curran and hurled herself from the bed to the floor.

The impact woke her. Stunned, she looked around the bedroom, searching for the friends who had rescued her. But they were nowhere to be seen. Neither was Curran.

Across the room, she saw a dressing table covered in small oval-framed photographs of her father. Beside it was an unglazed clay vase filled with dried country flowers. On the wall was a faded line-drawing of Nyon's market square. And she knew then she was still in her mother's house.

Slowly, almost reluctantly, she hauled herself to her knees. She reached blindly for the jumper she had thrown on the carpet with the rest of her clothes, and pulled a handkerchief from its sleeve.

It was soon wet with tears. She stayed in the same position for more than half an hour, weeping quietly and wondering how it would all end.

'I'm so sorry, Stephen,' she uttered between sobs. 'How could I even think – '

189

14

'I used to be afraid of dying,' Curran's father said as they opened the door to Pearl's apartment. 'Used to imagine you and Pearl cleaning out my wardrobe after I was gone. Giving away my clothes to charity shops. Throwing my toothbrush in the dustbin. But I tell you, boy, it's a thousand times more tragic when a father has to clean out the possessions of a dead child.'

He looked at Curran with an expression of dire sorrow that shocked the surviving son. Curran had seen his father age ten years at Pearl's funeral. Seen lines of laughter and character turn into lines of decay and regret. But he was not prepared for such a transformation as that which confronted him now. A vibrant, dynamic, humorous diplomat turned broken old man with patchy brown skin and unkempt strands of crinkled white hair.

He took his father in his arms and hugged him hard.

They packed Pearl's belongings in tea chests, pausing to tell each other stories about her triggered by the discovery of something or other. The framed cheque for $14.50 she received from the Fort Lauderdale *Suburbian* for her first published article; the scarlet party dress she was wearing when she fell overboard during a family cruise in the Caribbean; a silver-plated locket given to her as a keepsake by her first high-school boyfriend; a book-mark made of a long transparent plastic sachet containing a single pressed bloom from a wild strawberry.

'Don't know where she got it,' her father said, rubbing his fingers across it as if he was touching Pearl's skin. 'All

I know is that she had it when she was tiny and would never part with it. When she was sixteen, I bought her a beautiful leather bookmark with her name embossed in gold. She threw it away and stuck to her damned plastic.'

'Maybe the pressed flower meant something to her,' Curran suggested.

'Search me.'

The father waved a dismissive hand as if to indicate he could no longer talk about Pearl without the hurt becoming unbearable. To divert his thoughts, he asked Curran what was happening in England.

'To the country, or to me?'

'You, of course. Are things still bad with Dany?'

For better or for worse, Curran had always told his father everything. He was a valuable sounding board, even if some of his attitudes were lurching towards obsolescence. But this time was different. Curran did not want to burden the old man with his troubles. He had suffered enough torment already. He glossed over the subject by saying that there was no hope of a reconciliation.

'God . . .' The father sighed with exasperation. 'I like Dany so much.'

'You *love* her,' Curran corrected. 'You should see the pair of you together. Clasping each other's arms. Pouring each other drinks.'

'Got another woman?'

'No,' Curran lied. 'It's not like picking up the next can of beans in the supermarket.' The thought of Martha made him go off at a tangent. 'By the way, did you know a guy called Knapp when you were in the service? Maybe at the time you were in Geneva. In the early sixties.'

'Knapp?' The father did not have to ponder for long. 'I knew *of* him. Everyone did. He was a real high-flier, tipped for great things. Maybe even the White House. He had hooked himself to the Kennedy bandwagon.'

'What happened to him?'

'No one really knew. He vanished from the Geneva scene, that's all. The word was that he had gone under.'

'Underground?'

'Secret. CIA, that sort of thing.'

'And you never heard of him again.'

'No one ever hears of guys like that again. They don't tell you they are going – and you don't ask where they have gone. I dare say he is living under an assumed name, sitting beside some pool in the Bahamas sipping a banana daquiri, safe in the knowledge that he has served Uncle Sam.'

'Or dead,' Curran said, remembering what Martha had told him in the restaurant.

'Maybe. Who knows?'

The phone rang. Curran answered it.

'Is that the home of Miss Pearl Curran?' Knapp asked.

Curran said 'Yes' without thinking. The line went dead – and Curran cursed the telephone company.

'They'll call back if it's important,' his father said. 'Maybe it was someone from my yacht club. I told them I'd be here today.'

With such a hoard of memories to share along the way, it took them five hours to fill as many tea chests. Even then, the bathroom and the small side room used as an office by Pearl remained untouched.

'I'll clear them tonight,' Curran said.

'You're not coming home with me?' his father said with more than a tinge of disappointment.

'Someone's got to go through Pearl's business affairs. You don't want to do that, Pop. I know her trade. It'll be

192

easier for me to tie up the loose ends. Besides, you're pooped.'

Curran's father took the point, and was grateful. He pushed the back of a hand on to his aching back, stretched and said: 'I suppose it makes sense.'

'What time are the furniture people coming tomorrow?' Curran asked.

'The auctioneers? They said about four in the afternoon.'

Curran made a quick mental calculation. Martha's plane was coming in at 6 A.M. and she would be home by eight. He could sift through Pearl's notebooks and floppy disks tonight, grab a few hours' sleep, go to Martha's for a while and then come back to oversee the auctioneers and load the tea chests into his father's station wagon.

'Then why don't you get back here at three,' he said. 'I'll see you then.'

As the old man shuffled out, he gazed back at the apartment's walls, naked now Pearl's paintings and prints had been taken down. 'This is my daughter's place,' he said, looking tragic again. 'I can't believe someone else is going to live here.'

Curran slipped disk after disk into Pearl's word processor, called up file after file on to its screen . . . and came to realize how awesome was his task. Pearl, it was clear, had been a journalist in demand. She had written enough articles to fill a library, but had not erased her work after it had been published, preferring instead to retain it – as insurance against libel actions brought on by shabby editing, Curran assumed – and use new disks for new stories.

It could have taken him all night, but he struck lucky with the fourteenth disk he tried.

193

A list of twelve files flashed up, named UN.001 to UN.012. A glance at the first revealed it was the introduction of her unfinished feature on the early days of the United Nations. Curran called up the others in numerical order. Some contained weird and wonderful anecdotes about the fledgling world organization, others repeated choice quotes from past Secretary Generals like U Thant and Hammarskjöld. The final file, however, was written in the first person – and dealt with Pearl's recollection of her days as a child in Geneva.

Curran read quickly, hitting keys impatiently to scroll up. All the ingredients were there: the school, her treasured alliance with the Seven Swans. And then there was a paragraph which sent Curran's hopes soaring. It was written in Pearl's ebullient style:

I set out to find my favourite teacher, who we all called simply Mam'selle, but it was not easy. Like some winsome beauty in a medieval fairy tale, Mam'selle had fled the fire-breathing Miss Spice and headed for the hills. Switzerland's Jura mountains, to be precise (not every peak in Switzerland is an Alp, folks). There she would have stayed, locked away in splended isolation in the snowed-under town of Le Locle, had I not, quite by chance, been introduced to a teenage girl in Geneva who turned out to be her niece!

'Found her!' Curran cried. 'She found Mam'selle!' He wanted to call Dany there and then, but a glance at his watch told him it would be 5 A.M. in London, and, he prayed, she would be sleeping. He hit the next-page key to see what followed, but to his dismay, the screen became blank. The paragraph about Mam'selle had been Pearl's last.

Curran wondered why – and turned his attention to the notebooks piled in a pyramid beside the word processor.

Pearl's notes were in shorthand, but Curran managed to decipher most of them. He found the UN material within half an hour, but as he flicked over another page, his spine turned to ice.

The shorthand faded away into an unintelligible scrawl, and out of that came a child's writing – large spidery capitals of differing heights and widths.

The final entry read: 'WOODS. NO! GO AWAY, NASTY MAN!'

Knapp closed the door behind him, shutting out the watery nightlight that illuminated the stairwell. The lock had been easy to pick, and he was already convinced this would be his easiest assignment. He padded across the parquet floor of the lounge, taking care to avoid the barely visible silhouette of a low wooden table placed between twin chairs and a sofa. To make a noise would be a complication, though it would probably not affect the fate of his victim unduly.

The first door he opened led to the kitchen, a surprisingly large affair considering the locale. A single plate had been left in the sink, along with a single mug and a single knife, fork and spoon. Alone and isolated. That was how he wanted them to be.

His next view was of the bathroom, full of feminine paraphernalia like bubble bath, skin lotion, assorted shampoo bottles, hair gel and curling tongs.

There was only one door left – and she would be sleeping behind it. Knapp opened it with the lightest touch so it made not a squeal, not a squeak. The shape he hoped to see was under the duvet. Long and lean, stretched full out on the stomach with legs slightly apart. The sleeper's face was buried deep in the pillow, hardly a nostril clear to breathe in the night air.

Ah, the pillow . . .

Knapp had considered several methods of execution. Strangulation, perhaps, or the delivery of a carefully aimed blow that would snap a neck like a dry log. But the pillow provided the appropriate answer. Suffocation. After all, how did most adults rid themselves of unwanted children?

He smiled as he glimpsed a second pillow, cast to the floor by a sleeper who preferred her head to be low on the bed. It could only be construed as a gift, and he was not one to ignore gifts. He picked it up and balanced himself at the foot of the bed, ready to lunge forward and press down with all his might until her last flicker of life was snuffed out, the way it was meant to be.

He placed the pillow on her head with ease, but then something inexplicable happened. The sleeper awoke and struggled like a demon. Certainly, he had expected her to struggle, but not with this degree of power and determination. He pushed and pushed and refused to give in. Yet he was unable to hold the pillow in one place and knew his victim was drawing gasps of life beneath his whitened knuckles. He flung the pillow aside so he could pummel the resistance from her first – and saw for the first time that the sleeper was a man.

'You're not her,' he said with no attempt to disguise his surprise.

Curran, his lungs scorching, heard the voice as if it was coming from another world. He took in great gulps of the air that had been denied him and opened his eyes. It was dark and forbidding in the room, but Knapp took a step back into the shaft of silver that seeped through a gap between curtain and window – and Curran saw he was the man in the picture.

Definitely. Undeniably. Unbelievably.

Curran wanted to leap from his bed, grab him by the throat and batter him until he was told what the hell was happening. But he had been stunned and weakened by Knapp's attack and could not move a muscle.

Knapp did not wait for Curran's strength to return. Now that he knew what he was up against, he was confident of winning any conflict. But that wasn't the point. The man was probably a loyal American, and he wished no harm on such a patriot. It was only Pearl the traitor he wanted to kill.

'I'll be back for her,' he said. Then he spun solidly on his heels and disappeared into the night.

Curran's throat was raw and he could neither scream nor shout. He knew he needed to force adrenalin into his bloodstream to jerk himself into action, and as the feeling returned to his hands and arms, he smashed them into the mattress time after time until life flowed into the rest of his body.

He climbed from the bed, slapping his face – and Dany's hysterical jabberings over the phone came to him. Words that had somehow flown in and out of his mind, yet were returning now like an echo from a cliff.

'A tall man with grey hair. After me, after all of us. He killed Pearl and Louise. Don't know how, but he did.'

Curran heard running footsteps on the sidewalk below. He threw back the drapes, pushed up the sash window and leaned out. The bobbing head was directly beneath him.

'Pearl's dead, you bastard!' he yelled. 'You've killed her already.'

Knapp stopped in his tracks. He twisted his head violently and looked up. A street light turned his face into a distorted conglomerate of amber and black, but Curran could make out a smile.

'Is that so?' Knapp said. 'Then I shall not need to return.'

He turned to run again, vanishing instantly behind a parked truck. As his trailing ankle disappeared, Curran began to quiver like an accident victim in shock.

He knew then that Dany was right. The man in the picture was out to get them all.

15

Curran tried to convince the police, but they were a cynical bunch.

'You're telling us that a guy let out of the bin in England attacked a total stranger in New York,' a swarthy lieutenant named Favero said. 'It makes as much sense as Queen Elizabeth becoming President.'

'He didn't mean to attack me,' Curran insisted. 'He was after my sister.'

'But she's dead already.' Favero nodded to the tea chests to emphasize his point, and grinned at a pair of subordinates who were dusting the apartment for prints. 'Why would anyone want to kill a dead woman, huh?'

'Maybe he's deluded.'

'If anyone's deluded around here, pal, it's you.'

Curran was outraged, but clung on to the remnants of his temper lest Favero should up and leave and forget all about it.

'Did you check the airports? I told you he is an American called Crosby.'

'Sure – and no one called Crosby flew into New York on the day of your man's release, or the day after. You want me to check every other airport in the Americas for every other day between then and now? You want me to turn the whole NYPD over to this investigation? You want me to pull in every fuckin' Crosby in town? Shit, mister, if what you're saying is true – '

'Of course it's damn well true!'

'If what you're saying is true, what we've got on our

hands is a lily-livered son of a bitch who couldn't go through with it. Have you any *idea* of the number of motherfuckers who *do* go through with it in this city, day after day after fuckin' day?'

'All right, all right.' Curran held up his arms in a show of surrender. 'So what if I show you a picture of the guy?'

'You got him to pose for you?'

Curran brushed aside the ridicule. 'My paper published a photograph of his release from hospital. I'll get it wired to our New York bureau. Someone there will bring it round to you.'

'OK,' Favero said without enthusiasm. 'Is he the only one on the shot?'

'No.'

'So call me to tell me who to look for. I'll be waiting with baited breath.'

At Martha's, Curran hid his agitation under a mask of tranquillity. The child in him wanted to blurt out everything to her, so she would comfort and reassure him like a mother hen. But the other chunk of him, the chunk he forced to stay dominant, knew she must not become involved, for her own sake and for his. Who knew what could happen to her if he dragged her into the sights of his assailant? Oh no – better to have her as a refuge to which he could run; a soft warm haven in whose presence he could forget.

He saw the bruise as soon as Martha dabbed away her make-up. Rose-red with a blurred mustard halo, it spread from her cheekbone to her jaw on the left of her face. Curran touched it, taking care not to press hard. Even so, Martha flinched.

'What happened?' Curran asked.

Martha tried to smile, but it was still painful. 'I tripped and fell . . . in the departure lounge a couple of days ago.

200

There was an ashtray in the way. One of those damn great pillar things that looks as if it could hold up an office block. Blue it was. With a shiny metal top. Lucky I didn't crack my teeth.'

It was the way she said it that made Curran suspicious. Too much detail, too much unnecessary elaboration. Why hadn't she simply said, 'I fell over and hit an ashtray.' It was almost as if she was trying to justify her injury. In his time as a journalist, Curran had written countless stories of women beaten by cruel men. Invariably, as the story emerged in court or at an inquest, friends and neighbours would tell how the battered woman at first insisted that her bruises were caused by silly falls. The sort of thing that could happen to anyone. There was a kind of inexplicable shame about it, as if the victim either blamed herself for the perpetrator's attack, or could not bring herself to admit to others that she was unloved and brutalized.

'Martha, do you have another man?' Curran said out of the blue.

'*What?*' Martha was staggered by the question.

'Another boyfriend. Another lover.'

'No. Why do you – '

'Did anyone help you?' Curran interrupted.

'What?'

'When you fell over.'

'Another stewardess,' Martha replied without hesitation.

'I'll call to thank her tomorrow.'

'No need,' Martha said testily. 'I can say my own thank-yous, thank you very much.'

The joke made Curran relax. It was spontaneous, unrehearsed – and Martha had ridden his impertinence without concern. Either she was a skilled faker, which he

201

doubted, or she had indeed fallen on the damn ashtray. At any rate, the inquisition was not worth pursuing.

Martha disappeared into the kitchen. Curran heard cupboard doors click as she searched for something.

'I asked my pop about your pop,' he called, changing the subject.

Martha continued her search without replying – and Curran scolded himself for making her clam up again by mentioning her father. He felt foolish and naïve. The man had lived in a secret world and, to some degree, it must have extended to infringe on the life of his daughter. It was only natural that even now he was dead, she would be unwilling to discuss it. But her absolute silence, her refusal to even laugh off her reluctance, told him something . . . that there was a story buried deep within her, waiting to be told. Curran warned himself to suppress his natural fascination and wait for the right moment to listen.

Martha swept past him with an uncorked bottle of cabernet and two glasses.

'Isn't it a bit early for that?' Curran said, squinting at the parallel slabs of morning sunshine that were streaking through the windows.

Martha ignored him. She walked through the open door of her bedroom and put the wine and glasses beside the bed. 'For later,' she said as she turned to beckon him to her. 'After we've eaten.'

Their love-making had an intensity that took their breath away. The apartment was hot and there was no need for sheets. They stretched out together, front to front, relishing their nakedness and the escape of imprisoned passion.

They kissed every inch of each other's skin, stroked taut muscle and soft flesh, ran thumbs roughly along vertebrae, pushed hips against thighs, explored the sweeping undulations of each other's buttocks.

Martha twisted and stretched, shadows thrown by a venetian blind accentuating the rippled porcelain quality of her ribcage. She was in a mood to be teased, to be pleased – and Curran responded knowingly.

He reached for the cabernet bottle and poured a trickle into her pubic hair until she was wet. Then he drank, licking and sucking, deeper and deeper, until she opened herself to him and he found the anxious bud of her clitoris. As he pleasured her with his tongue, varying his rhythm, flicking down on occasion in pursuit of wine that had crept towards her anus, he stroked her abdomen and the underside of her breasts with fingertips that tingled as if he was touching a live wire. She became excited, gripping the rails of the bed's headboard and arching her back away from the mattress to increase her sensation. When she climaxed, her whole body writhed and tossed, taking Curran's head with it, and it seemed it was only her hold on the rails that prevented her from taking off.

They were on another planet now, and wanted to stay there. She dipped a new make-up brush into the neck of the bottle and returned the compliment, painting Curran's body with warm, burgundy streaks of liquid before licking them off and, finally, taking his penis into her mouth to give him the most exquisite pleasure.

It was another two hours before they poured what was left of the wine into the glasses.

Curran was woken by a peck on the nose and the smell of percolating coffee. Martha, in a white satin gown that clung to her contours, looked down at him and smiled. Their eyes asked each other the burning question.

Had it been lust . . . or love?

Curran warned himself not to be caught on the rebound from Dany. But then he remembered every sumptuous moment that had gone before and how, after the initial release of sexual energy, he had repeatedly made love to Martha. Not screwed her. Not fucked her. *Made love* to her. And she had done the same to him.

He returned her smile – and they both knew.

Knapp's eagle landed on the African tablelands, but at the instant talon touched soil, he was transformed into a man again. He walked up and down a line someone had scored in the parched soil with a stone, small clouds of dust billowing from beneath his bare feet. Around him, herds of zebra and wildebeest grazed and foraged, unaffected by the presence of such an illustrious human being. Small, needle-beaked birds followed their hooves, snapping up grubs from disturbed earth. In the distance, a giraffe tugged leaves from the plain's solitary tree.

There was a commotion away to Knapp's right, and he looked to see what had caused it. A pride of lions – seven females, a male and four cubs – was on the move, scattering lesser beasts along its route.

'I don't blame you,' Knapp called out to the fleeing animals. 'They look hungry to me, too.'

The lions suddenly changed direction. Knapp squinted to get a clearer view. He could no longer see their bodies, their tails or their hind legs. Just twelve heads on top of twelve pairs of forelegs, growing larger by the second.

It took him a moment to register what was happening, but then he realized. They were coming for him.

Panicking, he looked around for shelter. But there was nothing, not even a bush. As he glanced back to the

204

pride, the seven female hunters fanned out and broke into a run. In an instant, they had surrounded him.

They crept closer in an ever-decreasing circle, their bellies scraping the surface of the plain as their limbs dropped them into positions of attack.

They leaped in unison and Knapp was knocked to the ground. He heard their roaring and snarling as they bit hard into his flesh. One took his head and swung it from side to side, trying to break his neck.

A fight for the spoils broke out. Three lionesses sunk their teeth into his shoulders and arms. The other four took his legs and feet. Both groups tugged. Knapp screamed as he felt himself being torn apart. His belly was stretching. Muscles and tendons were snapping. Bones were cracking. Soon, he would be in two pieces.

The sound of a bugle drifted from over the horizon. Hagerty, Napier and Lipton led the cavalry charge, ridiculously dressed for the conditions in heavy, dark suits – dripping wet even though the air was as hot as fire.

Knapp freed his right arm from a lioness's grip and gave them a cheery wave. 'Over here,' he yelled, laughing at their appearance. 'You're too late, as usual. I think I'm done for.'

Hagerty waded into the lions with his fists and his feet. Knapp half expected Napier and Lipton to whack the beasts with umbrellas. But they, too, relied on their hands.

The lions were taken by surprise by the intervention. Though they knew they were under no real threat, that their strength and ferocity would overcome, they were lazy creatures. They lost heart and gave up, content to wait for an unchallenged kill. They sat back on their hind legs, licking Knapp's blood from their jaws with great curling tongues.

But the damage had been done. Knapp lay on the line in the dust, two legs and an arm removed from his torso and fatty entrails seeping from gaping wounds in his flesh.

While Lipton chased away the pride, Hagerty and Napier did their best to put him back together.

'You're broken,' Hagerty said.

'I know,' Knapp replied. 'The only thing that puzzles me is why you guys didn't find out sooner.'

'You gave us no clue,' Napier said.

'You thought I was so able, so in command.'

'We had no idea of the strain you were under.'

'I didn't show it. I couldn't show it.'

'You were faking,' Hagerty said.

'Don't we all?'

'But *why*?'

'I just drifted into it.'

'We thought you were strong.'

'I was. But it all became too much.'

'Any more secrets?' Hagerty asked.

'Are you keeping anything else from us?' a returning Lipton said.

'Something that has caused this sorry situation, perhaps?' Napier added.

Knapp looked up into the cloudless blue sky. The eagle was circling above with Yelena astride its back, her chiffon shawl and red hair blown back by the breeze. He waved to her with his remaining arm. She blew him a kiss. Knapp tasted it as it fell on his lips.

'Beautiful,' he murmured. 'I love you, darling Yelena.'

'What the hell's he talking about?' Hagerty demanded forcibly.

Napier's voice was more compassionate. 'Delirious,' he said. 'He's gone. The poor chap's gone.'

'What are we going to do?' Lipton was panicking.

'I can help,' Napier said in a reassuring way. 'I have connections. I know somewhere he can go.'

They patched him up as best they could. They pushed his severed limbs into shoulder and pelvic joints and held them in place with bandages they made by tearing their shirts.

'Over here,' Napier called.

Knapp's eyes followed the voice. He saw a cage on wheels, like those used by travelling circuses. He imagined it had once been brightly-hued and patterned. But time had washed away its colour and its heavy-duty iron bars were coated in rust.

Napier held open the door. Hagerty and Lipton dragged Knapp to the cage and lifted him into it, dropping him clumsily – uncaringly, it occurred to Knapp – on the floor. He heard clanking noises as bolts were slid into sockets and a padlock was snapped shut.

Then they left him. They turned and walked away into the plain without a farewell glance, throwing the key of the padlock into the dust. Knapp, dripping with blood, clear watery liquid oozing from gaps in the bandage, watched them go.

He knew he was trapped. Left alone to rot. Abandoned in a strange place.

The seven girls came to look at him in his cage, pointing at him with stubby little fingers, giggling at his predicament, their nasty, piggy eyes boring into his flesh, opening further wounds.

One of them, the child with the jet-black skin, picked up the key of the padlock and teased him by waving it in front of his eyes. Then she yelled: 'Let's play catch!'

The girls made a circle, just as the lionesses had done. Each tossed the key to her neighbour, laughing at butter-fingered attempts to catch it.

While they played, Knapp began to gnaw at the bars. He knew it would take thirty years to free himself. But when he did, they would laugh no more.

The alarm woke him at 6 A.M. precisely and he took less than half an hour to wash, shave and dress. As he looked in the mirror, he reflected that just as God and the Catholic Church were with Kennedy, so the Spirit of Right was with him. More telephone calls and his shadowy confrontation with the struggling patriot had confirmed that heavenly retribution had been taken against the girl Stefanie and the girl Pearl, as well as the girl Louise. Now, it was up to him to carry on his Messianic work.

Thinking ahead, as was necessary in such situations, he had packed his bag the night before, and was ready when the cab arrived at seven to take him to JFK Airport.

'Where're you flying to, bud?' the cabbie asked on the way.

'Nairobi,' Knapp answered hesitantly. 'Kenya.'

'Where all them animals are.'

'Zebra, wildebeest . . . and lions.'

'You going hunting?'

'Yes, that's right. Hunting.'

Dany broke free from Curran's grip and ran from the house into the street. Curran chased her along the pavement for fifty yards before catching her under the sprawling branches of a cherry tree, but there was nothing he could do. Tears tumbled down her cheeks. Pink blossom falling from the tree stuck to her wet skin.

She screamed and shouted and tried to push Curran's hands from her elbows. 'Let me go!' she yelled. 'I must go. Get away. Don't you see?'

Curran wanted to slap her to bring her to her senses.

But not here in the street. It would be too brutal, too public. Curious faces were already peeping from behind lace curtains.

He half guided, half dragged her back to the house. She took off again as soon as she was inside, bolting for the back door. He grabbed her as she turned the knob and spun her around.

'Stefanie is *dead*!' she shrieked.

Curran did not understand. 'What – '

Dany was wild, frenzied. She twisted this way and that, tried to claw at Curran with her fingernails. But he would not let her go.

'In her sleep, like Pearl and Louise.' She spat the words, trying to make him realize. 'Christ, I tried to call you, but you weren't at Pearl's or your father's. Where the bloody hell were you?'

She tried to struggle free again. Curran held firm. Dany kicked him in the shins, making him cry out.

'Let me go! I've got to get away. The same thing is happening to me. Don't you see? Don't you *see*?'

Now Curran slapped her, swiping the palm of his hand across her face with a force she could not ignore. The blow swept away her rantings, but she glowered at him with eyes that looked as if they would never forgive.

It was the first time in his life that he had struck a woman. 'I . . . I'm sorry,' he said. 'Now, tell me . . .'

Dany, panting as if she was taking her last breaths, spluttered out everything she knew. 'Stefanie's mother phoned to tell me. I asked her what the doctor had said. The diagnosis was the same. Heart attack during sleep. Best way to go, they said. Christ!'

Curran squeezed her arms to reassure her.

After a pause, she carried on. 'They said Stefanie was highly strung. A woman desperate to achieve, and under tremendous pressure to perform. Traces of cocaine were found in her blood. She was flying, they said, but came down to earth with one final bump.'

'Did you ask her mother about family history?'

'No previous instance of heart failure. Does that surprise you?'

Curran was aware of a creeping horror, as if millions of tiny insects were swarming across his flesh. 'No,' he said. 'Not any longer.'

He let Dany go and for a cruel, soul-searching moment, they looked blankly at each other as if they were a pair of stone statues.

When Curran spoke again, it was in a whisper. 'We both know it has nothing to do with heart trouble . . .'

'It's the man in my visions,' Dany said at once. 'The man hunting through the school records, to find our addresses. The man who is coming for us.'

She searched Curran's eyes for belief, and he made no attempt at concealment. The words that proved it tumbled automatically from his mouth. 'I saw him. He thought Pearl was still alive. He tried to smother me with a pillow, thinking I was her.'

Dany could neither cry out nor emit the slightest gasp. She heard what Curran said, but it was no longer within her comprehension. Her limbs became numb and her throat felt dry and constricted. For a moment, she thought she would never again be able to utter a word, but then Curran asked her if she had spoken to the other Swans, and she forced herself to answer.

'Sari and Mai-Lin,' she said distantly. 'Kipini's out of reach in the bush.'

'And are Sari and Mai-Lin having these visions?'

'No. I did ask, and ask again, but they said no. They're so upset . . .'

'No more clues, then.'

'Did you find any?'

'I've found Mam'selle. We'll call her in the morning. Then we'll contact the sleep researcher. I hope to God she'll agree to look inside your head.'

'She must,' Dany said. 'It's my only hope.'

She threw her arms around Curran's waist and held him as if she was clinging to the only branch on the edge of a precipice, then pushed the side of her head against his chest, firmly so she could hear the comforting rhythm of his heartbeat.

'It's madness, isn't it?' she said quietly. 'Do you think I'm going mad, Stephen?'

Curran stroked her hair. 'No,' he said.

Dany began to cry again and Curran felt her trembling in his arms.

'We never harmed anyone, so why is he doing this?' she said. 'Oh Stephen, I'm so frightened.'

Curran did not reply. All he knew was that he was frightened, too.

16

Knapp waited three days in Nairobi, in order to join a recognized tourist party. It was necessary for cover, but nevertheless a tiresome ordeal due to the nature of his fellow travellers. As he surveyed them on the creaky, thirty-seater turbo-prop burbling over the savannah, he could not remember a more despicable group.

Loud men with fat stomachs poking from absurd knee-length shorts and garishly printed shirts. Perspiring, double-chinned women in loose cotton dresses that had neither shape nor style.

Ugly, that's what you are, he thought as he ran his eyes along the aircraft's centre aisle. Wealthy, yes, but ugly and ignorant. You want to see the animals? Hah, they'll run away as soon as they catch sight of such grotesque examples of the human species.

The plane took six hours to reach the ranch. From the air, it was a spectacular sight, an almost shocking contrast to the barren, sun-baked scrub that surrounded it. Watered and lush, its sheer greenness was dazzling. And though no pond nor lake was visible, it had the quality of an oasis. It was laid out in a perfect square within 100-yard-long stone walls. The main thatched block – a long, thin building – was surrounded by clusters of acacia and giant cacti pruned in the shape of trees. Here and there, bushes peppered with vivid scarlet blooms cast elongated shadows in the late-afternoon sun. Between the main block and a white-walled annexe, a substantial plot of land had been ploughed, raked and planted out, giving rise to thoughts of kitchen gardens, runner beans, potatoes and cabbages.

Eighty yards from the ranch's perimeter, several acres of bush had been flattened and rolled to forge an airstrip. The plane set a herd of impala to flight as it bounced along the dirt.

The group, twenty-six in all, were shown to their rooms by Kenyan rangers in khaki uniforms. Knapp was forced to share with one of the fattest, ugliest men on the plane. But though he felt inner disgust, he neither argued nor complained.

Inconspicuous. That was the key word. Do nothing, say nothing to draw attention. Success – and survival – depended upon blending with the background. It would be difficult for him, given his position and natural commanding manner, but was utterly essential.

The tourists were invited to wash and help themselves from bowls of fruit and jugs of water left in each room, before being officially welcomed by the Ranch Director. Knapp changed into his lightest suit and waited for the call.

When everyone was ready, the group was ushered into a room which looked like a small lecture theatre. Rows of cane chairs were arranged in semi-circles around a cine screen and an elaborately decorated lectern which could have come from a church. Knapp sat at the back, beneath a projector of a size that betrayed its thirty-year vintage.

He waited for the entrance of the inevitable white face. The master of the ranch, an old refugee from faded European aristocracy now consoling himself amid the remnants of the Empire, cases of export gin and native servants.

But the Ranch Director was neither white, nor old, nor a master. The door swung open – and polite applause

213

greeted a striking black woman in her mid-thirties. Lean and athletic, she was dressed in matching blouse and slacks in olive-coloured canvas, with a mock leopard-skin belt pulled tightly around her midriff to make the most of her svelte contours. Her shining hair was pulled up by a bright-red polka-dot scarf, revealing black earrings with a halo of sharp orange like that from a total eclipse of the sun.

She walked casually and with poise, but it was her smile which immediately put her spectators, unnerved by such an alien environment, at ease. Wide, dimpled and rich, it had a friendly and familiar quality that seeped into them like a favourite wine.

Only Knapp was unimpressed. As he watched the woman take the single step on to the lectern, he knew at once it was *her*. The one who was bent on destroying *him*. He glared at her, his eyes filled with hatred, and fought a compulsion to throttle the life from her there and then.

Kipini, glancing at a set of notes, began her speech of welcome, making sure to enliven her voice so her audience would feel as pioneering as the thousands who had visited the ranch before them. 'Welcome to the Linitria Sanctuary, a vital part of the Kuypers Memorial Foundation, named after the great Dutch explorer who began the work which we have carried on since his death. Here, you are in the heart of Masai country, the tribe whose warriors, beauty and noble sense of honour will steal your hearts. You are also in the land of the black rhinoceros, the lion, the leopard and the antelope. Here, we feel sure, your senses will explore new boundaries. You will see stunning sunsets, you will hear the sound of the wild and you will touch the soul of Africa. And, yes, some of you will even be seduced by snakes.'

Kipini laughed – and the safari party joined in. Knapp

forced himself to smile, though it hurt his jaw. Kipini cast her eyes over the newcomers. As she did so, even though she exuded an air of undeniable intelligence and authority, Knapp detected a hint of shyness. She never allowed her gaze to rest on any one person, preferring instead to skip across heads until she could return to the safety of her notes.

Look at me, he challenged in his mind. *See I am here. Look, damn you.*

'Our mission here,' Kipini continued, 'is to protect wildlife, both flora and fauna, from the destructive encroachment of man. But we ourselves, yes, we in this plantation, must also not encroach. We must find a harmony between human activity and the well-being of the beasts. Otherwise everything could – '

Look at me. You were not reluctant to stare at me before. To pry with your eyes. Your little piggy eyes.

'The Kenyan government is very aware of this. The World Wide Fund for Nature and the Save the Rhino Fund also support our efforts to create new reserves and pay specialized personnel and scientists. And of course, we are grateful to animal-lovers such as yourselves for showing such an interest. The money you have paid for your holiday will help – '

Look at you – and look at them. You don't want them here. You just need their money. You must despise them, just as I do, so why pretend? Hatred and pretension. The cornerstones of your life, Little Miss Director.

'There were 20,000 black rhino in 1970. But today, in the whole of Kenya, there are fewer than 350. At the same time, the price of rhino horn has climbed from $40 a kilo to $600. There is a ridiculously high demand for the horn's so-called aphrodisiac qualities, and it is also used to make dagger handles – '

Look at me! See the daggers in my eyes.

'The ranch also funds itself. Around this plantation, we are raising 6,000 cattle and 5,000 sheep. To some extent, they are left to graze in the wild, which does have its dangers, particularly if a pride of lions takes an interest . . .'

There was more laughter. Kipini looked up – and saw him.

She glanced away, then looked back at him again, flicking her head to one side to gain a clearer view between the ranks of shoulders. He stared back without blinking – and she felt a fierce palpitation sweep across her chest.

Her smile disappeared as if it had been slapped off her face and she suddenly felt as lost as a child away from home for the first time. At the same moment, she was conscious that she was in front of an audience and tried to disguise her disquiet. She glanced down at her notes and tried to find her place.

It was hopeless. The words were there, on paper in front of her. But she could not see them. Could make no sense of them. Her mind had been distracted – and there was no going back.

She tried to pick up the thread of her speech as best she could, but she could not overcome a stuttering hesitancy. 'Er . . . there are sixty . . . er, rhino that is, in the territory of this sanctuary. If you include the . . . er . . . territory around the outlying base camps, which you will . . . which you will see in due course. It's a treasure. Er . . . a treasure when you think of the overall number of rhino.'

She could *hear* people shifting in their seats. Was she so garbled? Were they so embarrassed? She had begun eloquently and lucidly. And now, an instant later, she was a jumbled wreck. What on earth must they think? She glanced once again at Knapp, but he did not help. His stare was unrelenting, merciless. It chilled her backbone.

Why?

She could not understand.

She wanted to wrap up the speech and escape. She told the party they were welcome to wander around the ranch at their leisure, but warned them of the perils of pushing hands into bushes, or upturning rocks.

'Venomous African vipers,' she said. 'We have developed a serum in our laboratory in the annexe, but don't rely on it.'

Oh Lord! The warning had been so blunt, so heavy. She wanted to help them enjoy animals, not scare them to death. Why had it come out like that? The man. The man at the back. It was something to do with him. But what?

She skipped what should have been a lengthy and exciting itinerary for base-camp visits and went straight to the end of her speech. It had been deliberately written as a moving finale, but she sapped its atmosphere with her haste.

'I have the privilege of being in charge of a little piece of Africa. And when I die, I want it to be more alive.'

The group was left high and dry, not knowing whether to applaud or to demand answers to questions left floating in their heads. A few clapped, but most simply sat still in astonishment and concern. Kipini thanked them for listening and hurried out.

Knapp was the first to his feet, stretching and smiling at his neighbour to demonstrate that he, at least, was at ease.

He remembered the cabbie who drove him to JFK Airport. 'You going hunting?'

Oh yes, Mr Taxi Driver. The hunter has his prey in his

217

sights. The little girl. The treacherous little nigger girl. She had hidden herself far away from him. But he had flushed her out and he had got her on the run.

She would not be running for much longer.

Curran circled Crosby on a copy of the Mogden release photograph and wired it to the paper's New York bureau, with a request that it should be relayed on to Lieutenant Favero. When this was done, he found a quiet corner of the newsroom and reached for the nearest telephone.

He called directory inquiries for the Neuchâtel area of Switzerland to obtain Mademoiselle Barthié's number in Le Locle. But when there was no reply at her apartment, he diverted his attention closer to home, tracing Ciera O'Connell to the psychology department of Prince's College, part of London University. She, too, was out, but Curran made an appointment to meet her the following day, claiming he wanted to conduct an interview after learning of her fascinating work in a report of the Atlanta seminar.

He cleared his throat and braced himself for the next call, for he knew in his heart it would probably be futile. After bludgeoning his way through a battery of secretaries and underlings, he was finally connected to Ashe, the Medical Director of Mogden hospital. Curran introduced himself as a representative of his newspaper. He was polite but direct, hoping against hope to catch Ashe off guard.

'A man called Crosby, an American, was released from your establishment last month, sir. Could you tell me why he was there in the first place, and for how long?'

Ashe was nobody's fool in his dealings with the press. His loathing of what he perceived as their mindless interference had seen to that. His reply was crisp – and unhelpful. 'I am afraid I cannot tell you anything, Mr Curran, even if I so desired,' he said. 'Given that Mr Crosby was an American in a British institution, you will perhaps not be surprised to learn that his sojourn with us was covered by the Official Secrets Act. It is a matter of record somewhere in the bowels of Whitehall. But I have never seen his file, and neither will you be able to. The job I inherited from my predecessor was simply to monitor and restore the man's health. This I have done successfully.'

Curran remembered the shadow who smothered him, and felt a desperate urge to challenge Ashe's infernal arrogance. But he bit his lip and ploughed on. 'As Mr Crosby is now healthy, perhaps I could talk to him. Do you have a forwarding address?'

'No,' Ashe said with indifference. 'For the very same reason I outlined before.'

'Then if you don't know where he is, how can you check up on him?'

'No need, he is perfectly cured.' Ashe paused, then added pointedly, 'Will that be all, Mr Curran?'

Curran thanked him and hung up. No need for anger or insult. The call had produced no more and no less than he had expected, and there were others to be made that were certain to be more productive.

He tried Mam'selle again. This time, the phone was answered. But the voice that came on the line was not that of a woman, but a frantic man. After exchanges in a combination of halting French and English, Curran realized it was Mam'selle's landlord.

'She has gone, m'sieur,' he said with both anger and amazement. 'She just packed her bags and went. Not a word to anybody. Not a centime left for me. No one knew she was going – and no one knows where she has gone. *Merde alors!* What could have happened?'

'Mam'selle's running,' Dany said with conviction as Curran walked her to Prince's College through Bloomsbury's contradictory air of modern haste and Edwardian charm. 'She doesn't want to be dragged into this like the Swans have been. She's running away, just like she did before.'

'How can you tell?' Curran said. 'What makes you so sure?'

Dany was almost contemptuous of his doubt. Her stride quickened and her face became implacable. 'I just know,' she said, without so much as a glance in his direction.

Ciera O'Connell met them in the lobby of the college, an algae-stained concrete cube that bore testimony to the hideous folly of 1960s architecture. Curran came clean immediately, explaining that his interest in her work was personal rather than professional, introducing her to Dany and revealing enough about Dany's visions to stimulate her interest. Ciera did not hesitate. Casting a sly grin at Curran's audacity, she took them to her room on the fifth floor.

It would not have been difficult to guess her vocation. The heavy bags beneath her eyes, the waxy pallor of her skin, the hollowness of her cheeks, the anxious way she drew on a cigarette, the empty coffee mugs standing beside a scale-covered kettle. All betrayed a succession of sleepless nights. On her desk was a textbook by William C. Dement, who Curran assumed was a leader in the field of sleep research. It was called *Some Must Watch While Some Must Sleep*. Ciera O'Connell, it was clear, was one of the watchers.

Her room was as shabby as the ill-fitting grey tracksuit

220

she wore. A windowless, glumly-decorated affair, it was multi-purpose and served as her office, study, laboratory and – judging by the sink and water heater on one wall – her kitchen.

The adjacent wall was jam-packed with electrical machinery: monitors, computer keyboards and gun-grey panels covered with switches, knobs and dials. They were arranged on second-hand tables of differing heights – and the tangle of exposed wires beneath them, looking like a swarming colony of giant black centipedes, added to the sense of chaos. One corner was dominated by a machine which looked like a tea trolley covered with graph paper.

Ciera followed Curran's eyes to it. 'It's a polygraph,' she explained in a soft Irish accent. 'It measures brain activity and eye movement. Lets me know when the subject is dreaming.'

'Subject?' Dany queried.

'Whoever sleeps in the bed in the next room. Electrodes are placed on their head, face and neck. Terminals are pushed into a socket beside the bed. The socket is connected to the polygraph. Simple, really.'

For a few minutes, to break the ice, they exchanged pleasantries and generalities. Ciera turned out to be a divorcee from Dublin who had launched herself feet first into a mid-life change of direction. She used to be a secretary, she said, but had always yearned to be an academic and was now engaged on a PhD psychology course specializing in the study of dreams. Because she was a mature student, she explained, she was required to fund herself.

'I work days on the wards of a psychiatric hospital in Oxford and often work through the night here,' she said with a resigned grin. 'Sometimes I go thirty-six hours without sleep.'

She sighed at the thought and pushed at the front of her hair so it stood up on her scalp.

Curran and Dany, who could not make out if she was thirty-five or forty-five, offered their sympathy, but it was waved away by Ciera.

'You seem to be the ones with real trouble,' she said, lighting another cigarette. 'So tell me more.'

Dany told Ciera about her visions. About their dreadfulness, their startling intensity and the way they revolved around the time when she was a six-year-old girl at a school in Geneva. She also told her about the deaths of Pearl, Louise and Stefanie.

Ciera listened without interrupting. She paced up and down, flicking cigarette ash over the vinyl-tiled floor. Even after Dany finished, she kept moving, head bowed and silent.

Dany felt obliged to say: 'Will you help?'

Ciera did not respond – and for a moment both Dany and Curran felt their spirits sink. But then, out of the blue, Ciera whispered: 'Maybe . . . maybe. Mary, mother of God, it's just possible.' She paused, then uttered, 'SUD.'

'Excuse me?' Curran said.

Ciera looked up at them both and threw her cigarette butt away, stamping on it with a forthright foot. 'SUD,' she repeated. 'Sudden Unexplained Death.'

Dany asked Ciera to explain, but she refused. Unwilling to ignore an academic demand for precision, she insisted on having forty-eight hours to look up research papers, study textbooks and dig out any other information she could find on the phenomenon of SUD.

By the time Dany and Curran returned, she was prepared to share her knowledge, but remained circumspect.

'It's a syndrome which has been investigated in America,' she said. 'Studies have mainly concentrated on immigrants from South East Asia – Laotians, Vietnamese, Cambodians – simply because the problem seems to affect them more than most. More than 140 of them – spread around sixteen states – died not so long ago. But Americans and Europeans are also known to have been victims. They all went in their sleep.' She clicked her fingers. 'Just like that.'

'Why?' Curran asked incredulously. 'What caused their deaths?'

'I can only tell you about the Asian immigrants. I'm not familiar with the American and European cases. Even then, there are only theories, no hard facts, like just about everything connected to the whys and wherefores of sleep. They include the stress of resettlement, the disruption of traditions and religious beliefs, diet deficiencies and toxic substances in foods, medicines or folk remedies.'

'But that sort of thinking wouldn't apply to the Americans and Europeans, surely,' Curran said.

'Exactly. As I said, there are no hard facts. Nothing has emerged from post-mortem examinations. All that is clear is that each of the victims was asleep – and having night terrors.'

'Night terrors?' Dany said quizzically.

'As distinct from nightmares,' Ciera said. 'They are more vivid, more frightening – and far more medically traumatic. Night terrors are characterized by the sleeper talking, or crying out; convulsions brought on by rapid contraction and expansion of muscles, often making the dreamer toss and turn maniacally; a coma-like state from which the dreamer cannot easily be aroused and a furiously active nervous system. Night terrors cause heart rates to reach 160 to 170 beats per minute and can bring

223

on one of the fastest accelerations of heart rate known to man.'

'So SUD victims die of heart attacks?' Dany said.

'In a way,' Ciera explained. 'They do suffer ventricular fibrillation – the heart gives out, in other words – but I wouldn't describe it as the cause of death.'

'Oh?' Curran said curiously. 'What is, then?'

'People who were with SUD victims heard them groan and make gurgling noises. Often, they let out foamy sputum.' Ciera paused deliberately, because what she was about to say startled everyone who heard it. 'The only possible conclusion . . .' she went on slowly, '. . . is that they were literally frightened to death in their sleep.'

'Jesus . . .' The memory of Pearl's final convulsion, and the froth that had spewed from her mouth, returned to haunt Curran again. The knowledge that it would have been virtually impossible to save her did not ease the pain. If only he could have woken her . . .

It all rang true to Dany, who could still feel the fear in her bones from her last vision. She reached for Ciera's hand, held it as a child holds its mother's, and repeated: 'Will you help?'

Ciera again brushed aside the request. 'Tell me every single detail,' she said. 'About you, about your friends. Everything you know about your inner fears and their deaths.'

'Yes, of course, but – '

'No buts,' Ciera said harshly. Then, more softly, she added: 'I need to convince myself, you see. I don't want to go up any blind alleys, for your sake and for mine. I have to be confident that Sudden Unexplained Death is the likeliest hypothesis. It's very rare, you see, especially to threaten a woman such as yourself. I have to be sure.'

Dany did as she was asked, talking virtually non-stop

for two hours while Ciera listened, absorbed and made mental notes.

When the dream researcher was sure, when she had unnecessarily made the point that she was motivated as much by her own fascination as by a chance to be a Good Samaritan, she agreed to help – on two conditions. 'The first is that you stop drinking,' she told Dany earnestly. 'You say you have been drinking to ward off the visions. This is the utmost folly. Alcohol does suppress dreams, but the mind *needs* time to fantasize and if denied, it will bounce back with a vengeance the next time it gets a chance. These are called rebound dreams – and are far more vivid and fierce than ordinary dreams. Heavy drinkers can even hallucinate while they are awake. Your husband told me Pearl had been drinking before she died – and we know Stefanie had – and look what happened to them.'

'What's the second?' Curran asked.

Ciera kept her eyes fixed on Dany. 'I will help you – if you help me. There *are* techniques which enable me to look inside your mind while you are dreaming, but I am neither psychiatrist nor hypnotist. Clearly, there was a trigger which set you and your friends dreaming. It is up to you to discover it.'

When Dany excused herself to freshen up, Curran took Ciera aside and, in a quiet voice, even though he knew Dany could not hear, told her he was already pursuing the trigger. He spoke about Crosby and the blown-up photograph, and asked if it should be shown to Dany.

Ciera shook her head. 'It is clear your wife is damaged,' she said. 'We must be careful she is not broken beyond repair. The photograph could perhaps stimulate her senses, but it could also tear them to shreds. I suggest you carry on your inquiries discreetly – and independently.'

When Dany returned, managing a smile of hope as she came through the door, Ciera's face became fraught with concern, giving the lie to her insistence that her involvement was prompted largely by the chance for scientific discovery.

Though she had met Dany only two days before, she had quickly warmed to her. The tenacity with which Dany had applied herself and the charm of her childhood memories had reinforced such a feeling.

Ciera already knew she would not like to see Dany hurt. 'Take care,' she said, running her fingers along Dany's arm. 'For this trigger, whatever it is, is the catalyst for phenomenally powerful dreams.'

'I can feel it,' Dany responded. 'Something that happened when I was small. Something bad.'

Ciera nodded in sympathy. 'We can suppress our worst experiences, but they are always there, stored away on a shelf in the cellar of our mind, like an old bottle of wine. Often, when the wine is found again, it is more mellow, a far cry from the bitter taste it once had. But sometimes things go wrong. A foreign organism that makes the wine continue to ferment. Year after year, decade after decade. And when it is finally uncorked, it is explosive.'

Ciera glanced at Curran and thought again of what he had told her about Crosby. It occurred to her that Dany was living in the shadow of a twin threat. When she was awake, being pursued by a violent man who had already attacked her husband. And when she was asleep, being pursued by the projected, magnified and distorted image of some awful memory. Ciera looked back at Dany, her eyes a furnace of anxiety.

'Take care,' she repeated. 'You are in a great deal of danger.'

17

Knapp watched the rangers loading the four-wheel-drive convoy ready for the journey to the first of the base camps.

He smiled and waved, but made a mental note that they were all armed with high-powered rifles, and that he should be wary. Although Kipini was in charge of them, she was also in their charge. They revered her, that much had become clear already. And they would not take kindly to any attempt to harm her.

Kipini, rubbing sore eyes after a restless night, emerged from the shade alone – and Knapp took his chance. He hurried up to her and greeted her with a friendly: 'Good morning, Director.'

Kipini stopped in her tracks and did not respond. Normally, she would have laughed and told her guest to address her by her Christian name. But there was something about this man that demanded formality, both from him and from her. She glanced briefly at him, but his gaze penetrated her and she had to look away. She felt uncomfortable and wanted to carry on with her business, but he had trapped her between a picnic table and a cactus.

'Beautiful day,' he said, doffing a straw hat bought for the safari. 'But then every day is a beautiful day here, is it not?'

'Yes.' Kipini forced herself to reply, though she made no attempt to survey the sun-bathed scene of tranquillity. 'It certainly is, Mister er . . .'

'Dallenbach. Evan P. Dallenbach.'

'Mr Dallenbach. Of course. I'm sorry.'

She said nothing more, but he stood there, grinning and nodding as if he was listening to her animated conversation. She wondered what he wanted, but felt it inappropriate to ask. He glanced over his shoulder to see if the rangers had noticed this chummy exchange with the Ranch Director. One ranger flashed a pearl smile in his direction and he knew his object had been achieved.

Kipini was finally obliged to say: 'Can I help you, Mr Dallenbach?'

'Yes,' he said without expansion – and this time she had to look at him. The effect was staggering. She felt her insides churning and for one awful moment thought she was going to vomit there and then. But she suppressed the feeling and coughed to disguise her retching.

Knapp was not fooled. He knew fear when he saw it, and was not surprised. Fear was the price of a life of treachery.

'Is something the matter, Director?' he said in an overly sincere voice.

'No . . . no,' Kipini said. 'Just something I ate last night, I expect.' She hesitated, realizing what she was suggesting, and began to correct herself. 'Not that the food here is – ' Now she was transfixed. She broke off from what she was saying and stared into Knapp's eyes. Her gaze seemed to bounce from his retinae back on to hers, its power magnified a thousand times.

He did not blink once. It was uncanny, he thought. The girl stares at me. I stare at her. Just as we did those many years ago.

'Do I know you?' Kipini asked, mirroring his thoughts.

He feigned surprise at the question and shook his head.

'You haven't been here before?' Kipini persisted.

'Never. This is my first time. A virgin in Africa.'

'It's just that – '

Knapp waited. Surely she would not have the effrontery, here and now, in public, to admit what she had done. Surely she would not *dare*.

One of the rangers called to Kipini, asking her to check the provisions and equipment.

'Excuse me,' she said.

She brushed past Knapp, but felt the flesh of his arm against hers. The sensation was despicable. It was as if her skin had been burned or frozen – it didn't matter which. As she walked on, she could feel her legs going along with her breath. For a moment, she was sure she would collapse. But she reached the first vehicle in the convoy just in time, and clung on to its wing mirror for support.

A ranger asked her what was wrong. She repeated her story about tainted food. The ranger said he would fetch some medicine.

Kipini looked over her shoulder. Knapp stood with his back to her, his attention involuntarily switched to the obese room-mate who had waddled out of the ranch to join him.

Absurd thoughts raced through her mind. She tried to combat them, tried to tell herself she was being ridiculous, but it was useless.

For the first time since she had been at the Linitria plantation, she felt as isolated as a sailor marooned on a desert island.

She prayed that someone would find her soon. Before it was too late.

Curran drove to meet Martha feeling like an insect whose legs were being pulled off one by one by a sadistic schoolboy. He was deeply involved in Dany's plight. He wanted to worry on her behalf and wanted to care for her. Yet he was in *love* with another woman – and could no more shrug it off than throw himself from a cliff.

Heartache, torment and guilt. It sounded like so many headlines he had written in the past. Life was full of heartache, torment and guilt. And no one knew how to avoid it.

It was mid-morning when he arrived at Martha's hotel. They made love without waiting, their bodies hungry for the other's caress since the realization that they were more than just passing strangers.

For a while, as they kissed and touched and stroked, Curran could think of nothing but how Martha had come to mean so much to him in so short a time.

But as soon as he climbed from the bed, the thought of Dany – what she was doing and what was happening to her – crept remorselessly back into his head.

This time, the pressure of needing to share his burden became too much. He apologized in advance for talking about his wife at this time in this place, but then he let it flood out of him. His urgency made him gabble and stutter, but he managed to tell Martha about the Seven Swans, Dany's dreams and how they had been induced by a picture in his newspaper.

'It was of some people being released from a nuthouse. There was a man in the background. Smiling, waving.'

Martha resolved to be patient. She sat up in bed, gathered the sheets around her and tried to understand. 'Smiling and waving?' she said. 'Doesn't sound too threatening to me.'

Curran scowled at her and strode to the bathroom on the pretext of needing a mirror to comb his hair.

Martha realized she had been flippant, and tried to

rescue herself by calling after him. 'He was set free from . . . what did you say . . . a "nuthouse"?'

'A place up north,' Curran said. 'A secure hospital for the criminally insane, like Broadmoor and Rampton. It's called Mogden.'

Martha shuddered inwardly. She knew the name. It was where she and Hagerty had collected her father. She reached for her cigarettes and lit one, trying not to inhale too deeply lest it made her cough. 'Oh . . .' Her voice was unsteady and she kept her contribution brief. 'When was this?'

'Five weeks ago. Six maybe.'

'Oh . . .'

Christ! The reporters, the TV crews . . . the photographers. It all came back to her. It was the same day. The very same *time* her father had been released. She remembered Hagerty trying to convince himself that the presence of the press was of no import: 'Your father'll be part of the entourage, unnoticed amid all the excitement.'

'Part of the entourage . . .' Martha muttered.

'What?'

'Nothing.'

Martha felt the onset of deep sadness. She had intended to tell Curran about her father. Not yet, but some time soon. Now, she knew she couldn't. It was all too close, too tight. Her father and Curran's father. Geneva. And now Dany's visions and the day she collected her daddy from a secure hospital for the criminally insane.

She stubbed out the cigarette as Curran came back into the bedroom. He was about to tell her how the same man had attacked him in New York, but she stopped him short by wrapping her arms around his head and pulling him towards her until his lips touched her breasts.

231

She wanted to lose herself in more love-making. But she felt tragic and she knew why.

True lovers didn't keep secrets.

The giant towered above Kipini as she cowered with the others behind the fallen tree. His hair had been flattened into streaks by the sudden rain and his right fist clutched the stone he had used to do what he had just done. Half of a shattered flint. Long, jagged and sharp with a line of droplets clinging to its lower edge – some as clear as the rain, others sticky and crimson like dyed tears.

He stared glassily at Kipini . . . and reminded her of someone she knew. The man who had spoken to her at the ranch, before they left for the base camp. She was sure it was him. It had to be – didn't it?

Three other men in black suits were running towards them, shouting and yelling. But they were still too far away.

Kipini looked up at the giant and whimpered. 'Don't hurt us,' she begged. 'Don't do what you did to her. Please, sir . . .'

But the giant was unmoved. And like the animals she had grown up with, Kipini felt an instinct for survival.

'Run!' she cried. 'We must run!'

'NO! STAY EXACTLY WHERE YOU ARE!'

It was *his* voice. Now she was certain. But what did he want with her? Why had he been in Switzerland? Why had he come to Africa?

The giant raised his arm and tightened his grip around the flintstone – and in an instant his intentions became crystal-clear.

'Why were you watching?' he boomed. 'What business is it of yours?'

'None, sir,' Sari piped up.

'Spies!' the giant accused, ignoring their age, ignoring their snuffles and their pitiful, terrorized faces. 'Spies out to trap me, to destroy me . . .'

'No!' Stefanie was not sure what he meant, but knew he was wrong.

'. . . Unless I destroy you first.'

'Don't hurt us,' Kipini repeated.

'Hurt?' The giant smiled in a fatherly way as if he had, after all, recognized their tender years. 'It won't hurt. See – '

He spread the fingers of his left hand on the wet bark of the pine, stretching them as widely as possible until his thumb and little finger were pointing in opposite directions. Without hesitation and with not the slightest grunt or snarl, he brought the flintstone down on the hand with all the force he could muster.

It sliced into his second finger between wedding ring and knuckle, yet still he did not cry out. When he lifted the flintstone, Kipini saw blood and dirt fill the gaping fissure in his flesh.

The stone flashed down again and again and again. There were dreadful noises. Crunches, tears and rips. The top half of the assaulted finger flicked to one side, making an angle with the lower half, until a final blow severed it altogether.

It jumped into the air and hit Dany in the face before flying on into the undergrowth. Dany screamed so hard she hurt her throat.

'Don't!'

'Stop!'

'Jesus Christ!'

Kipini heard the cries of the three rushing men, but her gaze stayed fixed on the giant. For one brief moment, he hesitated to examine the stump of his finger, watching blood pump over his ring until gold disappeared beneath flowing scarlet. But he said nothing, felt nothing. And soon, the twin furnaces that were his eyes switched firmly back to the girls.

'You saw. . .' he muttered. 'You would all betray me, too.'

The stone in his hand hurtled towards Kipini and she knew she would be the first to die.

The only way to stop him was to wake up.

Please, God of all creatures on this earth, let me wake up. Now.

Knapp crouched low as he crept from his tent. A cobra slipped silently past him, but he was not concerned. Human beings were by far the more dangerous predators. Life had taught him that.

He glanced constantly to right and left, checking on the positions of the rangers. There were eight in all, two on each side of a corral that penned in the six rows of ex-army tents which made up Base Camp Three. One was tapping the side of his rifle as if to indicate he was ready for action. But the presence of the cobra confirmed Knapp's suspicions that the rangers were not as alert as they might have been.

Second-class, he thought to himself. Planet Earth was blighted by the overwhelming numerical dominance of the second-class. If only there could be more like him. Just the idea was invigorating.

It was 3 A.M. – and Knapp had expected to tread quietly. Yet the cacophony thrown up by the creatures of the night, massing around a waterhole two miles away, gave him unexpected cover. A chorus of insatiable frogs and crickets and bats, topped off by the trumpeting of a bull elephant, it seemed to be amplified by the rare

Kenyan air and was a stark reminder to the trespassers in the camp about whose country this was.

Knapp paused for a moment to pinpoint Kipini's tent. It was at the far side of the camp from his, that much he knew. But which row? He had watched her take her leave from the supper around the campfire and crawl into her tent to sleep. But that had been from a different angle. And now, if he was honest with himself, one tent looked much the same as the others. He scolded himself for not concentrating harder at the vital time, surprised that a man of his calibre should have been so slack.

'It happens to us all,' he murmured in self-defence. 'Even Khrushchev slipped up in the end.'

The campfire, surrounded by a cluster of red-robed Masai tribesmen who had wandered into the corral in the hope of an effortless meal, was still burning. Knapp decided to wheel around to the other side of it, so he could get his bearings from behind his position at supper.

He made deliberately slow progress, taking care not to trip over guy ropes or raise too much dust with his footsteps, but he reached his new hiding place within twenty minutes. He scanned the campfire and beyond. Visibility was restricted by the great grasshopper legs of the Masai, seated in a circle with bony knees stretching up to their chins and vast crescents of beads dangling from their necks. But when one moved to stoke the embers, he saw it. A tent two rows away from the line nearest the fire. Kipini's tent.

It had a white kerchief tied to one of its upright poles, shining like a beacon in the glare of the full moon. Knapp shook his head and smiled. Doubtless Kipini had told the party to seek out the white kerchief if they needed to find her in an emergency, but Knapp had missed the briefing. Two mistakes, he reflected. There would not be a third.

Within minutes, the white kerchief would be a signal of surrender.

He ringed the camp again, hopping lightly from toe to toe like the infant antelope he had seen the day before. Kipini's tent was slightly isolated from the rest, as befitted her status. That was good.

He took time to unzip its door flap, holding it in position lest a sudden rush of night air woke her. Once inside, he closed the zip – and they were cocooned together.

It was a large tent, big enough to sleep four or five. Its canvas filtered the light of the moon, but was not thick enough to black it out entirely and Knapp had no difficulty in seeing.

Kipini was in a lightweight sleeping bag on an air bed pushed against one side. The rest of the floor was crammed with the tools of her trade: maps, car keys, torches and handbooks fighting for space with a leather medical bag and a short-wave radio.

Knapp had to fight an urge to laugh out loud. No good you being the doctor, he told her in his thoughts, because you will also be the patient. And no good you being the radio operator, because it will be you whom they will come to fetch. Too many eggs in one basket, my dear. Always best to delegate and diversify. That way, you don't get caught.

Knapp crawled towards her on his hands and knees. The moment he reached her head, he saw she was restless. Her eyelids were flickering and she was uttering a string of incomprehensible words.

He watched her as she dreamed, and talked to her like the little girl she was. 'Such a pixie face,' he whispered. 'Such a turned-up nose. Such big brown eyes. Tell me, what did they see?'

Kipini's body jerked violently. She tried to turn over, to calm herself, but the spasm continued intermittently. Knapp seized his chance when her head slipped off the down pillow that was her one concession to luxury in the bush. In one swift movement, he grabbed the pillow and placed it firmly over her nose and mouth.

The pressure woke her, and Knapp heard her muffled cries trying to force their way through the fabric and feathers that were smothering her.

She lashed out with her arms and her hands, but, with no target in sight and no idea of what was happening, her flailings were useless. She tried to kick, but her legs were hemmed in by the sleeping bag.

Knapp felt the generator inside him feeding great bursts of power to his wrists. He held on as Kipini's resistance reached a peak – and smiled with the satisfaction of a job well done as it began to fade. Soon, Kipini's arms went limp and flopped by her side. Knapp moved his palms to the centre of the pillow and pushed harder.

'I let you go once, even though you were a *very* bad girl,' he said. 'But not this time, sweetness. Oh no, not this time.'

When he was sure she was dead, he released his grip, lifted her head and slid the pillow back into position.

Before he left, he curled his finger around a loose strand of her hair and tidied it by hooking it behind her ear. Softly, he sang her the first bars of a song which, in the circumstances, seemed appropriate.

'Sleep, little baby, don't say a word . . .'

18

Dany felt like Frankenstein's monster as Ciera fixed the electrodes for what she called the 'hook-up'.

'Ow! What are you doing?' Dany cried as she felt a stinging on the top of her skull.

'Scraping the surface of your skull with a spatula,' Ciera replied. 'Otherwise the electrodes can't pick up the current.'

'Current?' Dany shifted uneasily in her upright wooden chair and curled her fingers into the folds of her nightdress.

'Sit still,' Ciera said firmly.

'Sorry . . .'

Ciera carried on scraping. 'Our bodies are humming with electric currents, particularly up here, in the head. It's the outer surface of the skin which keeps 'em to ourselves.'

'Otherwise we'd all go around giving shocks to each other?'

'Something like that. Though we're only talking about fifty millionths of a volt, so I doubt if we would exchange huge flashes of lightning.'

Ciera pushed the first electrode on to the scratched skin, squirting a dab of glue on top to keep it in place, and drying the glue with a blast of hot air from some hidden machine.

'Don't worry – the glue will come off when you next wash your hair, if not before.'

Ciera repeated the procedure, substituting sticky tape

for glue, to position the remaining five electrodes. One to the side of each eye, one on the left earlobe, one on the chin and one on the jowl.

'What do they do?' Dany asked.

'You want me to get technical?'

'No – but I want to understand.'

Ciera was happy to oblige. Curious guinea pigs were often good dreamers, in the sense that they could remember what they saw. Ciera fed off good dreamers, but was especially pleased that Dany was showing early potential. Of all the dreamers in the world, Dany *needed* to remember.

'The current between the right and left-eye electrodes and the earlobe electrode measures right and left-eyeball movement respectively. The skull and earlobe electrodes measure brain waves and the chin and jowl electrodes measure muscle activity. When you are plugged in next door, I will get four readings on my polygraph. When the readings demonstrate certain patterns at the same time, I will know you are in REM sleep.'

'REM sleep?'

'REM stands for Rapid Eye Movement. It happens when you dream. Your eyeballs dart around, back and forth – and all sorts of other weird and wonderful things go on.'

'Like what?'

'It starts off with small convulsive twitches of the face and fingertips. Breathing becomes irregular. Very fast – pant, pant, pant – and then slow. Sometimes it seems as though people stop breathing for several seconds; you wouldn't believe it. Then the eyes flicker. I've gently pulled back the eyelids of some dreamers. They seem to be actually looking at something. It's all very strange. Blood flow in the head gets quicker and brain temperature soars. But the large muscles of the body are absolutely paralysed. Arms, legs, trunk, the lot. Men get huge erections. You should see them. Like a baked salami!'

Dany laughed. Ciera was a wonderful practitioner of her art, she thought. Forthright, but not severe. Intelligent, but not intense. Dany began to relax for the first time in weeks.

'So does this happen *every* night?' she asked.

Ciera tut-tutted. 'Usually five or six *times* every night. An adult sleeping for eight hours will normally spend one and a half to two hours in REM sleep . . . often made up of several short B-movies topped off with an hour-long feature film.'

'My films are horror films.'

Ciera rested a hand on Dany's shoulder and said: 'I know, dear. I know.'

Ciera fixed a tiny speaker inside Dany's left ear and led her to the bedroom next door. Dany carried her own pony-tail of wires leading from the electrodes on her head to a multi-coloured collection of small plastic plugs.

The bedroom was another ad-hoc affair. An old metal bed which looked as if it had started life in a Dickensian poorhouse was tucked into one corner amid a plethora of discarded cupboards, drawers and scratched filing cabinets.

Ciera apologized and joked about how her guinea pigs had christened it the Hilton. She showed Dany the bedside lamp and advised her to read for a while before settling down to sleep. Then, as Dany lifted herself into the bed, she plugged each wire into a jack box on the wall beside the bed's headboard.

'A cable runs from the jack box to my polygraph next door.' She took hold of the pony-tail of wires and swung them gently to and fro. 'Plenty of slack. They won't stop you sleeping.'

Dany slid her hand along the wires until it took hold of Ciera's. Her apprehension had returned, and she tightened her grip. 'Don't leave me!' she said with a sudden panic in her voice.

Ciera pointed to an infra-red camera which hung from the ceiling on the far side of the room. It was positioned at an angle to enable it to scan all but the foot of the bed.

'I've a monitor next door,' Ciera said reassuringly. 'I'll be able to see you all night.'

'Are you sure?'

Ciera tried to divert Dany's thoughts by telling her a story about her last subject. 'He was a student called Tony,' she said. 'Just before he went to bed, Margie – a colleague from across the corridor – came into my office and asked me how to spell measles. Tony's dreams were covered in spots all night. Everything he saw was through a filter of great red blotches! So you'll probably dream of great big salamis . . .'

Dany smiled, but it was not convincing and Ciera became more serious.

'Don't worry, Dany. I won't let you – ' She was about to say 'go', but thought better of it. 'I won't let anything happen to you.'

Dany opened her book and began to read. Ciera said 'Goodnight' and returned to her office. After half an hour, she saw Dany settle down on the TV monitor – and transferred her attention to the fevered scribblings of the polygraph. Like most first-timers in such an alien environment, Dany took a while to get to sleep. But by 2 A.M. she was dreaming.

* * *

'Come on, Dany, let go.' Mam'selle shook her hand, but Dany kept hold of it, as she had done since the men in black suits returned the Seven Swans to the schoolmistress in the woods.

Dany could not see what happened immediately after the reunion, but she knew now she was back in the comforting womb of her classroom. The twenty-four desks in six rows of four. Drawing books and paint pots scattered across the shelf under the panoramic window. The class calendar pinned to a cork board at the back of the room. As Girl of the Week, Dany had filled in imminent events the previous Monday, giggling with excitement as she scrawled the misspelled words Class Spring Picknick.

Now there was no laughter. Mam'selle, usually so carefree and relaxed, was agitated and bad-tempered. Finally, using all the strength she could summon, she prised herself free from Dany's grip. Dany burst into tears and threw her face into her hands.

'That is enough, my little girl,' Mam'selle said with unknown severity.

'But, Mam'selle,' Dany protested. 'We saw it. We all saw it. It was horrible. Awful.'

'You are shocked, Dany. It is natural. You became afraid when you got lost, that's all. You will be all right in a minute. Perfectly all right, you'll see.'

'No! It was real. It happened. Honest . . .'

'Dany, I am trying my hardest not to be angry with you. Girls sometimes stray and become lost. There is no need to make up such a story. No need at all.'

Dany tried again, but Mam'selle refused even to listen. She turned her back and busied herself by flicking grime from the drying dresses of the dirtiest girls, and brushing their hair in an advance attempt to placate parents certain to be angry at the state of their children.

'It was an outdoor picnic,' she announced loudly so all the girls could hear, absorb and pass on to mothers and fathers. 'The weather is always unpredictable at this time of year. The storm came from out of the blue. We all got soaked. We had to tramp through mud and, naturally, our clothes brushed against filthy wet trees and bushes. There, you see, it's not so unreasonable.'

'Mam'selle . . .'

'*Non, Dany! Ça suffit!*'

Dany screamed in frustration. It was a high-pitched scream that rebounded from the walls of the classroom like an echo. She couldn't stop. She screamed and screamed and screamed until she was sure her eardrums would shatter like glass.

'Dany . . . Dany.' The voice came to her from afar, but was enough finally to jolt her from unconsciousness.

When she was fully awake, she realized that the scream she could not stop was not a scream at all, but the sharp whine shrieking from the tiny speaker in her ear, set off by Ciera to wake her during REM sleep.

A shadow that was Ciera stood above her, microphone in hand, tape recorder strapped across her shoulder. 'Tell me,' Ciera said firmly. 'Tell me what you were dreaming about.'

Dany remembered every detail, every facial expression and every word that passed between her and Mam'selle. She rattled them off without any need for prompting.

It was only when Ciera sensed Dany was drying up, that the dream was slipping away into nowhere, that she intervened to squeeze out more information. 'Why wouldn't Mam'selle listen to you?'

Dany shook her head. It felt heavy and she knew she

wanted to sleep again. 'It was useless arguing with her,' she said. 'The men in the woods had convinced her that nothing had happened.'

'What men?'

'The men in the black suits.'

'Who were they? Why were they there?'

'I don't know.' Dany's concentration was waning. 'Leave me alone. I want to sleep.'

'Why were they there?' Ciera's demand was strident, and provoked an equally fierce response from Dany.

'I don't know! I've told you that once already. Now leave me alone, God damn you. Leave me alone and go away!'

Ciera knew there was nothing more to be done. She switched off her tape recording, tucked Dany's duvet around her shoulders and left the room.

Dany dreamed three more times during the night. Ciera woke her each time.

One vision centred on an old wrecked car – doorless, wheelless and covered in rust – that had been abandoned in the woods amid the brambles and the bluebells. Another was of a scarecrow that could walk and talk. The third was a repeat of the first.

In the morning, Dany could remember nothing.

Curran shook Jute by calling him at Mogden hospital.

The nurse was beside himself. 'What are you, crazy,' he said. 'I'll be sacked if they find out.'

'Don't worry,' Curran said. 'I told them I was your bank manager.'

'What's it all about? Why are you hassling me?'

'I'm running out of time. When was Crosby admitted? I need the answer.'

244

'I've got it,' Jute said as if he had known all along. 'I was going to contact you tonight.'

'Tell me now.'

'The eighth of May, 1960. Thirty years ago, as near as dammit. So . . . how much?'

Curran was in no mood to bargain. 'Another two hundred,' he said generously.

'Done,' Jute said. 'My bank manager *will* be pleased.'

Curran hung up, lost in thought. The eighth of May 1960. When the Swans were six years old – and in Geneva. It was beginning to add up.

Martha steeled herself and said: 'So where'd you go, Daddy?'

Knapp was absorbed in unpacking his suitcase, and did not reply. Martha clung on to a bedpost for support. She was nervous, but determined to challenge him.

'Why didn't you tell me you were going? It's a bit odd, don't you think? Just disappearing like that. How do you think I felt?'

Knapp grunted. Without looking at Martha, he said: 'You're not my guardian angel. You don't have to worry about me. I'm perfectly aware of what I'm doing.'

Martha gritted her teeth and persisted. 'So where'd you go?' she repeated.

'Oh good Christ!' Knapp threw a shirt to the floor in exasperation and turned to face her. 'Africa,' he snapped. 'I went to Africa. There, now will you stop grilling my ass?'

Martha wouldn't. 'Africa? Why Africa?'

Knapp fixed his eyes on hers to out-stare her, as he knew he would. 'What the hell do people go to Africa for? To see *animals*, for Christ's sake. Wild animals.'

'Oh . . .' Martha had to look away, flattened by the

245

ferocity of Knapp's glare and the apparent innocence of his answer. Knapp brushed past her with the subtlety of a bull. Martha was knocked off balance – and it was only her hold on the bedpost which saved her from falling. She was enraged and followed Knapp to the kitchen to continue the confrontation, but he stopped her in her tracks by turning, waggling a finger at her and growling: 'Don't!'

She let it go – and even volunteered to finish his unpacking, an offer which he accepted with grace. She asked him if he wanted her to stay the night, to keep him company. He replied that it was up to her.

They watched TV together in an uncomfortable silence, the picture before them constantly changing as Knapp pressed every available button on his infra-red channel control, unable to make up his mind what to choose.

'It's all crap,' he mumbled towards midnight. 'Visual valium for morons.'

'Then why are we looking at it?' Martha said.

'Why indeed . . .' Knapp pressed his final button, this time to switch off. Without further ado, he said, 'Goodnight' and went to his room.

Martha, clearing up the evening's debris of empty plates and bourbon glasses, was confused, but heartened.

It was the weakest glimmer of hope. But Knapp's 'Why indeed . . .' had been the first time, the very first time since she picked him up from Mogden, that he had conceded that she might – just might – have a point.

He was grateful again when she made him breakfast the following morning, and she decided to capitalize.

She poured him another cup of coffee and said in a concerned tone: 'Daddy . . . you're not still working for the government, are you? I mean, first Europe – and now Africa.'

Knapp thought hard before replying. He wanted to

scream at her to mind her own business. That he had already given her answers that should suffice. But the girl was showing promise. She had helped him unpack and had cooked him ham and eggs. Maybe, before she went back to work, she would clean the apartment.

'I told you about Africa,' he said calmly. 'I went on safari.'

'I thought safaris lasted at least a couple of weeks. You were back here within ten days.'

One more chance, Knapp thought, and then your interfering must stop. 'There was an accident. One of the people in the party got hurt. Bitten by a snake. Not fatally, but it was nasty enough to make a lot of us realize we weren't getting the protection to which we were entitled. We had a vote. Half of us decided to ask for our money back and come home. The other half stayed.'

Now, Martha thought. While he is being warm and thoughtful. While there is an opportunity to sweep away the barriers between us. Hagerty had warned her not to. 'Don't,' he had said. 'Not under any circumstances. It might cause a relapse.'

But her determination had carried over from the night before. She could not help herself. 'Daddy . . .' she began, reaching out to touch his face. 'We've never talked about what happened before you were locked away in that awful place. Hagerty has told me bits and pieces, but not everything, I'm sure. Will you tell me? Now?' She withdrew her hand as soon as she asked the question, half expecting him to erupt like a volcano.

He stayed where he sat, sipping his coffee and betraying not a hint of emotion. But behind his façade, he finally understood. Like the dawn of time, the *motive* for her constant bombardment of questions came shining over the horizon. It was the same motive that drove her to

247

pester him and cajole him, the same motive that spurred her futile attempts to ingratiate herself with him.

She was a spy for the Russians.

Khrushchev, damn the wily old buzzard, had gotten to his own daughter. And he was using *her* to undermine *him*.

He had to laugh at the cheek of it, and fleetingly wondered if Martha was an unwitting pawn. But he rejected the notion, on the grounds that her questions and her timing had lacked both innocence and spontaneity.

He chortled again as he pushed his coffee mug away with a single, firm finger. 'It won't work,' he said as he rose to his feet.

'W – what?' Martha stuttered. She took a step backwards, frightened by the eerie grin that distorted his face. But she was not fleet enough.

With a speed that took her by surprise, Knapp punched her in the jaw with a clenched fist. The blow lifted her off her feet and sent her sprawling.

As she lay spreadeagled on the floor, he looked down at her and shouted: 'Traitor! You and the others. You're all the same. Now get out and don't come back!'

Martha, sobbing, crawled on her hands and knees to collect her things, terrified that he would attack her again and maim her . . . or worse. He watched her go – and as she took one last glance at him, something dawned on her, too.

He was her father, but he was not normal.

She felt a combination of fear and pity as she scrabbled down the emergency stairway to the safety of the street.

She ran to the bar around the corner from her own apartment, turning up the collar of her coat to disguise her swelling jaw. As she downed her first bourbon, she felt a resurgence of the very determination which had led to the pain that was spreading across her face.

There were questions about her father that needed answers. And Hagerty would have to provide them.

Knapp was glad to be rid of her, and was only sorry he could not be a fly on the wall of the Kremlin when Khrushchev found out.

'Oh Nikita,' he said aloud. 'Maybe you'll have a chuckle, too. But I know you. You'll try to find another way of tripping me up. How you love to plan ahead. But you won't do it, you old jackal. There'll be *strength* in the White House, not weakness. Jack Kennedy's determination – and my power.'

He walked to his desk and opened a drawer, pulling his list of targets from beneath a sheaf of other papers on which he had scrawled memoranda to party colleagues and useful camp followers.

'You won't stop me, Khrushchev,' he said. 'And neither will they.'

He crossed out Kipini's name . . . and circled Sari's.

19

Sari was frantic as she spoke to Dany on the phone. 'It's Kipini,' she said, her voice shaking with disbelief. 'She's dead.'

Dany, numb from head to toe, could not reply.

'She's *dead*,' Sari repeated more emphatically.

Dany forced herself to speak. 'How?'

'They don't know. She was in the back of beyond in Kenya, and she was the only one there with any medical knowledge. By the time they got her body to Nairobi, a post-mortem was all but useless and . . . oh, I can't say it.'

Sari's panic was beginning to veer out of control. Dany, even though she was mortified, found herself in the role of calming influence, just as she had been when the two were schoolfriends. When Sari was ready, she said: 'Someone must know how.'

'It was Kipini's father who called,' Sari said. 'He was so dignified, but you could tell he was – '

'What did he say?'

'That it could have been natural causes – or murder.'

'Murder?'

'They don't know. But they are questioning some of Kipini's rangers – and an old flame of hers who turned out to be at the camp where she was . . .'

'Killed.' Dany finished off the sentence, for both women knew the truth.

They talked about what was going on, about how four of their little tribe had died within weeks, about how the three who remained needed to give each other strength, about Dany's attempts to mine her memories to find the solution – and about what they should do next.

'Does Mai-Lin know?' Dany asked.

'I'll call her next. Oh heavens – ' Sari had been threatening to burst into tears, and now she could hold back no longer. When she became coherent again, Dany heard her softly chanting: 'Swans don't cry, swans don't lie. Swans stay together until they . . .'

Dany wanted to hug her, to tell her everything would be all right. She cursed the 12,000 miles of land and sea that were between them and did her best to offer advice without sounding desperate. 'Tell Mai-Lin to take care,' she said. 'And you do the same. You have a good husband. Make sure he protects you. Make sure he understands.'

She glanced across at Curran. He was sitting on the edge of an armchair, shocked but desperate to hear more about Kipini's fate. Perhaps he did not qualify as a good husband, but he heard what Dany said and nodded at her as if to promise: You can rely on me.

At work, Curran called Lieutenant Favero in New York and told him of Kipini's death. When Favero asked him what the hell he was talking about, he finally lost his temper.

'Just get in touch with the cops in Kenya,' he yelled. 'Send them the photo. Ask if anyone saw the same guy who attacked me. Dammit, man, you've got to believe me. Just fucking do *something*, will you?'

Favero did not reply before hanging up.

Knapp flew to Sydney executive-class, choosing TWA as his carrier rather than PanAm, who, he now knew, were harbouring a spy.

Spy . . . spy . . . spy. The world was full of spies, and always had been.

One of the air stewards reminded him of Lyall, the gung-ho military attaché who had broken the news of the U2 spy-in-the-sky crisis two weeks before the 1960 Paris summit.

'What's a U2?' Napier had asked blithely as Lyall ushered them into the privacy of a side room at the Palais des Nations. The attaché looked at them darkly. The four diplomats on the receiving end of his glare – Napier, Hagerty, Lipton and Knapp – were accustomed to it, for they knew how Lyall despised their dialogue with the Russians, just as they loathed his rampant militarism – the legacy, they assumed, of his bloody work as a behind-enemy-lines Ranger in the Korean War. But this time there was something different glowing in his eyes. Something between gloom and anger. He was warning them to expect bad news.

'The U2 is a high-altitude reconnaissance aircraft,' he said. 'One was shot down by the Russians four days ago, on May Day.'

'Where?' Hagerty said urgently.

'Over Russian territory,' Lyall responded without delay. 'They hit it with a rocket. The pilot survived. His name is Garry Powers. He's being held by the Soviets.'

A hush descended over the room, broken only by the gentle tinkling of a chandelier's breeze-stroked crystal. The four diplomats stood with chins in hands, absorbing the news. They all knew what it meant. That years of gruelling toil in preparing the ground for the Paris summit had likely been shot down in flames by American reck-lessness and a Russian missile.

Lyall confirmed their worst fears with his next revel-ation. 'Khrushchev's gone berserk in the Supreme Soviet.

He warned of a devastating response and said Russia had rockets ready to be fired around the clock. There were shouts from the floor of "Down with the aggressors" and "Down with the bandits". Eisenhower has ordered an inquiry.'

'Good Lord.' Lipton could not phrase it in any other way, but the pain was still evident. They all felt it. It was the pain of impending failure.

Napier brushed his moustache, praying that a stiff upper lip would see him through. Hagerty banged his fist on a table, making a vase of flowers tip over and sending a bulbous rivulet of water winding across varnished walnut. Lipton pulled his watch from his waistcoat and checked it, as if wishing he could wind back its hands to give someone time to order Garry Powers to turn his blasted U2 around and head for home. One by one, they all turned to Knapp – and waited for the inspiration that only he could provide.

Knapp remembered their pleading, begging faces. What to do? What shall we do, Donald? How can we placate the Russians? What will we say at the conference table? He remembered the water from the toppled vase dripping on his feet as if hope itself was ebbing away. And above all, he remembered the *pressure*.

You see, he wanted to tell them, just this morning, just before we came here to be informed of this crisis, Yelena told me she was pregnant. And you know what? She wants to tell the world about it. About us. After all this time. Can you imagine? Can you imagine what it will do to me? It will finish me. Destroy me. No more marching to the White House. Kennedy will throw me to the dogs like an old bone. First Yelena and now this. There's only one thing to do.

And then he started to laugh. It was just a chuckle at

253

first, but it soon swelled into great booming bellows of hilarity that made tears the size of pearls run down his cheeks.

The other diplomats were taken aback. Lyall was outraged. In an instant, he slipped a hand inside his tunic, pulled a six-inch assault knife from its sheath and began waving it under Knapp's nose.

'Don't do that!' he shouted. 'They've got our boy, and you shouldn't laugh.'

Hagerty and Napier leaped forward to restrain him, but he carried on yelling.

'Commie bastards! It's a taste of this sharp metal they need, not all the goddamn talking and fraternizing and patting on the back that you guys go in for. Sharp metal, that's what showed 'em in Korea.' He flashed the knife to and fro in a criss-cross pattern. 'That's what I did to them. Carved them into diamonds of sliced flesh, then hung their bodies from a tree to warn their motherfucking comrades to expect more of the same.'

Hagerty squeezed his wrist to make him let go of the blade. Lyall was stronger, and held on. But the struggle made him realize he had lost control of himself, and he eventually allowed his grip to loosen. The knife clattered to the floor.

As the others led Lyall away, soothing his fury and apologizing for their colleague's inexplicable behaviour, Knapp's laughter subsided. A twinkle from the knife caught his attention and he stared at it vacantly, seeing its detail for the first time.

It was an uncomplicated weapon. Piebald bone handle, bronze sleeve and slippery, shining, straight steel blade. Its uncluttered purity reminded Knapp of the edge of a glacial crevasse.

254

'Beautiful but dangerous,' he muttered. 'Just like Yelena.'

Knapp chuckled again as the lookalike air steward passed by with a blanket for a fatigued passenger.

'You forgot your knife,' he called out. But the steward did not hear.

Martha told Hagerty she had flown to Washington especially to see him. He felt duty-bound to agree to a meeting, but did not want her in his office at State. He suggested they look at the Japanese cherry blossom in East Potomac Park.

They savoured the fresh spring zephyr amid the joggers and tourists on the perimeter road beside the Washington Channel. As they walked, Hagerty seduced Martha with his amiability, which bordered on the flirtatious, and his apparent command of the situation.

'I can understand your concern about your father,' he said, taking her arm. 'Especially if, as you say, he has struck you.'

Martha baulked at Hagerty's implied doubt of her story. 'Twice,' she said firmly. 'He's hit me twice.'

'Quite unforgivable, I agree,' Hagerty concurred. 'But as I have told you before, the adjustment your father is being required to make is immense. He must of necessity be under a great deal of stress. You know how it is, Martha. People under pressure often take it out on their nearest and dearest, for who else is there? How many times have you heard a harassed wife moan, "Everyone at the office thinks he's so damn wonderful – they should see the bastard at home."'

Martha found herself nodding in agreement. Hagerty was giving her the same line as before, she thought. His consistency was absolute. It caused her to doubt herself, but she was not yet convinced.

'What about his trips to Europe and Africa?'

'Your father is free to come and go as he pleases,' Hagerty responded. 'What reason did he give you for the journey to Africa, for example?'

'Safari. To see animals.'

'Well then.' Hagerty clapped his hands as if it was all much ado about nothing. 'A yearning for wide-open spaces. A desire to see Mother Nature at work. What would you do if you had been locked up for thirty years?'

It was the cue Martha had been waiting for, but she hesitated. Hagerty sensed what was coming and tried to head it off by offering to treat her at the park's snack bar. She accepted, and was happy to make small-talk as they sipped tea and nibbled Danish pastries. But as Hagerty dabbed at his mouth with a serviette, she came out with it.

'Does everyone under stress have the same violent streak as my father?' she said. 'Did you tell me the truth about why he was put in Mogden?'

Hagerty was ready. When one pack of lies is questioned, tell another under the guise of truth. It worked every time. Folk were so desperate to believe, especially damaged souls like Martha.

'Not totally,' he said. It was a shocking admission, yet he tranquillized it instantly with a smile and a new outpouring of information, delivered in a brisk monotone. 'He was never a spy. He never worked for the CIA. That was just a cover story to explain his disappearance. A story which, I regret, I was forced to perpetuate.'

He looked at Martha apologetically, but did not delay. 'Your father flipped during the run-up to the 1960 Paris summit meeting between Eisenhower, Khrushchev and the

256

British Prime Minister of the time, Macmillan. He had been a key figure in pre-negotiations that went on at Geneva and elsewhere. I was on the same team. We all thought he was a shooting star – in fact we called him the Comet. But what none of us knew was that he was as vulnerable, as unsure, as the rest of us mere mortals. It all became too much for him. On a flying visit to London, to talk to the Brits, he snapped and went berserk. He was working in the basement of a British government building close to Whitehall at the time. Looking up records, doing some kind of research. It *was* a classified establishment that did not officially exist. And he *did* set fire to it. Left nothing but a pile of ash and three charred corpses.'

Martha asked about the poor victims, but Hagerty refused to be sidetracked.

'Naturally,' he continued, 'the British were appalled. For one thing, years of hard, dangerous work had gone up in smoke. Espionage work that had cost many more lives of valued personnel than the three who died in the basement. For another, they doubted your father's motives. There were whispers about him working for the Reds, that sort of thing.'

Martha gasped, but Hagerty held up a hand to warn her not to jump ahead.

'It could have built up into some diplomatic incident – and at such a sensitive time,' he said. 'Neither Britain nor America could afford a public argument in front of the Russians, who would not only have been gloating, but also in a more powerful position for the Paris disarmament talks ranged against a divided Western alliance. So decisions were made. Instant decisions. Medical tests were carried out, and it was determined that your father was clearly unbalanced. Nevertheless the British, with some justification, demanded that as your father's act had

257

been carried out on their territory, secret territory at that, then he had to stay in Britain so they could keep tabs on him. We agreed. Reluctantly, but there was little else we could do. It was also apparent that it would probably be some time before he was fit again. So what the hell to do with him? He could not be nursed privately. And besides, without security he could have escaped. Imagine how the British perceived the situation. A madman on the loose, his head stuffed with classified information. Oh come on . . .'

'So it had to be Mogden,' Martha said.

'Under an assumed identity, yes. No one knew who he really was, and the story that he had gone under was put out among his former colleagues.'

Hagerty, confident his fable had been well told, smiled again and said, 'That's where we came in.'

Martha fell silent. It was so much to take in. She thought she understood, but was not sure. She thought Hagerty was telling the truth. But to her surprise, she felt she was not sure of that, either.

Hagerty ushered her away from the snack bar. As they left the park to look for a cab, he put his arm around her shoulder. The kind uncle again. Strange, she thought, it was reassuring and unnerving at the same time.

He turned her round so she faced him, and looked at her imploringly. 'Martha,' he began. 'You've heard me spout a lot of official-sounding words. Classified . . . summit . . . alliance . . . going under. What does that say to you?'

'That you shouldn't have told me,' Martha replied without hesitation. 'And that I shouldn't tell anyone else.'

Hagerty smiled with genuine gratification. He had seen a dew-drop appear on the pipe-joint, but he had wiped it away. Now, it was time to tighten the union and reseal it with a smooth plastic paste.

'It's rare, and I'm not sure whether it's healthy, but sometimes official considerations are outweighed by personal considerations,' he said. 'I told you because of who you are, and who your father is. We were very close. The tragedy of your father affected me, too. I loved that guy. I still love him today.'

As soon as Martha's cab turned the corner, Hagerty took another to State. He told his secretary he was not to be disturbed, locked himself inside his office to make sure, and picked up the phone.

He tried to call Knapp first, but there was no reply. So he called England and spoke in turn to Lipton and Napier. 'Our man has sprouted wings – he's travelling all over the place,' he said, deliberately avoiding the use of Knapp's name. 'He's hit his daughter, too. Twice.'

Lipton, who had drunk too much vintage port, made it clear he did not see a problem. 'Why should he not travel, old man? And perhaps his daughter is simply being damned annoying. You said yourself she was too clinging, too soon.'

Napier, who left a Cabinet meeting to take the call, was even more forthright. 'He has been declared sane. Three times, by eminent physicians. Lest you need reminding, we acted with the necessary extreme caution. The initial diagnosis confirmed twice, over a period of years. Then a further two-year wait before his eventual release. He is as sane as you or I. He will act like a sane person. I'm afraid you are fretting for nothing.'

Hagerty was forced to agree. But then again, over the years he had come to mistrust the complacency of the British. Especially people like Napier and Lipton.

* * *

259

'Get off! Leave me alone!'

Dany tried to shake herself free of the man in the black suit, but he held firm.

'Sssh,' the man said in a kindly way. 'I'm not going to hurt you. And our friend wasn't going to hurt you.'

'He was!' Dany protested. 'He was going to hurt all of us, wasn't he, Pearl?'

Pearl was rigid with fear, and could say nothing. Another man in a black suit bent to pluck her from her hiding place behind the tree trunk.

Stefanie pointed to both saviours. 'You . . . you tell him not to come back,' she said. And then she fainted. One second she was there, the next she was gone, lying unconscious among the docks. The other girls screamed. Sari whimpered: 'Oh no – not her, too.'

The first man fell on his knees and slapped Stefanie's cheeks.

'Leave her alone!' Dany yelled.

'Stop it!' Kipini shrieked.

'I'm trying to help her,' the man said. 'We're trying to help all of you.'

'No, you're not,' Dany said. 'You're like your friend. You're going to hurt us.'

'Look – ' the man said impatiently. The girls took a step back, and he calmed himself. 'Look, I mean it. We're here to help.'

Stefanie began to come round. As soon as she opened her eyes, they filled with tears. Her sobs grew louder, and prompted the others to weep, too. Soon all seven, their fear released at last, were crying their eyes out.

Dany knew they would all have cried for days and weeks had the rain not stopped as suddenly as it had started. The clatter of water on leaf died away, leaving an eerie silence that made the girls overly conscious of their own cacophony. Dany took her knuckles from her eyes and looked up at the sky. A trailing edge of grey cloud was being blown away, and a renewed spray of faint sunlight began to filter through the damp haze that remained. Dany felt a welcome warmth settle on her shoulders.

The two men shepherded their flock into a circle. One, a tall man with a thick moustache, dropped to his haunches in the centre of the ring. He glanced at the swan emblems on their blazers and nodded knowingly. 'L'École Internationale des Cygnes,' he said. 'Am I right? Were you out for a walk with some others? Are you lost? Do you know where your teacher is?'

'Teacher is?' Pearl said.

'We're with Mam'selle,' Louise volunteered.

'So . . . let's find her, shall we?'

'Where are the other men?' Stefanie demanded suddenly.

'They're gone,' the man with the moustache said. 'They're friends. We're all friends. Perhaps we can be friends, too.'

Stefanie looked at him, grimaced and shook her head.

'Oh well.' The man smiled and shrugged his shoulders. 'We'll still take you to find your Mam'selle. Come on.'

Dany looked over her shoulder to the clearing. The talking black scarecrow had gone. The nasty giant had gone, tugged away into the laurels by the third black-suited man who had rushed to their rescue. Only the rusty car remained. And that, Dany was certain, would stay there for ever.

Their terror came and went as they picked their way through the woods. One moment they were content, glad to be leaving that place and glad to be going back to Mam'selle. The next it all came back. His twisted face. The wet red on his shirt. The sharp flintstone in his hand. The groaning of the rope. The black scarecrow. His unstoppable march towards them.

261

'NO! STAY EXACTLY WHERE YOU ARE!'

Time after time, their progress was interrupted by renewed outbreaks of hysterical sobbing. The two men in black suits wrapped their arms around whichever girl was upset at any given moment.

'Don't worry,' they kept saying. 'You're going to be all right. Everything will be all right.'

It was Stefanie who asked the inevitable question. 'What were they doing?'

The man with the moustache turned and raised his eyebrows, reflecting her inquisitiveness. 'The man and the woman, you mean? Our friends?'

'Mmm.'

'Let me put it this way. Have you been playing in the woods today?'

'Hide and seek,' Dany said. 'I hid first.'

The man chuckled. 'Well then, that's what they were doing. Playing.'

'*What?*' Dany said incredulously.

'Oh, grown-ups play as well, you know. They play at being goodies and baddies, just like you.'

'And that man was being a baddie?' Louise suggested hopefully.

'That's right.'

'I don't believe you,' Stefanie said.

The man turned back to follow the woodland path, taking care to step over an exposed root. 'Why should I tell you fibs?' he called over his shoulder.

'Just forget what you saw,' the second man, who was bringing up the rear of the queue, chimed in. 'It isn't important.'

The words lingered in Dany's mind, growing louder with each repetition.

'Forget what you saw – it isn't important . . . Forget what you saw – it isn't important . . . Forget what you saw – it isn't important . . .'

'No!' she screamed. 'I can't! I won't!'

'It's all right,' Ciera said from nowhere. 'I've got it on tape. Go back to sleep.'

'Girls! *Les enfants!* Please . . .'

'Is that your Mam'selle?' the man with the moustache asked as he heard the distant cry. Sari nodded, and they followed the sound.

Mam'selle, standing in the midst of the rest of the class, wet and wretched and looking as if she too was lost in the woods, spun round when she heard their approach.

The seven girls ran the last few yards towards her. Dany gripped her hand and would not let go. Mam'selle tried to cuddle them all at once and burst into tears of relief. 'Oh thank God,' she said time and again. 'Thank God you're safe.' She stroked their hair, squeezed their shoulders, brushed their cheeks with the back of her hand.

The two men in black suits stood back to watch the reunion.

'They were lost,' the man with the moustache said. 'Alone in the woods. Imagining every noise, every crack of a twig, to be the approach of some ferocious beast. So completely terrified, poor mites.'

Mam'selle looked up. The men were a blur through her tears, but she was so utterly grateful to see them.

'*Merci,*' she gasped. '*Merci infiniment, messieurs.*'

'Our pleasure, mademoiselle,' the second man said courteously.

They allowed her ten minutes to settle and comfort her little charges, then asked her to join them away from the

263

children. When Dany persisted in clinging on, they told Mam'selle to shake her off. She did as requested, but Dany refused to wander far from her side. The three grown-ups turned their backs to her. But Dany could still hear what they were saying.

It was strange. The man with the moustache talked to Mam'selle as if she was a friend. But the second man, who had a big hooked nose and a bony face, was angry with her and spoke loudly. He sounded like Pearl's father did when Pearl's mother hid his cigarettes, and Dany knew he was American.

'They stumbled across a couple making love,' the man with the moustache said. 'We saw them, too, when we walked in on them later. The children didn't understand what was going on.'

'Nothing terribly untoward about that,' the American man said. 'But why were they there in the first place? Why did you let them go? This could be a serious matter, mademoiselle.'

'I know. I'm sorry,' Mam'selle said meekly, as if she accepted their authority without question.

'There could have been the most awful tragedy,' the American man continued. 'These woods are vast. Perhaps the girls would never have been found until they were corpses rotting in the mud. Have you thought of that? Well, have you, girl?'

Mam'selle put her hands together and bowed her head so her fingertips touched her lips, as if she was praying. Dany heard her begin to sob again.

'My colleague and I are quite simply appalled. And we are not without influence in Geneva, as you can imagine. Shall we use that influence to make sure such young children are never again left in the care of a schoolmistress who cannot be trusted?'

'Oh no, monsieur,' Mam'selle begged. 'Please . . .'

'Then may we suggest you take the girls promptly back to where they belong?'

'Yes, messieurs. Of course. Immediately.'

'While we ponder upon whether any disciplinary action should be taken for this monstrous outrage.'

'Yes, messieurs. Thank you. *Merci*.'

When Mam'selle turned round, she was as white as a sheet. Dany gripped her hand again and vowed to herself that she would never let go.

The next she knew, she was back in the classroom and Mam'selle was twitchy and nervous as if she had a fever.

'Come on, Dany, let go!' Mam'selle finally prised herself free. Dany screamed hysterically and ran to the back of the classroom. She plucked the calendar from its hook and threw it on the floor, flinging herself to the ground after it. Using her fingernails, she clawed frenziedly at the date under which she had filled in the details of the picnic.

She could see it as clear as day: 6 May, it was. Printed in red with a black shadow. But now she wanted to erase it for ever, to scratch it from her mind. She cried out as her fingernails broke one by one, but her determination carried her on and she used her thumb to rub the torn paper.

Ignoring Mam'selle's frenetic attempts to make her stop, she rubbed and rubbed. Until nothing was left of 6 May but a hole in a classroom calendar.

20

Knapp watched Sari as she swam in Redleaf Pool, a semi-circle of placid water claimed from Sydney Harbour by an iron-bar fence that kept out the sharks. It had a small beach, populated by a comfortable mixture of gay men and mothers with small children. Sari had three in tow, all boys aged between six and two, pushing model cars through tunnels dug in the sand. As she emerged from the sea, it was clear she was pregnant with a fourth.

Knapp followed her with his eyes as she climbed clumsily up concrete steps leading to the whitewashed café that overlooked the beach. Plain and plump, and wearing a shapeless black swimsuit, she joined two more glamorous friends at an outside table stacked with cocktails and taller glasses of iced Coca-Cola.

For a moment, it looked like the sort of scene Knapp had imagined would typify life in Sydney's affluent eastern suburbs. But the lines of worry on Sari's face told another story. And the way her friends glanced nervously at every passer-by suggested to Knapp they were not there to provide mere company.

Such a frightened rabbit, he thought to himself as he studied his prey. Have you confided in your friends, Sari? And will they save you? I think not, little bunny. I think not.

He watched her at a discreet distance for forty-eight hours, interrupting his vigil with an occasional telephone call to glean more information, until a picture-postcard of her life emerged. Despite her dreary ordinariness, which

Knapp found repulsive, she had nevertheless found contentment. She had a husband, a successful architect who had expanded and fashioned their solar-panelled brownstone house in Bellevue Hill with some panache, and who obviously saw *something* in her. She had a blossoming family. And she had the kind of material possessions expected of her type. A BMW car, Gucci handbag, Yves St Laurent sunglasses. She wore pressed cotton clothes of mellow ochres and greys that blended perfectly with the colours of the New South Wales autumn. And doubtless her damn kitchen was brimming with programmed this and computerized that.

The end result, it occurred to Knapp, was a human being who had restricted her aspirations to the stifling confines of marriage and reproduction. An automaton, waiting for others to switch her on. In that respect, she was dead already. But he knew he had to kill her just the same. Even robots talked.

He left her as she carried out her morning shopping at a delicatessen in Bondi Junction, again under the watchful eyes of her two friends. He would return that night, he decided, to do what had to be done.

He filled in time by taking in the pleasures of Sydney. A cruise around the harbour, lunch at the restaurant in the Opera House and a digestive walk in the botanical gardens nearby.

It should have been a relaxing interlude, but the excitement of the night to come made him feel urgent – and somehow sexual.

A plantation of orchids, waving gracefully in the breeze coming off the Pacific, accentuated the sensation. Symbols of feminine beauty and promise, open and enticing, they stirred in him an overwhelming desire to enter and ejaculate.

He hurried from the gardens into the city centre, where he bought a sack, a tow-rope and a bag to carry them in. Then he took a cab to King's Cross, Sydney's cosmopolitan magnet for gourmets and vice-hunters alike.

After a short search, he found a suitable candidate lounging against the wall to one side of a Malay restaurant. She was about eighteen, Knapp estimated, and Arabian in appearance. She was smoking a small cheroot that smelled of cannabis. Ash fell from its tip and settled on the creases of her leather mini-skirt, but she did not appear to care.

They discussed terms and when an agreement was reached, exchanged knowing glances. The girl laughed when Knapp told her that discretion was essential – and did not blink when he warned her of dire consequences should her tongue work loose.

'A man such as myself has connections,' he said sternly. 'I will find out.'

'Sure . . .' she said languidly.

'So.' He coughed to indicate he was changing the subject. 'What shall I call you? Are you another Miss Twilight?'

'Call me what you like,' the girl said, throwing the remnants of her cheroot into the gutter.

'Good.' Knapp took her by the arm and led her towards a taxi stand. 'Then I shall call you Yelena.'

Spurred on by the revelations thrown up by Dany's second session with Ciera, Curran returned to the library microfiche.

He had a date to work on – 6 May 1960 – and was elated that it tallied with the 8 May admittance date of the American, Crosby. He scoured the news pages of *Times* issues dated 5, 6 and 7 May in an attempt to unearth a tragedy or a crime that could have been witnessed by the seven little girls, thus sowing the seeds of their adult traumas. But the more column-inches he studied, the more his optimism dwindled.

'Nothing,' he told Dany gloomily when he returned home. 'The only event in Geneva was a further round of preliminary talks leading up to the Big Three summit in Paris. And the only big news story was the shooting down of the American U2 spy plane over Russian territory.'

Dany thought for a moment, trying to dust off her knowledge of modern history. 'The pilot,' she said firmly. 'Was it Garry Powers? Was the U2 the same as the Garry Powers thing?'

'Uh-huh. The U2 was shot down on May Day, but Khrushchev announced it in Moscow on 5 May. According to *The Times*, he "startled the Supreme Soviet".'

Dany sighed in frustration. 'I saw the wreck of an old car in the woods, not a bloody plane,' she said icily, as if Curran was somehow responsible.

'You didn't listen,' he said, reflecting her sharpness. 'I said the U2 was shot down over Russia.'

'So where does 6 May get us?'

'Nowhere. Are you sure you got the right date?'

Dany lost her temper. 'Of course I'm sure! No, I'm not. I think . . . oh Christ, I don't know.'

She pulled at her hair and grated her teeth. Curran went to comfort her, but she swung away from him. She had never felt more helpless. Curran, his powers of detection all but spent, had never felt more useless.

Dany ranted for more than a minute, tearing into Curran for having the nerve and the insensitivity to doubt her. She was disappointed in him, she said, for being such a callous bastard. Though she was being unfair, he let her shout. It was a release – and she needed it.

She stopped only when Yvette, woken by the sudden uproar, ran from her bedroom yelling, 'Mummy! Mummy!' Dany let the girl fly into her arms and held her tight. As she cradled Yvette's tiny body, still warm from sleep, it occurred to her that now, at this precise moment, mother and daughter were united in a need to be loved. It stoked her anger against the element needed to complete the chemistry: a man who loved them both.

'What do you care anyway?' she snapped at Curran. 'You've got yourself another woman.'

Curran was as winded as if he had been hit in the stomach by a ramrod, and felt an inexplicable flush of panic, like a small boy found smoking at school. 'How can you be certain?' he said foolishly.

His reply confirmed Dany's suspicions – and now it was she who was reeling. For a moment, they stood motionless, neither with the courage to look at the other, neither knowing what to say next. The presence of Yvette saved them. The child began to yawn, and it was clear she needed to return to bed. Curran volunteered for the task and Dany did not object.

The break in the confrontation calmed them both. Once they were sure Yvette was asleep, they opened a bottle of wine and talked. Dany tried hard to be reasonable, and apologized for being unreasonable earlier. 'A wife knows, that's all,' she said. 'Besides, you are a good-looking man and you are going through the process of divorce. You need a shoulder to cry on, a woman to touch.'

Curran chose to touch Dany, guiding her on to the sofa and massaging her back to soothe away her torment. Their fears about what could happen were left unspoken, but hung in the air like morning mist.

'I won't leave you,' Curran said. 'I promise I won't leave you until this is over.'

Dany wondered how it would end, and shuddered at the thought. She put a hand over her shoulder to grasp Curran's. 'Perhaps the Geneva newspapers?' she suggested quietly.

Curran was certain it would be useless, but tried to disguise his doubt. 'Perhaps,' he said.

The fresh scent of lemon from the trees in Sari's back yard mingled uneasily with a lingering whiff of charcoal smoke from the barbecue party thrown earlier by her neighbours. The pungent mixture drifted into Knapp's nostrils, but he did not let it distract him. He was more concerned with finding a way to break in. Doors had been bolted – and despite the clinging warmth of a humid night and the lack of a hum from the dormant air-conditioning system, every window was shut. Clearly Sari was trying to protect herself, which was amusing. But there were no police and no private security guards, which demonstrated uncertainty and hesitation. Two flaws that would prove fatal to most armies, let alone a plain, plump housewife and her talented, but suburban, husband.

It was a large, furry spider scuttling along the side of the house which gave Knapp a clue. He followed it as it turned to climb the wall and saw it suddenly disappear. Closer investigation revealed it had squeezed into a circular plastic fanlight cut into a large smoked-glass window. The fanlight, eight inches in diameter, had radial louvres. Pull a piece of string one way, and the louvres would open. Pull it the other way, and they would shut.

Knapp chuckled to himself as he saw they were open. The fanlight and the smoked glass suggested a toilet on the other side. And while Sari had been prepared to close all the windows in order to stop a feared attempt on her

271

life, she had not been willing to restrict the airflow in the toilet.

Such a clean, hygienic little girl. But so immature and foolish.

The louvres gave Knapp's gloved fingers a useful grip, but he did not pull too hard lest he make undue noise. Lights were still on next door as they cleaned up after the party. He heaved with constant and prolonged force until the fanlight gave way and slipped out of its grooved frame.

The spider scampered to safety as Knapp thrust his forearm through the resulting hole. By bending his elbow and contorting his wrist, he was able to reach the catch of the main window. Within a minute, it was open and he was inside Sari's last refuge.

For a time, he was disorientated. Sari's husband had gutted the inside of the house and transformed it into an open-plan spectacular of immense size. Traditional concepts of layout had been thrown away and forgotten. In their place were wooden floorboards stretching from one side of the house to the other, partitioned into sections by rough brick walls of varying heights – three feet between lounge and kitchen, four feet between lounge and dining area, five feet between dining area and study, and six feet around the bathroom and toilets, including the one from which he had just stepped. There was no plaster lining – brass fixtures were screwed on to bare brick – no carpets and no ceilings. Stainless-steel columns stretched from ground level to the roof timbers high above, and the upper-level rooms were built on a wide internal balcony which stretched around the perimeter of the building and was supported by angled oak beams. Each upper room was served by its own spiral staircase, again in stainless steel, leading from whichever living area was directly below.

Knapp was suitably impressed, and gave himself time

to find his bearings. Moonlight streaming in from the skylights that pock-marked the roof made his task simpler. They, too, were shut tight, accentuating the oven effect brought on by the closed windows. Knapp broke out in a heavy sweat and decided to carry on with his work before he was overcome by heat. What with the stifling atmosphere of Africa and now this, he was sure the girls were determined to make him suffer to the end.

He took off his jacket and tie, folding them neatly over the arm of a sofa and brushing them with a hand to make sure they would not crease. He unbuttoned the top of his shirt and folded back its sleeves, feeling businesslike as he did so. Finally, mindful of the wooden floor and steel staircases, he took off his shoes to ensure a silent approach.

His next job was to locate Sari. He chose a spiral staircase at random and climbed it. When there was nothing to be found but a room cluttered with drawing equipment, he slipped back down and tried again.

This time, he was more fortunate, his eyes catching sight of the foot of a double bed as soon as his head emerged through the trapdoor-like gap at the top of the stairs.

A single sheet was all that separated Sari and her husband from the night air, but they were both wringing wet with perspiration. She was a preposterous sight, lying on her back with her pregnant hump stretching skywards like a termite mound, straps across her shoulders indicating that, despite the heat, she had still insisted on wearing a nightdress. He was on his side, naked. A freer spirit, Knapp mused, trapped in the mediocrity of marriage to such a dreary mate.

He did not waste time looking at them, despite the temptations of superiority felt by those awake over those asleep. There were two problems to solve – one expected and one unexpected. The first was that Sari did indeed sleep with her husband, which meant he would have to be dealt with first. The second, the more serious, was the installation of a panic button on a chair pushed hard against Sari's side of the bed. It was a ludicrous device – a red blob, illuminated for detection at night, standing proud of a black plastic box – and Knapp fleetingly wondered what it was connected to. He concluded that, in the absence of any police involvement, it was probably rigged to an alarm made by her all-purpose husband. But that did not make it any less dangerous, and he knew this was a night to take care.

He had come prepared with a solution to the first problem – and pulled a small bottle of chloroform from his trouser pocket. He looked around for suitable absorbing material – suitable in the sense that forensic scientists would be able to find and identify the fibres left on the man's nose – and plucked a discarded vest from a dressing table.

He soaked the vest, conceding that chloroform was an old-fashioned method of administering unconsciousness. But then again, it was not his fault that he had been unable to move with the times. That responsibility lay with the girls – and one of them was about to pay for it.

Synchronizing his movements, he used one hand to thrust the vest against the husband's nose and the other to push the back of his head into the fabric so there was no escape. The man's body jerked as pressure was applied and his eyes flashed open. But there was nothing he could do. Knapp felt the same surge of strength he had experienced when he dealt with Kipini. It was as if laser beams in his body were exploding every atom of restraint, leaving him free to reach his full potential. At moments such as this, he felt invincible.

The chloroform was powerful and unrepentant. The fear and incomprehension in the man's expanding irises were glazed over by impending oblivion. He had no time to fight his assailant, no energy to utter a single curse or challenge. For him, it was over before it had begun.

Not so Sari. Stirred by the twistings of her husband's fevered body, she opened her eyes to see Knapp's leering smile. In an instant, she was as awake as if someone had splashed cold water in her face.

She cried: 'You!' and tried to turn so she could hit the panic button. But her swollen womb slowed her and Knapp grabbed her shoulder, tugging it hard so she was forced to roll back into her prone position. In an instant, he pulled the pillow from beneath her head and rammed it into her face.

She cried out, but could not be heard. She tried to scratch, but could find no target. All she had left was instinct.

Knapp watched with amusement as her right arm reached out, little by little, until it hovered over the panic button. He pushed the pillow harder – and Sari's arm was paralysed in mid-air.

'No use saying it's not fair or telling your teacher,' he said. 'No use being naughty and then pretending you weren't.'

Sari heard him and redoubled her efforts. He felt her legs kicking high in the air behind him, heard her sound-proofed protests being absorbed by down, watched her hair flicking across the sheets as she tried desperately to heave her smothered nose and mouth away from the claustrophobia that threatened to overcome her.

'No use telling tales and thinking you can get away with it. No use trying to stay awake at night.'

Sari was screaming, 'Why? Why?' but only her soul

could hear. She could not fight an onset of dizziness and knew her life was ebbing away. It was horrific. She could even *feel* her eyes rolling back into her skull. Her paralysed arm entered its death spasm, shaking uncontrollably as if connected to an electric wire.

Within seconds, it went limp and fell towards the panic button. Knapp stretched out a hand and caught it before any damage was done.

He folded it over her chest, tucked the pillow behind her head and closed her eyelids.

'Tsssh, you look as if you've seen a ghost,' Knapp said in a consoling manner. 'But no need to worry.' He took the corner of her top sheet and dabbed swelling beads of perspiration from her forehead. 'Go back to sleep. Go back to your dreams, plain little Sari. It's all over now.'

There were things to do before he could go, though none was unduly complicated.

With one flowing movement, he took the head of Sari's husband by the hair, pulled it across to her face so that the man's languid lips pressed against her cooling cheeks, then cast it back on to its own pillow.

Next, he dipped down to the floor and reached under the bed to grab the cord that led from the panic button. He took a penknife from his trouser pocket and cut the lead, taking care to slice separately through the live and neutral wires lest the knife should complete the circuit and set off the alarm. Once severed, he slipped the panic-button mechanism into his other pocket.

He was about to go outside the house to replace the fanlight when he was distracted by the sigh of a child, amplified by the openness of the building. He hesitated, wondering if he should slip on his shoes and leave at once, but finally his curiosity got the better of him.

276

He followed the noise, and after climbing another spiral staircase, found himself in a vast room that took up the entire length of one side of the balcony.

It was a splendid affair, bedroom and playground for all three boys. A vast Scalextric slot-car track meandered across the floor. Discarded clothes drooped across piles of toys. Corners of T-shirts, pants, comics and drawing books poked from drawers that had been left open. Model spaceships, mobiles and the like dangled from long strands of coloured string falling from the roof timbers. Knapp was particularly enchanted by a monstrous inflatable shark, originally used to advertise one or other of the *Jaws* films. After poking it so it swung lazily from side to side, he sat cross-legged on the floor, equidistant from the boys' beds so they could all hear.

He told them how it was a rare pleasure to be in such a room – and that at one time, he loved little children more than anything in the world.

'Take my daughter Martha,' he said. 'She was a diamond, a real sparkler. But then something happened. Something very strange. I began to look at little children – well, little girls to be exact – and I began to hate them.'

One of the boys, the six-year-old, rolled over and muttered something incomprehensible.

Knapp was quick to reassure him. 'I like you, though,' he said, smiling though he knew the boy could not see. 'You mustn't be afraid of me. One day, you can come to visit me if you like. In the White House, in Washington, in America. Tell you what – you can stop over in Los Angeles on the way. See Disneyland. It's wonderful, so they tell me.'

As he climbed to his feet, ready to go, he looked at each of them in turn and said: 'I had to kill her, you know. But you didn't wake up and see me, so I don't have to kill you, do I?'

He sighed as an afterthought came to him. 'Maybe it's just as well . . . or there'd be no end to it.'

21

The man hobbled towards Dany carrying a long flintstone dripping with blood. His shuffling gait and expressionless face gave him the appearance of a zombie. She knew he was dead, but undead, and wanted her to join him in the hellish world of the lifeless living.

'He's going to do to us what he did to her,' Stefanie said, and none of the girls doubted it.

'Run! We must run!'

'I can't. My legs . . .'

'Mam'selle!'

'Sssh, Sari. Be quiet.'

Dany looked past the approaching zombie, searching for an escape route in case she was able to dodge out of his path. But it was blocked by the rusting car and the scarecrow swinging from the branches of the sycamore tree.

The scarecrow looked at her and laughed. 'No, no, dear Dany,' it said with an evil chortle. 'You can't come this way, or you'll end up like me.'

The zombie was upon them. He was covered in blood and sweat and dirt, and his nostrils ran with thin mucus that flowed down his chin and splashed on to the fallen tree trunk.

He was talking to her. Saying something. But she could not make out what. She looked up at him and discovered the reason. He had lips, but the gap between them was filled with a membrane of skin. Every time he opened his mouth, the membrane stretched with it, preventing the passage of words.

All that came out was a vague mumbling. But it was growing in intensity, growing in anger and outrage.

'We can't hear you,' Mai-Lin said with exasperation.

'Don't hurt us,' Louise pleaded.

'Please . . .' Sari whined.

But it was no use. The zombie's patience snapped and he leaned over the tree trunk directly above Dany. Now it was she who was being splashed with his mucus, and her stomach folded over in revulsion. Rain bounced off his body, spraying her with water droplets and fine specks of blood. She saw him raise his arm into the air, ready to plunge the flintstone into her head.

'Stop!'

'Don't!'

'Jesus Christ! Stop, man. For pity's sake, stop!'

The cry came from the right, from three men in black suits crashing through the brambles.

The zombie glanced in their direction, but they could neither distract nor stop him. With tremendous force, he brought the flintstone down upon Dany. It split her skull at the temple – and great plumes of her lifeblood washed out over her face.

She tried desperately to cling on to her senses. But her attempts to look at the stone that had entered her head made her cross-eyed, and her hearing was fading. The last thing she remembered was the three men calling out the zombie's name.

'Dany! Dany!'

'No. That's my name.'

'For pity's sake.'

'You just said that. I heard you calling it in the woods.'

'It wasn't me. Please, Dany . . .'

'What?'

'Wake up! For pity's sake, wake up.'

Ciera, trembling from head to toe, lit another cigarette in an attempt to calm herself. She knew Dany was upset and felt the need to justify her actions. 'I couldn't let you go on,' she said, symbolically tugging the terminals of Dany's electrodes from the jack box in the wall. 'You were tossing and turning, turning and tossing. In a dreadful state. It was terrifying, Dany. If it had been you who had been watching, you'd have been terrified, too. If I'd left you any longer, you could have gone.'

'Gone?' Dany sat up in bed. The sharpness of her voice reflected the unequivocal hostility she felt towards Ciera.

'Gone the same way as Pearl, Louise and Stefanie. God, Dany, we're talking about *death*.'

The word brought Dany to her senses – and an instant flush of guilt swept across her chest. Now it was she who had to justify herself.

'It's just that I was so close,' she said. 'I had a name, Ciera, a *name*. And it went when you woke me.'

'I couldn't have known. It doesn't work like that.'

'Don't you understand the importance of it? Can't you sense the frustration?'

'I do – and I can.'

'Then why did you stop me?'

Words like irrational and unreasonable entered Ciera's thoughts – the very words used by Curran to describe Dany when he dropped her off at the sleep lab. Yet what could they expect? Zombies, flintstones covered in blood, a talking scarecrow that issued threats. The poor woman was in hell already.

'Let me try again,' Dany said bluntly.

'I won't.'

281

'You must. *I* must.'

'No. I can't take the risk. Neither can you.'

Dany snatched the electrode wires from Ciera and began to plug them back in herself, even though she had no idea which terminal fitted in which socket. As she sorted out the tangle, she muttered a message to both Ciera and herself. 'It seems to me that death is a possible consequence whether or not I take risks tonight. So why play safe?'

Ciera shook her head. Despite all her misgivings and all her downright fear, she could not help but admire Dany's courage.

Dany sensed Ciera's resistance was crumbling. She turned, smiled and said quietly: 'Will you help me with these bloody wires?'

She dreamed four more times before morning. In the final vision, the zombie and the scarecrow returned, along with the three running men. They called out the zombie's name, but this time it was lost in the squawks and the flaps of a flock of birds frightened from their perch by the trio's rush through the brambles.

All she could make out was that it began with the letter N.

Curran and Martha made love, but it was a mistake. It was an act played out almost formally, one which left neither satisfied. The silence that followed it spoke volumes.

We shouldn't have, they were telling each other. *We are deeply in love, but no matter the strength of that new love – that exciting new love – we have other things on our minds that possess an even more awesome power.*

Curran climbed from the bed and took two drinks from

282

the hotel room's refrigerated cabinet, a vodka for himself and a gin for Martha. He poured them into a pair of tumblers, adding ice and a splash of orange juice to each, and stirred them with an upside-down teaspoon.

Martha watched him, sensing the diversion he was creating by such elaborate preparation. 'We don't have to, you know,' she said.

'Don't have to what?' Curran mumbled, sipping at the vodka to see if he had achieved the right mix.

'Screw every time we set eyes on each other.'

'I want to.'

'Half of you does.'

'I know which half.'

'Don't joke. I'm trying to say that I think we go deeper than that now. We don't have to *prove* our attraction to each other time after time.'

'Don't you enjoy it?'

'Usually, yes. Tonight, no.'

'Was it something I did, or something I didn't do?'

Martha grew impatient.

'God, Stephen,' she said with exasperation. 'Stop pretending. And stop trotting out those tired old male clichés. They don't become you. For Christ's sake, you didn't enjoy it either, but at least I know it wasn't down to me. It's something else. Admit it. What's wrong?'

Curran sighed and swallowed his vodka in one long, gratifying gulp. In truth, he was glad of the cue. He had begun to tell Martha about the deaths of the Swans the last time they met, and she had been willing to listen. Now, he hoped, she would let him finish his story. He needed to tell it so badly – and he needed Martha to pump him with renewed energy and determination.

Without further hesitation, he pulled the photograph of Whittaker's release from his briefcase, told Martha of his

283

meeting with Jute and pointed to Knapp. 'Don't ask me why, but this guy is behind it all,' he said. 'This is an agency picture. Reuters'. It was wired all over the world and doubtless used by newspapers in countless countries. It startled Dany and I'm sure it sparked her dreams. It was probably seen by Louise and Stefanie – and did the same to them. He's an American called Crosby – and he's the trigger.'

Martha froze, transfixed by the sight of her father. His face was partially obscured by light reflecting off the photographic paper, but she knew those piercing eyes so well. And the way he was waving . . .

Inexplicably, Martha suddenly felt he was waving to her. A happy father glad to see his daughter after a gruelling trip abroad. 'Hi, Martha, how're you doing?' Wouldn't it be wonderful if it were true? For a moment, she had to fight a bizarre urge to return the greeting. But then panic took over, and she was forced to summon every last reserve of control in a desperate attempt to appear normal.

'Wh . . . what about the others?' she asked. 'Sari, Mai-Lin and Kipini. Why didn't they die in their sleep?'

Curran felt his blood flow quicken. Martha was helping him. She was his ally. At last, he was not alone in his struggle to find Crosby.

'I can only assume they didn't see the picture,' he responded eagerly. 'Maybe Kipini was in the bush. Maybe the Thai papers didn't carry the photo. Maybe Sari doesn't read newspapers . . .'

Martha wanted to tell him. She wanted to plunge her finger on to her father's nose and say, 'You're not going to believe this, but – ' She stopped herself just in time, but felt sickened by her cowardice. 'What about Pearl?' she

284

asked. 'She died in her sleep *before* this picture was even taken.'

'She went to Geneva just before she died. She was with her old teacher, the one the Swans called Mam'selle. Then, in her notebook, she wrote, "Woods – no, go away, nasty man!" She *must* have been there, in those same woods that Dany remembers in her dreams. It must have made Pearl remember, too.' Curran tapped Knapp's head on the picture and said: 'Whatever happened, I'm certain it had something to do with *him*. And he is the one who murdered Kipini.'

Martha's head was reeling. Kipini was murdered in Africa. Her father was in Africa at the time she was murdered. Her lover, the man she now treasured above all others, was connecting the two. And worst of all, so was she.

'He tried to kill me in New York, when I was at Pearl's place,' Curran went on. 'He thought I was her – didn't know she was already dead. It happened the night before I came to your place. I saw him. It was the same guy, no question. I didn't tell you, Martha. Didn't want you involved. Now, I can't help myself . . .'

Martha was struck dumb. First a picture of her father, then Africa, and now New York. It was too much to be coincidence. She spun around so Curran would not see her shock.

He was still talking frenetically, but she could not hear what he was saying. It was as if he was a timetable announcer at a busy rail station, drowned by the thunder of trains and the terminal's cavernous echoes.

It seemed an eternity until he realized something was wrong. When he asked what it was, Martha grasped the first ridiculous excuse that came within reach. 'God, I'm sorry,' she said breathlessly. 'All of a sudden, even though you're saying what you're saying, I can't keep my damn eyes open. Jet-lag, I guess. All these years, I've never quite tamed it. Can we talk in the morning?'

Without facing him, she fumbled for a nightdress in her suitcase and slipped it on. From somewhere, she found the strength to turn momentarily to kiss him lightly on the forehead, but then she returned to the refuge of the bed, lying on her stomach and pushing her face deep into the pillow so all he could see was her hair.

Curran felt like an Olympic athlete who falls at the first hurdle. So much hope, so much adrenalin. And then, in the space of a millisecond, nothing.

He told Martha he understood, though he did not. He wanted to ask her how she could abandon him the moment after joining him. He wanted to beg her to stay with him, to hear him through, to help him decide what to do next. But he was so staggered by the suddenness of her withdrawal that he could only offer platitudes. 'I'm too charged up to sleep,' he said listlessly. 'I'll have to read a while.'

Martha grunted a distant acknowledgement – and Curran lolled back into a chair, flicking on a tablelamp to illuminate a coffee-stained copy of his newspaper. He tried to concentrate on the day's news. But it was hopeless – and within five minutes he was again staring relentlessly at the picture of Crosby . . . and wondering where he would strike next.

Martha, wide-eyed with wild thoughts and fevered trepidation, kept her back to him. Only an hour later, when he slipped in beside her and leaned over to kiss her cheek, did she close her eyelids to feign sleep.

A strange thing happened as he slid down into the sheets. Although he stayed close enough for her to feel his skin, he did not curl around her and push his chest against her shoulder blades and his groin between her buttocks as he usually did. Instead, he turned over so the only contact between them was at the base of the spine. She, in turn, found herself inching away from him – until that last remaining union was lost.

It was a tragedy they both felt. To Curran, it was as if the blossoming flower of their love, nurtured to date by a luscious warmth, was in danger of being choked by an ivy that had crept unseen upon it. To Martha, it was as if her father had climbed into bed between them.

The thought made her flesh crawl.

Knapp saw the rocket closing on the U2's radar screen. He got on his pilot's radio to tell the boys at the base in Turkey.

'It's a SAM – and it's coming for my ass.'

He banked the U2 through a manic turn that threatened to catapult him into space. Immense forces of gravity distorted his face and made his internal organs feel solid enough to punch through his ribs.

The rocket seared past inches from the plane's belly. Knapp watched its bleep spiral away with relief, but he knew it would be back.

As he levelled the U2 to catch his breath, he glanced out of the cockpit. Yelena was riding on the wing, sitting on its leading edge with no need for support. Her pose was hedonistic, in keeping with the gossamer robe that stroked every contour of her body. Shoulders thrust back and chest thrust forward so that her spine curved in a graceful arc. Legs held together at a slight angle to her torso, and feet curled like a ballerina.

Every now and then, she disappeared behind thin wisps of cloud vapour, but it was clear she was enraptured by the thrill of it all. She opened her mouth to take great gulps of crystalline air; shook her head to relish the cool droplets of mist that clung to her hair and turned it from auburn silk to burgundy wine.

Knapp pulled open the cockpit canopy and waved frantically to catch her attention. 'You must listen!' he said.

The slipstream tugged the words from his mouth and hurled them into the atmosphere.

Yelena saw his lips moving, but could not hear. 'Louder,' she said stridently. 'You must talk louder.'

'We are lovers, aren't we?' he said, raising his voice.

'Lovers.' Yelena rolled her tongue around the word to savour it. She turned to Knapp and stroked her robe suggestively over her breasts and down to the smooth hemisphere of her womb.

Knapp refused to be distracted. 'Lovers,' he repeated. 'And that is the way it must stay.'

Yelena felt dismayed, but carried on her teasing. She slipped a thumb under a strap of her robe and pushed it over her shoulder, exposing most of her right breast.

Knapp glimpsed the top of her nipple and had to turn away before he caved in to her succulence.

'I love you and I want the world to know,' Yelena said. She leaned back, allowing her neck to flop so her tumbling hair stroked the plane's wing. Then she tugged at her robe until her breast was completely free and caressed it herself, rubbing a vibrant finger over the windblown, erect nipple. 'I love him!' she cried out to any God who was listening. 'I love him, I love him, I love him!'

Knapp felt a raging fire in his chest, but blabbered out what he had to say. 'I love you, too, Yelena. I do, I *do*. But it is impossible. I have a wife and a child. My career depends on having a smiling wife and a happy family.

288

You know that. There must be no hint of an affair, particularly with a Russian girl.'

'I *am* that Russian girl,' Yelena shouted frenziedly. Her hands tore at her robe, tearing it to shreds that curled away into the turbulence. 'Make love to me. Please. Here and now, on this aeroplane. I want you now. I *must* have you now.'

'God!' Knapp flung his face into his hands. She wouldn't listen – and there was nothing he could do except . . . no, the thought was too appalling.

'If it got out, it would be the end of me.' His words faded away, but she could hear him clearer now.

'Then let it be the end of you,' she said. 'And the beginning of us.'

'No! I won't! I can't . . .'

Knapp waited for her reaction, but it never came. He took his face from its shelter to look at her, but she was gone.

Evaporated. Dissipated. Just another collection of droplets in the clouds. Just another cluster of spores on the wind.

He did not know what to think or how to feel. In the cauldron of his soul, joy, grief, heartache and relief mixed together into a broth of utter confusion.

He tried to sort it out, but there was no time. The U2's wings sprouted feathers, its cockpit and nose turned into eyes and beak, and the great eagle's clarion call demanded his attention.

Knapp lay on his stomach in the nape of the eagle's neck. He saw the missile's renewed approach from below, watched in amazement as rocket turned into flamebird, and braced himself for a fiery impact.

But it never came. The flamebird reached the peak of its climb and levelled off to fly alongside the eagle, dipping

289

its head slightly to demonstrate at least a degree of respect. For today, at least, enemies were allies. So who was the foe?

The two creatures turned their heads in unison, until four vivid, ferocious eyes were fixed on Knapp.

'No . . .' he pleaded. But it was too late. The great eagle whipped up its back like a bucking bronco and sent him sprawling into nothingness.

The two birds toyed with him at first, swooshing either side of him as he fell through the air. Then the flamebird came nearer, burning off his pilot's suit and blistering his flesh. As the flamebird shot away, the great eagle took its place, brushing against Knapp's bare shoulders with the tips of its tail feathers.

Knapp hurtled on head first towards the ground. He screamed for help as he saw the clearing in the forest – and the concrete silo that was the firebird's home.

The birds let him drop until he was feet from extinction. Then the great eagle swooped, puncturing the skin on his back with its talons, hauling him up and away with the flamebird in pursuit.

He was carried for miles, dangling from the talons with no more hope than a common field mouse, until the great eagle reached its eyrie near the summit of a granite cliff.

Once there, the feast began in earnest. The great eagle rolled Knapp over, held him in place with one giant foot and speared his stomach with its beak, tugging strands of elasticized flesh until they snapped, and throwing its head back to devour them. From time to time, he offered morsels to the flamebird, which consumed them greedily. Knapp saw his intestines and kidneys torn away before the great eagle pushed inside his ribcage to dredge the rich, tender promise of his heart.

He watched everything until the flamebird, anxious for

a greater share, pulled out his eyes. As he plunged into eternal darkness, he heard Yelena call his name and whisper: 'You are to blame. It is all your fault.'

'Why me?' he screamed in self-defence. 'Why, why, why?'

He felt his remnants being sucked into the great eagle's stomach – and the bird's digestive juices began to reduce him to liquid.

When he was next whole, when he could next see, he was in a passenger jet taxiing to a halt in Bangkok.

'Pick up "Wifey",' Hockenhull called out to Curran. 'It's the page-eleven lead. Headline's done. Main deck reads HUSBAND WAKES TO FIND WIFE MURDERED. Subdeck: Riddle of death in bed. Grubby little story from Oz. Gimme three centimetres across two columns and twelve across single with a cross-head. Picture of the dead woman'll be here in a minute.'

Curran punched his keyboard until the story appeared on his screen – and gazed in abject horror at what confronted him: Sari's death, described in gruesome detail in little green words on a cold, soulless computer screen.

He read at the speed of light, hoping it would go away but knowing it would not.

The thrust of the story was that Sari's husband was suspected of her murder, despite his protestations of innocence. There had been no robbery at the house, it said, and Sari had no known enemies. There was a quote from a Sydney detective telling how despite appearances of a happy marriage, the husband paid regular visits to an exclusive massage parlour near Tamarama Beach, and had recently told work colleagues he was bored with his lot. Further down the story, there were quotes from two of Sari's friends, backing the husband's story that Sari had been terrified of a 'mystery man' who was out to 'get' her. But no one appeared to attach too much significance to this angle of the case, particularly since the husband's claims of the existence of a panic button could not be verified, despite his demonstration of an electrical alarm circuit that ended abruptly with two cut wires beneath the bed.

The detective concluded that it would have been 'possible' for the husband to have administered chloroform to himself after killing Sari. Traces of the chemical were found on her cheek.

'Kiss of death,' McKeachie, who was reading the story on his terminal, said dramatically.

'Wonder if he fucked her when she was cold,' Brookes called out. 'A stiff one for a stiff.'

Curran turned on him savagely, his voice trembling with the terror he felt inside. 'Who the fuck asked you? And when the fuck are you going to realize that this isn't all one big fucking laugh? That poor woman is dead. *Dead*, you bastard. Her husband is being blamed for something he damn well didn't do. And all you can do is crack fucking sick jokes!'

Brookes was stunned by the onslaught, but hit back with equal ferocity. 'OK, I'll cry,' he shouted. 'I'll cry every time I write a story about the dead or dying. And I'll drown in my own tears every fucking day.'

Curran did not hear Brookes's final words. His head went light and he was sure he was about to faint. He staggered to his feet, knocking over his chair, and rushed from the newsroom.

Hockenhull found him ten minutes later. He was three floors down in a remote corridor leading to the press hall, pushed into the corner of two breeze-block walls in a cold

292

sweat. Hockenhull put a hand on his shoulder and asked: 'What's up, lad?'

'Sick,' Curran said, his voice sapped of all strength. 'I'm sick, that's all. Flu or something . . . I don't know.'

'You sure?' said Hockenhull, who wasn't.

'Yes,' Curran lied. 'I shouldn't have come in tonight.'

Not for the first time, Hockenhull thought of consoling him about Pearl and his crumbling marriage to Dany. But it had all been said before – and Curran knew his colleagues were behind him, even Brookes.

'He was right, you know,' Hockenhull said. 'If you didn't laugh, you'd cry a bloody fountain.'

'I know. I'm sorry. Tell him I'm sorry, will you?'

'You going home?'

'I have to. You don't mind, do you?'

'Nah.' Hockenhull tried to introduce a degree of levity. 'I've already got some other mad bugger on that Oz story. By the way. Something you said . . .'

'What?'

'You said the husband had been blamed for something he hadn't done. What makes you think that?'

Curran looked at Hockenhull for the first time. 'I don't just *think* it,' he said with conviction. 'I *know* it.'

As Hockenhull watched Curran walk away, hands pressed against ears as if to keep out all further intrusions of evil, he was genuinely concerned for the poor man's sanity.

Hagerty did not want to see Martha again, but she was so adamant, so liable to veer out of control, that he had no choice. He even told her he would take the shuttle to New York and promised she would be both pacified and satisfied. And, of course, he told her not to worry.

At Hagerty's suggestion, they met at the top of the

World Trade Center, mingling with out-of-towners who were ooh-ing and aah-ing at the lesser towers that stretched up towards them.

'Funny, but it makes me want to jump,' Martha said as she gazed down at the toytown streets hundreds of feet below.

'It's a common sensation,' Hagerty concurred. 'Along with a feeling that we are all insignificant – a teeming family of ants who will all be stamped on one day.'

Martha turned to face him, her eyes already asking a thousand questions. 'Are you insignificant?' she asked.

'I can cope with heights,' he replied with a confidence designed to reassure her.

'And could my father?'

'What?'

'Cope with heights?'

Hagerty paused, reflecting on the proper answer. 'He did for a while,' he said finally.

'And then he fell off the ledge,' Martha said bluntly. 'Or was he *pushed*, Mr Hagerty.'

Her stridency made Hagerty reassess her. What had happened, he wondered, to the gullible girl-woman he knew? Why the formal 'Mr Hagerty'? And above all, why the sudden mistrust? He decided to throw her off balance with a head-on attack.

'All right, Martha. Enough of this playing around. What do you want from me?'

'I want the truth,' she said.

'I told you the truth in Washington,' he replied with equal firmness.

'The whole truth – and nothing but the truth.'

He could not raise his voice. He was in a public place. But he knew how to inject it with venom. 'Dammit, Martha. You're accusing me of holding back. Why do you

294

do this, when I have been so frank with you? What makes you want me to tell you the same things again?'

Martha told him. She told him about Curran and she told him of Curran's suspicions about her father. When Hagerty grinned, she described how Curran had been attacked in Pearl's apartment.

'Martha, sweetheart, your father was – is – one of the most respected statesmen of his time,' Hagerty countered. 'Smothering a complete stranger with a pillow is hardly his métier. We're talking about an intruder in a Manhattan apartment. It was night. How can your friend Mr Curran be sure? It was probably just some stupid kid from the Bronx.'

'But the other girl, Kipini, was killed while my father was in Africa.'

'Africa is a big country,' Hagerty said. 'He could have been 3,000 miles away from where this woman died. How can you possibly suspect your own father of being a murderer?'

The remark cut Martha dead. No matter how hard she tried to suppress it, no matter how hard she tried to concentrate on the facts and the coincidences, no matter how hard she tried to remember Curran's photograph, she felt a deep sense of shame.

Hagerty was quick to offer his sympathy. 'It's not easy to keep faith in a man with a history of mental illness,' he said. 'Even if he's your father.'

Tears welled in Martha's eyes. Hagerty took hold of her shoulders. They both felt relief. Martha because she still had her kind uncle. Hagerty because her doubt had been overcome.

Hagerty's only problem was the doubt she had sown in him.

* * *

Hagerty used an office at the United Nations to contact Napier. He told Napier everything Martha had told him – and waited for a response. It was more than twenty seconds before it came.

'But there's no proof that our man is involved in these goings-on,' Napier said. 'None whatsoever. It is merely a case of folk putting two and two together, and making five. A case of amateur interference.'

'Yes, but – '

'This man of hers, this journalist,' Napier interrupted. 'What did you say his name was?'

'Curran. Stephen Curran. Born in the States but a naturalized Briton.'

'It will be a simple matter for us to locate him.'

'You'll use your contacts at his newspaper?'

'I imagine so. Leave him to me, old boy. Leave Mr Curran to me.'

22

The doorbell roused Curran from a deep sleep. He waited for Dany to answer it, but when it rang again, he checked his watch with eyes that took time to focus. A quarter to nine in the morning. Dany would have left a few minutes ago to take Yvette to school. Damn!

The bell rang for a third time, suggesting the caller was not prepared to give up and go away. Curran cursed again and flung away his sheets melodramatically. As he climbed from his bed, he convinced himself it was the milkman after his weekly payment. An over-enthusiastic Irishman who, no matter how many times he had been told about Curran's shift work and the need for quiet in the morning, insisted on prattling on to Dany about the weather and his old mammy back in County Mayo, always in an extraordinarily loud voice.

Curran flung open the bedroom window, ready for another showdown. But it was not the milkman. Instead, a small rotund man in a severe black suit stood in the drive, flicking imaginary dust from his collar and clasping an official-looking briefcase embossed with a royal crest. As Curran cried, 'Yes?' the man took a step back and looked up.

'Mr Curran? Mr Stephen Curran?' The man, whose flushed face had been inflated by good food and excessive drink, neither smiled nor scowled.

Curran found it disconcerting, and fell back on a weak joke. 'If you're from the taxman, tell him I filled in my return a week ago.'

The man's expressionless mask did not falter. 'I am unconnected to the Inland Revenue,' he said. 'Nevertheless, I would like to talk to you, preferably before your wife returns from the school.'

Curran flinched at the man's knowledge of Dany's comings and goings, and muttered, 'My God.' The man heard but did not react. The only clue to his state of mind was a restless shuffling of the feet, indicating the onset of impatience. Curran told him to wait until he put on a dressing gown. As he opened the door, the man strode inside without further invitation.

Curran offered coffee or tea, but the man refused both.

'I am here on business, and I would like to be brief,' he said. 'I have a busy day ahead of me. I should have been at my desk already.'

'Your desk?'

'At the Foreign Office.'

'Ah . . .' Curran did not know what to make of it. He ushered the man into the lounge, told him to sit on the sofa, apologized for his state of undress and said, 'This is all very mysterious. Perhaps you had better introduce yourself.'

'My name is Lipton.' The man paused, searching Curran's eyes for any reaction. When there was none, he added: 'I gather you do not know of me.'

Curran shook his head. Inexplicably, he felt he needed to be alert, and breathed deeply to help himself come to his senses.

'Do not expect me to reveal any more about myself,' Lipton said. 'I hope my candour in offering you my name and my workplace are sufficient to satisfy you. I do, of course, realize you can find out more about me if you wish. You are, after all, a professional nosey-parker. Some call them journalists, though personally I believe

298

the term inapplicable to people at your rather slimy end of the tabloid market.'

The jibe was only confirmation. Long before Lipton made it, Curran knew he was an enemy. No battle lines had yet been drawn, but Curran found himself being sucked into a strange, impromptu duel in which victory or defeat might well depend upon who possessed the sharpest cutting edge.

'Nosey-parker will suffice,' Curran said. 'In fact, it is a rather charming term. Infinitely preferable to muck-raker, or gutter-reptile, or shafter of the Establishment.'

Curran chose his words. He used Establishment deliberately, for Lipton was clearly in its vanguard. And he was deliberately crude, to gauge whether his opponent would be offended by bad language. When he saw he was not, despite appearances suggesting otherwise, he realized Lipton was a foe worth reckoning.

'So . . .' Lipton said stridently. 'You do not know me. However, I know you.'

'How?'

'Because you have been asking questions. Questions that have been drawn to my attention.'

'Questions?' Curran could not conceal his bewilderment. 'What questions?'

'About the release of a gentleman from Mogden security hospital. An American gentleman.'

Curran felt the blood drain from his head as if someone had pulled a plug in his throat. For a moment, he was unable to speak, even though a thousand questions were battering the inside of his skull. Was this what he had been waiting for? A breakthrough in his search for the maniac on the trail of the seven girls? Or did it signal an entry into something far wider, something even more sinister? What possible reason, he asked himself, would interest a man from the Foreign Office in investigations that Curran, painful though such an admission was, knew to be blundering?

Lipton saw his discomfort, but made no effort to soothe it. He waited for Curran to speak, half expecting the journalist to make a futile denial of involvement in any such inquiry. Curran saw growing contempt in Lipton's eyes – and there and then, he decided to fight with all his strength.

'He is called Crosby,' he said in an attempt to shock Lipton by demonstrating his intelligence about the American. 'He was admitted on 8 May 1960. In the opinion of medical experts, he should have been given his freedom years ago.'

For the first time, a wry smile wound slowly across Lipton's face, though Curran could not tell if the unwelcome stranger was impressed, or relieved to discover the limited nature of his knowledge.

Lipton tugged at the bronze chain that dangled across his waistcoat. An antique watch with Roman numerals emerged from a small sewn-in pocket. Lipton glanced at it before allowing it to drop back into its pouch.

'Your wife . . .' he said. 'Best not to worry her unnecessarily. I must say what I have to say and then take my leave.'

'Say it,' Curran challenged harshly.

'Very well.' Lipton surprised Curran by producing a pack of cigarettes and stretching out his arm to offer one. A gesture of conciliation? Or a basic confidence trick? Curran refused in any case. Lipton slipped the pack back into his jacket without helping himself. Stranger still.

'I cannot tell you much,' Lipton said. 'What would you expect from the Foreign Office? But I can tell you to forget about this man Crosby. Otherwise I am afraid you will become entangled in something which you cannot possibly begin to understand. Something which burrows deeply into the fundamental security of Britain and the United States of America. Do I make myself clear?'

Curran did not believe him. He had an instinct for truth and lies, infused into his blood over the years by trying to separate the two while writing newspaper stories. Claim and counter-claim, that was what it was all about. And when did anyone from the Foreign Office last come clean on anything? What was the phrase that had crept into the English language via a representative of Her Majesty's Government? Being 'economical with the truth', if memory served him correctly. How economical, Curran wondered, was Lipton being?

'Well . . .' Lipton was anxious for an answer.

There was something about the man's manner – an element of arrogance, a hint of patronage, a whiff of concealment – that Curran was quickly coming to despise. And that smug throwaway line about Dany – 'best not to worry her unnecessarily' – reminded him of the *real* reason for his involvement.

'You have to worry about the safety of Britain and America,' he snapped. 'I have to worry about the safety of my wife.'

'Oh?' Lipton made it sound as if he was surprised.

'What do you mean, "Oh"?' Curran challenged.

'Well surely – '

'Surely *what*?'

'Forgive me, Mr Curran, but I thought – '

'Thought *what*?'

'I thought you were not exactly on the best of terms with your wife.'

Curran was outraged. 'That, sir, is a gross intrusion. How do you know? What right do you have?'

301

'I have every right,' Lipton said with quiet firmness. 'And it is my duty to know.'

'No . . . no, I cannot accept that.'

'Few people can. But it is a fact of life.'

'Have you come into my home to suggest I do not truly care for my wife?'

'No,' Lipton replied quickly. 'I have already told you why I came – and I can really add no more.' He rose to his feet and plucked his briefcase from the floor. He strode quickly to the front door and let himself out. As he reached the end of the drive, he turned and waited for Curran to appear. 'Forget Crosby,' he said as Curran reached the door. 'He has nothing to do with you, whatever you may think. You're on a wild goose chase that will only lead to needless anxiety.'

'I'll decide what I must do,' Curran countered. 'And I will *not* forget your Mr Crosby. I'll track him down and see what he has to say for himself.'

Curran slammed the door to rid himself of the sight of Lipton and put an end to the verbal skirmish.

But at the same time, he was aware the man had done his groundwork and could be a formidable adversary. As Lipton walked to his car, he was thinking the same of Curran.

Curran scalded his hand making coffee, his thoughts still concentrated on the round man who had come into his life without warning, without invitation, yet had assumed immediate relevance in a way that, if Curran was honest with himself, scared the pants off him.

He wrapped a tea towel around the blistered hand and walked into the lounge, slumping on the sofa which had a dip in the middle bearing testimony to the fat arse that had occupied the space only a moment ago.

302

He wanted Dany to come home, so he could tell her about the visitation. But his memory was returning through the haze of incomprehension. It was Wednesday, the day Dany went on from school to the gym to keep her muscles taut and – increasingly in recent times – her mind distracted. He wondered if Lipton had known about Wednesdays. If he had not, perhaps he was not quite as astute as Curran had imagined. If he had, then he had probably chosen the day deliberately, to make absolutely sure he would be alone with Curran for the time required to deliver his warning. Curran thought the latter more likely. Men like Lipton were inclined to give themselves elbow room to allow for unseen circumstances. Contingencies. That was the Whitehall word for it. The thought that Lipton had planned his visit so meticulously made Curran even more uneasy about the whole bizarre episode.

Suddenly, though reason told him Dany was in far greater danger than he, he felt alone and abandoned. To add to his misery, he had not seen Martha for days – and even then, she had been somehow remote. Since that time, he had found out about Sari's death in the most horrific way he could imagine apart from actually stumbling upon her body. And he had endured a couple of tough nights at the newspaper, where major stories about an air disaster and the announcement of a royal engagement – with all the pomp, circumstance and details of the blushing bride-to-be that surrounded it – had broken at the worst time possible. The effort he had been forced to make was monumental, and he was not sure he had succeeded. Even Hockenhull had yelled at him when he had run over deadline on a background story chronicling the royal romance from tabloid rumour to Palace announcement.

'Want me to write in the date of their first fuck?' Curran said in an attempt to cover up his lack of control.

'You can fuck yourself,' Hockenhull barked, his iron-faced scowl forbidding any further attempts at levity. 'You're twenty minutes late, and there are headlines and picture captions yet. Send me the story, or piss off out of here and let someone who can handle it take over. Newspapers can't carry bloody passengers.'

'You're only as good as your last story,' Brookes said quietly. He knew what it was like to be clubbed by Hockenhull's uncompromising attitude to his staff's off days.

Curran felt sick at the memory. Hockenhull had been an ally. Someone who could not hope to understand what he was going through, yet felt obliged to try. Now even Hockenhull had lost his patience – and who could blame him?

A passenger. It was the first time Curran had been called that, and it hurt.

He felt as if the heavy charcoal cloud he could see resting on the trees outside was about to squeeze through the window to settle on his shoulders. It made his head heavy, and he allowed it to fall on the arm of the sofa. As if connected by lever, his feet pulled up from the floor to rest on a cushion.

He sought the refuge of sleep, grateful for the soupy cocoon of darkness that was about to envelop him and spirit him to the promised land.

He did not care where it was, just so long as it was far, far away from where he was now.

Curran's dream was a dreadful coagulum of everything that was crashing around inside his head.

He saw Pearl juddering like a heavy lorry pulling away

from traffic lights, lips shining with spittle and fingers flicking maniacally like the limbs of an upturned beetle. He watched the spasm and reached out. When he touched her, she turned sickly green and coughed blood and sputum over her sheets. Her eyes never closed, but she was dead. Her body floated up from the bed, turned into a soft apricot vapour and disappeared through the ceiling.

The other Swans came to watch.

'Oo-er,' Louise said. 'Do you think she'll be all right?'

'Shall we fetch help?' said Sari, who looked like a plump cherub from an Italian water-fountain.

'Oh stop fussing,' Stefanie snapped impatiently. 'She knows where she's going.'

'Crosby did it,' Curran said. 'He's responsible.'

'But how could he be?' Mai-Lin shrieked. 'His name doesn't begin with an N.'

'I don't know!' Curran screamed. 'I just don't know.'

An N. An N. An N. An N. An N.

It was relentless, like the sound of a piledriver digging a well with no bottom. Only Dany's piercing cry saved him from being driven mad.

'Help! Help, Stephen, I need your help.'

Curran knew he would help her, and knew where to find her. On a rowing boat held fast by bulrushes on the Everglades. He was there in an instant, wading chest-high in water towards her. She turned full circle so he could admire her, a naked teenager whose blossoming womanhood made Curran catch his breath. Soft, fair down pointing arrow-like towards the cleft between her buttocks. Taut, unsullied flesh stretching over proud cheekbones. Eyes alive and sparkling with the incandescent hope of youth. Pubic hair glistening like jewellery in the sunlight. Bronzed shoulders as smooth and unblemished as polished wax. Satin nipples crowning breasts that were somehow heavy and light at the same time, and yet to be softened by years and suckling infants.

Curran clambered aboard in a sweat. He wanted to make love for the first time, for the very first time, and his drenched clothes fell away so he, too, was naked. The swamp's wonderful, all-encompassing humidity seemed ideal for such wet and sticky passion. Blood surged into his penis, making it hard and willing. The lust inside his chest threatened to break his ribs like so many dry sticks. He leaned forward, ready to hold her, his every fibre tense in the expectancy of relishing such an entreating, luscious body as this.

Yet she told him to wait.

And then, in front of his very eyes, she went through the strangest metamorphosis he had seen. Her skin cracked like an eggshell and coloured lines of plastic pushed through the fissures until she was covered from head to toe by thin, meandering lines of blue, yellow, green and red.

At first, Curran could not make out what they were. It was only when globules of solder-like metal burst from Dany's forehead and neck that he realized. The globules, molten at first but soon cooled and dried by the breeze, moved across her flesh until they became attached to the loose ends of the thin plastic flesh.

It had to do with electricity, he thought. Electrodes, terminals and wires, like in the sleep laboratory.

'You see,' Dany said glumly. 'I am a robot. An android. Call it what you like. Will you still love me?'

Curran stared at her for long, fretful moments. He wanted to love her, almost *needed* to love her. But something stopped him. What was it?

'I don't know!' he screamed. 'I just don't know.'

He dived from the boat and swam away.

'Come back!' Dany cried. 'Please, Stephen, come back.'

Curran twisted amid the floating lilies to look at her. She was the beautiful teenage nude again, standing swankily in the boat with her legs slightly apart, one hand on her hip and a curled finger on the other beckoning him to return.

'Not now,' he called, treading water. 'I won't let you down, but I need a love of my own.'

He swam to Martha, submerging his face beneath the surface of the water to hasten his progress.

She was waiting in nirvana – a palm-fringed coral island washed by small waves topped with soft, foamy surf. She lay back on a blanket on the beach, stretching her long legs to rub her toes against Curran's as he took his final step towards her. She was even more luxuriant than Dany, a full, experienced woman who saw the desperation on Curran's face and let him do what he wanted to do. He kissed her, caressed her, enjoyed giving her pleasure with his tongue and with his lips. After she had shuddered with ecstasy for the second time, she smothered them both with almond oil and pulled him on to her. He slithered inside her without the slightest friction. Then they enjoyed. Writhing, squirming together. Legs entwining and slipping. Palms skidding across the hills, valleys and plateaux of their bodies.

Martha made a fist and forced it hard across Curran's back. Yet the oil meant he felt no pain. He dug his fingers into the fleshy roof of her abdomen, then let them slide this way or that until he was forced to dig again. And all the time, their exhilaration and abandonment were building and building until the final moment could be held back no longer.

Curran's chest heaved and his shoulders shook from side to side.

'I love you,' Martha whispered.

'And me you,' Curran said tenderly.

'So what is going wrong between us?'

Her words were like arrows slicing into his heart and the moment she spoke them, she disappeared.

'I don't know!' Curran screamed after her. 'I just don't know.'

All he did know was that he had to run, to keep going. For if he stopped it would be all over.

He ran across oceans and across the great land masses. His face was frozen by the icy Arctic wastes, scorched by the searing desert wind. The muscles in his legs felt like liquid steel. Yet still he ran.

He arrived panting at his computer terminal in the newspaper office and flung himself into his chair.

'Ey-up. The bloody passenger's back,' Hockenhull snarled.

First exhaustion, then Hockenhull's merciless venom. But he had to go on.

'Crosby,' he uttered between breaths. 'Must find Crosby.'

He tapped the letters into his Command Field.

C-R-O-S-B-Y.

He hit the Execute button to call Crosby on to his screen. The American's face appeared not in computer greens, but in black and white. His image was blurred and peppered with tiny dots, like a blown-up photograph. And he was smiling, just as he had been when he saw the cameras at Mogden hospital those long weeks ago.

'Found me yet?' he asked.

Curran, perspiring heavily, shook his head.

'Not easy, is it?' Crosby grinned.

Curran shook his head again. He was in a daze – and his vision fuzzed at the edges. Another face flashed on to the screen, this time in full colour. Fat, grotesque and vaguely threatening. Lipton. The man from the Foreign Office whom Curran had met only that morning. What did he want?

'Forget Crosby,' Lipton said.

'Why?'

'Forget Crosby.'

'You've got to tell me more.'

'Forget Crosby.'

Curran hit a key to make Lipton disappear, but he wouldn't go. Curran tore the keyboard from its plug, but Lipton was still there, that condescending half-smile appearing on his bloated purple lips.

'Why are you involved in this?' Curran yelled at the electric face. 'How are you involved in this?'

'In what?' Lipton said. 'Forget Crosby.'

Crosby appeared again, then Lipton, then Crosby, then Lipton, until the two images were alternating at the speed of a stroboscope. Stripes of light flashed across Curran's bowed head until he could stand it no longer . . .

He woke with a skull-splitting migraine.

23

The water taxi dropped Mai-Lin at a jetty outside the soaring Lor Nam hotel. She glanced back to see if she was being followed, but her only companions were a cluster of Western tourists and a bent old Thai man waving his walking stick in greeting to a waiting friend. Mai-Lin felt comfortable enough to linger a moment and take in the panorama of the wide Chao Phryia river that was Bangkok's central thoroughfare. Its muddiness made it light brown, almost yellow in colour, and the life it had once supported had been killed off years ago by the oil and chemicals now poured into it every working day. The price paid by a nation which for some reason unknown to Mai-Lin had set its heart on becoming South East Asia's 'Fifth Tiger', following the concrete path of industrialization pioneered by the other four Tigers: Hong Kong, Singapore, Taiwan and South Korea.

The result, it occurred to Mai-Lin, was that the city she loved was slowly being raped. Burgeoning prosperity was one thing, but how could it hope to support the millions of peasants who had abandoned the land and swamped the city to seek so many promised fortunes? How could any responsible city father allow the trucks, the buses and the tuk-tuk motorbike taxis to belch out their poisonous, stinking clouds of black smoke? Mai-Lin despaired at the increasing number of women walking the streets with handkerchiefs clasped to their mouths.

First, it was the fish in the Chao Phryia river that had

been suffocated, Mai-Lin reflected. Next, perhaps, it would be her.

Precisely the same thought occurred to Knapp as he watched her turn and walk into the hotel.

Mai-Lin marched straight through the foyer to an unmarked door a few yards beyond the gaudy entrance to a gaudy bar. She opened it and stepped into a long corridor with dim lighting and peeling paint that suggested it was for hotel staff only. Mai-Lin walked the length of it, opening another door marked Fire Exit at the end, and strode out into daylight once again.

She crossed a courtyard and headed for a small, crumbling building which had a tattiness originally caused by neglect, and now accentuated by the sparkling magnificence of the hotel that swept up to the clouds beside it. Once inside, she skipped up stone stairs two at a time and burst through swing doors into a grime-stained office that, from time to time, was her place of work.

Like the three smart young men who yelled a greeting from across the room, her clothes and her cultured manner were strangely out of keeping with such filthy surroundings. She wore a startlingly vivid geranium mini-dress, like the expensive designer numbers worn in casinos by mistresses of the moneyed. It was held in place with thin straps, barely noticeable on her slender olive shoulders, and she set it off with matching high heels, fingernails and heart-shaped earrings. She had pulled back her thick black hair and tethered it behind her head with a butterfly grip, scarlet with white polka-dots. Her make-up was understated but harmonious, suggesting painstaking application. The red leather handbag she threw on her desk had a gold snap-fastening encrusted with what looked like miniature rubies. In short, Mai-Lin was a woman who exuded class.

It was a humid afternoon – when wasn't it humid in Bangkok? – and she pulled a string to set off the noisily ancient fan on the ceiling above her desk. She fetched a paper cupful of refrigerated water as the inevitable shower of dust despatched by the fan settled, then perched herself on her armless office chair. She slid a cigarette into a fake ivory holder, lit it and reached for the telephone.

Mai-Lin was shocked by the feebleness of Dany's voice – and asked ridiculously if she was all right. Dany, rubbing early-morning eyes burning in their sockets after yet another interrupted night, put on a courageous front and replied that she had seen better times. The two women, comforted by their shared plight, managed a brief chuckle.

They talked with quiet disbelief about the terrible loss of their friends. Dany spoke of her latest visions and experiments with Ciera O'Connell – then asked Mai-Lin how she was sleeping.

'Better than you,' Mai-Lin replied. 'I haven't seen his face, remember. But I wouldn't say I was sleeping like a baby, either. Not since this whole thing began.'

'You frightened?'

'Everyone is frightened by the unknown.' Mai-Lin spoke calmly, surprising Dany, who expected the panic that she herself felt.

'He's picking us off one by one. You know that, don't you?'

'It's obvious now.'

'Do you want to come here?'

'To England?'

'So we can face this together. We're the only two . . .' Dany's words tailed off as she realized the full implication of what she was saying. Five dead. Only two still drawing

312

breath. The zombie in the woods was coming closer all the time.

'I can't,' Mai-Lin said. 'The targets here are busy. All sorts of stuff is being traded. Purified. Unpurified. Processed. Raw. The farmers can't grow enough poppies. I can't get the time off.'

'Mai-Lin . . .' Dany gasped, incredulous that Mai-Lin could still show devotion to work at a time when her life was hanging by a thread.

'I don't want my home to become the cesspit of the world.' Mai-Lin said it deliberately to show Dany she meant every word. 'Has it become so unfashionable to *care*?'

'But – '

'Stefanie was the leader,' Mai-Lin interrupted. 'Then there was you. The rest of us just followed.'

'I don't – '

'Times change. People change. Little girls grow up into women. I'm a lot tougher now. It's what happens when some shithead comes at you with a four-inch blade.' Mai-Lin drew a finger across her dress, feeling the ragged, bumpy scar beneath the fabric that stretched from her navel to her right hip. She didn't like to do it often, even though the scar sometimes irritated her. And she rarely looked in mirrors when she was naked.

'But you are still vulnerable,' Dany said with genuine concern, wondering if Mai-Lin's overt bravado was a sham, or at least a shield to protect her from fear. 'Have you asked for protection? You're in the ideal place.'

'You told me the New York police didn't believe Stephen.'

'Yes.'

'And that you haven't been to Scotland Yard because

313

you have nothing concrete to offer them – and you think they'll react in the same way.'

'Yes.'

'So why should my people believe me?'

Dany searched desperately for an answer, but Mai-Lin spoke again before she could think of one.

'I hope he comes here first,' she said aggressively.

She reached across her desk and slickly flicked open her handbag with thumb and forefinger. Without fumbling, she pulled out an automatic Beretta pistol. She stroked its cool barrel across her chin and said: 'I'm ready for him.'

Knapp liked Bangkok. A tropical warmth that seeped through every cell of his body to soothe ageing bones. A relaxed attitude to life, unburdened by a plethora of unnecessary rules and regulations. Easy sex.

If he wasn't needed so badly in Washington, it would be a good place to settle.

As his cab made its way towards Patpong under the dim street lights of the Silom Road, which even at this late hour was jammed with buses, trucks and shirt-sleeved men on small Japanese motorcycles, he reflected that maybe the two cities weren't so different. Certainly Bangkok had been Americanized during the Vietnam War, when it became the R & R mecca for hordes of battle-weary GIs. When the soldiers moved out, the tourists moved in, but the legacy of the war remained. Most of the water taxis which plied the river were fitted with powerful engines plundered from the legions of US Army trucks abandoned at the close of the conflict. And the go-go bars, discos and fleshpots in Patpong and Nana Plaza had bluntly sexual Western names which had once held out hands of comfort to men who had forgotten the

314

sensation of touching a woman's skin. Pussy Galore, Eve, the Silver Dollar Saloon. All the golden oldies were still there.

Thoughts of Vietnam never failed to anger Knapp, for it should have been him and not Lyndon Baines Johnson who took over the reins when Kennedy went to ground. Indubitably, he would have made a better job of it than that drawling, inept bastard – a fact which everyone would swiftly recognize when he finally returned in triumph to the White House.

Better late than never.

The cab stopped near Soi Patpong 2, the smaller of the district's two compact sex markets. Knapp, briefcase in hand, paid his fare and walked along a flashing neon alleyway to the Heaven's Gate club, an up-market joint aimed at foreign businessmen calling in en route from Europe to Japan with credit cards and zippers at the ready. He chose it for two reasons. It was worked by fresh young hookers, one of whom he would choose to see to his needs later. And it was worked by Mai-Lin.

A squat, frantic doorman looking bizarre in top hat and tails held out a card detailing the night's programme of events.

'Pussy shoot ping-pong,' he jabbered, guessing the approaching man's nationality. Knapp brushed past him and strode into the club. The doorman grinned as his commission rose by another 200 baht.

The floor of the club was dominated by a huge circular bar in smoked glass and chrome, surrounding a raised stage, also circular and lit by a single spotlight. It was not yet midnight and the stage was empty apart from a lone bamboo chair.

Punters milled and chatted, some already on the look-out for the night's fare. Smoke curled into the air through

315

conical beams sprayed by soft pink lights scattered here and there on a low mirrored ceiling. On the far side of the club, well away from the bar, was a dance floor on which several pixie-faced Thai girls, most with a discreet number tagged on their lacy bikinis, were provocatively pushing out their crotches to the beat 'n squeak of Michael Jackson.

Knapp chose a table in the shadows closer to the bar than the dance floor, and ordered a bourbon. He had considered showing himself to Mai-Lin, but had swiftly rejected the idea. She was not as isolated as Kipini, not as stupid as Sari. Four days of following her tight little ass had taught him that. Words like canny, astute and intelligent came to mind.

Even so, it would not be difficult to kill her.

Mai-Lin walked in at 2 A.M., swiftly settling on a high stool at the bar. It was less than a minute before a man offered to buy her a cocktail. She accepted with a smile – and talked to him amiably while sipping at a foamy lime concoction through a kinked straw.

After fifteen minutes, though, she made an excuse and left his side.

'No joy there, sweetheart,' Knapp muttered under his breath as he watched from the darkness.

Mai-Lin spent a few minutes in the powder room before returning to lean against another part of the bar. A second man approached her and she accepted another drink.

'Better luck this time,' Knapp said, raising his glass to toast her good fortune.

He knew Mai-Lin's game. She was neither whore nor hostess. She was not even interested in the vice peddled by the club's Australian war-vet owner. She was concerned only with drugs. Who wanted them. Who supplied them.

316

Her employers were the Bangkok city police, and it was her job to work the clubs, to be friendly to their patrons, to glean information about the comings and goings of drug-running personnel and their powdery white cargoes – information that would later be relayed to the main police HQ from a scruffy nondescript building at the back of the Lor Nam hotel, the front for a front.

Knapp could guess her line of chat. Flirtatious small-talk at first. But slowly, imperceptibly, she would drift towards the subject of heroin, opium and cocaine. If her target at the bar showed signs of interest, she would hint that she was a negotiator for a syndicate prepared to supply or receive, depending on where the target stood in the chain. If he was a supplier she would gently – with a knowing chuckle and another drink – try to persuade him to name names of colleagues and associates. In that way, dossiers could be built, laboratories and warehouses located, raids timed to perfection.

If, however, the target remained immune, either through genuine lack of interest or professional discretion, she would cut him short and trot off to the powder room, where another expensive cocktail would be despatched down the toilet to ensure she did not become woolly-headed. Then she would try again.

Knapp had to admit she was a good operator. She had the looks and the confidence – and could do nothing less than intrigue anyone who met her. Men who gazed into her glistening chestnut eyes were entranced. And to ensure their undivided attention, she emitted a fragrantly-perfumed promise of sublime seduction.

Briefly, Knapp wondered if she was prepared to bed a target in the name of upstanding citizenship. But as she dropped the second man and latched on to a third, he felt only anger.

Trickery and deception, that was what she was *really* about. A spy, just as she had always been. Watching people, trying to trip them up. Ruining lives. Throwing people behind locked doors, from which there was no chance of escape.

Maybe she was good at what she did, but what about her victims? By this time tomorrow, Knapp mused, he would have taken his revenge and rendered her unable to hurt him again. And he would dedicate his action to the countless other innocents whose existences she had so rudely interrupted.

Mai-Lin left at 5 A.M., when her targets' drunkenness finally conquered useful conversation. Knapp stayed on, watching with amazement as a naked girl took to the circular stage to blow table-tennis balls from her vagina, a great cheer welling up from the surrounding crowd with each resounding pop.

As the artiste took her bow, he wandered across to the dance floor. Ten girls were still swaying, though the music was slower now as befitted the hour. A group of young Thai men stood in a corner close by, glasses of Mae Khong whisky in their hands. Knapp guessed they were the husbands or boyfriends of the girls before him, there to take their charges home if there was no money to be made this night.

Knapp chose Number 42, the most mature-looking of the group. From the corner of his eye, he saw the girl's spouse smile as he made his pick. He paid 500 baht at the bar and was told the girl would ask him for a further 1,000 baht in his hotel room once he had finished. He nodded his acceptance.

The girl loyally took his arm as they left and showered

him with compliments in pidgin English. 'You big important man?' she asked, pointing at his briefcase.

Knapp, his mind still on the kill to come, felt growing
excitement. He tapped the briefcase without thinking of
the rope and sack inside it, and said: 'Soon, sugar, I will
be the biggest, most important man in the world.'

Mai-Lin lived in a condominium on Sukhumvit Road, a
swank part of Bangkok populated by expatriates, wealthy
Thais and *mia noi* – the second wives kept by government
officials and business executives. She could not have
managed it on her police salary alone, but a generous
monthly allowance from her father more than bridged the
gap. She wished she could have turned down the handout
– it was the only chink in her armour of fierce independence. But in truth, Sukhumvit Road suited her. Her
early years in Geneva had internationalized her and she
felt comfortable among the cosmopolitan bunch that
milled around the area. And though it was only a few
miles from the moral desert of Patpong, it was a world
apart. A perfect refuge.

The bell rang at noon as she was having a brunch of
water melon and sugared lemon juice under the balcony
sunshade. She walked to the door, wiping her lips with a
finger, and made her usual precautionary check through
the spy-hole.

As soon as she saw Knapp, standing motionless in a white
suit, she knew he was the man she had been waiting for.
Her eyes told her, the acceleration of her heartbeat told
her, the sudden sickness in her stomach told her. There was
something dreadful about him. Familiar and wicked at the
same time . . . the most dangerous chemistry of all.

She watched him as he leaned forward to press the bell
again – and thought of what he had done. He had

murdered dear Kipini. He had murdered dear, dear Sari. He had killed Pearl, Louise and Stefanie as surely as if he had laid hands on them. He had reduced lovely, sympathetic Dany to a shambolic wreck.

And now, he has come to reduce me to so much water, gristle and bone.

Mai-Lin could not believe he was really there, less than a yard from where she stood. She saw Pearl's coffin being dropped into the ground, and imagined Knapp's warped smirk of delight at such a scene. Though she tried desperately hard to hold herself steady, though she tried to tell herself she was a seasoned professional who had met similar situations with coolness and aplomb, she could not prevent sparks of apprehension jumping between the hair tips on the back of her neck.

She was experienced enough to know that the next step was fear – and moved to counter it, to assert herself over the forces of evil. She fetched her Beretta from a drawer beside her bed, screwing on a silencer as she returned to the door. Knapp rung the bell a third time. He knew Mai-Lin was in – and she knew that he knew.

She felt an urge to shoot him through the door as he stood there, to rid the world of this disease-ridden specimen of mankind. But she resisted it. She had a vocation. She had a duty to find out *who* he was – and *why* he had set out to annihilate her little group of childhood friends.

'Are you armed?' she called out.

His reply would have sounded aptly proverbial, considering the part of the world in which he found himself, had he not laced it with sarcasm. 'If a man is carrying a weapon to dispose of an enemy, does he inform that enemy of the fact?'

'Then I will inform you. I have a gun and will not hesitate to use it.'

320

'I don't doubt it – and it was kind of you to tell me. Such a thoughtful little girl.'

Mai-Lin felt unsure again. Her habitual foes were crudely violent. Screaming swine who would stick a knife through the stomachs of their own mothers as long as the *deal* was right. This man was different. Perhaps not the velvet-gloved assassin. But a velvet-voiced one certainly.

There were no hysterics from Knapp, no snarling threats. Just a calm, reasoned assurance that what must be done will be done. Mai-Lin warned herself not to waver.

'You must agree to be searched,' she said.

'That would be a trifle undignified.'

'You must agree.'

Mai-Lin saw Knapp grin as he replied: 'Oh, very well then.'

She opened the door as far as the retaining chain allowed, pushing the barrel of the pistol through the gap. Knapp smiled again and raised his hands in the air as if he had been told to reach by a cowboy. When she first saw his face clearly, without the blurring restriction of the spy-hole, she was immediately struck by his age.

'You're so much *older* . . .' she said without thinking.

Knapp bowed his head in recognition of the fact. 'I'm afraid so, my dear. Time waits for no man . . . or woman, for that matter. Only a few tender years ago, you yourself were just a little girl. Making mischief. Telling tales.'

Mai-Lin knew he defied logic. If he was so old, he should have been that much less of a threat. Yet the trim cut of his suit showed his body was in fine shape. He had killed with those same gristly hands. And he had watched his victims die with the same sharp eyes that were looking at her now.

His eyes, his eyes . . .

321

She wished he would not look at her so. He was boring holes in her, making her feel somehow exposed.

Mai-Lin unclipped the retaining chain and flicked the pistol to usher Knapp inside. 'Take off your shoes before you enter a Thai dwelling,' she said brusquely. 'Put them beside the mat next to mine.'

Knapp chuckled to himself. He had killed Sari in stockinged feet. Now he would claim Mai-Lin in the same ridiculous attire.

'You are so very . . . what's the word . . . traditional,' he said.

Mai-Lin ignored the jibe. She ordered him to turn round, spread his legs and put his hands on the wall. Ignoring his protests that she was being over-theatrical, she frisked him for a gun or a blade. When she found none, she thrust busy hands inside his pockets, searching for identification.

'Darn it,' he muttered. 'I must have left my passport and credit cards at the hotel. It doesn't do to be parted from such things in a strange city.'

Mai-Lin grew more confused. A man with no name who had come to kill her without a weapon. How, then, when he must have known she would be armed? What did he have in mind? Her turmoil manifested itself in impatience. She pulled on his shoulder to turn him around and snapped: 'Why are you here? What do you want? Who are you?'

'So many questions.' Knapp waggled an admonishing finger.

'Which need answers.'

Calmly, Knapp told Mai-Lin he was on her side. He knew her line of work and had come to inform her about a large consignment of heroin soon to be shipped from the Golden Triangle, via Bangkok, to the United States.

'Nonsense,' Mai-Lin replied. She stepped away from Knapp, holding her pistol with both hands and pointing it at his chest.

'Then how do I know about you?' Knapp protested. 'How do I know your name and private address? How do I know you work Heaven's Gate and the other vice dens of Patpong? How do I know of your shambolic shack behind the Lor Nam hotel?'

'You followed me. You bribed some of my more corrupt colleagues for information. It's not difficult. You know how much the average policeman earns in this city?'

Knapp knew every wage packet of every rank, but shook his head.

'Peanuts,' Mai-Lin went on. 'It leads to more than a shade of private enterprise. Small men lining their pockets, trying to be big shots. It'd go down well where you come from. How much did you pay?'

Knapp opened his arms in a gesture of innocence, wondering whimsically why he had bothered to invent his guise as an informant when it was so blatantly unnecessary.

He studied Mai-Lin. She was wearing a baggy silk dressing gown and her hair was still wet from her morning shower. The combination made her look more vulnerable than the stylish woman-about-town he had watched the previous night.

As if she could read his mind, Mai-Lin straightened herself in an attempt to beef up her stature.

Knapp ignored her posturing and looked over her shoulder at the apartment. No surprises here, he thought. Cool tiled floors, furniture made from woven rattan cane, a mammoth Grand Tower air-conditioner. And high on the wall beside the entrance to the balcony, a Buddhist altar supporting a small bronze Buddha statue, a selection of *dork mai* holy flowers, candles, joss sticks and an offering of fresh fruit and water.

Knapp nodded in its direction. 'To ward off evil spirits?' he suggested, without smiling.

'Yes . . . no.' Mai-Lin found herself stuttering. Knapp's gaze was upon her again. And now finally, with the utmost crushing certainty, she knew she could no longer hold back the fear.

It had the effect of paralysing the muscles in her arms and her legs. She tried to fight it, tried to free herself from the magnetic cocoon he had thrown around her. But it required immense effort even to move her lips so she could speak.

'Where were you in May 1960?' she blurted out. 'What were you doing?'

Knapp did not reply. He stared at her, watched as her body was gripped by tremors.

'Why were you in the woods? Why did it happen? Why wouldn't you leave us alone?'

Knapp took a step forward. Mai-Lin managed to twist her wrists a fraction so the Beretta was pointing directly at his heart.

'Why have you come back after all this time? What did we ever do to you? We didn't harm you. You must know that!'

Knapp took another step.

'How could we? We were so young!'

Knapp, unrelenting, shuffled closer still. 'I knew you would be ready for me, day or night,' he said. 'You're the type. That's why I did not bother to wait until the sun went down.'

Mai-Lin knew she had to pull the trigger of her pistol now . . . or never.

She summoned every ounce of effort she possessed,

324

trying desperately to send a message to her fingers. Curl and pull. Curl and pull.

Remember Pearl – curl and pull. For Louise and Stefanie – curl and pull. To avenge Kipini and Sari – curl and pull. To save Dany – curl and pull. Please, for the love of everything I cherish, curl and pull. Curl and pull!

It was useless. Knapp, his face suddenly crimson with fury, his eyes glaring with hatred, kept coming.

'So demure, so in control,' he sneered. 'Such a loyal and devoted servant of all that is good. Such a beacon of worthiness. Such an example to us all.'

Mai-Lin whimpered. She was neither demure nor in control. She was no more than a terrified six-year-old girl in the woods outside Geneva.

Knapp's arm lashed out and knocked the Beretta from Mai-Lin's hands with one blow. Automatically, she found herself following the gun's flight to see where it landed. It had the effect of freeing her from Knapp's hypnotic gaze – and she felt suppleness and confidence surging back into her body.

Without looking back to pinpoint Knapp's head, she high-kicked her right leg. Knapp was caught on the left cheekbone with sufficient force to stop him in his tracks. But he did not cry out.

He, too, was experiencing a burst of inner strength, both physical and mental, that stemmed from inside his head, crashing against the lining of his skull before thrusting down the nerve highways of his spine and into every fibre of his being. He had felt it before, when he dealt with Kipini and with Sari, and knew precisely what was happening.

When fear and pain are eliminated, there is nothing left to hinder ultimate power.

Mai-Lin ran across the room, turned and slid a coffee

table into his shins. He brushed the table aside and followed her, making sure he stayed between the girl and her gun. She went on the attack, leaping at him and clawing at his face with long fingernails, pushing herself away instantly to give him no chance to counter.

She wanted to see the weals on his cheeks and his jaw, but dared not look in case he trapped her again with his eyes. Everything would have to be done as if she was a blind woman.

She came again, lunging under his shoulder to hit him on the neck with the taut side of her hand. He pushed her away with a force that took her by surprise. She slid on her dressing gown across the polished floor and cracked her head on a large ornamental urn. The instant she stopped, she flipped over to deny him a chance of pinning her down. Then she was on her feet again, rushing towards his bulk with the intention of ramming her fist into his testicles to take his breath away.

He saw her coming and moved a fraction. Her knuckles smashed into the top of his thigh, but it was she who winced with pain. The man felt as solid as a redwood tree and she knew she would have to think of something special to fell him.

She spun on the spot like a top. His flailing arms tried to grab her, but she was too quick. She dodged under his elbow, jerked herself on to her ankles for leverage, pulled her right arm back behind her shoulder and flattened her palm in readiness for the final blow.

She would thrust her fingers directly at his voice box, crushing it and pushing it back into his windpipe. His next breath would be his last.

'Mai-Lin,' he said out of the blue.

She could not help glancing at him – and he had her at his mercy.

He slapped her face so hard that she fell backwards on to the floor with the barest hold on consciousness. Through the haze, the only shape she could make out was a square, growing larger as it loomed closer. At the last moment, she recognized it as the cushion from the wicker-work chair she had bought the previous week.

'Why do little girls fight and argue so?' Knapp said.

24

Ciera took Curran aside minutes after he arrived at the sleep lab with Dany. 'You must stay tonight,' the researcher said urgently.

Curran looked across at Dany, who was sitting limply on her wooden chair, waiting for the electrodes to be stuck to her skull. He had never seen her so wretched. Fatigue and anxiety had drained her to the point of collapse. Her eyes were sore, red-rimmed and void of hope. Her heart was so heavy with despair that even though she knew Curran and Ciera were staring at her, she had no wish either to return their gaze or avoid it. No, she decided, she would just sit here . . . and wait.

'The night of reckoning?' Curran said.

'Uh-huh. She's been building up to it. Her dreams have become more vivid, more detailed – and she has been more terrified by them. I am convinced that tonight she will finally see everything she is ever going to see. But at the same time, the extreme intensity of her vision could endanger her life.'

'Like Pearl, Stefanie and Louise?' Curran said unnecessarily. 'Sudden Unexplained Death?'

'Only in Dany's case, it will not be unexplained – and not unpreventable. But in a situation like this, there will always be a fine line between life and death. You know that what we are doing here is wrong. That Dany should be in hospital . . .'

'But –'

'But then we would never be able to look into her dreams – and we would never know what this is all about.'

'Exactly,' Curran said, relieved that someone else had said what he was thinking. 'Thank you, Ciera. Thank you for everything.'

'Don't thank me – help me. I want you here tonight so I don't have to shoulder such responsibility alone.'

Curran could see that the normal yellow-greyness of Ciera's vitamin-starved skin had been further jaundiced with worry. He nodded once and said: 'Of course.'

Dany ignored every attempt at conversation, every attempt to reassure her that all would be well. She went to the sleeping room without saying a word, her thoughts dominated by the friends who had died in their beds. She knew that like them, she was about to endure the ultimate terror – and might never wake up.

Her silence made Ciera more disconcerted than ever and put Curran on a knife edge.

The two watchers sat side by side gazing at the blue-lined paper flowing under the thin inky needles of the polygraph like a stream caressed by the tendrils of a weeping willow. The needles swept up and down, leaving hills and troughs on the paper, regular and unmuddled as Dany dropped off to sleep with apparent serenity.

There was a chill in the air of the sleep lab, as predictable as it was unfathomable, and Ciera briefly left her seat to fetch a jumper, tossing it across her shoulders as she returned. Curran found himself buttoning his jacket. They looked at each other and laughed nervously. Then they talked incessantly, fearing that any break in their conversation would allow the atmosphere to take control.

Curran told Ciera how Yvette had been sent to stay

329

with her grandmother in Switzerland. Ciera spoke with pride about how she had plumbed in a new sink at her flat herself, because she could not afford a plumber.

More than an hour went by. And then, without notice, the polygraph needles recording Dany's eye movements accelerated frenziedly until they were scratching vast black, fuzzy-edged puddles on the paper below them.

Ciera looked darkly at Curran and said: 'This is it.'

Dany knew the man was closing in on her. Coming from nowhere to kill her, to close her eyes for ever. She could *feel* him as she had felt him in the archives room of her old school. She could feel his unstoppable power, his warped and ruthless determination, and imagined it was what Pearl, Louise and Stefanie had felt in the moments before their deaths.

When her mind drifted back to the woods, she could see exactly what he had done and why he had done it. She could hear every word he said. She even knew what he was thinking. A fusion of time and destiny took her inside him, and he inside her.

Everything was so clear.

The seven girls ducked down behind the tree trunk, and a sparkling row of fourteen curious eyes settled on the strange sight that confronted them.

In a small clearing beyond, a man and a woman, he aged in his early thirties, she looking several years younger, faced each other beside the rusty shell of an abandoned car.

The man threw his jacket over a dead branch that hung low from a sycamore tree, and stood stiffly with hands on hips in an open-necked white shirt and beige trousers. The woman was all in black, her full-length dress, done up tightly at the collar, brushing the yellow blooms of the dandelion cluster beneath her. The girls all thought she was pretty, but her beauty was partially obscured by the hand she held on her forehead. It was funny, the girls whispered. The hand was there as if to protect herself from the glare of sunlight, yet she was in the shade.

'Perhaps she's got a headache,' Pearl said.

'Her other hand's in a funny place, too,' Stefanie said.

'It's on her tummy,' Louise said.

'That's not her tummy, silly,' Kipini chided.

'What is it then?' Louise asked indignantly.

'It's called a womb,' Kipini corrected. 'My mummy told me that's where I came from.'

'Where is it?' said Louise, becoming confused.

'It's inside you.'

'Oh . . .'

The woman's head slumped. A knot of thick red hair tumbled from her shoulder. When she spoke, she sounded to Dany as if she was terribly sad.

'So, now I have told you of my intentions.'

The man held out his arms imploringly, casting a handful of pine needles to the ground. 'All I want to know is why?' he said.

'If you do not know, you should know,' the woman replied forcibly.

'I don't understand.'

'It is time to tell the world – and be done with it.'

The man raised his voice. 'No! It is a secret and shall remain a secret.'

'You cannot expect me to agree to that. Not now.'

'You must! You have to . . .'

'I do not *have* to do anything. You do not own me.'

Stefanie butted in. 'She's angry.'

'She speaks funny,' Dany whispered.

331

'She's not American.'

'Or English.'

'Neither am I,' said Mai-Lin.

'You speak funny, too.'

'*Girls! Les enfants! You must come back to me.*'

'I want to go back to Mam'selle.'

'Be quiet, Sari.'

'Ssssh.'

The woman circled her womb with her hand, as if she was soothing sore flesh. 'And what of my baby?' she demanded. 'What of *our* baby?'

The man scratched the back of his neck and transferred his gaze to the ground before muttering: 'There are ways and means . . .'

'No!' The stridency of the woman's cry made the girls jump. 'I will not! I want to have the child. It means so much to me.'

'But . . .' The man spun round and slammed a frustrated fist into the bonnet of the rusty old car. When he turned to the woman again, his face was accusing. 'You tricked me,' he said, flicking a finger in her direction.

'No . . .'

'You did it deliberately.'

'No.'

'You became pregnant on purpose to trap me.'

'No.' The woman shook her head in sorry disbelief at what she was hearing.

'It was the only way you thought you could get me – to have me for yourself.'

'No! No! No!' She covered her ears to try to make herself deaf, but she could still hear his fury.

'Why did you do it? You must be mad! You know that if people find out about us – about *you* – then I will be finished. It is too much to ask of me.'

'Is it? Why should it be so?'

'Jesus Christ! You *know why*. Don't come the little innocent with me, girlie. You know what this ball game is all about.'

The woman could not prevent her tears. But she knew that as well as being tears of sorrow, they were also tears of anger. She wiped them from her eyes roughly with the back of a wrist.

'I know what is coming now,' she said with certainty. 'You are going to tell me you will lose your position in the service.'

'You know damn well I will!' the man screamed. 'And the rest. I will be shamed, disgraced, pilloried. I will lose my job, my family and my whole fucking future. Do you know what I am talking about?'

'I am aware of where your ambitions lie. You want to soar like an eagle.'

'I will lose everything . . . everything!'

'You will not lose my love. And you will not lose our child.'

'Jesus Christ!'

The man clenched his fists and stamped a foot on the ground hard, as if he was squashing a venomous spider.

'He's flipping his lid,' Stefanie said without knowing whether or not to be pleased with such grown-up language.

'He's very angry,' Louise said nervously.

'Gosh . . . look.'

The woman took hold of the man, curling her arms around his shoulders, pressing herself against him. She tried to kiss his lips, but when he turned away, she settled for the side of his face. She kissed him time after time, pushing quivering fingers through his hair, sliding a palm down his spine, rubbing her thighs against his. She could

not tell if she was trying to seduce him or simply attempt-
ing to calm him.

Either way, she failed. He wedged his fingers between
his chest and hers and pushed her away with an uncompromising strength she had not previously encountered.

Now it was her turn to feel rage. 'How *dare* you,' she
cried. 'Does not our romance, our tender feeling for each
other, mean a thing to you? Three years of a shared love.
Secret, yes, but also cherished. Three years . . .'

'Shut up, damn you. Shut up!'

'How can you talk to me so?'

'I can talk to you any way I like.'

'And I can talk to others any way I like. I will tell them
of our love and our child. I will tell them of my happiness.
I must, I have to. I can no longer keep it inside me. My
heart is burning a hole through my chest. Do you not see?
Now is the time for us both. We must spend the rest of
our lives together. You and I and our baby.'

'No! Shit . . . no!'

The man could no longer move. He stood rooted to the
spot, paralysed with indecision, fear and resentment. He
could not bear to look at the woman. His eyes fell to the
floor of the woods and traced a dizzy, curling path through
the brambles, the weeds, the grass and the dirt.

Just as he was certain he would faint and topple over,
he saw it.

A long, thin wedge of smashed flintstone, poking from a
dust puddle with its sharp edge facing upwards. As smooth
as ice on one side, rough and jagged on the other.

Its contrasting appearance triggered an explosion of
opposites that burst across the man's mind like shrapnel.

An awful, terrible idea – yet irresistible. A beautiful
woman who had been his lover for three years – yet a
witch out to destroy him. A dazzling career that was

reaching for the highest heights – yet stood on the brink of an abyss.

An abyss.

An abyss.

The word would not leave him. It careered past the back of his eyeballs, raced through the ripples of his brain and hurtled into the gnarled bundle of nerves that stood at the summit of his spine.

No, he could not let it happen.

In one swift movement, he bent to pick up the stone, clasped it firmly in his right hand and scored it powerfully up the woman's leg from ankle to thigh.

The flint opened a gaping gash – and the woman screamed in agony.

'Hush!' the man cried, his voice suddenly childlike. 'Be quiet. You mustn't tell a soul.'

The woman screamed again and turned to run. But the man stopped her with his free hand and jumped in front of her with one apelike bound. The woman crossed her hands over her womb to protect her baby in case the man should try to punch her in the abdomen.

She looked at the man and tried to find the gentle lover who had cared for her so. But all she saw was a man possessed. A man who had lost control. Every muscle in his face was twitching frenziedly. Yet the hand gripping the scarlet-tipped flintstone was steady and alert.

She emitted a whimper of the purest fear. 'Please,' she begged. 'What has happened . . .'

He knew he had to stop her talking, before she told the damn universe of their secret. He punched her on the jaw with his left hand and leaped on her as soon as she hit the ground. He tore clumps of grass from the earth and stuffed them into her mouth until all she could do was shake her head.

Still, it was not enough. What if she spat out the grass? What if she got back to Geneva? What if all the others heard what the hell he had been doing?

'Darling Yelena,' he uttered. 'For so long my friend . . . yet now my most heinous enemy.'

He remembered the military attaché, Lyall, and the way he dealt with his enemies. *'Carved them into diamonds of sliced flesh . . .'*

The man did as the Ranger had done, using the flintstone for his blade. First he tore the woman's clothes, then he tore her flesh. Fine jets of blood spurted from severed arteries until the man was covered by a clinging, glistening crimson film.

He needed to pull the stone hard towards him each time, for its sharpness could not hope to compare with a knife. But nothing could stop him now. He dug into the woman time after time. He criss-crossed her chest, her stomach, her pelvis, her legs. And finally, of necessity it occurred to him, he criss-crossed her face, making sure there was nothing left of her mouth.

She coughed and spluttered at first. When she managed to rid herself of the grass in her throat, she cried for help. And even after the assault on her mouth, she continued to emit a distorted yelp like a mongrel with a collar pulled too tightly around its neck. The seven girls, too petrified to utter a sound, watched her try to inch her way backwards, rubbing her shoulder blades from side to side on the dirt. But she got no further than a foot or two before her body was consumed by tremors, as if she was lying on ice.

Her final act was to raise her arm towards the man. She stretched out her fingers imploringly and let out a grunt that Dany swore sounded like, 'Why?'

The man was unmoved. He looked down at the woman

with contempt and pushed her hand aside so it flapped down beside her leaking stomach.

Mercifully, finally, she was silent and still – and always would be.

The man shuffled on his knees to the rusted car and searched inside it. Within a minute, he found what he was looking for. The tow-rope was was frayed and stained with the residue of rust, but a tug to test its strength satisfied him that it would do. He trussed the woman's arms to her limp, blood-dampened torso and slipped a loop around her neck. Then he dragged her to the sycamore tree hosting his jacket, threw the loose end of the rope over the dead branch and pulled. After he tied his final knot, the woman was left hanging.

'I'll leave you there,' he muttered as he looked up at her face, a patchwork of death-white strands of skin, crimson chasms and coagulating globules of blood. 'As a warning to others, you understand.'

After a moment of thought, he added: 'I cannot be denied, you see. And neither can those who want to see me where I should be. At the pinnacle, my darling sweetheart. At the very pinnacle.'

To the girls, the woman – with her shredded black clothes and her matted red hair – looked like a scarecrow dangling on a string. It was only the way her bulk swayed in the breeze and the protesting groan of the rope that reminded them she was a real person.

That, and the squirts of blood they had seen as the man gouged her with the stone.

Black clouds blotted out the sun and disgorged their heavy load of rain without delay. Pearl cuddled closer to Dany. Louise could restrain herself no longer and shouted, 'No! No!'

The man heard and spun round. Through the swirling

337

curtain of rain, he saw a fallen, horizontal pine. And above it, barely visible, were seven straw bonnets . . . and seven pairs of eyes.

He felt no panic, not even apprehension. All he knew was that the children – for that is what they appeared to be – had found out about the woman. And he couldn't have that.

He threw the stone casually into the air and watched it spin before catching it again. Ignoring the brambles that clawed at his trouser legs, he walked towards the girls.

Dany jerked maniacally in the bed. Ciera rushed into the room and went to shake her awake, but Curran held her back.

'Let me go!' Ciera protested. 'She could die. You know she could.'

'No . . .' Curran tried to stay calm, though he could see Dany's vision had possessed her body and soul. 'We have to let her go on, don't you see? We have to let her see everything that happened, once and for all.'

'But – '

The man came closer. Dany cried out and broke into the heaviest sweat Curran had ever seen.

'We can't,' Ciera said. 'I'm responsible. I'd never forgive myself if – '

'Be strong!' Curran addressed it as much to himself as Ciera.

The researcher felt Dany's pulse. 'It's racing,' she said. 'She can't go on like this much longer. The heart won't take it.'

'Leave her,' Curran said. 'Be cruel to be kind.'

The blood-covered zombie was upon her. Dany began to pant like a dog, the tips of her fingers flicked like windblown leaves and her stomach folded in on itself.

'Please,' Ciera begged. 'She's turning blue.'

Curran could not say another word. All he had left was one more grain of willpower.

The zombie raised the flint into the air and brought it down on his outstretched hand. '*It won't hurt. See –* ' One blow. Two blows. Three, four. Bone and gristle crunching. The severed finger flying through the air towards her, slapping against her cheek. The zombie lifting the stone again, ready to punch it through her skull.

'No!' Dany screamed. She went into spasm. Razorblade colics sliced through her body, making it curl in agony. Her mouth opened, exposing a protruding tongue lolling lifelessly on her lower lip. A rivulet of foamy saliva flowed on to her pillow.

Ciera struggled from Curran's grasp and reached over to grab Dany's shoulder. She shook it forcefully, but her hand was knocked away as Dany's arms went haywire.

'Dany!' Ciera yelled, her voice hoarse with panic. 'Dany! Wake up, Dany!' Curran joined in the chorus and shouted as loud as he could.

Dany whipped over where she lay, completing almost a full circle before crashing down on to the mattress once more.

Her arms stopped flapping, her tremors subsided and her tongue receded into her mouth. Soon, she was lying perfectly still.

'Oh no . . .' Curran's utterance was despairing. 'Oh God, no.'

Ciera's shoulders collapsed as if someone had taken a prop from under them. She glared at Curran, trying to transfer as much guilt as she could on to him, though she was only too aware she would never be able to forgive herself.

Only a single step was required to reach Dany's side,

but Ciera was reluctant to take it. She summoned the courage from somewhere and automatically took hold of Dany's wrist to feel if any pulse remained.

After a while, she turned to Curran and said without expression: 'It's normal. She's still sleeping.'

'Jesus Christ, Knapp. Stop!' The three black-suited men appeared through the trees as if by magic, launching themselves at the zombie as the flintstone flashed down towards Dany's head.

It all became a tangled blur. Shadows lunging at other shadows. Tall shapes mingling with short shapes. Arms, legs, faces, hands, feet, hips, shoulders.

It was too frenetic, too muddled – and the potential outcome was too terrifying to contemplate.

As tears threw an opaque shield over pupils, Dany lost her power of sight. All she could do was touch the rough bark of the fallen pine, smell the fresh perfumes pummelled from bluebells and daffodils by the hammering rain – and listen to the frenzy erupting around her.

'Hold him!'

'Kick him!'

'I can't – he's too strong.'

'You have to. You must.'

'Christ!'

'Shit.'

'He's gone mad . . . fucking berserk.'

'Hit him – now!'

'Aaah!'

'You got him – now hold him. For Christ's sake, hold him.'

'He's covered in blood.'

'Hold him! Kneel on him!'

'He'd have killed them. The kids – he'd have killed them.'

'Who are they? What the hell are they doing here?'

Dany blinked as hard as she could. Her tears were dispersed by her eyelids – and she saw the zombie, who she now knew was named Knapp, pinned to the ground by the men in black suits. He was struggling ferociously beneath them, his fists beating their shoulders and his feet kicking their hips. But little by little, they were getting the better of him.

'Go on,' Dany uttered in support. 'You've got to win . . .'

It made the three men glance round. Thick moustache. Round and red. A face so bony it could have been a fleshless skull. Dany picked out their salient features as she scanned them one by one.

The man with the moustache somehow managed a flicker of a smile to comfort her, but it vanished as he turned towards the clearing and saw the dangling scarecrow.

'Look!'

'Where?' the round red man said.

'Over there. Look!'

'Shit . . .' the bony man gasped.

'What is it?'

'*Who* is it?'

'Oh God . . .'

'What have you *done*, Knapp?' the bony man shrieked, unleashing a battery of punches that finally forced the zombie into silent submission.

'Keep him here,' the bony man ordered. 'I'll take a look.'

The man with the moustache turned again. 'Wait a

minute, children. Stay here and we will sort this out. There's nothing to be afraid of.'

The bony man ran to the clearing, leaping clumps of brambles, leather soles slapping into sodden ground as he landed. 'It's a girl,' he shouted as he reached the scarecrow. He stopped dead, watched it sway for a moment, then groaned, 'Oh Christ. Oh Jesus, Jesus Christ!'

'Dead?' the round red man called.

'Look at her – what do you fucking think?'

'Did he do that? *Could* he?'

'Get her down and see if she's carrying identification,' the man with the moustache suggested quietly.

'Jesus Christ . . .' The bony man was retching as if he was about to vomit. 'I don't believe . . .'

'Need help?' the round red man offered.

'No – stay on top of him.'

The bony man stretched up to pull the noose from the scarecrow's neck.

'Stay calm, gentlemen,' the man with the moustache said. 'Don't worry, children.'

Dany's tears flowed again – and her blindness returned.

'Got her. Oh God, oh Jesus. How could anyone do this?'

'Any identification?'

The rustling of a hand flicking through pockets. Even at such a distance, Dany could hear it.

'If she's got it, I'll find it. Oh, this is terrible, awful. She's sticky with blood.'

'Brave it out.'

'Hold him down!'

'Stay there, you swine.'

'God, she's a Red.'

'Who?'

342

'The girl. The dead girl. She's got her papers on her. She's Russian.'

'Good grief . . .'

'You mean Knapp's murdered a Russian girl?'

'The day after the balloon goes up about the U2.'

'This is serious.'

'That's the understatement of the twentieth century.'

'He's killed a Russian girl.'

'I don't believe it.'

'Khrushchev will.'

'He's fighting! Help me!'

'Knock him cold.'

'Then what?'

'We'll have to think of something.'

'Something wild – and something fast.'

Dany's sight was restored only when the rain stopped and the sun emerged from behind the clouds to illuminate the woods. The zombie called Knapp was lying amid the docks, his arms splayed out like Jesus on the cross. He was moaning and shaking his head as if waking from a deep sleep. The round red man stood above him, watching his every move.

The man with the moustache leaned over the tree trunk, his face vast, oval and distorted as if Dany was looking at him through a magnifying glass. He smiled and asked for names.

The girls, who did not trust him – smile or no smile – would not have it. When Dany shook her head, the man's lips hardened and he transformed his request into a demand. 'Names. Quickly now.'

A renewed wave of fear swept over the girls. Perhaps this man would turn into a zombie, too. Unless they co-operated. Unless they did as he said.

'Dany.'

'Pearl.'

'Tell him your name, Kipini.'

Stefanie was about to announce hers when the man with the moustache stopped her short by holding up a rigid hand. He had been distracted by the intertwined swans on her blazer – and stared at the badge as if it were a light shining in darkness. His expression was one of recognition – and shock.

He wheeled around and glared at the zombie accusingly. His voice shook with trepidation. 'Dear Lord, Knapp, it could have been my daughter watching you butcher – '

The zombie heard, but did not react. He had lifted his head – and was watching the bony man pull the torn remains of an old jute sack from the rusty car. When the bony man dropped the sack on the scarecrow to cover its disfigured face, he clambered slowly to his feet to get a better view.

He whispered, 'Yelena . . .' before his knees folded and he crashed once more to the ground.

Ciera decided it was safe to break into the dream and went into the room with her tape recorder already switched on and rolling.

Dany was oblivious to Ciera's entry. She had tucked her knees under her chin. And she was sucking her thumb.

25

Curran was spurred by the emergence of the name Knapp in Dany's final vision. As he boarded the plane to New York, he cursed the diversion caused by chasing a man whose surname began with N. It had been an honest mistake. In her previous dreams, Dany had remembered the name without the silent K . . . as would any six-year-old.

Now, for the first time, he had a genuine lead, something to cling to, someone to find. A man called Knapp who was in Geneva at the same time as the Seven Swans. There was only one place to start, one person to question.

Martha Knapp.

Curran felt like an old piece of timber savaged by the elements and gradually splitting in two. One half of him prayed the shared name was pure coincidence and that he would be able to go on loving Martha without reservation. For that, in his heart of hearts, is what he yearned to do. The other half was desperate that there should be a connection. That Martha would be able to tell him where to go and what to do to find the monster who had wreaked such death, destruction and sorrow.

His jet landed at JFK two hours before Martha's next flight took off, and they arranged to meet in an airport bar. As soon as Martha saw him, she frowned and remarked how tired and bedraggled he looked. It was a sign of caring, and Curran was thrown into further disarray. He asked for a large vodka and propped himself on a bar stool. Martha said she never drank before work, and

345

settled for an iced mineral water. The situation reminded them both of how they met and they shared a knowing smile. But Curran could not maintain it for long – and Martha sensed his inner turmoil. She put a hand on his and asked: 'What is it, Stephen? Tell me. That's what I'm here for now.'

'I'm not sure if you want to know,' he said.

The reply troubled her – and she began to guess what he was about to say before he said it.

He told her of the panicked shouts and yells that had echoed through the Geneva woods thirty years before. He told her of the struggle to subdue a man who had gone berserk.

He left out the murder of the girl and the fact that she was Russian. He wanted to spare Martha such grotesque details – and in any event they were unnecessary for what he had in mind.

'There was something new,' Curran said, looking at her intensely. 'The man was called Knapp.' He shook his head, trying to determine how he should phrase his next utterance. He came up with, 'Strange, eh?'

Martha did not force him to say another word.

In a way, it was a relief to unburden herself, and she did not hold back on anything. Choosing her words carefully, she spoke about her early days in Geneva; how her father had vanished from her life without explanation; how he had reappeared just as mysteriously in a secure hospital for the criminally insane in England; how she had met him on his release and how he had ill-treated her since their reunion.

'He's not dead,' she said, her eyes full of apology. 'I lied to you.'

'It doesn't matter,' Curran said.

'He hit me,' Martha went on, almost in a whisper. 'I never fell on any damn ashtray.'

Curran could not help but feel sympathy, but told himself he had to be strong. 'Was he the man known as Crosby?' he asked, trying not to reveal the desperation he felt inside.

'Yes.' Martha's chest began to heave, as if she was on the verge of panic.

'Is he still known as Crosby?'

'No.'

'Then what is his name?'

'Dallenbach. They gave him a passport and papers in the name of Evan P. Dallenbach.'

'They?'

'The State Department. Through a man called Hagerty.'

'The State Department? Why them? Is – was – your father a spy or something? CIA?'

'Maybe, but I don't know now. I don't know anything for sure any more. Truly, I don't . . .'

The conundrum veered out of control in Curran's head until it was almost too much to bear. He asked the bartender for another vodka, though he knew it would fog his thoughts further.

Martha rescued him by volunteering hard information. 'He's the man in your photograph. The trigger. He was in Africa at the time Kipini was killed and he hasn't been in his apartment for ages. Enough time to reach Sari, anyway. I've had my suspicions for . . .' She fell silent, unable to shake off a sense of betrayal. Then she said: 'Oh God, Stephen, he's my *father*.'

Curran leaned forward to take her in his arms. She clung tightly to him, digging her fingers into his waist.

He was all she had left in the world.

She looked up, her face as forlorn as that of a starving child, and said starkly: 'Stephen, what did my father do in Dany's dream?'

The question punched the breath from Curran. What to do? What to say? He simply did not know.

'Tell me!' Martha demanded.

'You're too upset,' he countered, playing for time. 'Not here, not now.'

'You'll find a better time and a better place . . .' Her urgency was replaced instantly by resignation. '. . . so you can mop me up afterwards.'

'Something like that, I guess.'

'It was that bad, huh?'

Her eyes locked on his and she had her reply. Yes, Martha, Curran's were saying, it was that bad. And worse.

Martha took a pen from her purse and scribbled Knapp's address on the back of an envelope. She pushed it across to Curran, then climbed from her stool before her treachery overwhelmed her and forced her to snatch it back.

'I'll see you when it's all over one way or the other,' she said.

Curran held out a pleading hand. 'Martha – '

'When it's all over,' she repeated.

She walked away with her head lolling to one side.

Curran shocked himself with his bestial thirst for revenge. He wanted to find Knapp's apartment. He wanted to buy a gun and bullets. He wanted to smash his way into the apartment and hold the gun at Knapp's head to force a full and final confession. He wanted to march Knapp to the nearest police station and listen as he repeated the confession to uniformed witnesses.

And if that did not work, if Knapp resisted, he wanted to blow the bastard's brains out.

It was not the thinking man's reaction. It was not even rational, for he had never handled firearms and had not a clue about loading, kickback and the like. Or how it would feel to threaten – and perhaps even take – another's life. But it was damn well real.

Yet something Martha had said stuck with him. 'He hasn't been in his apartment for ages.'

So he is unlikely to be there now.

'Enough time to reach Sari, anyway.'

And then where? To Bangkok, for Mai-Lin? Or to London, for Dany?

Curran could not afford to delay. He ran to the PanAm desk and pleaded for a seat on the next London flight. The pony-tailed clerk hmm'd and haa'd and uttered platitudes like over-capacity and fuller than a can of sardines. But when Curran said he was a close friend of Martha Knapp's, she winked and said there might be a way.

Before he boarded, he called Lieutenant Favero – for what it was worth – with his new information. 'Evan P. Dallenbach,' he reiterated before hanging up. 'He's the one. He's Knapp . . . and Crosby, too. Check him out. Please . . .'

Martha should have been on the flight, but another stewardess said she had cried off sick. 'Literally,' the girl told Curran, sounding upset herself. 'I haven't seen so much water at Niagara Falls.'

The journey was the most frustrating Curran had known. So long, such a waste of precious time. Even now, he thought, even as I sit here trapped in this airborne toothpaste tube, Knapp might be turning the door of my house, treading the carpet on my stairs, choking the life from my . . . wife.

The word came as a surprise, but a pleasant one. For better or for worse, for richer or for poorer, Dany was still his wife. And she would always be the golden temptress in the boat on the Everglades. The idea she might be harmed filled him with a pumping anguish.

By the time the jet touched down at Heathrow, he was ready to run to her side. But as he hurried through customs, a gloved hand settled on his shoulder. 'Mr Curran?' a voice said from behind. 'Come with me, please.'

26

The office was everything Curran expected . . . and he despised what it represented. Dark oak panels; subdued lighting from ornate tablelamps; stained and varnished floorboards supporting a heavily patterned Axminster rug with bronze tassels; a solid hand-crafted walnut desk inlaid with leather and ivory, presided over by a plump man with a bronze watch chain curling across the waist-coat of his three-piece grey suit. In short, the head-quarters of the Establishment in Great Britain. Curran wondered how many tall stories had seeped into the walls, and prayed that Lipton would not seek to tell another.

Lipton harboured no such intention. Hagerty had primed him. 'I've had another call from the Knapp girl,' Hagerty had said. 'She's hysterical – on the verge of a breakdown. She knows everything but the final full stop.'

'How?'

'The newspaperman – the lover. He told her. Christ knows how he found out, but he did.'

Reluctantly, the two men agreed that the gutter jour-nalist's pursuit of the truth could not be thwarted by mere kidology. Instead, a decision was taken to be more candid with him. Totally frank had been the phrase used by Hagerty. And though such a concept was alien to Lipton, he was determined to try his utmost.

Curran remained edgy. He had successfully demanded a diversion in the Foreign Office car's route from Heath-row to Whitehall, so he could call at his house and check on Dany. She had been as well as could be expected, but

Curran was now convinced that any moment he was not with her – any moment at all – could be her last, and he was anxious to return.

He had to protect her. It was all that mattered now. He was where he was only in case Lipton could help.

The early signs were not hopeful. Lipton's complacency had not deserted him. He even sounded as if he found the whole affair slightly tedious. But suddenly, he pushed a button on his intercom and told his secretary that under no circumstances should he be disturbed. Within seconds, he was talking succinctly about murder and its consequences.

'It was indeed perpetrated by Knapp,' he said without restraint. 'The victim was a young and rather beautiful Russian interpreter named Yelena Markova, his mistress. They met at an international conference in Geneva and both worked in the city. Their relationship was evidently close, as she became pregnant with his baby. Knapp underwent a complete and instant mental breakdown when it seemed the affair would inevitably be made public, effectively ending a meteoric career which most observers felt was certain to end with a top post in the White House. Who knows, if he had decided to run for the American Senate and so on, he could have become the President himself. He had all the prerequisites, as I am sure you are aware.'

Curran, leaning forward with his chin supported on entwined hands, nodded.

Lipton waited for a question, but carried on when none was forthcoming. 'The murder in the woods happened on the day after Khrushchev's announcement to the Supreme Soviet that an American U2 spy plane, piloted by Garry Powers, had been shot down with a missile over Russian territory. In such circumstances, with tension at breaking point, the murder of a pregnant Russian girl by a senior

American diplomat would have been blown up out of all proportion by the Soviets – and by media people such as yourself.'

Curran resented the snipe, but preferred to ignore it so Lipton's flow would not be interrupted. 'And the Paris summit was looming,' he said to demonstrate his knowledge of the events of May 1960.

Lipton raised an eyebrow of surprise, but grunted confirmation. 'That would have been scuppered for certain,' he said. 'But the situation could have exploded into something far, far more serious. Who knows, it could have put the Cold War in the freezer for years. It may even have turned the Cold War into the real thing. Believe me, the potential was there.'

'I believe you,' Curran said, though the words momentarily stuck in his throat.

Lipton, his point made, moved on. 'You have heard of the three mysterious men in the woods that day – the men who finally felled Knapp?'

Curran nodded again.

'Well, I was one of those men.'

'Oh . . .' For the first time, Curran was certain the meeting was about to bear fruit.

'There had been rumours of Knapp's affair. Only whispers, you understand, circulating among just a few of his closest colleagues. No one knew who the girl was, or for how long Knapp had been seeing her. But those of us who considered ourselves to be his friends were deeply concerned, for we knew that if it became public, it could destroy him.'

'So . . .' Curran tried to sound encouraging – and Lipton was receptive.

'On the morning of 6 May 1960, Knapp was seen in a highly agitated state at the Palais des Nations in Geneva.

This was not surprising in itself. The U2 affair had placed an enormous strain on us all, and undoubtedly contributed to Knapp's subsequent breakdown. Nevertheless, it was unusual to see in a man known above all for calm in a crisis. I was among those who asked what was wrong, but he snapped at me and told me to mind my own business. It was most unlike him. I talked about his state of mind with two close colleagues, one British and one American. We all agreed it had something to do with this – possible – secret romance. When we saw him driving away in the afternoon with an unknown girl at his side, we determined to follow. We had no intention of being blessed Peeping Toms, you understand. No intention of intruding upon his privacy. But we thought we owed it to ourselves – and to Knapp – to be in possession of the facts. Our intention was to confront him later and to make him realize his foolishness.'

'But something went wrong,' Curran guessed.

'Up to a point. We lost him briefly. The roads were awfully narrow and winding. And it was not until we saw his parked car by chance that we were able to resume the pursuit.'

'On foot.'

'Quite so.'

'And you saw what my wife saw.'

'The aftermath rather than the act itself.'

'Quite so.'

Curran's mimicry, with its hint of sarcasm, threw Lipton on the defensive for the first time. 'We wanted to safeguard his future, that's all. We had no idea the girl was a Russian . . . and no idea of his dire mental state. We could not have known what would happen in those woods.'

'But it did.'

354

'Yes – and the three of us had to make decisions. Difficult decisions. On-the-spot decisions.'

'Which were?'

'To bury the body of the interpreter Yelena. And to spirit Knapp away. Between us, we furnished him with the new identity of Crosby and, through contacts, he was admitted to Mogden hospital.'

'Why Mogden?'

'He had to go somewhere. We couldn't put him in a padded cell in the middle of the desert. Mogden was deemed suitably secure, remote and discreet.'

'Why not simply kill him? Get rid of the problem. That's what you people do sometimes, isn't it?'

'You don't understand,' Lipton said with exasperation. 'He was a brilliant man, who commanded friendship and loyalty from his colleagues. He was sick when he did what he did.'

'How did you account for Knapp's disappearance?'

'A simple matter. In close diplomatic circles, strictly between ourselves and the upper echelons of the Soviet service, we admitted he was having an affair and leaked stories that he and the woman Yelena had run off to start a new life together who knows where. Stories, by the way, that passed into official records, should you care to inspect them.'

'And Knapp's wife? What of her?'

'Ruth? Like everyone else, she was told something different: that Knapp had gone underground as some sort of secret agent. It was done to spare her feelings. Later, she was informed there had been a mishap, and that her husband was dead. She never got over it, you know. She was ill for years before she died. I must confess it was a tragic spin-off.'

Curran searched Lipton's face for a trace of sincerity,

but could find none. He was enraged – and wanted to ask how in God's name Lipton could write off the sorry fate of Knapp's wife in a few paltry sentences. But there were other considerations more pressing, more close to his own heart.

'The little girls,' he said. 'Throughout all of this, there has been no mention of the little girls.'

Lipton's response was swift and unequivocal. 'We were sure they would forget all about it. They were only six years old, for pity's sake. We gave them a reasonable explanation of what they had just witnessed. That the man and the woman were just playing, that they liked to dress up and pretend they were monsters and witches and suchlike, just like children do. We tipped off their teacher that they had stumbled across a couple making love, so she would understand if they talked about it. There was really no problem. They accepted everything with the minds of children.'

'But things changed once they had the minds of adults!' Curran said fiercely. 'The memory stayed with them somehow, developing and maturing somewhere deep inside them. Three of them died when the full horror of it returned. Two others have been killed by your Mr Knapp. And my wife is in the gravest danger.'

Lipton glanced around casually as if searching for his customary cup of afternoon tea. And Curran, despairing, knew the man simply could not understand. To him, the girls were an annoying irrelevance, an opinion confirmed as Lipton veered the conversation back on to its previous tack.

'Of course, it is not so much Knapp's career that is at stake today, but rather those of the men who took part in the consequent deception – myself, a senior executive at

356

the US State Department called Hagerty . . . and a man named Napier.'

It was the way Lipton delayed the final name that gave Curran the clue. As Lipton confirmed his guess with the slightest of nods, he gasped at the implications. 'Not *the* Napier?'

Lipton nodded again. 'Alexander Napier,' he said. 'The Prime Minister. He left the diplomatic service to face the voters, with spectacular results.'

'Christ . . .'

Lipton took advantage of Curran's disarray. 'So you see – '

'See *what*?' Curran challenged, quickly regaining his aggression.

'So you see why, of course.'

'No, I don't. Tell me.'

Lipton sighed. He was becoming tired with Curran's attitude, doubtless born out of the basic ignorance of those who hacked out lies, speculation, dirt and drivel in the name of popular journalism. 'Are you a political man, Mr Curran?' he asked.

'Not over here, no,' Curran answered honestly. 'That part of me will always be in the States, I guess.'

'But you would be interested in bringing down a Prime Minister . . .'

'It depends.'

'Surely you would become the most notorious journalist of your generation by doing so?'

'Perhaps. I don't know.'

'But then again, should you embark on a trail of allegation, you will face a problem.'

'Which is?'

'Proof. You have none.'

'You have just told me – '

'It will never pass my lips again. You don't have a tape recorder about your person, do you?'

'Then why?'

'For a reason. To help you understand why courses of action were undertaken. How they did no harm to anyone. And why it would be wrong to punish those involved now for the entirely reasonable decisions they took decades ago. Decisions that if revealed now by, shall we say, careless prattling, could be taken out of context.'

'No harm? No *harm*?' Curran lost his temper and began to shout. 'No one cares about the girls, do they? They cared about a spy plane, a chunk of scrap metal. They cared about the name and reputation of a diplomat, a savage murderer. And they cared about a damn summit meeting, which was called off in any case and never damn well happened. Now they care about protecting themselves and their lofty, feather-bedded positions. *But no one cares about the girls!*'

'We *do* care about the girls.' Even over the phone, Hagerty sounded more convincing than Lipton, but there was still something in his voice – a slight harshness, a trace of coldness – which made Curran mistrust him. He glanced across the room at Dany. She was swaying to and fro in a rocking chair, staring out of the window to the sun-filled garden beyond, utterly convinced she was experiencing her last days on planet earth. She had not left the house since returning from the sleep laboratory after her final vision, and her skin had taken on a waxen, neglected texture that aged her by ten years. She only needed a shawl to complete the picture of a grandmother who knows her time has come. As he watched her – pitied her – Curran barely heard Hagerty's impassioned reasoning.

358

'Just as Knapp was put in Mogden with the best possible intentions, so he was released with the best possible intentions. He had been pronounced sane several times, dating from years before his release. Though it would have been simple to arrange, we thought it inhumane that he should remain all his life in captivity. In other words, we thought it appropriate to grant the man his freedom.'

'With disastrous results,' Curran said plainly.

'Yes. Things have gone terribly wrong.'

'And he must be returned to captivity.'

'Yes, of course.'

'You told me you were now in a position to follow Knapp's trail . . .'

'They say better late than never.'

'And . . .'

'He was almost certainly responsible for the deaths of Kipini and Sari. Mai-Lin was found dead yesterday in her apartment. I'm still waiting to hear from my people in Bangkok, but I think we can assume – '

Somehow, Curran had known it would come to this. Even the news of Mai-Lin's death neither shocked nor surprised him. It was more like confirmation of the inevitable. Surely, it was all happening to someone else. Tragedies always did, didn't they?

'Oh yes,' he muttered. 'I'm sure we can assume.'

'So then . . .' Hagerty prompted.

'That leaves Dany.'

'I'm afraid so.'

At the mention of her name, Dany got up and walked out. The alternative was to sit there and listen to speculation about her imminent demise, and she could not bear that.

In a way, Curran was relieved. It enabled him to speak more openly. 'She is clearly in great danger.'

359

'I would not dispute that, Mr Curran,' Hagerty said. 'But we need her to catch Knapp.'

'Bait?' Curran could not disguise his horror, but Hagerty was swift to stamp on it.

'How else do you suggest we trap him? We have been unable to discover anything about his movements until it is too late. The one certainty in the whole scenario is that he will come after your wife. Agreed?'

'Agreed,' Curran said reluctantly. 'Do you want me to arrange something with the police here?'

'No!' Hagerty's insistence was startling. He acted quickly to calm himself, but a trace of tension remained. 'I must insist there should be no police involvement.'

'Why?' Curran asked starkly.

'For obvious reasons. Didn't Lipton explain?'

'Then who will protect Dany? I can't stay awake twenty-four hours a day.'

'I will make the necessary arrangements. There are men available, working out of the embassy in London. Skilled men. I'm sure I don't need to elaborate.'

'What if I don't agree? What if I call in the police?'

'Then the whole affair will become public.'

'That concerns you. It does not concern me.'

'Oh, but it does.' Hagerty's voice was suddenly threatening. It was a type of threat Curran had never before encountered. A threat by a man who evidently wielded power. Unseen, but awesome power.

'Go on . . .' Curran managed to say.

'If Knapp becomes known to the masses, I will make sure his daughter becomes known also.'

'Martha?' Curran glanced over his shoulder, lest Dany should return.

'Have you any *idea* how her life would be scarred?' Hagerty said without mercy.

'I'll protect her,' Curran said with sudden defiance. 'She can live with me.'

'You may love her, but could you live with the daughter of the man who has done all this? Could she live with you, knowing that her father tortured your sister, tormented your wife and slaughtered their friends?'

Hagerty hung up before Curran could reply. It was a basic, but devastating tactic, yet Hagerty did not feel pleased with himself. As he walked to the window to see what Washington was doing today, he was forced to wipe bulging beads of sweat from his forehead. 'Pressure,' he muttered to himself. 'It gets to everyone in the end.'

It crossed his mind that he had engineered a trap over which he could exercise total control from a comfortable, familiar office 3,000 miles away.

It crossed his mind that if Dany and Curran were to die, and Knapp snared, that would be an end to it.

27

Cloud masked the moon, leaving just a street light to push faint illumination into Dany's bedroom. She lay on her back, her eyes open and alert, her heart pumping fiercely, as it had been since she climbed into the bed four hours earlier. Beside her, Curran was asleep, breathing loudly, his chin stubble grating on the pillow, his hair dishevelled and in need of a wash.

Dany was glad he had agreed to sleep with her again. She had told him it would make her feel more secure. She had half expected him to reply, 'Just this once – just until all this is over.' But he didn't, and she was grateful for that, too.

She stroked his back. He stirred slightly and grunted as if he had enjoyed her touch. Perhaps she could love him again. Perhaps he could love her.

There was more protection on either side of the bedroom door: two of Hagerty's men, sitting bolt upright on uncomfortable wooden chairs that diminished their powerful stature. Dany had expected them to wear jeans and leather jackets and to smile with sparkling Hollywood teeth. But they were far more sober. Dark suits, white shirts and unembroidered ties. Clean-cut and plain, they spoke with an unlavish precision that symbolized efficiency more than glamour. Only the bulges under their jackets, where they wore their guns, gave a clue to their chosen profession.

Dany knew there were three more of their type on the far side of the bedroom door, concealed behind cupboards and chairs. That meant Knapp would have to deal with six men, five trained and one willing, before he could attempt to kill her. Yet *why* did she still feel so frightened?

The answer, it occurred to her, came as she was finally on the verge of sleep.

From the corner of the one eye that remained open, she saw the two guards rising to their feet. It was the way they did it that troubled her. Silently, stealthily, glancing across at her as if to check whether she had noticed. She pretended she hadn't, and they stretched to relieve stiff muscles.

One walked across the room towards the bed, and she squeezed her eyelids shut as he approached. Within seconds, she felt his breath on her face. It smelled of nicotine and she had to suppress a cough of revulsion. He was close to her for what seemed an age, but finally there was no more breath, no more smell, and she knew he had moved away.

She waited ten seconds before daring to open her eyelids a millimetre. She saw a silhouette resting his head on hands that were pressed together and flattened. The first man indicating to the second that she was sleeping like a baby.

What now? What would they do now they were satisfied of her unseeing, unfeeling, unknowing state?

Her eyes followed the first man's shoulders, her ears followed his footsteps. He returned to the door, took the other by the arm and muttered something incomprehensible.

There was the slightest hint of a click – and she realized they were opening the door. Light from the landing sprayed inside the bedroom for an instant and was gone again.

Dany waited, listening for further movement. Her heart began pounding again – and she was certain that if anyone was still in the room, they would be sure to hear it. After another half-minute, she was equally certain that Curran was her only companion.

She glanced over the sheets timidly. There was no one there.

Why have they gone? Why did they leave? The questions had no logical answers. Dany was instantly as afraid as she had ever been. A moment ago, the two men were her protectors. Now, she was convinced, they were her enemies.

Oh God, someone help me.

She shook Curran until he woke. As he stirred, groaning with the misery of yet another rudely interrupted sleep, she whispered: 'The guards have gone. Stephen, the guards have gone!'

'W–what?' he uttered, barely registering consciousness.

'They've gone. They've left us alone. Oh God . . .'

The panic in Dany's voice injected Curran with attentiveness.

'Gone?' he said. 'Gone where?'

'I don't know!' Dany tried in vain to keep her voice down, and glanced at the door as if it would tell her whether anyone had heard. Her fear was instantly absorbed by Curran, though he tried to conceal it for her sake. He pulled his sheets to one side, exposing his flank, and said: 'I'll go and see what's happened.'

'No!' Dany cried. 'Don't leave me alone!'

'Come on, Dany.' Curran tried to sound reassuring, for his own benefit as well as Dany's. 'It's the only way to find – '

'No!' She interrupted him without compunction. 'If you

leave this room, something terrible will happen. I know it. I *feel* it.'

'What?' Curran wanted to say she was being ridiculous, yet his own feelings of disquiet would not desert him. A hot fluttering erupted inside his chest. 'They've probably just gone to make coffee,' he said in an attempt to calm himself.

'They brought a kettle, coffee, milk, sugar and mugs up here with them,' Dany countered, pointing to a tray resting on the floor beside an electric plug. 'Look, the stuff's there.'

Curran looked. As he saw the outline of the kettle through the darkness, he knew the ultimate decision had to be made.

It was ironic. No matter how sophisticated, how intelligent, how experienced, it all came back to the same old basic question. Man or mouse? The answer, of course, was that, like most men, he was something in between. And thankfully, there were precious few occasions when any were called upon to demonstrate the traditional qualities of manhood: raw courage, determination, strength, fearlessness and protection of the weak. But this was one such occasion, and it was as awesome as it was inevitable. Curran felt like a First World War soldier about to go over the top for the first time. He did not know what would confront him – but he knew it would be bad.

'Don't go, Stephen.' Dany tried one more time, but it was futile. Curran was already out of bed, pulling on underpants, jeans – and a pair of trainers in case he was called upon to run.

'You mustn't go . . .' Dany's voice was weak and helpless, reflecting her state of mind. She was afraid for herself, yes. But now, at this instant, she was more afraid for Curran.

He picked up a full bottle of wine from Dany's dressing table and tested its weight in his palm. It was capable of felling one man, he reasoned, but how many would be waiting? He glanced at Dany once before moving to the door – and she was startled by the terror he betrayed. He turned his attention back to the door. It could have been the door to hell for all he expected to find on the other side.

'Don't go,' Dany said again.

But he was gone.

Dany sat up and pulled the sheets around her in a vain attempt to ward off the terrible chill that had swept across her body. Her shoulders shook and her teeth chattered as if she had been abandoned in the middle of some vast, frozen lake.

The waiting was unbearable. The silence was unbearable. What was he doing? What had he found? Was he about to enter a kitchen full of confident, professional operatives sharing a joke and a beer? Or was he being led like a lamb to the slaughter?

Her answer came thirty seconds later. A blood-curdling scream echoed in the hall below, followed by the dull thud of something heavy hitting the wooden floor like a sack of sand. It had been Curran's scream. She was sure of it.

Christ! So soon. So quick. With no comebacks. No second chances. He had left her side and now he was dying or dead. Killed because of her.

'Stephen!' she cried out helplessly. 'Stephen!'

When there was no reply, her voice trailed off into a whimper that only she could hear. 'Stephen, please, come back . . .'

She didn't need to see him to know what he looked like. Mouth distorted by one final, primal scream. Eyes open, still asking a thousand questions. Limbs curled and pointing in every direction like the tentacles of a beached jellyfish. Blood from his wounds forming winding rivulets on the hallway floorboards, spilling into the gaps between them, mixing with the dust below to make a ruby-grey conglomerate like porridge and raspberry jam.

She wanted to remember him as he had been on the Everglades. The wide-eyed exuberance, the nervous smile, the voice cracking with sexual tension and expectancy. But she could not erase that final look of terror on his face as he walked through the door, and knew she would remember it as long as she lived.

As long as she lived . . .

She felt a renewed, frenzied panic, knowing she would be next. What to do? Run downstairs to see if she could save Curran before his life ebbed away? Leave the bedroom and make a bolt for it? Stay in the room and hide? Try to jump from the window?

What to do? Oh Mother of Christ, why doesn't somebody tell me what to do?

Too late.

There was a noise of rushing footsteps on the stairs, rising in a crescendo until Knapp burst through the door like a stampeding bull. He held Curran in his right arm, supporting him with a wrist punched under a shoulder and curled across the dead man's chest. But as soon as he saw Dany, he dropped the body wholesale, allowing it to crash again to the floor.

In the light from the landing, Dany could see glinting dark liquid seeping from a gaping wound across the side of Curran's neck. Knapp followed her eyes and said: 'The worst is over. His jugular pumped it all out downstairs.'

There was a sadistic glee in his voice – and he smiled broadly to emphasize the point.

'No . . .' Dany whimpered. 'You can't. You mustn't.' She tightened her grip on the sheets around her, pulling them into her until they were taut and stretched.

'A cotton shield,' Knapp observed. 'Not very robust, my dear.'

Dany pulled on her cocoon again. The top sheet ripped on her shoulder. Knapp laughed as if to say, 'Told you so.'

'The others . . .' he growled. 'Your friends?'

Dany could barely talk. The sight of Knapp, the memories such a sight evoked, made her numb with fear. 'Guards . . . to keep you from me,' she managed to mutter.

Knapp, in no apparent hurry, chuckled again. 'They didn't though, did they? I'm afraid you were too young, too naïve to realize. They are the type of men who do as they are told; obey orders from higher authorities; know when to respect their superiors.'

The thought made him beam with pride and delight. For the first time, Dany noticed the glow of his eyes. It was not a normal, warm, fireside glow. It was more Neanderthal, more savage. It made her feel like a small rodent in the presence of a towering hunter – and she knew that to have any chance of survival, she must run.

She leaped from the bed, hoping to take him by surprise and rush past him. But he was equal to her agility and caught her elbow as she crossed in front of him, using her momentum to spin her around before releasing her so she bounced back on the bed.

'You and the others,' he said with a menacing sneer. 'Seven little girls. Seven little blabbermouths. Seven chances for me to be hung alongside my lovely Yelena. No, I cannot risk that. Not a man in my position.'

Dany panted on all fours, ready to make another dash. 'You killed her!' she screamed at him. 'Not us! It was *your* fault!'

'And you want to make sure I pay for it. You have never given up the pursuit. Your treachery now is as great as it was then.'

'It is *you* who have pursued *us*. Don't you see? Don't you care?'

'Kennedy needs me. America needs me. The world needs me. It is calling out to me. I must respect that calling. Yelena was beautiful, but misguided. She could not stop me. And you cannot stop me.'

'I don't want to stop you. None of us wanted to stop you. We had forgotten you, don't you understand? We were only six years old. Only little. Only tiny. We had forgotten. It was you who came back into our lives.'

Now!

Dany slid from the bed to the floor and scrambled on her knees as fast as she was able. She passed Knapp's toes and she passed his ankles. She could see Curran's lolling head and lifeless hands and the landing beyond, and somehow knew that if she could scramble over the body, she would be safe. She urged herself on. Come on, Dany. Come on!

She was halfway across Curran, her knees between his shoulder blades, when Knapp reached down and slid his hands under her shoulders, plucking her high into the air as if she was made of duck's down. Before he threw her back on the bed, he slapped her buttocks. 'Go back to bed, naughty girl,' he said.

'Oh Jesus,' Dany cried, for she knew now there was no escape.

Knapp's eyes rolled. Spittle seeped from his lips. He

pulled a flintstone from his pocket and wiggled it to show Dany the moonlight glinting from its jagged edge. 'Remember this, my little cherub? It's so sharp you could cut your finger on it. I saved it for you . . . for you are the last.'

In an instant, he was upon her. He was so much bigger than her and his weight pushed her down into the mattress, pinning her arms at her side. He yanked the pillow from behind her head and thrust it into her face. She tried to kick, tried to punch, but it was hopeless. He was demonic, and with such possession came unconquerable strength.

She felt a deep shard of pain as he scored the flint across her chest.

'You have to face it again, little one,' he said. 'Only this time, there can be no escape.'

He cut her again and again, the stone clattering across her ribs before tearing deep into her stomach and abdomen. Yet the pillow denied her the chance to cry out to relieve the agony.

He was killing her twice. By butchery and by suffocation. 'Criss-cross, criss-cross,' he said. 'Then I'll hang you up.'

She was burning on the outside and on the inside. Her skin burned as he carved great fissures in it with the stone. Her throat and her lungs burned as they were constricted by lack of air.

She could feel blood spurting from the fatty tissue beneath her flesh. She could feel it matting her body hair, cascading down her sides, saturating sheets and seeping into the mattress. The dam across her nose and mouth was unbreachable. The black curtain across her eyes was complete.

The hurt became unbearable. The violence became

unbearable. She knew she could not survive. Her only hope was to flee to another world.

It was not true what they said about your whole life flashing before you, but the highlights were there.

She was sitting cross-legged on the classroom floor in Geneva, listening as Mam'selle read *Alice in Wonderland*. She was laughing with Pearl as they jumped hand in hand into the swimming pool. She was staring excitedly at the snowdrifts as a mountain train took her up to the ski lodge with Louise and Mai-Lin. She was clapping her hands until they hurt at Stefanie's first fashion show. She was writing a congratulations card after the birth of Sari's first child. She was standing ten yards from a lioness with Kipini. And she was dressed in flowing white, saying 'I do' to Curran in a tumbledown village church.

But that was all in the past now.

Her new world came to her as a horizon. There were no tunnels to walk through, no bridges to cross. It was just *there*, shooting fanned stripes of colour into a magnolia sky which had the soupy thick texture of stone paint. The colours were dazzling and vivid. Every hue of the rainbow was represented. And there were others she had never before experienced.

It made her feel fresh and whole again – and she was glad to have reached it. She began to walk to the horizon. Head held high, hands at her side.

She walked and she walked, naked and carefree, the soles of her feet soothed by flower petals strewn in her path. It led her across a desert plain that was neither hot nor sandy and on across a lake of water that was neither cool nor wet, each step taking her further away from *him* and his despicable world, his nauseating world, his world of hatred and fear and violent retribution. The world from which she had – mercifully – finally escaped.

And then a great explosion tore her paradise apart. It erupted behind her – a flash of silver azure accompanied by the loudest crack of thunder she had ever heard. She spun round like a top to see what had happened.

Knapp – expressionless, unmoved and with no fight left in him – was being held by the two bedroom guards.

The flash had come as they threw the light switch, the thunder as their wooden chairs clattered to the floor.

Curran, too, was jolted awake. Dany stared at him disbelievingly. She reached over and ran a finger across his neck, but found no gaping wound. She looked down at her chest and her stomach. Her skin was still covered by her nightdress – and there were no punctures, no gashes, no puddles of red. She glanced over her shoulder. Her pillow was there, warm where her head had been resting.

The three other guards ran into the bedroom, and all grabbed a piece of Knapp to make sure the trap had indeed been sprung.

Knapp broke down and cried. He was helpless, a child in their arms.

28

A week later

Curran leaned back against the black saloon and gazed over to the gate he knew so well from the blown-up photograph he had thrown in a lay-by bin on his way to Mogden hospital.

There were no photographers this time, no TV cameramen. No lenses for Knapp to wave at with his four-fingered hand.

Hagerty looked out from the back seat of the car, grimacing at Mogden's unchanging countenance, as bleak in late spring as it had been in winter. 'It's not the White House,' he said sadly.

'No,' Curran murmured. 'But it's where he should be.'

'It's where we should have kept him.'

Curran let out a sound that was half gasp, half laugh, born out of irony and the barely suppressed rage that still swirled inside him. Hagerty may have been expressing regret. But it was too little, too late. Far, far too late.

Curran had emitted the same sound when Lieutenant Favero called him just before he set out from London.

'We are making progress now we have a contemporary name,' the lieutenant announced, his attitude for the first time one of earnest concern. 'Your claims are being taken seriously, Mr Curran. There does seem to be a trail of damage – and the Federal authorities have taken command of the case. They are anxious to interview Evan P. Dallenbach, and you. This is the last you will hear from me. I am simply calling to let you know you are about to hear from the FBI.'

Curran had slung down the phone without being able to utter a word. What was he supposed to say? Thank you?

He looked at Hagerty and wondered if the high-up from State knew the FBI had the scent. Probably. And could he stop them? Probably . . .

The hospital gate creaked open and a male nurse appeared, inspecting its hinges to discover where it needed oil. Martha, her head bowed, walked through slowly with the Medical Controller, Ashe. He had a supportive hand on her elbow, but she pulled it free as they approached the black saloon.

Though he had talked long and hard to Ashe on the telephone, Hagerty could not help but give the principal a withering look of disgust. Ashe, his silver hair blown back by the early-morning breeze, rode it out. But Curran could tell he felt shame.

How much did he know of Knapp's story? How much had he been told? Curran wagered he knew little, and had been told lies. Nevertheless, by signing the form that declared Knapp sane, he had made a serious misjudgement. As soon as he had seen Martha to her keepers, he swivelled around and returned to the haven of his insular domain.

'He'll wait a few months before resigning,' Hagerty said with deliberate certainty.

Martha, the maelstrom inside her making her feel nauseous, glanced at Curran. She had not expected to find him there, and could not be certain if she was glad.

'How is he?' Curran asked.

'Oh . . .' Martha's sigh was leaden. 'He's still heavily sedated. He neither knows where he is, nor cares. He neither knows who I am, nor . . .' She could not bring herself to complete the sentence.

Curran guided her away from the car so they could talk in private. They looked at each other uncomfortably, almost as if each was embarrassed by the other's presence. Hagerty was right. They both knew they could not remain lovers. There had been too much pain, too much suffering. Best to let it be before fingers of blame were pointed, before sides were taken, before loyalties were compromised.

A tragedy among tragedies. That was their story.

'You know we can't go on,' Martha blurted out finally. 'Not like before . . .'

Curran nodded. Martha tried desperately to rationalize, though even she knew it was unnecessary.

'You see, I have to come to terms with what my father has done. It's not . . . it's not easy, Stephen, and I really don't have room for too much else. I can't settle into any . . . any relationships, you know what I mean?'

'Do you still care for him?'

'Oh God . . .' Martha's hand rose shaking to her mouth. She gripped her jaw as if it would somehow hold her entire being together. 'Don't ask me that. Not now. It's too cruel.'

'I'm sorry.'

He understood now. Understood what Hagerty had told him about Martha's aching, hopeless adoration for a father who was not as other fathers. Understood that she was overwhelmed by the final, intractable knowledge of his evil.

'What will you do?' he asked.

She shrugged her shoulders and tried bravely to smile. 'Change my name,' she said. 'Knapp sounds sort of . . . dirty . . . now. Soiled napkin. Soiled Knapp.' She laughed, but it was not genuine and she quickly reverted to her future plans, delivering them in a tense staccato rhythm. 'Start again. Change my job. Move to the West Coast. Vanish. That sort of thing.' She looked at Curran and rubbed the red haloes that were making the fringes of her eyes burn. 'And you? How will you pick it all up? Will you stay with Dany?'

Curran had already thought it through. 'Yes,' he said.

'For the sake of Yvette?'

'She needs to be cared for.'

'And because you still love your wife?'

'This whole awful experience brought us closer. Much closer.'

'And you love her . . .'

Curran hesitated, for there was no easy answer. He thought he could love Dany again. He thought she could love him. Certainly, he *hoped* they could love each other. Only time would tell.

'I'm glad she survived,' Martha said.

'Of course,' Curran replied, sounding too formal for comfort.

'And do you still love me, Stephen?'

This time he did not delay. 'Yes,' he said. 'I'll always love you.'

He supposed he meant it, though a dark part of him remembered how she had failed to finger her father when he had shown her the blown-up picture in the hotel room. If she had, if he had known the killer's name earlier, then maybe Dany would have been saved the final, dreadful trauma that had left her lying in her bed, broken into so many little pieces. And maybe Mai-Lin would have been saved. You see, he told himself, already there are questions . . .

They exchanged a single, deep, poignant kiss – a kiss of past joy and present melancholy – before Martha turned to go.

376

Curran grabbed her sleeve before she took a single stride. 'Take care of Hagerty,' he warned darkly.

Martha was puzzled. Ever since her father had been captured, her kind uncle had been at her side, holding her hand. 'But he saved Dany,' she protested.

'To save himself,' Curran persisted. 'Don't trust him, Martha. What he did with his cohorts thirty years ago was wrong. What they did in February was wrong, and unleashed the most hideous consequences. Hagerty knows it. I know it. But he told me he will destroy you if I say anything.'

Martha closed her eyes and turned her face to the heavens, as if praying to God to take her now. She sucked in a chestful of air to give her a last pulse of strength, then looked at Curran in a way that nearly made him weep. 'Destroy me?' she said quietly. 'I have already been destroyed. What more do I have to lose?'

She walked slowly to the black saloon. As she climbed inside, Curran saw Hagerty put an arm of consolation around her shoulders. But as the car slipped away across the moor, she edged to one side until she was free of his embrace.

The Moscow hotel room was more spartan than those he had shared with Martha, but it was comfortable enough. Curran lay on the bed and made his final decision.

In a way, Martha had already made it for him. '*Destroy me? What more do I have to lose?*'

The FBI were on the trail, and could just make it by Hagerty's linebackers. And if it all came out, Hagerty would have more to worry about than dragging Martha in the dirt.

'Besides,' Curran repeated aloud. 'What they did was so hideously wrong.'

377

He reached for the telephone. Christie's secretary put the call through to the editor's office.

'What d'you want? I'm in morning conference.'

'To tell you I'm taking six months off to be with my wife,' Curran said. 'Whether you like it or not.'

'Bloody impertinence.'

'And to play you this . . .' Curran took an Olympus microcassette recorder from his travel bag. It was the same recorder – matt black, four inches by two – that he had picked up at home when the Foreign Office car interrupted its journey from Heathrow to Whitehall. The same recorder he had tucked in the breast pocket of his shirt as Lipton told him the full story of Knapp's crime and the subsequent cover-up by a civil service mandarin, an influential US State Department official close to the President and the British Prime Minister.

'You don't have a tape recorder about your person, do you?'

Yes, Mr Lipton. Yes, I do.

The internal Soviet flight was bumpy and nerve-racking, just as Hagerty had predicted, and Curran trusted the rest of his information would be equally accurate. In return for a renewed vow of silence and complicity, Hagerty had provided him with a name, an address and details of how to reach it. Curran sat on the old Ilyushin turbo-prop comfortable in the knowledge that he would repay Hagerty with headlines that would finish him.

It was a deception of which Hagerty himself would have been proud.

Curran shared the journey with a pretty young interpreter named Gala, an Anglophile who had happily ridden the new wave of freedom in the USSR. She was an outgoing

Belorussian girl with vivacious blonde hair that fell over her shoulders in great curls, and was disappointed that such an adventure had been tainted by Curran's sombre mood.

They landed at the oil city of Baku in mid-afternoon, and Hagerty's directions took them to the old woman without difficulty. Their taxi meandered through a maze of derricks, pylons and power cables to a newly-built tower block on the Apsheronskiy peninsula outside the city. It overlooked the Caspian Sea, but the location was a mixed blessing. A fierce wind howled off the water, even though the day was clear, and the sea's beauty was lost under a film of oily scum.

The woman was a widow in her early eighties who lived with her son and his family in a two-room apartment. At first, she was unwilling to let Curran in, particularly since her son was at the well and her daughter-in-law had taken her grandchildren to buy new shoes. But when Gala explained a little of the reason for his visit, she ushered them through the door with a hand that immediately began to shake.

Curran watched her as she made tea. Her shoulders were round and her left leg appeared shorter than her right, but she seemed in good health otherwise, suggesting a resilient constitution. Her ample belly pushed out a beige cotton dress printed with wild red flowers. She wore a grey cardigan that had seen better days – and thick, opaque stockings, the like of which Curran had not come across for years. She could have been like thousands of old women in Baku, just another kept alive by a loyal son and the proceeds of petroleum products. But her solid forearms and listless, hang-dog face gave her away.

She was a woman who had worked the land before

379

being forced into the concrete and steel of Baku – and she was a woman who had known deep, everlasting sorrow.

Gently, cautiously, caringly, Curran – through Gala – told her the truth about what happened to her daughter in May 1960.

The old woman reacted as he had hoped. With grief, yes. But also with relief.

Through her tears, she told Curran of her pride in Yelena and how the young, exuberant girl had fought her way out of their remote farming village to go to university and to take up such an important post with the Soviet diplomatic corps. 'I knew what they said was not correct,' she said. 'I knew she would not disappear without telling me. I knew that wherever she was, she would write. She loved her mother, you see, just as I loved her.'

Curran told the old woman how he found her.

'The man who guided me asked me to regretfully inform you that this story can never be officially acknowledged,' he said.

The old woman nodded knowingly. It was a familiar theme.

'But I am going to ignore him and tell it anyway,' Curran went on. 'I simply wanted you to know first . . .'

The mother managed a brief smile of gratitude and said, 'I just thank God someone *cares* about Yelena.'

She took Gala's curls between her thumb and forefinger and rubbed to feel their texture. If only, she thought, this hair was auburn.

'Yelena did the job you do,' she said, gazing into Gala's blue eyes. 'And she was beautiful, like you.'

She turned to Curran and looked at him imploringly. 'I think about her every day,' she said. 'And I dream about her every night.'